A THREAD OF HOPE

Nikko sprang up from the couch. "Fox, what are you working on?"

Fox shook his head and waved his hand in dismissal. He took another two steps toward the door. But then he seemed to reconsider. He turned to face Nikko. "We may be able to code you into the biogenesis function," he blurted out.

"The biogenesis function?" Nikko couldn't keep the scorn out of his voice. "That's no refuge. It's a fantasy."

The biogenesis function was Fox's pet project—a theoretical complex of assembly codes that would define every element of Summer House and its internal environment in a sequenced construction plan. Wrap the code in a packet of assembly Makers, drop it on an appropriate substrate, and—in theory at least—it would be possible to replicate the entire House.

In theory.

"The biogenesis function is never going to exist, Fox. It's too complex."

"Its complexity can hide you," Fox said softly, in a voice that betrayed his own uncertainty.

"I don't want to be a string of code! I want to be alive. I would do anything to stay alive."

THE BOHR
MAKER

Linda Nagata

BANTAM BOOKS

New York Toronto
London Sydney Auckland

THE BOHR MAKER
A *Bantam Spectra Book* / *April 1995*

SPECTRA *and the portrayal of a boxed "s" are trademarks of Bantam Books, a division of Bantam Doubleday Dell Publishing Group, Inc.*

ISBN 0–553–56925–2

Published simultaneously in the United States and Canada

*Bantam Books are published by Bantam Books, a division of Bantam Doubleday
Dell Publishing Group, Inc. Its trademark, consisting of the words "Bantam Books"
and the portrayal of a rooster, is Registered in U.S. Patent and Trademark Office
and in other countries. Marca Registrada. Bantam Books, 1540 Broadway, New
York, New York 10036.*

PRINTED IN THE UNITED STATES OF AMERICA
RAD   0 9 8 7 6 5 4 3 2 1

To my husband Ronnie,
whose support and confidence
made this book possible.

CHAPTER

1

Just past dawn a dead man came floating down the river. The current carried him under the old river-straddling warehouse, where he fetched up against one of the fluff booms Arif had strung between the rotting pilings. Phousita found him when she came to gather the night's harvest of fluff. He floated facedown. His head had wedged under the fluff boom; his long black hair swayed like a silk veil in the current.

Phousita glanced nervously overhead. The trapdoor that opened onto the main floor of the abandoned warehouse hung open. She debated with herself a moment. It would be so easy to slip into the water, ease the dead man's body off the boom and guide him back into the current before Arif discovered he was here. She would never have to worry about who he might have been or what bitter spirits still haunted his flesh. Let someone else farther down the river have him!

But her conscience wouldn't let her do it. Even in the dusky light under the river warehouse she could tell he'd been a wealthy man. Such fine clothes! And he might have money on him, jewels. The clan was hungry. She glanced again at the trapdoor. "Sumiati," she called softly.

The termite-eaten floorboards creaked, then Sumiati peered through the door. She had an empty bucket in her hands, ready to pass it to Phousita. "So fast today! Did you fill the first bucket already? It's about time our catch improved!" Her dark eyes widened when she saw the body. She sucked in a little breath of surprise. "Phousita, he's still got his clothes! Hold him! Don't let the current take *tuan* away. I'll come down. Look how beautiful his robe is. Oh, do you think we're the first to find him?" She put the bucket down, then turned to climb through the trapdoor, moving awkwardly as she bent over her pregnant belly. She hung for a moment from the insulated wire rope, looking like some rare, ripe fruit. Then she dropped gracefully to the narrow metal plank that Arif had lashed between the pilings. It shivered under the impact.

Phousita reached out a hand to steady her. Sumiati was a small woman, but even beside her, Phousita was tiny. She stood no taller than a petite child of seven or eight, though she was nearly twenty-five years old. Despite her size, her body was that of a woman: slender and beautifully proportioned, endowed with ample breasts and rounded hips, but on a scale that seemed unnaturally small. With her pretty round face, her dark eyes, and her thick black hair carefully coiled at the nape of her neck, she might have been a diminutive spirit out of some forgotten mythology.

Her unusual appearance had once attracted many clients after hours in the business district. But she'd promised Arif she wouldn't venture down there anymore. She was hungrier these days. The clothes from this dead man would buy a large quantity of rice.

And yet she hesitated. Easy wealth was so often cursed with misfortune. "I don't like finding the *tuan* here," she told Sumiati, instinctively using the traditional honorific. "There's no telling what evil influences *tuan* carries with him. Let's work quickly, then I'll shove him back into the river."

Sumiati looked suddenly concerned. "Maybe we should call Arif."

"No!" Sumiati jerked at the sharp tone of Phousita's voice. Phousita hunched her shoulders; she looked across at the dead man. "No," she said more gently. "No need to wake Arif. We can do it." Pulling the close-fitting skirt of her sarong up above her knees, she eased herself into the water until her tiny feet touched the clean gravel that cushioned the river's concrete bed. The current swirled in cool streams around her waist, gradually soaking her faded blue breastcloth. She reached back to help Sumiati down, then grabbed the empty fluff bucket and started wading toward the dead man, one hand on the fluff boom for balance.

Arif had constructed the boom shortly after he'd moved the clan into the abandoned warehouse. He'd gathered rare old plastic bottles, the kind that didn't disintegrate in only a few weeks. He'd cut them in half and then lashed them to a plank stripped from the warehouse. They floated half-submerged in the water and when the fluff came floating down the river they trapped it, like huge hands grasping at the feast. The system had worked well for many months. It would still work, if only there were more fluff in the river ... or fewer hungry people. Her gaze scanned the thin line of brown foam bobbing against the boom. A dismal catch. Not enough there to feed three people and there were thirty-nine empty bellies in the clan. Forty, counting Sumiati's soon-to-be-born. Phousita tried not to think about it.

Fierce rays of yellow light lanced under the river house as the sun leapt up over the city. Phousita touched the dead man's head. Bright white flecks of bone and torn pink flesh could be seen through his black hair. The back of his skull had been caved in by a blow. The current still washed dilute puffs of blood from the wound. He must have been only minutes in the water. She lifted his head carefully by the long hair. His face was pale, nondescript European. His eyes were closed. A single *kanji* glowed in soft, luminescent red on his cheek. She couldn't read it. "Look, *tuan* was robbed," she said, pointing at the torn lobes of his ears where earrings must have been. Sumiati peered over her shoulder.

Out of principle Phousita touched his neck, checked for a pulse. It was a ceremony the Chinese doctor insisted upon, even when the patient was obviously dead. Perhaps it helped ease the frightened spirit still trapped within the body. Sumiati looked on, a worried pout on her lips until Phousita shook her head. Sumiati smiled.

"Even if *tuan* was robbed, he still has his clothes," she said. "Maybe the thieves overlooked something." She quickly checked his pockets, but found nothing. Phousita worked at the fastenings on his robe. In minutes they had the body stripped. Phousita stepped back in relief.

Sumiati's eyes glowed as she held the fluff bucket stuffed full of fine clothing. "Push him off the boom," she urged. "Let's hurry. We have to take these to temple market. It's a long walk, but we'll get the best price there. We can take some water to sell too. And then we can buy rice. Enough for everyone to eat until their stomachs complain! And clothes. Henri and Maman need new clothes. And medicines, of course. You'll know the ones to buy. And the Chinese doctor is always glad to see you. . . ."

Phousita smiled at Sumiati's nervous chatter. The dead man had indeed brought them good fortune. And now she could send him on his way. She reached for the dead man's arm. Twisted it gently, to ease him off the boom. Hurry now. In a moment he would be gone.

"Phousita!"

Her hands jerked back in guilty surprise. She looked up as Arif dropped through the trapdoor. He landed on the metal plank. His slim, hard body—clothed only in worn shorts—was poised in a fighter's stance. Arif was always fighting, she thought bitterly. And he'd do anything, anything at all to survive.

He stared at her, cruel violet eyes so out of place amongst the swollen, exaggerated features of his laughing, yellow, bioluminescent joker's face. Sumiati, blind to his moods, started to bubble forth in her good-natured way with the tale of their find, but Arif cut her off with a gesture. "Phousita," he growled softly. "What are you doing?"

Phousita glanced at the nude body of the dead man. Without his clothes he seemed a pale, ghostly thing. "Take the basket up, Sumiati," she said softly. "Arif will help me now."

Sumiati nodded, confused. Arif helped her out of the river and onto the plank, then stepped back, out of her way. She climbed the rope. "Close the door behind you," he said. He still stared at Phousita. In the harsh shadows under the warehouse, his ogre-ugly face glowed brilliant yellow with its own generated light.

By his own admission Arif had been a wicked child. His mother had sold him to a sorcerer who poisoned him with a spell that exposed his sins upon his face. With his ridiculously elongated nose and chin, his cheeks as round and full as overripe guavas, and his glowing yellow complexion, he resembled one of the comical servants of the *wayang* theater. Except his eyes.

His gaze flickered upward as the corrugated metal door closed with a creak. Soft footsteps moved off across the warehouse floor. When Sumiati was out of earshot, Arif spoke: "He's food, Phousita." He walked to the end of the plank. "Why would you throw away food?"

Suddenly Arif dove, slicing like a sunbeam through the water, his thick black hair, tied up in a short ponytail, trailing behind him. He surfaced next to Phousita, startling her with an explosion of bubbles. He threw his swollen yellow head back and laughed, then hugged her tiny figure quickly, his arms encircling her waist. "Don't be afraid, Phousita," he crooned. "The old witch filled your head with all kinds of lies. It's just a body. *Tuan*'s spirit is gone."

Phousita was trembling. She sank into Arif's arms while the cool river rushed past. "You don't know what kind of man he was," she whispered.

"It doesn't matter."

"It matters if we take his body into ours."

"Not his body. Only the fluff that grows from it. You helped me plant them before. You ate the fluff."

She laid her head against his chest. He'd dismissed her reluctance then too. "Sutedjo and Piet were part of our clan," she said. "We knew them; they would wish us no harm. But this man is a stranger; we don't know what evil he's done."

"It's gone with him."

"His spirit clings to the body."

But Arif's patience had eroded. "Spirit rides in the head and his head's smashed in," he snapped. "Stupid country girl, *he's gone!*" He ducked under the water. A moment later, he surfaced on the other side of the boom. Grabbing the dead man's wrists, he twisted the body roughly off the boom. "I wish you'd never met that old witch! She chased your brains away. You want to be a sorceress like her? Fah! She was just a stupid old hill woman. I'm glad she's dead. I wish I could have planted her too!"

Phousita slapped the water. "Stop it, Arif. Stop it! You pretend you know so much. You don't know! You hear rumors on the street and you think they're true. Shiny new magic. But even the new sorcerers don't know everything. Arif!"

He wasn't listening. He'd turned his back on her, hauling the dead man up the river. She took a deep breath and ducked awkwardly under the boom. Fear filled her as water swirled past her face. Then she burst to the surface, gasping and splashing for air. She didn't know how to swim. Arif had promised to teach her. Oh, why did she get angry? It did no good. Arif only wanted the best for her, for everyone in the clan. It hurt him when she let her doubt show.

"Arif." She caught up with him; helped him drag the body against the current. They reached the edge of the river house. Arif stopped. Phousita glanced down through the clear water to the gravel beneath her feet. Scattered there she could still see the remnants of Sutedjo's bones, bright white slivers that hadn't yet turned to fluff. She glanced up. Arif studied her with violet eyes. "It wasn't the old witch who cured you, Phousita. It was the Chinese doctor. The old magic is dead."

He ducked under the water, hauling one leg of the dead man with him. Phousita used her tiny body as an anchor to keep the corpse from drifting downstream while Arif secured the man's foot to a mooring stone on the bottom. He surfaced, took the other leg, hauled that down too.

Over the next few days the body would slowly dissolve into a rich harvest of fluff that would float to the surface and gather downstream against the fluff boom. The clan would never know the reason for their good fortune. They'd attribute the abundant harvest to luck.

Fluff hadn't existed when the old woman was alive. That was only a few years ago. Phousita could remember it easily. She'd been perhaps twenty-one, still trapped in a child's body. The river had been a stinking sewer then, a deadly thread of water draining the city's filth. When the fluff first started collecting on the river's banks, they'd paid no attention to it, assuming it was just a new kind of pollution. Then Arif had seen the rats eating it. . . .

Now the river ran clear. The water was clean, drinkable, though the city's filth still washed into it with every rain.

Arif surfaced again, took the dead man's right arm. "Help push him under," he said gruffly. Phousita nodded. Arif stretched the arm of the corpse beyond its head, then reached underwater for the mooring stone. He found it, and glanced over his shoulder at Phousita. "Now." She placed her palms flat against the cold, slippery chest and leaned hard, forcing the body under.

Something gave way beneath her right hand. She could hear it more than feel it, a sharp metal *snick!* The chest opened like a blinking eye. A golden needle shot out of the black orifice, to bury itself in Phousita's breast. She reared back in horror, swiping at the spot of blood just above her breastcloth that marked the point where the needle had disappeared. She stumbled through the water. Her chest was on fire. She could hear herself bleating like a terrified child: "Unh! unh! unh!"

The corpse twisted in the current, the shoulders rolled. She saw a little white tear in the dead white chest before the corpse turned facedown again. Her gaze shifted to Arif. The horror in his eyes must have echoed her own. *Help me.* She tried to say it, but her mouth had gone dry. Her tongue grew puffy and swollen as the needle's poison spread through her system. The bubbling song of the river seemed to rise in volume, building like a wall around her before it collapsed into a chaotic buzz. Her vision blurred. She could see Arif reaching for her. But the current was swifter. Her eyes closed as its cold hands caressed her face and swirled through her hair.

CHAPTER

2

"Name?" the majordomo program asked.

Nikko, who was in truth only a program himself, a modern ghost, an electronic entity copied from the mind of his original self, had little patience for Dull Intelligences. "The name's Nikko," he growled. "Rhymes with psycho. Nikko Jiang-Tibayan. I've only been here a hundred times you decrepit excuse for a secretary."

He could hear Kirstin laughing, somewhere over the electronic horizon, a dim sound in the majordomo's limited sensorial world. "Are you going to admit me or not?" he snapped.

"Of course, sir. The lady is expecting you."

A pathway opened, and the electronic pattern that constituted Nikko's ghost slid through it into Kirstin's mind. Physically, his ghost occupied her atrium, an accessory organ that had been induced to grow as a filamentous tissue in her brain. But the atrium had drawn on her sensorium to create for him a psychic environment that was a precise duplicate of the room which

Kirstin occupied. From her point of view, he was simply an overlay on her physical reality, a virtual companion—invisible to anyone but herself—yet she could host him in the real-space of her house. And though he was only a ghost, she could see him, scent him, touch him, taste him again . . . as she'd done many times before.

Today, though, he carried with him a sense of urgency, a certainty that his time was running out. He had a few more weeks at most, Dad said. The end was impossible to predict precisely, but it wouldn't be long. Nikko could already feel the gathering presence of death, manifest in the clumsiness that had begun to afflict him as his nervous system degenerated under a preprogrammed genetic code . . . a clumsiness that was replicated perfectly by his ghost.

Kirstin held a hand out to him, the gold rings on her fine fingers bright against the perfect ebony of her skin. She smiled a cool, possessive smile as she anticipated his touch—no, the *simulation* of his touch, a tactile hallucination of the atrium, inspired by this electronic ghost inside her mind.

He took her hand, his own extraordinarily long, china-blue fingers twitching uncontrollably. She frowned at this latest disability, but for the moment she chose to overlook it.

Still, he felt her scorn. He would have scowled at her then, if he could. But his face wasn't made for that. He was, after all, only an experimental model, a singular prototype of an artificial human variant that had since been banned by the Commonwealth. A unique freak. The myriad small platelets that composed his enameled hide could conceivably perform a clumsy imitation of most human expressions. But Dad hadn't attached much importance to that aspect of Nikko's design. Instead, he'd rerouted the cranial nerve that would normally control the tiny muscles in the human face to service the kisheer, the symbiotic organ that sealed his mouth and nose and ears under vacuum, pro-

viding him with oxygen on the Outside. But Nikko
didn't spend much time mourning his lack of expressions. A cold stare served most of his purposes well
enough.

"I've been asking to see you for nearly a week," he
growled at Kirstin. His fingers wrapped across the back
of her hand and then around her wrist, though he was
careful not to flex the muscles in his arm. The atrium
would simulate that. In the tiny pseudogravity of
Kirstin's home, an object would take over two seconds
to fall one meter to the floor, and a lover could be
swept off her feet with only a small investment. But
Nikko wasn't in the mood for games like that. He said:
"Maybe I'll find another lover, if you don't want to fill
up my last remaining days."

"Ah Nikko, as charming as ever, I see." She lifted
his hand, to stroke the smooth enamel of it against her
dark face. Her coppery hair was coarse and kinked,
floating in an undisciplined cloud around her shoulders.
Her features were Northern European: a blocky nose
and a heavy, rectangular face. The cream-coffee eyes
that measured him seemed too light for her skin. Nikko
found her plain. But he wasn't here out of love, as she
well knew.

He gazed past her in sudden surprise. She had a
painting of him on her living room wall! He recognized
her style. "That's a romantic bit of trash," he said, as he
slid carefully around her to take a closer look.

"What's wrong with it?" Kirstin exclaimed, her voice
a curious mix of amusement and anger. "I thought
you'd like it."

He glared at the piece. If she'd depicted him under
conditions of atmosphere his kisheer would have lain
across his shoulders like a short gray cape. But instead
she'd placed him in the vacuum forest of glassine trees
that grew on the outer walls of Summer House, displaying him with the respiratory organ in active position, its
supple gray tissue raised over his mouth and nose and

ears like a veil. There was something feral in the poised stance she'd given him; he crouched, his toes wrapped securely around a low branch while his intent gaze seemed to track some object offscreen. His hands were half-raised, ready.

"Is that how you see me?" he asked. "Like an animal? In my 'element'?"

"Take it as a compliment, Nikko."

"When it's meant as an indictment?"

In the portrait he seemed something other than human. His head was smooth and hairless with a high forehead. His face was half-masked, his flat Asian nose and petite ears barely visible beneath the kisheer. He had no eyebrows. Dad had substituted a dramatic ridge of black. His eyes were blue, and quite human-ordinary—though behind their protective crystal lenses they were difficult to see. In the portrait he was nude, as always, his body a smooth, elongated masculine sculpture covered in living armor designed to protect him from the zero pressure of the void, gleaming in a shade of blue called nikko. An accessory organ closed over his genital and anal zones like a living loincloth, a bow to the modesty of society, and protection for him under vacuum.

"I'm an historian," he told Kirstin. "Not a zoological exhibit."

Kirstin's arm slipped around his waist. She pulled herself against him. Her breasts felt too soft and vulnerable against his enameled skin. But bedded in them, the hard thrust of her nipples seemed to warn of her armored soul. "You're beautiful," she said. "And I won't have you much longer. Why shouldn't I remember you as you really were?"

His face couldn't show contempt, but his voice communicated it well enough. "So why don't you paint me plugging you in your bed?"

She grinned. "And admit to the world that I practice bestiality?"

He pulled away from her. "I am *not* an animal!" He was what every person inhabiting the thousand celestial cities of the Commonwealth should be—a graceful being adapted to the new environment, able to function in vacuum without pressure suit or air supply, equally at home in a corridor of one of the orbiting cities. And that was why the Commonwealth despised him—he was the future they were afraid to accept.

Kirstin taunted him with her cool gaze. "Don't chide me, Nikko. I wasn't the one who made you what you are. That was your dear old dad. Fox Jiang-Tibayan: he thought he could be a better designer than the Goddess herself. Too bad for you he didn't examine the consequences before he started."

Nikko felt his long fingers close into a fist. *The Goddess.* Mother Earth was a fucked-up old tyrant. She could use a little outside help in the evolutionary process. But Kirstin didn't see it that way. Her Gaian philosophies condemned any artificial advance in the physiology of the human species—a view that meshed nicely with the secular laws of the Commonwealth.

Kirstin approached him again. She laid two fingers against his smooth chest. "You're an historian," she said, tracing a slow circle on his skin. "You studied under Marevic Chun and you've dedicated your life to stirring up trouble. You've had fun, haven't you? Selectively exposing scandal and corruption to wound the corporations that compete with Summer House. Even attacking the police. But you've never looked into your own history."

"You're wrong," he said, turning away from her, uncomfortable with this subject. "I know that litany."

She smiled. "Ah, but you've only had it from one side. You know that Fox created you on the authority of a research permit, but did he tell you that he obtained that permit by bribe and threat and political favor? You're an historian, Nikko. You should know the facts. I testified against the permit, but it didn't matter. Fox knew all the right people." Her chin tilted up and she laughed lightly, remembering. "You should have seen him. He was so pleased with himself. He never considered what would happen when the permit expired."

The permit had been issued by the Congressional science advisory committee for a period of thirty years. Dad had been required to build the expiration date into his design. At the time he hadn't seen that as a problem. In thirty years, Fox had expected artificial humans would be commonplace, and that he would have no trouble in getting the permission to reverse Nikko's condition. But instead the passage of time had ossified the nascent bigotry of the Commonwealth. There had been no extension on the research permit that allowed Nikko to exist. In a few more weeks, it would expire.

Kirstin slid her hand up to his shoulders. Her fingers dabbled at his kisheer: a gesture calculated to arouse him. He'd come to her as a last resort. Kirstin Adair, Chief of the Commonwealth Police, charged with enforcing the laws that limited the use of nanotechnology. It was one of her duties to ensure that society remained human. Yet she also had the authority to grant him a reprieve.

Nikko was an historian. He'd learned his trade from Marevic Chun, one of the founders of Summer House. She'd taught him how to hunt the data trails, to dig beneath the civil veneer most people and corporate entities presented to the world, to forage amongst forgotten electronic notes, reports and memos, to finagle interviews with reclusive people and ghosts, all to reconstruct the veiled events of the very recent past and with any luck to embarrass the Commonwealth and the police, to expose their corruption, to generate a backlash of disgust that would drive the trend line of history toward a more liberal political climate that might allow him to live.

He'd failed in that. But he'd succeeded in other things. He'd used his skills to track down Kirstin's past, and he'd come to understand her, long before they met.

Without further words, they retired to the bedroom. Nikko's gaze swept across the collage mounted on the wall above the bed: an impressionistic mélange of teeth and bone and hair and shreds of skin in bright, artificial colors, all knit together with airbrushed genetic patterns he hadn't the skill to read.

Kirstin had already slipped out of her gown, leaving it to drift slowly to the floor. Her one-hundred-and-twenty-odd-year-old body waited for him on the bed, as fresh and full as any teenager's. He joined her.

She pulled him toward her in her silent, hungry way. His belly slid across hers: smooth, hard enamel skating on yielding flesh. Her nails slipped across his armored breast. He flexed his arms and slowly sank against her. His mouth found hers. He knew what she felt: kissing him was like kissing a china statue come to life. But his mouth and tongue were as soft and warm as hers and more intricate, a sea of papillae designed to mesh with the kisheer when he needed that to breathe.

His kisheer had shriveled in his body's excitement. It lay like a wrinkled kerchief around his neck. She licked at it, teasing it open. His hand was on her throat. He stroked her fine black skin, feeling her pulse beat a fierce rhythm beneath his sensitive fingertips.

Suddenly, unexpectedly, her teeth sank into his kisheer. He screamed in pain and dove against her. "*Stop it!*" he hissed, while his fingers squeezed a gentle warning against her throat ... fingers long enough to encircle her entire neck. . . .

But she hissed at him in turn. "*You* need *me*, Nikko."

She knew what she was doing. She controlled the situation. It was her atrium, and she could throw him out at any time.

She bit deeper. The pain began to cloud his brain. He felt himself begin to overheat. He couldn't dump heat with the efficiency of a human-ordinary. So he did the only thing he could: gave in to her completely, hating her, even as her body took command of him, drawing his sterile seed out in a prolonged burst of wracking, shivering lust.

Later, as he daubed at the blood still oozing from his kisheer, he had to remind himself that none of this was real. He was, after all, only a ghost of his true self, existing within Kirstin's atrium, nothing more than an overlay on the reality of her world.

But ghosts were not simple, inconsequential fantasies. A scarred ghost could return home and scar its master. Over the years, many of his ghosts had never returned to him. He knew that some had simply been erased. But sometimes, he suspected, a damaged ghost would choose not to return home, to save him from its pain.

He lay back on the bed, feeling his body settle slowly down upon the sheets. Kirstin snuggled against him, her hand stroking his belly over and over again. She loved to touch him.

He put his arm around her. He knew he should say something sweet now, make himself endearing. But he didn't think he could pull it off.

His gaze fixed on the collage mounted over the bed. The thing repulsed him. It was Kirstin's perverted way of displaying the human trophies she'd collected over the years: illegal body parts gathered from her victims, artfully arranged in collage to suggest the jagged slopes of a forested mountain. Here, diamond teeth became an exposed escarpment. There, the cropped bits of hair grown of actual gold were trees blurred by mist. Silver-gray skin stretched in mystery across the gullies, blue skin a pale canopy of sky. And running through it all, like woodland spirits, the twisted, translucent genetic patterns describing modifications to human systems that went beyond the bounds of the law.

Kirstin could claim a long and illustrious career of enforcing the law.

The law: there was no simple, profound statement that could contain it. The law of the Commonwealth was a very human thing, built on conviction and avarice, riddled with loopholes, as alive as the genetic record of the species and in as constant a state of change. An edifice built to address a primary concern: what is *human*? With the passing years, the answer to that became ever more difficult to define.

Unlike the ancestral type, a modern human need not grow old. Aging was considered a defect in the human genome, not as a defining parameter of the species. But the inclusion of artificial genetic structures was forbidden. There were exceptions. There were clauses. But a basic summary of the law could be held to say: mix and mingle active human genetic material as you like—change your color, change your size, change your face. Replace the genes for disease, for aging, for personality disorders with more socially acceptable versions. But do not mingle the human inheritance with nonhuman or artificial instructions. Do not augment the human mind with machine intelligence.

The law had much to say about nonhuman intelligence. Commonwealth society could not have functioned without an army of Dull Intelligences to oversee routine regulatory and analytical functions. But adaptive, volitional, or conscious machine intelligences were banned. By law, creativity was a function reserved for human minds.

Kirstin was a firm believer in the law.

She touched his shoulder. "You remind me of Leander Bohr in his last days."

Nikko shuddered. Leander Bohr. She brought up that name to torment him! Bohr had been a Gaian terrorist when he'd taken on a very youthful Kirstin as protégée and lover. He was still considered the greatest molecular designer who'd ever lived. Entirely self-taught, so the legend said. Unnumbered orphan from the slums of Berlin—some contemporaries swore Leander hadn't known how to read until he'd designed Bohr's Maker. Then the molecular machine taught *him*, illegally rewiring his neural architecture in the process.

Legal Makers were programmable molecular machines endowed with a Dull Intelligence that would enable them to execute only one function, or at most a series of functions leading to a single objective, such as the construction of a ship's hull or a set of clothes. By contrast, the Bohr Maker's capabilities were more openended. It could adapt itself to the needs of its host through an illegal self-programming feature.

At its essence, the Bohr Maker was a microscopic packet of instructions. But once the instructions were executed, it became a molecular communications and design system that would insinuate itself throughout the body and mind of a single host, resulting in profound physiological change. The host individual would own the talents of an expert in molecular design, along with the physical mechanisms to execute those designs.

Most Makers had a learning function that would allow them to refine their programming through experience. But the Bohr Maker could develop entirely new programming functions, at a rate that far exceeded the best human minds. The Bohr Maker was illegal under the law, not only because of its status as a volitional intelligence, but because its activities compelled the corruption of human physiology.

"I feel strange," Kirstin mused, her breath blowing soft over Nikko's kisheer. "Almost regretful. I haven't felt this way since those final hours with Leander."

Nikko felt the dry wings of panicked butterflies beating in his belly. He felt as if he were about to float away from the bed. "Did Bohr know he was doomed?"

She smiled indulgently. "I didn't have the same reputation then, Nikko dear. But *I* knew he was doomed. It's the same sense I have with you."

Nikko rolled away from her. She was toying with him. Daring him to ask for a reprieve . . . so she could turn him down.

He lay on the bed, staring at Kirstin's collage. Futility weighed on him in defiance of the tiny gravity. He felt he could hardly move. But Kirstin was as moody as a rock. "I'm glad you came today, Nikko darling," she said cheerily. "I've really had a bad day."

"Oh? What went wrong? No mutant babies for lunch?"

"If only." She laughed. "If only I could selectively terminate certain constituents of our research division . . . that Jensen Van Ness in particular."

Nikko felt his heart begin to thunder in his chest; his kisheer went still across his shoulders. Jensen Van Ness. Had she finally fixed him at that address? "Van Ness," he muttered, as if the name were a mere historical curiosity. "He was with the cops the day you brought down Leander Bohr; part of the investigative team, right?"

Kirstin ran a long-nailed finger down his forearm. "That's right. Why have you never interviewed him?"

"Who says I've never interviewed him?"

"I do keep an eye on these things, you know." She leaned over him, fixing him with an analytical stare . . . as if she could draw the truth out of him by mere force of will. But his face remained impassive, as always.

"You should make an appointment with Van Ness," she continued. "I think you'd like him. Because he's just like you—he has no *perspective* on the graceful state of human existence within the Commonwealth."

"Imagine that." Nikko's bitterness leached into his voice. "He's got to be a hundred and something years old. You'd think he would have learned by now."

She ignored him. "Van Ness got in my way today. The bastard. His one claim to fame is that he dissected the neural tissue from Leander's toasted corpse and isolated the Bohr Maker. Anybody could have done it. But he's lived off the moment ever since. And every time I petition to have the Bohr file destroyed, he logs a counterpetition claiming it as essential research material." Her lip curled in contempt. "He doesn't want his accomplishment erased. That's all."

She shook her head, setting her mane of coppery hair swaying. "The Bohr Maker is too dangerous to retain. Police Makers can't compete with it. We'd have to violate our own laws against adaptive artificial intelligence systems to make anything that would really threaten it. It has all the advantages. If it ever got loose, it could rearrange the balance of power in the Commonwealth as easily as it rearranged Leander's brain. But Van Ness doesn't give a damn about that. He'd rather risk the security of the Commonwealth than lose his prize."

Very quietly, Nikko said: "I don't blame him."

Kirstin gave him a withering stare. She knew how badly he wanted that Maker. She knew he'd tried to get to the file through her. Perhaps she suspected he'd also tried to get there through Van Ness.

She hissed softly. "Like I said. Neither one of you has any perspective."

Nikko suppressed a sigh. Things were going very badly. He should go home. There was no point in staying here.

But instead he forced himself up. "Get dressed," he said. "Take me to the balcony." He couldn't wander without her. Here he was only a ghost overlaid on her reality, dependent on her senses for a picture of her world.

Obligingly, she slipped her gown back on, then took his arm. They drifted together across the plush carpets, intermittant toe-taps enough to keep them aloft while they pretended at love. The door warden winked its amber electronic eye and a glass panel slid open.

Kirstin lived in Castle. The city was the seat of Commonwealth government, a bubble of life at the end of the space elevator that rose out of India. Atmospheric rockets had been banned for decades, and the elevator was the only means of travel between Earth and the orbital cities, creating an information bottleneck presided over by the police. The police maintained Gates at both ends of the elevator which logged the identity of every traveler going to or from Earth, while scanning them for illegal molecular material. In the early days of its construction, critics had mocked the elevator as the Imperial Highway, and the name stuck, as resonant names usually do.

Nikko gripped the glass cage that enclosed the balcony and looked out on the Highway. It was less than a kilometer away, a great ribbon of black glass and amber lights rising out of the Castle's courtyard, straight up past the hundreds of spires of intricately worked glass and white ceramic perfection that were the Castle towers, past the gel lock and the transparent bubble that encased this fairyland. On into the empty spaces of the Gulf until it vanished in the dark and the distance. Black on black, the Imperial Highway stretched for over forty thousand miles until it met the Earth.

It was night in India.

Every half hour an elevator car the size of a ten-story building would appear on one of the Highway's six Castle-bound tracks, decelerating rapidly as it approached the Castle gates. Fifteen minutes later another car would leave on one of the six Earth-bound tracks. Nikko could make that journey only as a ghost. His physique had been designed for the variable G of Summer House, his own native city, where the highest pseudogravity reached only three-quarters Earth normal. This was one of his few regrets.

He breathed in the pleasant atmosphere. It was a few degrees warmer here than inside, reminding him of the balmy interior of Summer House. He felt his dark mood begin to ease. Perhaps he could find it in himself to charm Kirstin after all.

He let himself drift down into a chair beside her, as a 'bot rolled onto the balcony, carrying a pot of tea on its flat back. It squatted between them, performing as a table.

Kirstin lifted the teapot and carefully poured a syrupy stream, then set china splash lids on the full cups. Steam rose in white tendrils through the sipping slots.

Nikko reached for his cup. His enameled fingers clacked against the bone-white china: like meeting like. He felt the searing heat and the steam in his nostrils. He lifted the cup. If a third person had been present, the intruding eyes would have seen the cup still upon the table, undisturbed, while Kirstin drank her tea alone, because a ghost could not really affect the physical world, not so much as by picking up a cup.

But within the cloistered reality shared by Nikko and Kirstin, this long-fingered hand that seemed to move the cup was a faithful depiction of the actual hand of the real Nikko Jiang-Tibayan, complete with the same disabilities. His hand twitched in a sudden, grotesque spasm. Scalding tea sloshed against the cup's lid, emerging like a dark ribbon through the sipping slot to collapse in a burning line across his wrist. He swore at the pain, and his hand snapped down, inadvertantly launching the cup toward the tiled floor. It fell like a tiny missile, shattering on impact, shards of ceramic perfection flying apart in a fountaining explosion of unhappy disorder.

Kirstin watched the pieces fly overhead, then fall back down again in long arcs. Globs and streamers of dark tea added to the illusory mess. She looked at Nikko and clucked in studied scorn. "You're getting so clumsy, Nikko darling. And my fine antiques! If you were real, and no ghost, I daresay I wouldn't have the nerve to bring them out at all."

His hand twitched again. He hated himself. He sat very stiff in his chair and stared out at the thread of the

Imperial Highway. "What do you expect?" he asked softly. "I'm dying."

"Oh, please. That's in such bad taste."

"You can stop it." He bit down hard on his lip, horrified at what he'd just said. He hadn't planned it. The words had just rolled off his tongue. He turned stiffly, to see what effect this blunder would have on Kirstin.

Her face was lit with the faintest of smiles. "At last, at last," she crooned. Her brown eyes seemed to chide him. "Nikko darling, I love you for your stubbornness. But I see even you have limits. And finally, after—what has it been now? two years in my bed?—you come to the point of this charade of love. 'Kirstin, dearest,'" she said, mocking his deep voice, "'I've screwed you faithfully. Now won't you grant me a reprieve?'" She laughed. "My sweet gigolo."

His kisheer unfolded across his shoulders in a short cape, the thin film of it aquiver with his silent rage. *Gigolo.* She was kind. *Whore* was the word he might have used. Fuck for your life.

"You're a hard old hypocrite," he told her. "But you won't have much longer to enjoy me in your bed. How do you think you'll feel when I'm irretrievably gone?"

"Oh, Nikko, you flatter yourself. Remember, you're a ghost. I've never even touched you, really. And you've never touched me."

"Ghost or flesh: we know what's real."

"You won't be the first lover who's died in my arms."

"There won't be anyone else like me."

"So true. Freak."

He bolted to his feet. He couldn't help himself. He caught hold of the glass cage that enclosed the balcony to arrest his momentum, then turned back to look at her. One long-fingered hand coiled in on itself as he recalled the smooth, soft vulnerability of her throat.

But he was only a ghost, and he'd never touched her.

"You know I need you," he said, his words emerging mangled past his shame. "What would you have me do?"

She smiled, her teeth an icy wall that seemed to flow out around him. He felt himself trapped in her voracious bite. "I would have you beg."

He was a dying man. And imminent mortality breeds its own desperation. *Beg.* He let go of the cage bars. He felt himself drift down to the tiles, legs bent. He landed on his knees. He watched himself, a ghost outside a ghost as the words she'd commanded spilled from his throat in a voice choked with frustration. "Please, Kirstin. You're the only one who might save me. Please grant me a reprieve. Just let me live."

"No." Her gaze cut across him in scathing triumph, from his head to his bended knees. "You're an illegal creation. An abomination in the eyes of the Goddess, and I will not abide your existence beyond your lawful span—no matter how fine a fuck you are."

He shuddered—a nikko-blue china teacup deliberately flicked off the table for the pleasure Kirstin would take in watching him shatter against the floor.

"Stop playing with me!" he screamed. "What do you want from me?"

"Nothing I haven't already taken."

"You can't let me die."

"I've been meaning to ask you—after you're gone, do you think you might will me your carapace? That fine china exoskull would make a marvelous addition to my bedroom collection."

His hands twitched. His fingers tapped like the legs of some monstrous spider against the dark skin of her finely muscled thigh. She'd gone too far. There were some affronts that even a whore couldn't overlook.

But it was all right, he told himself. He was glad

she'd done it. Because now the rules of the game would change.

He felt his anger blossom into a kind of fierce joy. Now there were no rules at all.

"Enjoy your moment," he told her. "Because I'll see to it you don't outlive me."

She laughed at the absurdity of his threat. "Oh, Nikko. I'm going to miss you. I really am."

But it was all right. He prepared his ghost to leave while she watched him with mocking eyes.

"You'll be back," she said. "Because you'll always carry the niggling hope that I might change my mind."

"Don't believe it." He left her, to retreat home across the net.

CHAPTER

3

Visions tumbled through Phousita's mind like paper images tossed about by an impish wind: scraps of memory, half-forgotten knowledge, outright fantasy, all aswirl, visible for a moment, then gone, gone, gone away to nowhere, swept around a corner, she couldn't catch them, hold on to them, every bit of her life slipping by. And something that wasn't a part of her life, recurring. A face. It appeared and disappeared, and alone amongst all the other images, appeared again. It matched nothing in her memory, this angular face, lovely as an angel. White skin, blond hair, unnaturally angry eyes. A song surged around it. She reached out to touch it and it faded again.

The song went on. It seemed to tug at her, and unwillingly, her eyes fluttered open.

Sumiati's lilting voice rolled over her and she found herself staring at the familiar mildew-stained graffiti that covered the wall beside her hammock. Afternoon sunlight streamed through the cracks between the boards, striping her fingers as they clutched at the hammock's coarse nylon webbing.

She could see the angel's face again. It seemed to drift just behind her eyes, a haunting, spectral image. Fear permeated her body like a poison. She lifted her head. Her hair clung in sticky threads to her sweat-dampened cheeks. Cautiously, she looked over her shoulder, half expecting to see the angel himself.

Sumiati squatted nearby, tending a pot of rice set to cook over a small gas fire. She sang a soft pop tune, mimicking words from a language no one but Arif understood. Two children played quietly beside her, seemingly oblivious of the oppressive afternoon heat. Silently, Phousita eased her aching body from the hammock. She swept her oily hair out of her face and shivered. What witch had sent her such an evil dream?

"Hey," she called softly. "Sumiati?"

The kids looked up from their game and started jabbering excitedly. Sumiati turned around to stare, her mouth a small circle of surprise.

"Sumiati, I don't feel very well," Phousita said. Her hand rose tentatively to a half-remembered wound on her breast. She frowned, perplexed, as the soft touch of her fingers elicited a mild jolt of pain. She looked down to see a tiny circle of angry red flesh.

"*Phousita!*"

Her head jerked up. Sumiati hunkered by the fire, staring at her as if she were a ghost. The children had fled.

"Phousita," Sumiati whispered. "Is it you?"

Phousita looked down at her hands. "I had a dream . . . about a dead man . . . and an angel."

"It was no dream! Oh, you said *tuan*'s presence here was a bad sign. Phousita, you were right." Despite the bulk of her pregnancy, Sumiati rose gracefully to her feet, her eyes suddenly brimming with tears. "*Tuan* was evil! You were so deeply asleep when Arif pulled you out of the river, we couldn't wake you. We thought *tuan* had killed you, and stolen your body to house his own wicked spirit. Phousita—" She caught Phousita's hands in hers, squeezed them tight, kissed her cheek. Her eyes were shining. "I'm so glad it's you."

But Phousita wasn't so sure. The image of the angel that occupied her mind—this was not the face of dead *tuan*. Still, she sensed something new inside her, a foreign presence rapidly growing in strength. She squatted by the cooking pot, staring into the blue gas flame. Compulsively, her fingers kept returning to the wound on her breast. *It was no dream.* Then *tuan* must have been a sorcerer. What spell had the needle cast when it entered her body?

Sumiati squatted beside her. She adjusted the height of the flame, then glanced at Phousita. "You know, I've never seen Arif so angry."

"Oh?" She looked up, surprised.

Sumiati nodded. "Yes. He said he would drive *tuan*'s spirit from your body or kill you himself."

Phousita glanced around nervously.

"He's gone," Sumiati assured her. "He took the Knives and went to temple market to sell *tuan*'s clothes. He's going to bring the Chinese doctor back with him, *whether he wants to come or not...*." She nodded knowingly.

Phousita's eyes widened in surprise. The Chinese doctor never left his little shop to visit patients. How would Arif convince him to come? And then, "I don't need a doctor," she realized. Any money Arif got from the clothes would be wasted on the doctor's fee. The clan needed that money for food! Fish and fruit for the children, more rice, cooking oil. And of course medicine, when the next plague swept through the city. Phousita rose to her feet. "I have to find him."

But Sumiati was shaking her head. "Arif warned me you might wake up and try to leave. He said I must keep you here. He left some of the Knives...." Her voice trailed off in embarrassment.

"Sumiati!" But the girl refused to look up. Phousita stamped her bare heel against the broken vinyl floor. She started toward the door, the only way out of this little room at the end of the warehouse where she and Sumiati and the littlest children took their naps.

A boy and a girl stepped out of the shadows beyond the door to block her way. Phousita could read fear in their eyes, but their hands were steady as they passed a knife back and forth in a deadly juggling act, the blade moving so quickly it seemed to be in a dozen places at once. The leaping blade of the knife wove a fence of steel across her path.

She stared up at them. Little Sri was only seven, yet already taller than she. Phousita had delivered her in the shelter of a cardboard box on a dark morning when the rain hammered down as if it were determined to flood the world. Maman was a year or two older (nobody was quite certain). Arif had rescued him from a municipal cop who was beating him for sleeping on the sidewalk after dawn.

Phousita had become surrogate mother for both of them. She knew they loved her. Would they really cut her? She didn't believe it, but their eyes begged her not to test them. Arif was their master. He'd trained them in this deadly game and he would beat them if they didn't obey.

Her fist clenched in sudden anger. To force children into such a terrible choice! To give pain, or to receive it. . . . She would have no part of that.

Her hand opened. She smiled gently and beckoned to them. "Come. We'll help Sumiati with the sewing." Gratitude shone in their eyes. She stepped back, and the flashing blade of the knife disappeared.

Through the last hour of the steamy afternoon Phousita and Sumiati tended to chores while the river grumbled beneath the rotting floorboards. There were clothes to be mended, children to be bathed, and more pots of rice to be cooked. (There was only one pot and one stove so that the rice had to be scraped into a large plastic tub after each batch was finished.)

Voices drifted in from the street—idle chatter of the homeless, the hungry, waiting for the cover of night before they tried to approach the river. Twice, alert sentries called the Knives out to defend the warehouse against trespassers. Shots rang out once. At the sound of the rifles Phousita and Sumiati hurried to the windows to peer past the crumbling cardboard shades.

A hunting party from the Islamic Resurgence occupied the cracked concrete of the riverbank. Two men stood guard, their ancient weapons at the ready while a third carefully searched the blood-soaked clothes of an emaciated beggar caught feeding on the fluff. The Resurgence claimed a devil had cast the spell that cleansed the river; they shot on sight anyone who dared to eat from the devil's hand. Someday soon they'd discover Arif's fluff booms under the warehouse and then they'd burn the old building down. The clan would make its home on the street again.

Phousita watched until the beggar's body was kicked into the water, then she turned away, picked up a broom, and began to sweep at nonexistent dust while once again the face of the white angel filled her inner vision. Altogether, it was a quiet afternoon.

"Arif is here!"

Phousita started awake at the whispered warning. Twilight had fallen. She lay in the half-light, numbed by the sweltering heat left behind by the long afternoon. Her shoulder ached where she'd been sleeping on the hard floor.

"Phousita?" the voice whispered again.

She stirred herself with an effort. "I'm here. I understand." A figure at the door turned away and disappeared. She looked around. Sumiati and the children were gone. She could hear a commotion in the front of the warehouse, the cheerful, bragging, bantering chaos that always accompanied the end of the day when the clan's foragers returned from the city. Her hand rose, to touch the sweat-slick skin surrounding the wound on her breast. In her belly, hunger growled and scraped like a beast in a barren cage.

Sumiati had left the last pot of rice on the floor to cool.

Phousita became profoundly conscious of this fact as she sat listening to the distant noise of the new arrivals. The pot was very close. It was possible she could reach it simply by raising her arm. Her belly roared in urgency. Never had she felt hunger like this! Perspiration trickled down her cheek as she fought to ignore the sweet aroma of the rice. Suddenly, she could stand it no longer.

"ARIF!" she screamed, and her fists pounded against the crumbling floor. "Arif come free me. I'm dying, dying." She pressed her face against the floor. The torn linoleum scraped her skin. The rice pot drew nearer. She couldn't understand how it did this. She tried to turn away from it. Her hands shook as she sought to burrow into the floor. Her fingers burned as the rice pot touched them. She snatched them away, but the pot pursued her, searing her palms with steam as she removed the lid. She flung it across the room and screamed again. She pounded her forehead against the floor, again and again and again. Pain thundered in her skull, but the hunger would not recede. She collapsed, sobbing hysterically, her cheek pressed against the searing metal of the cooking pot.

"*Where is she?*" "*Get out of the way!*" "*It's plague, I knew it.*" The voices seemed to blur together, melted into one by a blinding yellow light. Strong arms lifted her, rolled her gently until she lay on her back. "Eat, Phousita." Someone placed rice in her mouth and she swallowed without chewing. Another mouthful, and another. The blurred figures around her began to resolve

into recognizable faces. Sumiati. Sri. And the hand that
fed her? She caught the wrist; looked up into the cool
brown eyes of the Chinese doctor.

He was a young man, by his appearance not much
older than Phousita, with a pale, translucent complexion and thick black hair tied neatly behind his neck.
"Eat, Phousita," he said again.

She stared at the rice in his hand while saliva
pooled in her mouth. She swallowed hard. "No one else
has eaten," she whispered.

"No one else has plague. Eat."

"I'm dying?"

"We don't know that yet. Eat."

"Arif." She squinted against the glare of a lantern,
searching for his nightmare face amongst the crowd that
squatted around her.

"Here." He touched her elbow.

She twisted around to face him. "Free me," she
whispered. She reached up to brush her fingertips
against the hilt of the knife he carried strapped across
his chest. "Don't waste the clan's food on me."

His clown's mouth fell open. He shook his head,
but at the same time he started to reach for the blade.

The Chinese doctor batted his hand away. "*No!*" he
barked. "You kidnapped me. You dismantled my office
and brought it down here. Now it's my turn! I want to
find out which plague's infected her—*then* we'll consider the knife."

He turned to the children behind him and began
snapping orders. A flat blue-gray box was handed to
him. He opened it, revealing a glass window flooded
with tiny amber symbols. Phousita recognized some of
them. She'd been to Zeke Choy's shop many times.
He'd shown her this *computer* before; taught her the
names of the letters. He placed the device carefully on
the ground, then accepted a small satchel from one of
the onlookers. He opened it, examined the contents,
set it aside, then looked around for the third and final

item. A small sky-blue case was passed into his hands. He set it on the ground, then opened it carefully. On one side was a tiny keyboard and a black-on-gray display. On the other a glass window shielded what seemed like a thousand slender tubes, some containing colored liquids, some clear. The clan muttered in admiration. The Chinese doctor was a sorcerer of wide renown; still, to think he could command so many spells. . . .

Zeke Choy scowled at his audience. "Damn superstitious fools," he muttered.

Phousita looked up as someone nudged her elbow. Arif. He smiled at her—a manic expression given the exaggerated features of his face. She knew it was meant to be reassuring. He helped her to sit up. She was weak, hardly able to support her own weight. Her head felt muzzy, and hunger still raged in her belly. But she tried to put her discomforts aside, so that she could attend to the doctor as he began the rite.

From the satchel he removed a tiny glass rod and a piece of paper. The paper opened to reveal a *lancet*. Phousita was familiar with this procedure. She'd performed it herself on plague victims who'd been too ill or unstable to journey to Zeke Choy's shop. She turned her hand palm up. The doctor took it, lanced a finger and used the glass rod to capture a bit of her blood. He would use the blood to divine the nature of her affliction. If it were an old plague, perhaps he could cure it. If not. . . .

She watched him insert the glass rod into a small hole in the face of the *computer*. The onlookers muttered encouragement and whispers of hope. He was a great sorcerer. Everyone knew it, though the doctor himself would always insist it was not so.

A chime sang. Phousita shivered as a sense of fatalism settled over her. She was old, nearly twenty-five— even Arif was her junior. Most members of the clan didn't live beyond fifteen.

Many times she'd imagined this moment, played out in her mind the feelings and fears that would haunt her in this inevitable time when she would finally face the reality of her own death after having witnessed the deaths of so many others. Her heart raced in a thready beat but she kept silent as Zeke Choy studied the pattern of letters on his computer screen.

He seemed puzzled. His brow knit, his scowl deepened. Phousita felt a cold sweat break out across her face. A wave of dizziness took her and she sagged against Arif, who held her tight. A wail of mourning arose from the gathered clan.

The doctor looked up in irritation, his thin hand chopping the air. "Stop it! Stop it, will you? It's nothing!"

The wail cut off abruptly.

"Nothing?" Sumiati said, her round face confused in the lantern light.

"*Damn vultures,*" the doctor muttered. A curse, but the meaning was unclear.

"*Tuan,*" Phousita asked timidly. "It is not plague?"

"No, no, of course not," he growled. "The poor sap you found in the river must have been a civilized gent. He hit you with a registered defensive toxin, that's all. He was probably from the EC. The fatal toxins are illegal there. This drug was designed to knock an attacker down fast and keep him under until the police arrived."

"The Commonwealth Police?" Arif demanded, his fist closing tightly on Phousita's arm. Sumiati moaned in fear.

The doctor snorted. "No, the *municipal* police," he said. "Crimes of assault are prosecuted in the EC."

Phousita didn't know what he was talking about, yet she sensed the words were a veil, intended to hide a more significant discovery. Apparently Arif suspected too.

"There's more," he hissed, deliberately omitting the

polite address *tuan.* "You've found another curse in her blood. What is it?"

"Nothing!" the doctor barked. "Give her a decent meal and she'll be fine. Phousita!" Phousita looked up, startled. "You're the shaman here. Now that your *wayang* goon has dragged me halfway across the city, I might as well get some work done. Who needs medical attention?"

Over the next hour he saw five children as well as Sumiati, then he shared dinner with the clan. From time to time during the meal he glanced at Phousita, his gaze searching. But he said nothing, and despite the return of her strength, she began to grow afraid, certain now that he hid something from her.

At the end of the meal, he announced his intention to call for a cab to take him home. "You hauled me on foot across the city, but I've no intention of walking back." He retrieved the *computer,* opened it, and tapped thoughtfully at the keys. "Where are we?" he asked after a moment, looking up at Arif.

Arif shrugged disdainfully. "There is no address here."

"The street, man! What is the name of the street?"

"Riverside. That's all."

The doctor muttered angrily under his breath, while tapping quickly at the keys. He seemed to find the results satisfactory, because his scowl softened as he sat back on his heels. "They know the place. I'll wait on the street."

"It's not safe to wait on the street," Phousita said quickly. Arif started to argue with her—of *course* his Knives would be watching—but she silenced him with a look. "I'll wait with you. No one will trouble you if they see me there."

"You've got a dangerous reputation, eh?"

She bowed her head, mortified. "The street people here know I belong to Arif."

"Ah." He gathered up his bags and she hurried to

assist him, but he wouldn't accept her help. The clan bowed deeply as he turned to go. Remembering his manners at the last, he turned back and executed a peremptory bow, then left by the room's only door. "Phousita!" he bellowed, when he discovered himself blind in the lightless passage.

Arif stood beside the door, an evil grin on his face. He dropped a flashlight into Phousita's hand as she hurried past him. She squeezed the tube and the darkness in the corridor scurried away.

"That's better," the Chinese doctor sniffed. "I thought for a minute I'd have to feel my way out."

She led him in silence to the front of the building, past the guards and onto the street.

The wayside was crowded with hovels—pitiful shelters made of woven mats, cardboard, and plastic sheets. The street was slick with rain. A baby fussed nearby, and someone sang in a deep, guttural hill tongue. "Ah, there's the cab," Zeke Choy said, seeing a light approaching in the distance.

"We're alone now," Phousita said. "Please tell me what else you divined in my blood."

The doctor looked suddenly uncomfortable. "That's the trouble," he said softly. "I can't tell you. I don't know what it is."

"But the *computer*—"

"I try to keep the data base accurate, but new plague appears all the time. You know that."

Her heart thundered. "Then it is a plague."

He shook his head. "Phousita, I don't know *what* it is. But I'll find out; I've still got the sample. In the meantime, well...." He shrugged.

The light of the cab drew nearer. He raised his satchel to gain the driver's attention. But he jerked his hand back down as a woman screamed in terror from a nearby alley. Immediately, the street village was plunged into silence.

Phousita grabbed the doctor's elbow and drew him

backward until they were pressed against the door of the warehouse. "What is it?" he hissed. She shook her head, uncertain. The street was dark. Gas fires, stars, a few scattered flashlights: in the diffuse light she could make out the thoroughfare and the village that crowded the wayside, but she saw nothing that would—

She caught her breath as two great beasts trotted into view from the alley. They paused for a moment in the center of the thoroughfare, their armored heads swinging slowly back and forth as their nostrils tested the air. She could hear them snuffling. "Police dogs," Zeke Choy muttered. He said it like a curse.

Phousita stood very still, wondering whom the dogs sought tonight. They were the servants of the Commonwealth Police. Their massive heads reached as high as a man's shoulder. Phousita had seen one crush a woman's skull in a single bite.

The dogs trotted slowly down the street, pausing now and then at a rickety shelter to lower their heads and examine visually the cowering inhabitants. In the harsh headlights of the approaching cab, their armored skulls glinted purest silver.

"Bloody useless corruption of science," the Chinese doctor muttered.

The lead dog stopped at the sound—a great black beast with mottled brown patches in its fur. Its eyes seemed to be made of glass laid over a gaping, black abyss. It approached.

Phousita felt her heart thud. She pressed herself against the door, guided by some instinct that insisted against all reason that maybe, maybe, she could make herself invisible. She dearly wanted to be invisible.

Zeke Choy though, seemed unconcerned. He stood quietly as the dog sniffed him, its sensitive nostrils carefully examining his hands, his clothes, the bags he carried. "Nothing illegal there, you fascist, imperialist pigs," he muttered. "Every molecule is licensed and registered."

Phousita stared at him, dumbstruck. She didn't understand what he'd said, but she was used to that. But who had he said it to? The *dog*? And did he expect the animal to reply? He was a great sorcerer, yet.... She looked at the animal. But it made no attempt to speak. Instead it turned its attention on her, its great, hot breath whooshing across her skin. Its companion joined it, standing back a few paces, examining her with its soulless eyes.

"Leave her alone," the doctor growled. "She's nothing to do with you."

Did the dogs obey him? They backed off, still sniffing suspiciously as if they were unsure of what they'd found. But finally they moved off, continuing their search farther down the street.

"They've no business here, no jurisdiction," Zeke Choy said. He looked at Phousita. "Don't let them scare you. The Commonwealth isn't interested in people like you and me."

Phousita had never imagined herself as a peer of the doctor. But she bowed her head and nodded.

The cab had stopped a few meters down the road. It pulled up now and Zeke Choy threw his bags in the open door. "Come to my shop in a few days. I'll examine you again. And don't worry ... there won't be a fee."

She started to object, but he shook his head and ordered the cab on. Phousita ducked inside the shelter of the old warehouse as soon as he was out of sight.

CHAPTER

4.

"Y ou were with her again, weren't you?"

Nikko started at the unexpected voice. His gaze shifted from the dark eye of the camera lens to the door of his apartment. It had opened, admitting his father.

Wordlessly, he turned back to the camera. The four-centimeter lens floated on the end of a tentacle. The tentacle sprouted from a data-storage plate lying beside him on the couch amidst a jumble of straps that would allow him to wear the camera as a backpack. Guided by a Dull Intelligence, the camera had turned, recording an image of Fox.

"Why do you continue to visit her, Nikko?"

Nikko's ghost had left Kirstin and come home to Summer House nearly an hour ago. He'd absorbed its impassioned memories, and now he was involved in dictating them into the camera's data base. For the past several weeks he'd been assembling a documentary exploring his struggle against his own preprogrammed death. He felt it to be the most important piece of work he'd ever done. He did not like to admit, even to himself, that it would probably be his last.

He held up his hands, so that Fox couldn't overlook their ugly twitching and trembling. At this level of Summer House the spin-generated pseudogravity was nearly two-thirds Earth normal, and his shaking hands reflected the strain. "Kirstin's star material," he said, staring into the faithful lens of the attentive camera. Sarcasm put a bitter edge on his voice. "What better way to get people to watch a documentary detailing my state-sanctioned murder than by including the antics of the ever-popular Chief of Police? Her involvement guarantees the biggest audience any treatise of mine has ever enjoyed."

"You won't hurt her," Fox said. "She'll deny everything. She always does."

The tentacle swung around, tracking Fox's part in the debate. The image it recorded was of a tall, pale man with a head of thinning red hair and a system-wide reputation in molecular design. Oddly for a designer who specialized in physiological applications, he actually looked well aged—near sixty on a physiological scale, though his chronological age was even more—ninety-seven, according to the records. Fox would claim he preferred the "dignity" of obvious maturity. Nikko figured it was just another act of penance on the part of a guilt-ridden father, but on the subject of Fox and Fox alone Nikko kept any such acerbic opinions to himself.

"You're wasting your time with her, Nikko. She's using you. She'll never grant you a reprieve, no matter what you do for her."

"I know it, Fox." Nikko felt this truth as a knot deep in his gut. To ease his own tension, he asked, half jokingly, "I don't suppose you've added a new Maker to your bag of tricks lately? Something that might help her change her mind?"

It was the wrong thing to say. Despite Nikko's unique beginnings in his father's lab, Fox had proved to be a typical parent, given to self-doubts and worry over his own role as a father. He'd spent much of the last thirty years tormenting himself over the wording of the research permit. And now Nikko had inadvertently given him a chance to indulge in another round of guilt. "Nikko, you know what my behavioral Makers will do. If I had one that good, I would have used it by now."

"Huh." His kisheer trembled briefly about his shoulders. "You could make one that good. But you won't."

To Nikko's mind, that was the wound that lay between them—not the damned research permit. Fox was Summer House and Summer House had made its reputation on marginal-tolerance Makers: those programmable molecular machines that came questionably close to modifying human, environmental, or artificial intelligence systems beyond the limits imposed by Commonwealth law. But the law was an artificial constraint. Its restrictions had created a seething, boiling frontier of creative energy, crushed between the successes of the past and the limited present. It was an unstable situation, ripe for provocation. . . . But Fox had always refused to cross the line.

"Camera off." The tentacle sank down against the storage plate, while Nikko's tremulous fingers hammered against his thigh in an angry, staccato beat. "You really want to help me, Fox? Then design a Reaper Maker that can reach Kirstin. Let me take her down before I go under."

Fox gave him a look of open contempt. "You want me to risk the security of the House for a simple revenge killing?"

"Gotta start somewhere." His kisheer rippled like an angry cat's tail. "You've been playing it safe too long."

The Commonwealth had been created to keep people safe from the new technologies, to protect them from themselves and from one another. Its creation hadn't ended the existence of the old nations of Earth. The EC, California, the Atlantic Seaboard Union, Australia, Japan, and hundreds of other countries were still functioning political entities, with their own laws and their own customs. But like the newer Celestial Cities, they'd ceded some of their sovereign rights to the Commonwealth. They'd all agreed that biological and technological law would be determined by a Commonwealth judiciary, with severe penalties for any transgression.

Not every country on Earth had joined the Commonwealth. Many had retained a paper independence, for reasons of nationalism or because of religious ethics. But even in these backward countries Commonwealth law was enforced, by specific agreement if possible, but if not, then by espionage. For no independent body could be allowed to develop technology surpassing that of the Commonwealth, or the police would become helpless and the Commonwealth would crumble overnight.

Perhaps the effort to control technological change had been laudable in the early days. But to Nikko's mind it had gone on too long, imposing too many rules, too many restrictions, too many limits in what could be a limitless world. Why designate the present human form as the end result of evolution when there were so many other possibilities? Nikko dreamed of the day when he could blow it all wide open.

"We can't win by defying the police," Fox told him. "You've got to stop thinking like a child."

"I don't want to defy the police. I want to break the Commonwealth."

"I want it too! You know that. And it will happen. But the time's not right."

"The time?" Nikko's kisheer moved across his face like a mask, its tendrils starting to fuse with his skin and the soft tissue of his mouth and nose. He yanked his head back. With a mental effort, he forced the kisheer down. "There won't *be* any other time for me, Dad. I've done all I can. You've done all you're willing to do. Nothing left now but to close up accounts." He fought to calm the trembling kisheer, hating it for all that it revealed about him.

But Fox took no notice. He was shaking his head. "It's not over yet," he said. "You still have a few more weeks. Sit tight, Nikko. Don't expose yourself. I need this time. I might have a way to hide you, but—" He turned away, his hands pulling at his red hair in frustration. "Love and Nature! I'm not ready to talk about this yet." He stomped toward the door.

But Nikko had tasted a hint of something forbidden. He sprang up from the couch. "Fox, don't fade on me now. What are you working on?"

Fox shook his head and waved his hand in dismissal. He took another two steps toward the door. But then he seemed to reconsider. He turned to face Nikko. "We may be able to code you into the biogenesis function," he blurted out.

"The biogenesis function?" Nikko couldn't keep the scorn out of his voice. "That's no refuge. It's a fantasy."

The biogenesis function was Fox's pet project—a theoretical complex of assembly codes that would define every element of Summer House and its internal environment in a sequenced construction plan. Wrap the code in a packet of assembly Makers, drop it on an appropriate substrate, and—in theory at least—it would be possible to replicate the entire House.

In theory.

"The biogenesis function is never going to exist, Fox. It's too complex."

"Its complexity can hide you," Fox said softly, in a voice that betrayed his own uncertainty.

"I don't want to be a string of code! I want to be alive. I would do anything to stay alive."

Fox nodded grimly. "I know. You've proved that with Kirstin." He started for the door again.

Nikko's kisheer trembled in anger. But his bitter retort was silenced by a sudden wave of dizziness. A psychic breeze seemed to blow over him, sweeping away his strength. He stared at Fox's retreating back in confusion. He wanted to call out to Fox for help, but words eluded him. He watched the door open; watched Fox leave. The door closed, leaving him alone in the room, questions crowding his mind but the will to speak them oddly gone. He sagged back down onto the couch, his body weak, his mind reeling. The sensation frightened him. He didn't know what to make of it. It occurred to him that he might be dying much sooner than expected.

A figure moved near the door. He saw it on the periphery of his vision and relief washed over him. Fox had come back. "Dad?" he croaked.

The bout of dizziness was passing, though the tremor in his hands seemed to have gotten worse. He lifted his head. But it wasn't Fox standing near the door. It was a little gentleman, whom Nikko was quite sure he'd never seen before. "Who the hell are you?" he growled. "And how did you get in here?"

The stranger was small and lithe, with skin as milky-white as Nikko's little brother, Sandor, and with hair as blond. He drew himself up, his chest puffed out like some cartoon caricature. "You've taken something that doesn't belong to you!" he announced imperiously. "I command you to give it back. Give it back, or—"

Nikko laughed. He couldn't help it. This little man was about as fierce as a tiger cub imitating a tiger. "Nature save us twice," he chuckled. "And whose joke are you?"

The stranger's scowl collapsed. His puffed-up belligerence vanished like yesterday's rumors. His eyes roved restlessly from side to side as if he were mentally searching for guidance.

"Oh, bother." He turned half away from Nikko, his left hand working in a nervous fist. A faint flush troubled the moonlight complexion of his face. "I just can't pull this sort of thing off," he muttered. "I've never had it in me. Well. I still have to do it, don't I? Of course. That's why I came." He stomped his foot heartily, then gazed up at Nikko, his jaw thrust forward in a comical display of determination. "Look," he said at last. "You've got to give it back, that's all. Just give it back. You don't really want it, you know."

"What?" Nikko asked. A gentle wave of anxiety rippled through his kisheer.

"The Maker! The Maker of course. The one that you've stolen. Oh, you're good." He shook his head in what seemed to be a gesture of admiration. "People have tried before. Of course, of course. Nothing new under the sun. Everything there is to do, has been done, time and time again. So many people. Impossible to be the first or the only anymore." He frowned. "Except of course you've done it. That's why I'm here. That's right. You were the first to succeed. Oh, you're good. But—"

He shook his head again, this time in a seeming gesture of despair. "How I run on! Do forgive me. Back to the Maker: it'll bring you nothing but trouble. That's what I wanted to say. The police won't rest until they have you—"

At mention of the police, Nikko's kisheer went still. So he had a trail to cover. What Maker did this gentleman mean? Where? He searched his memory. He had ghosts pursuing several research projects, but he'd received nothing illegal lately. He stared at the little man, mystified. But of course his uninvited guest could read nothing of that on his expressionless face. "Are you a cop?" Nikko asked softly.

"No, no of course not. If I were, I wouldn't have bothered to come here. You'd already be arrested."

"Then who—" He jumped as the door opened.

Fox had come back. Nikko turned to him with a rush of relief. But Fox would have none of it. He didn't even glance at the little man. His pointing finger and his red-faced anger were directed solely at Nikko.

"You've been drawing Sandor into your schemes again! I've just had a call from Castle. You've been tampering with his schedule. I won't have it, Nikko! Risk yourself if that's what you feel you must do. It's your business. I can't stop you. But don't involve your brother!"

Nikko looked between Fox and the odd little gentleman. "You don't see him, do you, Fox?"

Something in Nikko's voice must have registered with Fox, because he hesitated, and glanced around as if he suddenly sensed something odd afoot. His gaze swept across the little man without slowing.

Nikko felt his heart freeze. When it started beating again, it thundered in his chest.

The little man looked chagrined. "Didn't you know I was a ghost? That was the whole point of this effort! How could I hope to terrify you in person? Well. You've finally worked it out. I certainly am a ghost."

A cold, thorny lump of fear settled in the bottom of Nikko's stomach. "I didn't open my atrium to you," he whispered.

The little man grinned in relief. "Exactly!" he cried. "*I* opened it. I can command it. You see, that's the point. I've gotten past your defensive Makers and now I can admit anything into your atrium. And I can order your atrium to admit anything to your mind. I can destroy you." He looked down, as if a trifle embarrassed at this last statement. "Well, I don't want to, you know. But if you don't give up the Maker, I'll have to do it. I will. And that'll be that for you."

Nikko's kisheer began to tremble again. It was one thing for this man to invade his apartment. Another thing entirely to invade his mind. He started to rise from the couch.

"Nikko!" Fox demanded. "What's wrong with you?"

Nikko commanded his atrium to shut down. It wouldn't obey him. He commanded it to evict any present persona. Nothing happened.

"Useless," the little man said. "Until I turn control back over to you."

Nikko turned to Fox. Fox could rid him of this ridiculous parasite. Fox knew defensive Makers better than anyone. . . .

"I've been poisoned," Nikko hissed.

"Oh stop!" the little stranger said. "Keep this to yourself. Don't let it get out of hand." He deliberately stepped in front of Fox. "Look. I've got one of your ghosts. The very thief, in fact, who stole my Maker. I'm going to dump it on you. I have to do it that way, you see, so you'll know that I can. But I'll be back. I want that Maker." He vanished.

Nikko stared at the spot where he'd been standing. Then his chin snapped up as a tone in the mid-range hummed in his head. He'd never heard the signal before and it took him a second to dredge up the implanted memory of an emergency beacon. A ghost was coming in, and it wouldn't stop at Summer House plexus to await an invitation. It would drop directly into his atrium and he had no way to stop it. The tone stretched from one second to three. Only he, Fox, and his brother Sandor possessed his emergency code.

"Nikko!" Fox shouted. His hands were on Nikko's shoulders. "What's wrong with—"

The ghost flooded his atrium. A disembodied face flickered into existence. He recognized Sandor. The fingers of his left hand hammered against the smooth enamel of his thigh. "Sandor?" he croaked, uncertain. Sandor was only eighteen and Earth-side for the first time. *Leave him out of this!* Nikko thought fervently. *Let it be me.* For he'd developed the vice of ghosting behind his brother's face. Sandor was human-ordinary . . . far more difficult to trace than Nikko. And Sandor had a pretty face, a face that people seemed to warm to almost instinctively.

"It's Nikko!" the ghost barked, removing all doubt. "We've got trouble—"

The unheard-of happened. The ghost slipped out of the atrium and poured itself into his mind. Not the slow soak of an ordinary return, when the atrium gradually layered the memories of the ghost onto his original self. But a sudden, horrible awakening, a discovery of a past he hadn't lived and couldn't be responsible for.

A moment later the available blood sugars in his brain had been consumed. He dropped to the floor.

Scattered impressions swept over him as his heart pumped tides of energy to his brain, enough to sustain a pulsing consciousness. The soft carpet against his forehead . . . now against his back. Soft light in his eyes. Fox, voice anxious, shouting, shaking him by the shoulders . . . the foot of the sofa pressed into the carpet. . . .

Earth-side: the quest for the Bohr Maker.

Ah ha! The Bohr Maker! That was what the little gentleman had meant. Then he'd done it, he'd actually done it. He'd lifted the Maker right out of police files. Oh, the little man had been right. He was good. But then—

Disaster. Failure.

"Nikko!" a stranger shouted at him. "Wake up! Answer me!" A sharp slap to his face, then another. "Nikko!"

"Leave me alone!" he growled. He rolled over onto his stomach, shoved himself up on hands and knees. His head still swam. An IV ran out of his shaking arm.

"Stay down," the medic urged, applying gentle pressure to his shoulder. "We only want you awake, not ambulatory." She almost succeeded in tipping him over.

"Leave me alone!" Nikko roared, slapping her hand away. He sat back, panting. A niggling pain stung his arm. He looked down at the IV; yanked it out. It left a drop of blood behind.

"Dammit!" the medic cursed, trying to slap a patch on the wound.

An arm encircled his heaving shoulders. Fox leaned close to him. "Nikko, you fainted," he said softly. "Sit still a moment, before you go down again."

"Leave me alone," he whispered.

The odd little man might return at any moment. Nikko didn't think he could stand that. He wanted the atrium out of his head. He wanted it out *now*. He wanted it off. He issued the order.

To his surprise, the atrium obeyed him. It shut itself off. He sagged against Fox in relief.

"That's right," Fox crooned, hugging him. "Relax. Lie down—" Nikko shoved his arms away and struggled to his feet. He had the Bohr Maker! But Fox would never condone that. Too dangerous to cross the police. . . .

His legs felt rubbery, his brain abuzz. He leaned against a wall and forced himself to laugh. "Told you my time was up," he said to Fox, trying to turn the whole incident into a dark-humored joke. "An attack like that has to be a precursor to The End."

Fox clearly didn't believe him. "That wasn't part of the syndrome," he said. "You were with a ghost."

"No." He pushed himself away from the wall. Scooping the camera pack from the couch, he slung it over his shoulder and staggered drunkenly toward the door, feeling as if his blood had been drained and replaced with water.

Fox caught his arm. "I want you in the hospital."

"I'm all right!" Nikko shouted. He yanked his arm out of Fox's grip and shrugged into the camera pack. "And like you said, Dad. It's *my* business."

The door slid open for him. He lurched across the corridor to the transit node.

"Nikko, let me help you," Fox pleaded.

"Not this time, Dad."

He plunged into the thick jelly of the transit's protoplasmic column. Summer House immediately evacuated a transit bubble around him: an oval cell of soft, fleshy brown walls, with an extruded seat that would cradle him against acceleration. Tentatively, he switched on the atrium, just long enough to tell Summer House his destination. "Anywhere outside, by the fastest route."

The bubble that contained him shot into the transport system, whisking him through the city and between the great cells of the oceans to the outer walls. He shrugged his trembling kisheer up over his face. The respiratory organ's supple tissue fused with the papillae in his nose and mouth, and sealed across his ears. A burst of mildly euphoric chemicals accompanied the closure, easing him past the gag reflex that Fox had not quite engineered out. A moment later, a flood of sweet oxygen flowed from the accessory organ into his respiratory tract. He breathed it gratefully. The oxygen was harvested from waste carbon dioxide in his blood and breath, in a process fueled by his own metabolism. In theory, the system could operate indefinitely, allowing him to live for weeks in the void, without respite. He might even hide from the police for a while, in the vast glassine forests. The thought teased at his mind, though it stirred dread in him rather than hope. He didn't think of himself as a creature of the void, but rather as a creature of the strand, moving freely between the worlds of air and vacuum. And besides, he could not *eat* with the kisheer in place. While his body's waste products could be effectively recycled by his genital organ, the thought of living off an intravenous line seemed absurd to him. He would not live out his last weeks as a refugee. He would not let the police—or anyone else—force him to that.

A warning chime sounded. A moment later, Summer House spilled him into the void.

CHAPTER

5

He emerged near the top of the inhabited portion of Summer House. The zone of the vacuum-adapted, glassine forest that Kirstin admired began here, on the narrowing slopes of the cone-shaped habitat. Over the years, the forest had spread almost a quarter way up the thirty-two-kilometer tether that bound the habitat to a chondritic asteroid.

Habitat and asteroid: they functioned as counterweights on the ends of the tether. The whole arrangement spun once every five and a half minutes, generating a pseudogravity in the habitat that at its maximum was three-quarters that of Earth. A hundred kilometers away, the cylindrical shape of the city's magnetic launch tube winked in metallic gold.

Nikko climbed the forest. Though the gravity at this elevation was less than two-thirds Earth normal, it was still hard going. He felt crippled by his trembling hands. It was a struggle just to get his fingers to work in concert. But he pushed on through the tangle of black glass trees, driven by a primal, irrational instinct to flee—as if he could run away from the bastard who'd poisoned him. It was senseless, he knew it. But he needed the exertion to burn out his terror, his awful sense of helplessness.

In a few minutes he reached the top of the habitat. The grade changed abruptly from a steep slope to perpendicular as he moved onto the tether, but otherwise there was no change in the composition of the airless forest.

He kept at his frantic pace for nearly an hour, climbing three kilometers up the tether before he finally collapsed, exhausted, at the base of one of the thousands of black glass trees. His fingers twitched frantically, like worms cast into a fire. There wasn't enough strength left in them to make a fist.

He sucked air in harsh gasps from the kisheer. The organ didn't seem to be producing enough oxygen. It was starving him. He wanted to spit it out. He longed for atmosphere. But he knew that desire would pass. He didn't have to fear the void. He'd been designed for it. All he had to do was relax. . . .

Ignoring his hands, he lay still, gazing up at the tree's coin-shaped silver leaves, waiting for his breathing to slow. Incoherent snatches of memory boiled through his mind, so that his thoughts resembled a fragmented dream . . . or nightmare. Visions of hell: beggars squatting in the paltry shade of a dying banyan tree, their cracked plastic bowls thrust in his face. Uniformed thugs armed with kem-wands. Himself, a fugitive, trapped inside the cardboard walls of a squalid little hotel room, the heat so torrid he felt as if he'd been buried in hot sand, impossible to breathe it, to move through it. Regret and fear as thick as the air. Riotous laughter from another room. The Bohr Maker.

How could things have gone so wrong? Where had he been? He couldn't tell, just yet. His brain was exhausted; his recollections confused. *Relax*, he told himself. And things will fall into place.

So far only one thing was clear: he'd been poisoned. Someone had infected him with a Maker that had slipped right past his own defensive molecules to meddle with his atrium, revising the access codes and tearing his mind wide open to the whims of a stranger. Anger started to boil again inside him as he thought about it. Summer House had been placed in a deliberately remote orbit: sunside of Venus and at an angle to the plane of the ecliptic. It was not easy to get to. Someone must have begun moving against him months ago to have a Maker in place at Summer House. Someone had been stalking him, watching him for Nature knew how long, and he'd never even *suspected*.

As his heart began to calm and his breathing to slow, he bestirred himself long enough to climb the slick trunk of the tree, moving in clumsy fits and starts until he lay prone on one of the major branches.

The black-trunked, silver-leaved trees were one of only two plant species developed for the airless forest. They grew in graceful arcs from the vertical axis of the tether, turning away from the spin's outward pull. Between them grew brittle shrubs—a shadowy habitat for a population of small, furtive creatures resembling lizards. Nikko had no idea what the lizards were afraid of, as no predators had ever been introduced to the forest. Most likely their behavior was just a bit of historical trash preserved by chance long past its age of usefulness.

He'd climbed three kilometers up the tether—a fraction of its length, but high enough that he could look back down from his perch on the tree branch to the inhabited portion of the House below.

The House was an organic, living habitat, controlled by a network of nearly ten thousand neural centers. Oceans formed the outer walls of the inhabited section: great cells of water that mimicked aquatic environments of Earth. Sunlight was piped through the insulating oceans to hallways and corridors and beyond, to the great rain forest that filled the city's core.

The tether was an extension of the living habitat, binding it to the counterbalancing asteroid affectionately known as the "mother rock," as it had contributed over half its original mass to the construction of Summer House. Now the asteroid functioned as a reservoir of organic materials. Glazed with cometary ice and then coated with a stabilizing paint to minimize sublimation, it glistened like a small white star at the far end of the tether.

Time passed and Nikko's mind began to calm. Gradually, his whirling memories settled out in orderly sequence, and he found himself reliving the Earth-side experiences of his abducted ghost:

He recalled first the contempt he'd felt as he stared at Jensen Van Ness. Only a few hours ago the man had been a senior researcher in the Commonwealth Police, a molecular designer second only to Fox in renown.

Now Van Ness was a fugitive. He huddled cross-legged on the filthy carpet of a ramshackle hotel room in the Spill, his hollow gaze focused inward, his lips trembling, his shoulders hunched in acute dejection. He seemed oblivious to the fleas that crawled from the carpet into his clothing. But Nikko could feel them.

Nikko was only a ghost, existing within Van Ness's atrium. But the synthesized environment that contained him provided a high level of verisimilitude, down to the simulated bites of simulated fleas on the soft, human-ordinary skin of his ankles—for as always, Nikko had come to Van Ness disguised within his brother Sandor's physical appearance.

He knew his role. "It'll be all right," he lied, trying to ignore the horrible itching around his ankles, and the steaming heat that drove perspiration from every pore. "We'll get out of this."

But the voracious fleas worked in concert with the

heat to wear at his ever-limited patience. *"So pull your-self together before you kill us both!"*

Van Ness didn't respond. The treacherous bastard. He'd tried to steal the Bohr Maker on his own, for himself, without Nikko's knowledge. He'd taken the Maker and fled his home. But doubt and fear had caught him in the Spill.

Suddenly Van Ness gasped, as if trying to recapture a breath that had vanished from his lungs. His chin trembled, his head came up. His anxious gaze fixed on Nikko.

His appearance was that of a twenty-year-old, though Nikko knew he was well over a hundred. He had luxurious black hair—too well behaved to be natural—and a red *kanji* tattooed on his cheek, proclaiming him a life member of some snooty executive club. Hair and tattoo: they were the only two features Nikko really noticed. For the rest of him, Van Ness fell into the overflowing mental file of nondescript attractive.

"Why?" he pleaded. "Why did you do this to me?"

Nikko could frame no quick, diplomatic reply. To Van Ness, he was an obscure but talented young historian out of RedCam, a corporate group both geographically and politically far from Summer House. He'd come to Van Ness with a flattering proposal for a documentary on the unsung heroes of the police research division. But in truth he'd come only because Van Ness had access to the Bohr Maker—and a reputation that whispered of his vulnerabilities.

For some fifty years it had been Van Ness's task to constantly upgrade police defensive Makers so that they remained superior to any new corporate introductions. He'd been secure in his position—perhaps a little bored—so that when this fresh young historian from RedCam approached him, he'd been happy to talk. It hadn't been long before the conversation rolled around to Leander Bohr.

Van Ness claimed he'd known Bohr. He bragged about how he'd collected the charred tissue of Leander's brain and, from it, decoded the basic structure of Bohr's Maker.

Adaptive artificial intelligence was illegal in the Commonwealth. Dull Intelligences were common, but machine intelligence that could match the diversity of human thought was banned. The Bohr Maker was the most infamous example.

According to Van Ness, being infected by the molecular-scale machine was like being host to an intelligent force without a personality. Bohr had written into it his own talents as a molecular engineer, backed up by an immense computing capacity. When first introduced to a host, it would proceed through an infantile learning period during which it would automatically work to improve and enhance its environment. Eventually, it would subsume itself to the will and persona of its host—a host now equipped with the skills of the greatest of molecular engineers, and the physical apparatus to practice those skills within the host's own body.

Nikko *wanted* the Bohr Maker. Its talents had helped Bohr evade a police manhunt for five years. It could help Nikko do the same. It could heal him, and change him just enough that police Makers would no longer recognize him. Then he could lose himself in the vast, organic body of Summer House, while he worked secretly toward the collapse of the Commonwealth.

So he'd disguised himself behind his brother's face and won the affections of Van Ness. This human-ordinary ghost had visited Van Ness many times at his residence in Southwest Australia, and eventually Van Ness had made the suggestion: *I could open the Bohr file. And then someone clever, someone like you, could easily smuggle the Maker's pattern off-world.*

But Van Ness was an old man carrying a century's

accumulation of ego. He'd decided he could handle the theft alone.

Nikko found himself shouting in a sudden seizure of frustration: "Why'd you synthesize it?" He didn't worry about being overheard. He was only a ghost, and no one else could see or hear him. "You were supposed to bring out the Maker's pattern, not the Maker itself!" It would have been so *easy* for Nikko to smuggle electronic code past police Gates. And of course he would have brought a ghost of Van Ness out at the same time. He'd already grown a second body for him, under an alias in the mausoleum at RedCam. Van Ness had even visited it briefly, less than a week ago when he'd still been only toying with the idea of betraying the police.

But Van Ness hadn't stolen the pattern. He'd synthesized a hard copy of the Maker's components and stolen that, because he didn't trust Nikko through the resurrection.

The spineless bastard. He'd been very careful. He'd developed a tiny packet to contain the Maker. The packet had separate chambers, one for the Maker's computational core, two to store its initial manipulator arms. The chambers were divided by soluble membranes. When exposed to an aqueous medium they would dissolve, allowing the components to unite and the Maker to become active. The packet was ensconced in the hollowed-out core of a defensive needle. As Van Ness had explained the system to Nikko, he'd seemed especially pleased with that aspect of the design. The needle gun he carried hidden in his chest was registered with the police, so its presence wouldn't arouse suspicion. Like the chambered storage packet it contained, the needle would dissolve upon contact with flesh, or another aqueous medium, releasing its toxins. But so long as the needle remained in its launch cradle, invisible under his skin, it would be dry and safe. Van Ness had even arranged the thread of a neural connection between the Maker's computational core and the

Dull Intelligence that supervised the use of the needle gun. He could communicate with the Dull Intelligence, and so, indirectly, he could also communicate with the Maker's core.

It was a good system. But Van Ness had lost his nerve.

"You tricked me into this!" he shouted at Nikko. "It's your fault. You don't love me. You're nothing but a whore. And you poisoned me with a behavioral virus, didn't you? I would never have put myself in this position, never, never, never. Not for you. Not for anyone. If you'd just left me alone. You've ruined me! My life, my career. The police will execute me! And you're not even here, just a ghost. But I'll see to it the police find you too. . . ."

Play it calm, Nikko thought. It had been a mistake to let his temper show. It was the heat, he told himself. The heat and the horrible fleas. Damn, but he hadn't expected Van Ness to guess about the virus! He'd used the virus to give Van Ness a little courage, that's all. To instill him with some much-needed backbone.

"The police haven't even found you yet," Nikko said gently. He crouched beside Van Ness and hugged him, trying not to shudder at the hot, wet touch of the man's sweat-soaked clothes. Van Ness smelled horrible. That and the stink of piss from the carpet made Nikko want to gag. Too bad Van Ness's atrium delivered so well on reality.

"Love and Nature," Nikko sighed. "What an awful hot stinking place this is." He stroked Van Ness's sweat-slick cheek. "You know, we can still get the Maker out. You just have to trust me."

Van Ness went preternaturally still. His gaze fixed on the door. "What's that noise?"

Nikko listened, but all he heard was drunken laughter from an adjacent room. "What?"

"Shh!"

Then he caught it: voices whispering outside in the

local language. "Hotel guests," he said with a shrug. "Beggars. Criminals. Who else would stay here?"

"No, it's a police dog! Can't you hear it sniffing?"

Nikko listened again. He could hear odd sounds. But Van Ness's senses were clouded with fear and Nikko didn't trust them. "It's probably nothing," he said. And if it were a dog, well, the game was up, that's all.

No dog materialized. "We can still get the Maker out," Nikko repeated.

This time Van Ness looked at him. His eyes were wild and bloodshot, his face bleached and furrowed with worry. He pushed Nikko away and stumbled to his feet. "I don't care about the Maker. I just want to get out of this alive. I want to get back to my home, back to my job, back to the life I had before I met you. And the police will take me back too, when I show them the virus you planted in me. The police are supposed to protect me from outside attack! It's their fault I'm here. It's not my fault. They have to pardon me."

Nikko stood up to face him, his gaze deliberately hard. Van Ness had to be brought back into line. "They won't pardon you. They'll execute you, and you know it. The law is very strict on these matters. You should have resisted the virus, or gone for help. Besides, you head the division responsible for developing defensive molecular security. It was *your* lapse that exposed you."

Van Ness's hands began to shake. He cursed and spun on his foot, beginning to pace frenetically from one end of the room to the other, three steps each way, back and forth, back and forth. "If you're that good at molecular design," he shouted. "Then you don't need the Maker!"

But Nikko wasn't that good at molecular design. The behavioral virus had come from Fox's collection ... and Fox would never consider designing anything as potent as Bohr's Maker.

"I need it," Nikko said calmly. "Besides, we always

knew you'd probably have to sacrifice this physical copy." He reached out to touch Van Ness's hand, but Van Ness pulled away. Nikko let his own hand fall back to his side. "You've already been to visit your other self on RedCam. You know everything's ready. So trust me. Let me take your ghost out."

"Oh no!" Van Ness squawked, his finger jabbing the air like a knife. "Don't try to lead me on. I'm not stupid. I know I'm trapped here. The police will have my pattern in the data Gates by now. My ghost will never get through."

"Your ghost doesn't have to go through the data Gates," Nikko said. "You've established a communications link with the Maker's computational core. So download your ghost into the Maker. Store it there. Let me carry your ghost out, along with the Maker."

Van Ness stopped pacing. He shook his head in wide arcs like a wounded beast seeking a route of escape. His knees were actually shaking now. "Trust Bohr's Maker?" he croaked. "Put my existence in its—"

"Why'd you synthesize it if you don't want to use it?" Nikko hissed.

Van Ness had intended to inoculate himself with the Maker—that's what he'd told Nikko—just as Leander Bohr had done long ago with the Maker's original incarnation. But Van Ness was not Leander Bohr. He was afraid of the Maker—afraid it would get away from him, or worse, change him so much that he would no longer recognize himself.

"It doesn't know anything," Van Ness mumbled, his voice so soft and obscure Nikko suspected he spoke to himself. "It's a virgin copy. It was designed to function in a human brain; use its host's memories as a data base. But I haven't taught it anything; it wouldn't know what to do with me."

"Then teach it," Nikko said. "Let it feed on the open data net. Use it. It's your only chance."

"I will use it," Van Ness said. "But under controlled conditions. I can't trust it with my life."

Nikko groaned. "You have to trust it. You have to download your ghost into it. You know it'll work. You know the Maker will preserve you. You'll be as safe as the Maker itself, and I can't make you safer than that."

Someone shouted on the street outside. Van Ness jumped as if he'd been touched with an electronic prod. "I won't do it!" he screamed. "I see what you're trying to do and you won't get rid of me that easily."

Nikko drew three deep breaths to bleed his temper. He had one offer left to play. Let Van Ness see the advantage of it! "I'm coming through this city tomorrow," he said. "In first person."

Van Ness's eyes widened. "You'll actually be here?"

Nikko nodded somberly. This was a lie, of course. He wouldn't be here. He could never come Earth-side. His body would fail in such a deep gravity well. But Van Ness knew him under Sandor's human-ordinary face and Sandor *was* Earth-side.

Nature save me! He hated to involve his brother, but he could see no other way. So he carried on with the lie. "I've been working in the islands for almost three months now. But I've just had myself summoned to Castle. I'll be coming through the city this morning. You can walk right up to me and lay the Maker—and your ghost—in my hands."

"What alias are you using?"

"Sandor Jiang-Tibayan." He winced. He'd just condemned his brother, if the police came in on this too soon. But he needed the Maker. He *needed* it. Sandy would understand.

Van Ness looked glassy-eyed for nearly a minute as he used the atrium to access the net and confirm Sandor's identity. "You're from the House," he muttered at one point. "Not RedCam, at all. But the House." He blinked nervously, as he began to understand the breadth of Nikko's deception. Then, *"Liar!"*

he screamed. "You're not coming through today. It's tomorrow. Tomorrow! I can't last that long. The dogs will find me. You requested a day's delay! *You* did. You want the dogs to find me!"

Nikko shook his head in confusion. He'd had Sandor transferred to Castle. The orders had been easy enough to fake. He ran a check out of his own data field, only to confirm Van Ness's findings. Sandor had requested a delay in transfer. *Damn!* Everything had gone wrong on this venture! Just everything! Maybe it was time to pull out and start covering his trail.

"You thought you could get me," Van Ness croaked. "You thought you could hang this crime on me. No. There, I've done it. I've fed *your* identity to the Maker. Name and face. Ha ha. You're the one it'll finger, not me. And I've entered your name and your face in my atrium notebook. The police will find that too."

But it wasn't Nikko's name and face that Van Ness could identify. It was Sandor's.

Nikko felt the skin at the back of his neck pull tight. Van Ness was crazy, completely over the wall. Nikko knew it; knew it by the instinctive loathing he felt for the man, though he'd never encountered madness before. Even so, Van Ness could make good on his threats, *would*, if he had the chance.

Nikko had to fight back. He began searching the Spill's illicit directories, accessing information via the data field he occupied. He was only a ghost, enthralled to Van Ness's atrium. The atrium would simulate a physical attack on Van Ness. But he didn't think it would allow him to kill his host. And even if the simulation did go that far, by destroying Van Ness he would destroy himself, and have no way to recover the body, or the atrium notebook, or the Maker. No way to recover the secret of Sandor's identity, now that the Maker knew him, and the atrium notebook too.

But in the Spill help could be hired. He began making phone calls, only to be interrupted by a knock on the door. Van Ness heard it and closed his eyes; then doubled over and held his stomach. "Answer it," Nikko said. Van Ness whimpered, shaking his head no. The knock sounded again, louder this time. A man's voice called out in the local tongue. "Stop acting like a fugitive and answer it," Nikko commanded.

Like a sleepwalker, Van Ness moved to the door. He opened it a crack. *As if that could keep the dogs out*, Nikko thought. Peering over Van Ness's shoulder, he saw a dark-skinned, scrawny man in the street outside. "I get cure, I get cure," the man repeated over and over again, kneeling down on the floor and opening a briefcase to prove to Van Ness it was so. Nikko strained to see the case, but Van Ness wouldn't look at it, so he could get only a peripheral view. And the light was bad.

"You crazy, hah?" the man said, looking repeatedly between Van Ness and the case. "You shout. You talk self. No problem! I get cure, chase dat ghost right out!"

Nikko laughed. "A witch doctor! He thinks you're nuts. He wants to help you."

"Get away!" Van Ness shouted. "Get out of here!" He launched his foot at the case, sending it tumbling upside down. Vials bounced helter-skelter into the street. The man roared in fury, but Van Ness continued his assault, stepping far enough out of his room to kick the case again. It slammed into the canvas wall of a squatter's tent erected just inside the gutter. The witch doctor started screaming imprecations. Perhaps he was a famous man; he certainly drew attention. Heads popped out of doors all along the front of the hotel. Sleeping beggars in the street began to stir. Van Ness panicked.

He jumped over the makeshift shelters that had sprouted like mushrooms on the street after midnight. Splashing through puddles of rain and excrement, he took off down the street. Nikko ran helplessly after him.

Whoops rang out behind them, and again, just

ahead. Van Ness kept going until he reached the corner, then he risked a glance back. Two young men pursued him, their faces split by manic grins. Ahead, another youth holding a length of metal pipe blocked his way. Van Ness dodged past the boy.

A second later Nikko found himself cut off from the world, trapped in a terrifying cocoon of nonsensation. He couldn't see, he couldn't hear, he couldn't smell, taste, or feel. Because Van Ness no longer had any of those senses. Van Ness was dead. Nikko wrote an address for home and fled before the atrium's residual power ran down.

Nikko lay still for a time, staring down the length of the tether to the inhabited sector of Summer House three kilometers below. The experience Earthside seemed like a dream, a very bad and vivid dream. But of course it was real. Van Ness was dead. And when the police recovered his body and deciphered his atrium notebook, Sandor would be a wanted man.

Silently, Nikko cursed himself. How could he have been so stupid as to give up Sandor's identity?

He switched on his atrium, no longer concerned with the risk to himself. He had to synthesize another ghost. He had to hire a mule and find Van Ness's body and destroy it—before Sandor was made to pay for his brother's crimes.

CHAPTER

6

It was still night when Phousita awoke with a start. She shoved herself up on one elbow and stared at the eerie yellow bioluminescent glow of Arif's sleeping face. Darkness lay thick all around her. She could hear the breathing of other sleepers, the light wash of rain against the roof, the drippity-drip of water where the roof had gotten leaky. She could smell the sweat on Arif's body and the musty odor of the warehouse.

Yet the dream that had disturbed her played on, as if she were still asleep. She blinked and rubbed her eyes. No change. There was the old woman, kneeling on the corner of a nearly new woven mat, her wares spread out before her in the sunlight: powders ground from dried cat bones, amulets made of feathers and bits of plastic, the tails of rats, flayed, stretched, and dried (the old woman claimed it was snakeskin), black pumice carefully stored in a glass jar (the cinders of shooting stars), dried flower petals, bowls of foul-smelling liquids, mummified geckos, shiny beetles, nameless bugs. Every day the old woman had displayed her pharmacopoeia in the marketplace, offering charms and potions for every need. Here she was again.

Yet she was *not* here.

Phousita stared into the early morning darkness listening to the rain, while sunlight baked down on her head and shoulders, and the old woman smiled up at her as she used to do when Phousita returned from an afternoon of foraging in the streets. How light Phousita felt under the glow of that smile! The old witch could inspire cheer in the worst of circumstances. Phousita loved her so. She greeted Phousita, jabbering in the hill dialect no one understood. Phousita smiled anyway, proudly showing off the bananas she'd found buried in a rubbish heap behind a little restaurant.

A mosquito whined in the darkness of the warehouse. Phousita slapped at it frantically. How could she be in two places at once? How could she see darkness and sunlight with equal clarity? Past and present as if they were two views from the same room?

She must have cried out, because suddenly Arif's eyes were open, staring at her. She closed her own eyes as the old woman invited her to sit down in the shade of the cardboard box that served as a home for both of them when the market closed at night. *"Arif!"*

He took her hand, pulled her down in his arms. The hilt of the knife he wore strapped to his chest pressed painfully against her breast. "What is it?" he whispered.

She pressed her head against his shoulder. "The old woman—she's *here*!" Phousita drew back and started to point, but was suddenly unsure of the direction. Finally, she indicated her head. "I can see her, as clearly as I see you," she hissed. "She serves me water purchased from the water dealers while we eat the bananas I've found. She tells me it's been a good day. Her charms enjoy a powerful reputation. Many people come to buy them. Soon she will have enough money to take me to the Chinese doctor. Can you see her, Arif?"

He shook his head and scowled. "Stupid old witch. We don't need her. Tell her to leave."

Instantly, she was gone. Phousita uttered a small cry of surprise. Tears sprang to her eyes. The old woman had been the first person to show her love.... *"Arif!"* She clenched his arm, her nails biting into his flesh. "It's you. Now I can see you."

He rolled her over on her back, stroked her belly as if she were a child. "Of course it's me," he crooned. "I'm right here."

"No!" She stared past him into the darkness at a new vision. "It's the first time I've ever seen you. That night with *tuan*, your master, in the foreign hotel near the mosque. Oooh, I'm so afraid. They say a ghost possesses you. Horrible night! How I want to leave. Don't touch me! Are you an animal? I can smell the incense and the blood, your anger, everywhere. *Tuan* still holds the knife. They've beaten you, and you're crying—"

He clapped a hand over her mouth. In a strangled voice, *"Stop it!"*

The scene vanished. Only darkness surrounded her now. She lay back against the floor, shaking. "It's gone," she whispered.

Arif stared down at her. He looked hurt, ashamed. He'd lived then as a slave in a brothel on the edge of the marketplace. His master had been a horrible man, but a great sorcerer. He'd enlisted a ghost to occupy Arif's mind and command his body. It was the only way Arif could be controlled. But even that failed in the end, when Arif came upon a blade. While the ghost wandered, he cut out his master's heart.

"I'm sorry," Phousita whispered, reaching up to touch Arif's lips. "But I was there. Again." She groaned, as a horrible, cramping hunger announced its presence in her belly. She rolled on her side, then slowly sat up, one arm pressed against her stomach to ease the pain. "Come with me?"

He frowned suspiciously, his long, comical nose bending downward. "Where?"

She breathed quickly, shallowly, trying to subdue the pain. "To the foreign hotel. We never went hungry when we worked together."

"We planted another *tuan* yesterday," he growled. "There'll be fluff in the morning."

"I can't wait until morning! I need more. Now." She staggered to her feet. Around her, the breathing rhythm of the sleepers had changed. Many of them were awake, listening. She didn't care. "Come with me, Arif."

He shook his head, his gaze hard. He tried to grab her hand, but she dodged. With a little jump she cleared a body. She could hear the breathing. Someone pretending to sleep. She listened carefully to the soft noises around her and from them constructed a mental image of the room and its occupants. As if her ears had become eyes, she knew where everyone was, what they were doing. She darted away, her feet touching briefly on bare patches of floor and then she was free of the room, racing down the lightless corridor. Behind her she could hear Arif bellowing some unintelligible order, but it was too late. She hit the door with her forearms. It sprang open. She ran out into the street, while the two Knives who'd been assigned to guard the door stared after her with startled faces.

She slowed for a moment, looking back at them. What was she doing? She and Arif had made a pact: no more prostitution. It was their conceit that they could live without it. They'd founded the clan on that bargain and rescued other children from that fate.

As if in answer, her stomach twisted with a cramp that doubled her over and left her gasping in agony. She was on her knees before the pain began to ease. *"I have to eat,"* she whispered. And the clan had no food left. *"I have to eat!"* There was never enough food. Too many mouths in the clan. Even with the riches they'd taken from *tuan* there wasn't enough.

"Phousita!"

She looked up as Arif bounded out the door. Without thought, Phousita leapt forward to meet him. Her hand darted out. She snatched his knife from the sheath on his chest, then leaped back. Arif brought himself up sharply, poised, quivering at the point of the knife. She looked at the weapon in surprise. It was firmly clenched in her outstretched hand, the tip pressed against Arif's chest. He glared at her, his eyes burning with betrayal. Her gaze darted back to the knife. Would she really use it against him?

Yes.

Tears streamed from her eyes as she pressed the blade a little harder against his chest. She could smell the blood as it trickled from the wound. "I love you, Arif." But she could no longer control her own body. Something else lived inside her now, and it was stronger than she.

Too, it was very, very hungry.

"Arif, come with me, please. They always pay more for two."

He nodded stiffly, his violet eyes like deep pits in the soft glow of his face. She lowered the knife. Her nostrils flared as she drank in the scent of him. He smelled of anger and of love. She turned and ran through the dark streets, making for the lights beyond the slums.

Later, much later, Phousita tried to apologize. "I'm sorry, Arif. I couldn't help it. It's dead *tuan*. He's a powerful sorcerer and he commands me now. I had no choice."

Morning had come. The sun peered around the corner of a huge department store across the street. Already, urgent crowds jostled on the sidewalk; vendors were setting up their stands. Taxis and trucks raced quietly past, oblivious of the wary pedestrians trying to cross the street.

Arif sat huddled beside the plastic wall of a market stall dealing in lamps and oils. He cried softly, his face hidden between his knees. Phousita sat patiently beside him. She watched perfect memories dance like visions behind her eyes while she waited for him to calm down. He always cried on the morning after (as if every time were his first time.) He'd never told her why.

Yet now she *knew.*

She gazed at him, her heart full of sympathy. She said: "Your mother used to sell you on the streets as a punishment for your wickedness. So the pain returns. You know she was right every time you sell yourself."

He turned his head to look at her, tears still running down his swollen yellow cheeks. Anger narrowed his eyes. "You're lying."

She blinked. She'd spoken the truth. (But how did she know that?) Softly: "Perhaps she was not your mother."

He bolted to his knees. His hands seized her throat and his strong fingers began to squeeze. "She *was* my mother," he hissed. "She was! She lied when she said she'd found me. I was *not* thrown away! *No one* threw me away."

Phousita couldn't breathe. Darkness crept up on the edge of her vision. She gulped, then forced her body to go limp. As she collapsed to the sidewalk Arif let go. She lay still, her head swimming. For a moment she thought she might lose the bellyful of food she'd just bolted down. But the nausea passed. Arif took her hand, helped her up, then swept her into his arms, crooning over her like a child. "I'm sorry, I'm sorry." The woman in the market stand scowled at them, and Phousita tugged at Arif to get him to move on.

They walked nearly a mile, arm in arm, before Arif spoke again. "How did you know that about my mother?"

"I don't know." Phousita stared at the sidewalk, swept clean by the inhabitants who'd slept here last night. She'd been wondering the same thing. Certainly she hadn't known it yesterday. And Arif had said nothing overnight. "I think . . . I didn't know it. It was just on my tongue, and I said it. Perhaps dead *tuan* put the words in my mouth. He must be an evil sorcerer."

She stopped before a booth that sold thin strips of barbecued meat skewered on steel picks. She slipped a coin from her sarong and paid it to the vendor. Though her belly was still swollen with food, she could feel the hunger stirring again, as if the spirit that rode her knew she would find nothing more once they returned to the riverfront. She offered meat to Arif, but he refused, his face tight with despair. He'd eaten nothing. It was a covenant of the clan that all food should be saved and shared at the evening meal. So she'd betrayed everyone, not just Arif. Guilt tried to work at her, but it was drowned by the heavenly taste of the barbecue. She finished the meat, then carefully licked every trace of fat from the picks before returning them to the vendor. She and Arif moved on. Several minutes later: "I know things that I cannot know."

Arif looked at her warily.

"I know that *tuan* who bought us last night has a wife he loves dearly and two grown daughters, both employed by the Commonwealth."

"It's possible," Arif allowed.

"I'm not guessing. I know this."

"*I don't.*"

"Ah." His doubt didn't disturb her. She could see clearly in her mind the steady sequence of unfolding memories, her own, and others she didn't recognize. She smiled. The vendor at the barbecue stand had been much impressed by her unusual figure: a well-endowed woman, perfectly proportioned, in a body no larger than that of a slight eight-year-old girl. "Why do you suppose *tuan* is willing to pay so much for sex with freaks like us?" she asked.

"Who cares?"

She shrugged, remembering again the face of the angel. This was not the face of dead *tuan* whom she'd found in the river. So who might this angel be?

It would be good to find him, she realized.

She glanced shyly at Arif. "I think I'm becoming a witch." She waited for some reaction from him, but he said nothing. He stared straight ahead as they walked, carefully avoiding the squatters who occupied the way. She tried again: "Dead *tuan* that we pulled from the river was an evil sorcerer, and he's turned me into a witch." She'd been approaching that conclusion all morning. Now that she'd said it out loud, she felt inordinately pleased. She'd always admired the old woman for her ability to cure people with her potions and charms. And the Chinese doctor: he was the greatest sorcerer of all, almost a god.

"If you become a witch, we won't have to whore again," Arif said.

Phousita smiled and nodded. "Yes. That's so."

CHAPTER

7

Kirstin Adair sat on her balcony, drinking tea and attending to the backlog of calls that had accumulated during her hour with Nikko. She pulled them up one by one from the majordomo program into her atrium: a succession of routine business and little emergencies well-known to any high-level administrator. After almost thirty years as Chief of Police she could handle them with unconscious ease.

Individual cases rarely came to her attention. Most were routine violations of ordinance: the inclusion of illicit genetic material at conception; proscribed neurological and physiological talents; assault Makers—germ weapons designed to force deleterious or illegally advantageous mutations in target individuals; terrorist Makers, designed to attack essential elements of cities/corporations/families/individuals; Makers designed to spy on corporate competition or estranged lovers; Makers possessing generalized machine intelligence; Makers possessing self-aware personalities; unregistered behavioral viruses; unregulated modification of plants or animals or the creation of artificial plants or animals; duplicate personas existing in duplicate bodies.

Molecular technologies had allowed the celestial cities to be built; they'd been used to restore many of Earth's ecosystems. But molecular technologies demanded limits. They could not be allowed to run wild, or Gaia would be broken, torn to pieces, and the pieces changed so that they could never be put back together again. These days, it was the function of the police to ensure that never happened. But the war had been going on long before the Commonwealth, and Kirstin had been part of it even then.

She'd been lucky. She'd had a daddy who'd been a professional adventurer, a movie maker, a writer, and a rugged philosopher never short on grants and sponsors to fund his next expedition. He'd had only contempt for the heated, sound-insulated, locked and guarded comfort of a condominium, and he had custody of his daughter for six months every year. He taught her to be strong: physically, emotionally, and intellectually. To be sensitive: to the presence of a greater entity around her. In South America, New Zealand, Antarctica, the Himalayas: she learned to sense the voice of the natural world. Gaia spoke in a complex language of predator and prey, of growth and dormancy, of birth and migration, of seasonal change, of storms, of currents, and finally, of cruelty and death and *necessity*. Kirstin had come to feel part of the natural world, perfectly adapted to it, one strand in a web hung in four dimensions, spanning billions of years, a creative system of immeasurable potential.

But her father's period of custody would inevitably end, and she'd be thrust back into the crowded, mechanical, parasitic isolatorium of the city. She stood out from the pack at school like a wild marten amongst trained rats, her individuality drowning in a sea of sheltered classmates. The rat packs lived their lives between the air-conditioned mall, the air-conditioned condo, the air-conditioned school, and they thought they were *elemental* because they moved in tribes and carried guns and knew how to lie to mommy. Disconnection. Cold winter: Daddy had come five thousand miles just to see her. Now he was lying in the street outside Mommy's condo, blood welling from his mouth, cut down by trained rats. Kirstin saw it happen. But she never screamed. She never cried. Instead, she woke up to the truth: Gaia was under attack by an infestation of human rats feeding on the carnage of unsustainable technological explosions that tore through the body of the Goddess like bullets, blood oozing from the ruptured web of life.

But Gaia was old and strong and wily. She always produced corrective mechanisms. Feedback reponse: a predator appears. There were too many rats to exterminate, but the problem could still be neatly managed. First, disarm the rats. Then feed them, protect them, let them grow soft. See that their nascent separation from the real world is made complete. Withhold from them the power to ever threaten Gaia again. And if some among them still insist on straying outside their niche? Kirstin smiled to herself. That's why she was here. That's why the cops existed. To pick off the maladapted and maintain the integrity of the herd.

And if she enjoyed her work, so what? Did the wolf feel guilty about bringing down the sickly and the weak when it pursued a herd of deer? No. Like Kirstin, it happily performed its role in the body of the Goddess.

Not alone, of course. She kept herself aloof from the routine duties of the Commonwealth police, leaving the daily challenges of enforcement to the discretion of her officers. As Chief of Police, she focused her own attention on guiding the political currents of the Commonwealth, ensuring that cities and nations both inside and outside the Commonwealth were governed by reasonable individuals who respected molecular law. Cities occasionally attempted to pass a local ordinance easing some Commonwealth proscripton, thinking they might develop a trade advantage.... Or corporations would push the boundaries of the law to impress a restless client.... Or one of the nations outside the Commonwealth might be persuaded to attempt the development of illicit Makers.

And why? Citizens of the Commonwealth had everything they needed: perfect health; perfect bodies; safe environments; fine homes; family life; entertainment; art; opportunities to travel.... They ought to want for nothing. But of course there would always be a certain percentage of the dissatisfied. Snakes in the Garden of Eden.

Fox Jiang-Tibayan was one of the worst. To even *conceive* of creating something like Nikko was repugnant. To have the talent to persuade a timid Congress to approve such a scheme was diabolical. But Kirstin had made Fox pay for it in the years since. She'd had him to trial three times on marginal-tolerance technologies; and charged him in at least a dozen other cases that were settled out of court. The harassment had worked. Fox had become a conservative designer—at least on the surface.

And yet—Kirstin's lips turned in a sly, feral smile— she owed Fox a debt of gratitude. Without the research permit that permitted Nikko's existence, she would never have been able to inspire the wave of public outrage that had carried her into the office of Chief of Police.

She chuckled softly to herself. And Fox had given her Nikko too.

Nikko wasn't human. He was a frantic animal, amoral in his pursuit of continued life. Kirstin found him exciting, in much the same way she might find it exciting to toy with a panther. Taming it. Controlling it. There were so few challenges left. Dealing with the likes of Nikko kept her wits and her instincts sharp for the greater game of preserving the Commonwealth.

Too bad his time was almost up. She'd miss him. She'd feel his loss . . . the same way she might feel the loss of a favorite pet.

Kirstin wasn't half through with her backlog of calls when a new one came in under priority code. It was from Allende, the Director of Internal Security for the Commonwealth Police. She frowned. Allende wasn't one of her people. He was a Congressional appointee; a small-minded man with a tendency to work behind the back of the Chief of Police. Kirstin generally had a good relationship with the Congressional body. She'd approved of the Reform Act, which had eliminated the presidential office, decentralizing its authority across Congress. But at times there were conflicts.

While the senators were occasionally called upon to clarify existing laws, or grant approval to marginal tolerance research proposals, or to determine the eligibility of a state petitioning for Commonwealth status, their primary duty was to oversee the workings of the police. For that reason they occasionally felt the need to assert their independence from the Police Chief. The creation of a watchdog officer in the person of Allende had been their most recent rebuke. Kirstin found the situation grating. She needed to trust her officers—all of them—and she did not trust Allende. She'd been angling to get rid of him for months.

"Proceed, Allende," she said, wondering which of her officers he was harassing this time.

The atrium acted as an interface, processing the incoming signal and feeding it directly to her brain so that she "heard" Allende's voice, though her ear sensed nothing.

"Chief Adair. We've got a problem in our research division. Secure subject."

"So come." She issued him a formal invitation; Allende's ghost arrived a few seconds later. Ensconced in her atrium, nothing he said or did could be directly detected from the outside.

He appeared in the chair Nikko had occupied: a stout, dark-skinned man with hard eyes and heavy hands, dressed in the black tunic and shorts of a police uniform. By his stiff posture, she knew he didn't want to be here.

He nodded without smiling. "We have a serious problem." His gaze wandered nervously. Sweat actually began to appear on his pudgy cheeks. "Jensen Van Ness, one of our senior researchers, physically resident in Southwest Australia, used his security clearance to access the Bohr files. He synthesized the Bohr Maker, destroyed the file, then skipped. That was yesterday. Almost thirty-two hours ago now. I've tracked him through the Gates. He left the Commonwealth last night, for Southern India . . . or perhaps the Sunda Free Trade Zone. Of course the dogs are on it. All Gates are aware of his profile. Sector commanders have been alerted and decontamination procedures are being prepared.

"I expect to have him in custody within the hour. In the meantime I think we should review our internal security arrangements. This incident only proves what I've said in the past: our researchers are allowed far too many liberties with classified files."

Kirstin listened in silent fury while Allende's spiel ran out. The Bohr Maker. Hadn't she warned the Congressional Committee on Molecular Law time and time again to get rid of that obscene file? But Van Ness had always gotten in her way. Now he was gone and the trail was cold and Allende was sitting here, trying to shift the blame to her account.

She leaned forward, fixing him with an icy glare. "You pompous bastard. You tried to handle this on your own, didn't you? How many hours has it been since you knew Van Ness was gone?" Allende seemed to shrink as every muscle in his body tensed. *"How many hours?"* Kirstin snapped.

"Ten." He sat up a little straighter. "It's been ten hours. My staff has pursued every investigative channel in that time and we'll have him in custody—"

"You didn't think I needed to know this immediately? The Bohr Maker was stolen, and you didn't inform me?"

"My staff—"

"You wanted to bring him in on your own, didn't you? You wanted to grab a little glory. But you've put the police in jeopardy, instead. Van Ness possesses a terrible weapon. And because he destroyed the file, we can't duplicate it. We can't use it against him. But you didn't think I needed to know."

"We'll have him within the hour," Allende insisted.

But Kirstin knew he wouldn't have come to her unless the trail was stone-cold. "You'd better bring him home within an hour, Allende, or I'll have your head."

After Allende's ghost had gone, Kirstin abandoned the rest of her calls to the holding tank, changed into police uniform, and headed for the office.

The Bohr Maker. Her lips twisted as she thought about it. It was an obscenity before nature. An affront to the Mother. An evolutionary bomb that could explode in the body of Gaia, destroying the natural order, ripping through the soul of a four-and-a-half-billion-year-old goddess.

Leander had understood that. He'd never copied the Maker. He'd kept it to himself. He'd respected and loved the Mother, just as Kirstin had, and he'd used the Maker only in her defense. Leander Bohr had been a great man. But life as a fugitive had begun to weigh on him. He'd begun to talk to Kirstin of abandoning the Mother, of using the Maker to create an artificial world far from the sun, just large enough for the two of them. . . .

Kirstin had betrayed him to the police, feeling sure the Maker would be destroyed. But Van Ness had fought against that and now the Maker was loose again.

Van Ness didn't possess Leander's ethical sense. In his hands, the Maker might soon be running wild.

She found Allende physically present at the office. He told her: "The dogs in Sunda have scented a peculiar line of sub-Makers that may be associated with Bohr's Maker."

"There are records on this," Kirstin said. "Can you confirm the link?"

"We're working on it." His eyes seemed to glaze over as he accessed police files through his atrium.

Leander had designed his Maker to create molecular machines less sophisticated than itself. These sub-Makers could be sent out into the world as microscopic information-gathering systems. Of the millions of copies it might generate, most would be lost, and after a preprogrammed period of time they would self-destruct. But a few would drift home to the Maker. The lineage of these molecular complexes was well-known.

Allende's attention returned to the real world. "With minor discrepancies, they match the patterns of known Bohr sub-Makers. Van Ness is in Sunda."

Kirstin smiled. So the thief hadn't left Earth. That was something—though he might be hard to find in Sunda, a primitive political entity that existed outside the network of nations comprising the Earth-bound members of the Commonwealth. Some nonmember states objected to police activities within their territories ... not that they could stop an investigation. The Commonwealth Police recognized no political boundaries in the enforcement of molecular law. How could they? Illegal technologies weren't made safer by being developed outside the Commonwealth. And if a feral technology superseded the police arsenal and made the cops obsolete, who would be left to enforce the law? No one. The stability and security of the Commonwealth could vanish—literally—overnight.

So the police recognized no territorial limitations, and consequently, even the most disaffected member-states remained firmly within the coalition. They had no realistic option. Secession wouldn't gain them technological freedom, but it *would* deprive them of a political voice within the Congress of the Commonwealth.

Kirstin called up a chair. She dropped slowly into it, facing Allende, her arms crossed over her chest while she waited for his hour to run down. In an hour she'd be rid of him. She'd dismiss him for dereliction of duty—and let the Congress try to argue with her!

She waited, watching him with a raptor's intense stare as he continued his investigation. He worked without console or voice, his attention fading in and out as he consulted with his officers through his atrium. As time grew short, the sheen of sweat on his face grew heavier. He glanced at Kirstin more and more often, with the white-eyed look of a frightened herbivore. His reactions actually gave her physical pleasure, and she grinned at him, which only fed his nervous state.

Then, with only three minutes left on his time he suddenly sagged forward, expelling a mighty breath of relief. Kirstin scowled. He noted the expression and responded with a triumphant grin. "The dogs have found Van Ness."

A few minutes later, Kirstin stood between the huge animals. It was early morning in Sunda, and she waded hip-deep in the crystal-clear waters of a river that flowed beneath the decaying hulk of an old warehouse—or at least that was the illusion generated for her by the atrium of the alpha dog.

She'd gone Earth-side as a ghost, to observe the progress of the investigation. The dog's atrium had reconstructed for her the smell of the falling rain, the sound of treading feet in the structure overhead, the taste of the slightly bitter water, and the feel of the river's current as it washed past her legs. She gazed at the young boy who clung to one of the building's vertical supports, seeing him just as the dogs saw him with their artificial eyes. But the boy couldn't see her.

Nevertheless, she scowled at him, thinking *Parasite*. He was one of the millions of unwanted children infesting this backward country, plaguing the city, a scourge of human rats. An older girl had abandoned him beneath the structure when the dogs showed up. She'd screamed in fear, then shinnied up a rope that hung from a trapdoor, before slamming it shut behind her. Kirstin could still hear her screaming, somewhere in the structure overhead.

The boy—he couldn't be more than six or seven— was trying to hide from the dogs behind the column, but his hands and legs were shaking so badly he kept slipping and splashing into the water. Kirstin grunted in satisfaction. The police dogs were designed to intimidate. They were a terrible derivation of mastiff and Great Dane. Their huge square heads reached a man's shoulder and they massed nearly eighty kilograms apiece. The Sunda government permitted them in its territory in exchange for certain trade concessions— primarily molecular technologies that kept the present rulers in power.

Kirstin shifted her gaze back to the body of Jensen Van Ness. He'd been secured to the riverbed—sometime yesterday, judging by the body's state of decomposition. The microscopic Makers that kept the water clean had already dissolved a good twenty percent of the flesh, converting it into edible fluff; white ribs glinted brightly through tattered muscle. The skull was almost completely exposed. The body had been stripped.

She watched thoughtfully as a bit of fluff floated downriver. The current swept it up against a long boom constructed of old plastic bottles that had been cut in half. Many of the bottles were full of fluff. Kirstin glanced at the body again, then chuckled in grim amusement. Rats would eat anything.

She ordered one of the dogs underwater, then dove after it, down to the river bottom to get a closer look at Van Ness's body. The atrium collected enough data through the dog's eyes to extrapolate a palpable model. She was able to probe the skull with her fingers. Van Ness had suffered a massive head wound.

She surfaced, throwing her head back in a great arc to clear the water from her eyes. The drops splashed against the structure overhead, but they left no wet marks. These could be added, but on an investigation she preferred the environmental mock-up to accurately reflect the outside world. The only phony thing she wanted in it was her own apparent presence.

She sniffed the air, searching through the dog's enhanced senses for a trace of the Bohr Maker. The body was free of it; Van Ness had not inoculated himself. Then where had he kept the stolen sample? Had he forced someone else to carry it for him? (Someone who objected?)

She waded through the water, the dogs at her heels, until she stood at the foot of the column, staring up at the boy. What had the child been doing down here? One of the dogs stood on its hind legs, stretching its head upward until it could run its sensitive nostrils across the boy's leg. The child moaned in fear; but the dog found nothing. It dropped back down into the water.

Yet the Bohr Maker still existed. Somewhere, someone had a sample of it because every now and then as the dogs patrolled the riverfront they'd detected its telltale sub-Makers. Leander had designed the Maker to be elusive, almost undetectable without a sample of the infected cells. Leander had been a genius.

She turned, ready to wade back to the concrete riverbank when the trapdoor opened. The dogs turned around.

A swollen, luminescent yellow face with a great hooked nose and comically rounded cheeks looked through the opening. *Nature stop us,* Kirstin thought in disgust. In the celestial cities of the conservative Commonwealth, mutagenic Makers had long ago been outlawed. But they were still common in the Free Trade Zones, generally used against some poor, unsuspecting sap for the amusement of minor powers. So long as the mutations were harmless and limited to somatic cells, Kirstin had agreed the police should tolerate them—for diplomatic reasons.

She started to whistle for the dogs when suddenly she noticed their tense posture, their flaring nostrils. Had they picked up a trace of the Bohr Maker? From this goon?

One of the dogs growled and surged through the water, then leapt for the open trapdoor. The goon ducked out of sight while Kirstin looked on, laughing in delighted disbelief. Surely the beast was too large to fit through the opening? But no. It caught itself with its forepaws and hung dangling, its head and shoulders through the hole. Its mate came up underneath it, reared up on its hind legs and offered its great head as a platform. The first dog kicked off and vanished inside the building.

Screams rang out overhead, the cries of children shrieking in terror. The pounding of running feet on unpadded floors rolled like thunder. Kirstin slogged through the water, grabbed the rope, and pulled herself up after the first dog.

Back on Castle, Kirstin's corporeal self sat with Allende, reviewing Van Ness's communications log. He'd entertained a lot of visitors. Some of them as famous as himself. Others unknown. She had officers tracking down the records of everyone who'd visited him in the last three years. "No way he did this alone," she muttered.

Allende grunted agreement. "It's not in his psychological profile."

In a way, this exercise was a waste of time. They'd know who his accomplice was as soon as his atrium notebook was removed from the body and translated.

She left the records, to stand by the tall glass windows, her gaze fixed on the dark line of the Imperial Highway.

Behind her, she could hear a sudden, harsh intake of breath from Allende. She turned slowly, to meet his narrowed gaze. "We've just arrested two youths who may have been involved in Van Ness's murder," he told her. Then his lip curled. "Doesn't sound like we'll get any leads out of them, though. It seems to have been a simple mugging. When the Islamic Resurgence turned up, they dumped the body in the river."

"Nature save us! How long until that notebook is ready to read?"

Kirstin's ghost followed the dogs through the city's rain-soaked, labyrinthine streets as they tracked the various scents of the children who'd inhabited the warehouse. They'd brought down six so far; none had shown any trace of the Maker. The rest had disappeared like rats into the maze of crumbling buildings.

At mid-morning she decided to return to the site of the warehouse. The air stank of smoke all up and down the riverfront. She looked ahead for the warehouse. At first she thought the dogs had become disoriented. Then she realized the collapsed heap of charred girders and melted plastic slag was all that remained of the building she'd visited earlier that morning.

Apparently the Islamic Resurgence didn't approve of squatters who attracted the attention of police dogs.

"Now here's an interesting name," Allende said.

Kirstin's original self broke off her review of the

ghost's memories and allowed Allende to shunt an entry
from Van Ness's visitor log to her atrium.

"One Sy Gaudreau." Allende read the entry aloud.
"Affiliation: RedCam Corporate Group, Farsight City.
An 'historian.'" He pronounced the word as if it
smelled of decay. "You know the kind? They dig up
dirt on corporations, then expose them, or blackmail
them."

"I know the kind," Kirstin said. Nikko was the best
of them. "Alert the Gates to his physical description.
And trace that address. It's probably a fake. RedCam's
too conservative to tolerate an historian. Dissect the
plexus. See if those calls weren't routed from somewhere else."

His gaze shifted minutely. The order had been sent.
Kirstin had just turned back to the window when a
long, low whistle escaped Allende. "Data finally coming
in from Van Ness's notebook. Love and Nature, that
bastard was *weird*. Uh-oh. Uh-oh. Oh sweet mercy, you
were right about that fake address."

Kirstin glared at him, one eyebrow raised in irritation.

Allende grinned back, his pudgy face twisted in a
simian leer. "You're going to love this, boss. Van Ness
recorded the name of his accomplice. One Sandor
Jiang-Tibayan. Out of Summer House."

For a moment Kirstin was struck dumb. Then fury began to burn: a slow, deep fire under her heart. *Jiang-
Tibayan*. Sandor she'd never heard of. It didn't matter.
There were only two Jiang-Tibayans who amounted to
anything, and Fox had never had a criminal mind. So it
was Nikko. He was probably using this Sandor as a
mule, playing games with Van Ness behind her back.

She'd been holding her breath unconsciously. Now
she let it go. Her gaze focused on Allende. "Alert the
Gates to the profile of this Jiang-Tibayan. Issue a warrant to the local police force in Sunda. Send it through

our ambassador, so they know we mean business. I want this mule arrested!"

Then she called the mausoleum at Castle and made reservations. "I'm going to Summer House," she told Allende. "In hard copy."

Physical travel between the celestial cities was uncomfortable and dull and could consume weeks, or even months of time. Most citizens never bothered. Those who did travel generally transferred only their personas, downloading them into duplicate bodies kept stored in distant city mausoleums: hard copy.

Kirstin had accumulated hard copies of herself in mausoleums throughout the Commonwealth, most of them never used and known only to herself . . . like the one at Summer House. She would download her persona, and she would be there. She'd have Nikko under her hands.

"We have officers at Summer House who can handle the investigation," Allende was saying. "There's no need for you to go."

"Oh yes there is." This was personal. She wanted to take Nikko out herself.

She launched herself out of the office, and headed for the mausoleum. She'd have to put this body on ice before bringing up the one on Summer House. It was a Commonwealth convenant that only one physical copy could be active at any given time. That would take half an hour, at least. And another half hour to awaken the body on Summer House.

But then she'd be able to hunt down Nikko and take him, face-to-face.

CHAPTER

8

Sandor Jiang-Tibayan stared unhappily out the window of a Summer House corporate helicopter, as it automatically carried him on a pre-programmed course across the Strait of Malacca. The helicopter banked right, then left, flying around (never directly over) one of the hundreds of old oil-drilling platforms that studded this section of ocean. The rigs had been towed to Malacca, anchored firmly on the bottom and then christened, each one a separate nation.

Sandor was supposed to be working as an apprentice in a project to install a security system for the newest member of the community, a platform that would become regional headquarters for Summer House. But yesterday he'd been summoned to Castle. Nobody seemed to know why. He'd protested the order, sure that it was another one of Dad's schemes to get him off-Earth. But his boss told him to go anyway.

Fox had exaggerated ideas about the dangers of working in the Free Trade Zone. Things were all right here for the House. The cops left them alone and the locals welcomed their business. The ecoterrorists were a bit of a problem, but that's what security was for. Sandor liked it Earth-side. He'd been to Australia and Tonga and he liked what he saw. He'd even talked to his boss about applying for a permanent position.

He sat up a little straighter as the helicopter crossed the shoreline, continuing inland over an agricultural plain. He could just make out the city in the distance—a maze of white buildings huddled under a dark ceiling of rain clouds. The city was in the Free Trade Zone ... not part of the Commonwealth. His boss wouldn't let him take weekends here, so he'd only seen the airport.

As the helicopter descended, clouds veiled the fierce gaze of the mid-morning sun. Soon rain began to run in rivulets across the window. Moments later the helicopter landed, its hull rattling under a fierce tropical deluge. A hangar extended out from the terminal to cover the helicopter, and the roar of the rain suddenly ceased. Sandor disembarked, then boarded a slidewalk to the main building. It would be at least an hour and a half before his flight to India and he was already bored.

He decided to summon his resident ghost into existence. "Hey Nikko, wake up. Guess where we are."

The ghost crouched on his shoulder, a tiny humanoid figure encased in a smooth, blue, armored hide. It was House policy that apprentice corporate members be accompanied by a resident ghost at all times Earthside—an electronic babysitter to keep young minds out of trouble. Fox had wanted to issue one of his own ghosts to fill the position, but Sandor could guess how much fun that would be. So he'd begged Nikko to spare him a dedicated ghost.

Things had worked out. Sandor had been only a few months Earth-side, but he'd already muled for Nikko four times, playing the role of a radical historian out of

RedCam to get interviews Nikko swore he never could have gotten on his own. Sandor didn't mind fronting for his brother; it was fun. Nikko knew the most interesting people.

Now Nikko's gaze swept the terminal. "What are we doing here?" he asked. It had been a few days since Sandor had activated him.

"On the way to Castle," Sandor explained. "Somebody up top wants me to run up the Highway, but they won't say why."

"Layover?"

"Ninety minutes."

Nikko chuckled. It was an odd sound, coming from a face that never smiled. "Want to take a walk around the terminal?"

Sandor grinned. His boss wouldn't let him take weekends outside the Commonwealth, so all he'd seen of Sunda so far was sky and sea. But he could count on Nikko to overlook the rules. "Let's drop into the city. I want to know why this place is off-limits."

Nikko's head swiveled to gaze at him, the tiny black lenses that covered his eyes glittering in the overhead lights. "You're kidding."

"Uh-uh. Let's go."

"Have you got a bodyguard?"

"Oh, come on, Nikko."

But to Sandor's disbelief, Nikko was shaking his tiny head. "You want to see the city? Then hire a mule and ghost it."

"It's not the same!" he said, outraged.

"And a good thing too. It's an ugly neighborhood out there, Sandy."

"*Nikko!*"

"Sandor," he corrected automatically. "Show me you're not dumb, and stay inside the terminal with your own kind."

"My own *what*?"

"Look at yourself."

"I don't have to. I know what I look like." A lean eighteen-year-old, blond hair, milk-white skin, blue eyes.

"You're a walking jewelry store: earrings, cheek stones, coiffure pendants, rings, bracelets, necklace, even a chain for your boot. Leather boot?"

"Synthetic. So's the silk. Anybody could get it. Big deal."

"That's right," Nikko said. "Big enough to kill for. This isn't the Commonwealth."

"It's different, I know. That's why I want to see it."

"You wouldn't get a block without being assaulted. Uh-oh. Police dog. Look innocent."

Startled, Sandor stumbled off the end of the slidewalk. The animal sat on its haunches, studying the column of arriving passengers with a blank-eyed stare.

"What's it doing here?" Sandor hissed. He scowled at the ugly animal. "I thought they were confined to the Commonwealth."

"They run wherever the police have an interest. In answer to your first question, it's checking chips."

Sandor hefted the bag as he walked around the motionless animal. A patch of skin on his forearm hid the ID chip that identified him to any police officer who cared to know. It functioned as a passport for travel between the sovereignties. Usually the police checked chips at Gates. Sandor guessed they had no authority to set up a Gate here. "So I'm clean enough, right?' he asked Nikko.

"Why? Guilty conscience?" Nikko laughed again. The House worked at the edge of molecular law, and occasionally they pushed the technology beyond police tolerance. Sometimes their client corporations protected them; sometimes not. Sometimes the cops reversed a decision on a previously accepted molecule. Sandor's back seemed to tingle as he walked away from the dog but it made no move to intercept him.

"Love and Nature, Nikko. *What's that?*"

He stopped to stare at a trio of human-creatures squatting against the wall of the concourse. One of them seemed to have melted. His flesh hung down in black, decomposing wattles beneath his throat while the skin on his hairless head had grown so thin it had become translucent and Sandor could see patches of white bone shining through it. The sockets of the pitiful creature's eyes had stretched halfway down his cheeks. Dried mucus clung to his bloodshot orbs. His nose wobbled like a bit of dead flesh at the level of his lips. His partner suffered the same afflictions, though her state seemed less advanced. The stench was horrific. A child huddled with them, a little girl, healthy-seeming, except for a crusty-looking growth of dull blue enamel on her stunted forearms that was nothing like the smooth blue enamel platelets of Nikko's skin. Nikko was strong and beautiful in the way of natural things. These . . . these *people* (they were a family group, he realized, father, mother, daughter), how ugly and unfunctional and unnatural they seemed. The crowd flowed around him as he stared. A few individuals turned uncomfortable eyes on him, but no one else dared to look at the plaintive creatures waiting mournfully beside empty bowls.

Sandor had never seen anything like it. Why would anyone accept such hideous, nonfunctional modifications? "What are they, Nikko?"

"Victims of a cruel joke," he growled. "Someone cast a spell on them."

"What?"

"They've been scarred by uncataloged Makers."

"Oh." Sandor frowned. "Involuntarily?"

"Sandy, you are *so* green."

Sandor shook his head. He'd heard of such things before, but—— "This is Sunda. Makers are illegal here."

Nikko snorted. "Come on, little brother. You know better than that. Makers are everywhere. The only difference is, here they're not regulated. You can buy anything here—a new face, a new body. A curse. Now let's move on."

"But the police are here," Sandor said, stubbornly rooted in place. "They'd never allow this sort of thing in the Commonwealth."

"This is *not* the Commonwealth. The police maintain a presence here, and they'll move on anything they consider threatening to the Commonwealth. But petty molecular crimes they'll ignore. This is not their jurisdiction."

"Petty crimes?" he asked. "Is that what you call— Hey look!" The little girl had noticed his attention. He knelt down and smiled at her, and she approached him cautiously. Her hands were knotted, and nonfunctional. She held an empty bowl squeezed between her crippled arms. "So . . . uh, what does she want?" he asked Nikko.

In a flat voice: "She's a beggar, Sandy."

He scowled, uncertain. "Begging for . . . ?"

"Coins, trinkets, food, anything. That's how her family survives. Will you give her something?"

"Sure." He slipped a bracelet off his arm. If people needed help, they should be helped. Why Sunda had elected to boycott legitimate Makers he didn't know, but he doubted this child would agree with that decision. He dropped the bracelet in the bowl.

She stared at it a moment, wide-eyed. Then she bowed frantically. A moment later she'd run back to her father to display her prize. Sandor stood up, grinning. He scanned the overhead signs, then cut left toward the corridor identified with SpanAir.

"Feel pretty good about yourself?" Nikko asked.

"Sure do. I don't see why—"

A commotion broke out behind him. A woman screamed. He spun around. A solid *thunk!* and a child started sobbing hysterically. Sandor barely had time to step aside as the little girl raced past him holding her arms pressed against her head, her face streaked with tears and blood. *Thunk!, thunk!* Two uniformed men stood over the prone figure of her father, swinging their clubs mechanically against his fragile body. The woman huddled shivering against the wall.

Sandor's hand closed into a fist. *"Fascists!"* he hissed. He dropped his bag and charged back through the crowd.

"Stay out of it!" Nikko screamed in his ear, his voice touched by a rare note of panic. "Sandor, this is not the Commonwealth. This is not—"

He stopped listening. He grabbed one of the uniforms by the elbow and wrenched him aside. The shorter security guard he grasped by the wrist, aborting the flogging. "Mercy, man!" he shouted. "He's done nothing wrong. He's bothering no one."

The short guard stared at him with stony black eyes. After a moment, Sandor thought to release his wrist. Slowly, the guard lowered his arm. He tapped the club gently against his leg. The other, taller guard stepped up beside him, his expression officially polite. "You're interfering in an official matter," he said.

"They've done nothing wrong," Sandor insisted. His gaze shifted to the man on the floor. He could see no sign of life in the bruised, malformed frame. This close, the odor of decaying flesh was almost overwhelming.

"On the contrary," the tall guard said. "Begging is illegal. This family's been warned many times to keep out of the terminal. They continue to return, and so we must employ these brutal methods. But it has nothing to do with you. Please continue with your vacation."

Sandor continued to stare at the body. "You've killed him, haven't you?" he asked.

The guard shrugged. "If you would move on...." His hand invited Sandor to leave.

"Get moving before they get mad," Nikko advised. "Believe me, you don't want to get arrested here."

"But they killed a man."

"This is not the Commonwealth."

"You keep saying that!"

"It's worth repeating. Now let's *go*. These thugs hate ghosts and now they know you've got one on your shoulder. Move on before they decide to censure *you*."

All pretense of politeness had vanished from the hard eyes of the taller guard. Sandor stepped back hesitantly, then quickly turned and walked away. He could feel a crimson flush of shame wash his face. He looked around for his bag, but it had vanished. "Naturally," Nikko said.

"So what?" His hands coiled into fists so tight he could feel fingernails biting into skin. He wanted the pain. Ugly fascist pigs! Un-nature. Dirty world. "You knew what it was like here, didn't you, Nikko? Why'd you never tell me?'

"Grow up, Sandor." Then, "Uh-oh. Police dog just ahead. Copy two. It's fixed on you. Why? I don't like this at all."

The dog trotted toward them, the crowd parting before it as if it employed a priority transportation program. Except for Sandor. He refused to step out of its way. No matter. Because Nikko was right. Apparently it had come for him.

It stepped aside just far enough to let him pass. Then it turned around and followed at his heel, its great head almost on a level with his shoulder, its hot breath washing across his back as it snuffled, searching his person for illegal molecules.

"Be easy, Sandy," Nikko crooned. "It's got nothing on you."

But Sandor felt his anger wind tighter with every step. His fingernails bored deeper into his palms. When the dog sniffed at his heel he could stand it no longer.

He spun around and struck out with his foot, cracking the animal in the jaw. It yelped and jumped backward. "This is not your jurisdiction!" he shouted at it. "Leave me *alone*!"

The dog lunged. Sandor twisted aside, but it struck him with its head, a glancing blow to the chest that knocked him to the ground. He tried to roll away, but the animal was quicker. It pinned him, its great jaws clamped snugly around his throat. Mortal fear caused his anger to collapse like a bubble under pressure. *This is not the Commonwealth.* Here the police charter was meaningless. Here, he had no civil rights. The dog could kill him.

He thought of Fox. Dad had been bitter when he'd left Summer House. Earth was the same as Hell, in his mind. But Sandor had gone anyway, leaving his original body lying in cold storage in the Summer House mausoleum. If Fox had to revive that body, he'd see to it that the House never let Sandor Earth-side again.

Nature, the House would never let him *stay* Earth-side. Not after this run-in with the cops. Copy two was washed up. What happened to it now didn't really matter. He'd like to preserve the memory of this trip, and yet. . . . "Fuck off," he said, employing language he'd first heard a few weeks ago on the drilling platform. He stared into the beast's mechanical eyes. "You're violating my civil rights."

The dog remained motionless for what seemed like an eternity, but finally it released its grip on his throat and stepped back.

Amazed, Sandor rolled to his feet, one hand rubbing at his bruised neck. Briefly, he considered launching another kick at the dog. Then his gaze fell as the significance of this moment hit him. He'd never committed an act of violence in his life . . . until today. What had happened?

"Move on, Sandor," Nikko commanded. "Just move on."

He took the ghost's advice, because he didn't know what else to do. Turning his back on the dog, he started again down the corridor, pretending not to see the sympathetic stares of other travelers. He tried to understand what had happened. The House warned violence was contagious. Guess so. Suddenly, being sent back to Summer House didn't seem such a bad idea.

He wandered aimlessly, until he spotted a door that seemed to open onto daylight. He headed for it.

As he passed through the door, humidity enfolded him like a warm, wet blanket. He sucked in a heavy breath. Taxis lined the curb; agents shouted at him. The sun glinted fiercely off the wet pavement. In the distance he could see the city's towers, their summits almost touching the bellies of broken black clouds still heavy with rain. Curiosity stirred in him. "Don't even think about it," Nikko growled.

"Mr. Tibayan? Sandor Jiang-Tibayan?"

He turned, startled to hear his name. Two men, both dressed in green uniforms consisting of a short-sleeved tailored shirt and knee-length pants, looked him over. One had a very fair face, with Asian features. "You are Mr. Tibayan?" he asked.

"Yes, of course." Sandor glanced from one to the other nervously.

"We are officers of the municipal police." He flashed an ID card.

Sandor glanced at it and Nikko nodded. "Looks authentic," he said.

"Mr. Tibayan, you are under arrest for interfering with the official duties of an airport security guard, and for attempting to vandalize an authorized security device."

"You mean the dog?"

The light-skinned officer nodded. His companion stepped forward, a flexible wand in one hand. On Sandor's shoulder, Nikko cursed. "Preparing distress packet," he muttered. "Authorize send, Sandy, *right now.*"

Sandor's jaw dropped in confusion. But Nikko was his guide; he did as he was told. The message went out. "What's going on, Nikko? What—?"

The second officer raised the wand and gently touched it against his head. Instinctively, Sandor stepped back. Nikko said: "Kem-wand, kid. Been nice to know you." And a thousand tiny fires ignited in his head. He screamed. His legs buckled. His head hit the pavement with a thunderous *crack!*

A voice spoke out of the dark, a voice that purred soft, threatening reassurance. "You're coming out of it now, aren't you? There, there. A naturalizing Maker shouldn't have hit you that hard. What have you got inside that pretty skull? Not legal wiring, I'll bet."

A blood-red light suddenly blazed in his eyes. He blinked and the color thinned. Pink. Blinked again, and the white glare seemed to burn his retina. Behind his eyes his skull throbbed. His shoulders were on fire: his arms had been bound behind his back. He hung suspended from his wrists in a dark, stinking room, with a white light blazing in his eyes. He could barely breathe.

"Nikko?" he asked softly. He felt as if his brain had been packed in foam, set aside for storage. And one of his senses had failed him. "Nikko!" he called, more urgently.

He could see, he could hear, he could taste . . . blood in his mouth. Sweat beaded on his bare chest, his abdomen, his naked groin. He'd been stripped. And he'd lost one of his senses. "*Nikko!*" he screamed.

"He's gone."

The voice in the dark. He tried to lift his head to see. A sharp *thawk!* and his back exploded in pain. He groaned, his muscles cramping. Another blow across his back and the soft voice spoke. "Why are you here?"

"*Goin' to India!*" Sandor gasped. So hard to breathe with his arms pinioned behind him; and he needed air to bleed this pain away. "Call home. Let them know—"

Thawk! "What is your business here?"

"Nothing! Who—"

Thawk! "Why did you leave the terminal?"

Desperately: *"Air."*

"You had a rendezvous."

"No."

"With whom?"

"No one!" Someone threw a switch. The blazing light flickered as an electric shock nearly doubled his body over. It passed and he wanted to scream. But he had no breath left. Couldn't breathe. What was happening to him? *"Nikko."*

"We have a picture of you. You came here to buy a stolen Maker. But these instruments of Satan are illegal in Sunda." He chuckled softly, perhaps amused by his own hypocrisy. The government in Sunda remained in power only because of the advantages conferred by their Makers. "We have friends who've advised us about your activities. They say you're only a foolish child, and that we should spare you. But first you must tell us: where is the original thief?"

"I don't—" An electric shock interrupted him. His teeth fused together, biting his tongue. Blood flowed in his mouth. When the shock ended, he gasped for breath, aspirating the blood. He choked, his body writhing for air. He blacked out for a few seconds.

"We would like to let you live," the soft voice said, pulling him back to consciousness. "Wouldn't you like to return to your home? You can. Just tell us why you came to Sunda."

Sandor tried to nod, eager to tell them anything. "Install ... security. On a ... platform."

"You belong to Summer House."

"Yesss...."

"Where were you supposed to meet the thief?"

They didn't believe him! They thought he was somebody else. The realization horrified him. He couldn't tell them what he didn't know.

"Where did you intend to meet?" the soft voice repeated.

"Nowhere!" Sandor screamed. "I don't know—"

Another electric shock racked his body. His muscles spasmed so hard he thought his bones would break. He started to black out again, but the sharp sting of a needle inoculated him with a terrible, detailed awareness. He could hear everyone in the room; smell his own piss on the floor.

He could not sense the atrium. It would not respond to his entreaties. He couldn't call out, couldn't summon data, couldn't summon Nikko. "My mind is dead," he whispered.

"Ah, but your body is very much alive. Sometimes a body can be a burden."

Another electric shock, touching every cell, confirming the awful diagnosis. "*Alive. . . ?*"

"Tell me," his torturer crooned. "Tell me. We'd love to send you home."

The House skirted the legal boundaries of molecular technology. Subtle advantages could be mingled almost imperceptibly in the complex human system. Most had to be controlled through the atrium; but one had been developed as a last resort that would function even after the atrium was gone. "*Not alive,*" Sandor whispered. "*Don't hurt when . . . not alive.*"

He powered down. Voluntary control of the autonomic nervous system. He stopped his heartbeat. Terminated all motor function. His last breath eased noisily out of his lungs and his bowel failed. His ears he kept alive. And his brain.

Loud scuffling in the dark. Voices spoke, but Sandor didn't know the language. Someone shouted in rage. His head thudded against the floor. The dull wallop of fist against flesh as they tried to restart his heart. Cursing.

Silence.

He let himself breath, imperceptibly. His heart squeezed out a hundred beats.

Later, four men removed his body. *Shoosh* of a car door, soft hum of its engines. A long time. He breathes

occasionally; lets his heart run. The car stops. *Shoosh.*
Hum of crowd voices not too far away. After a time,
voices soft with tension. The door closes; the car pro-
ceeds. Only a few minutes this time before they stop
again. Groans and curses. His body's moved. Rippling
sound of water flowing. More voices. A great shout!
Then—

The fizz of bubbles filled his ears and all the street
sounds vanished. Something crunched under his head
with awful clarity, sound that moved too fast. In a panic
he released his heart. It thundered in his chest. He
opened his mouth to suck in a lungful of air. Water
choked his throat. Motor function swept back into his
limbs and he thrashed. His arms were strapped to his
sides. He bumped along underwater, driven by a fierce
current, pinned to the bottom by an awful weight that
nearly crushed his shoulders. He twisted, thrashed. Finally got his feet under him and *pushed*. His head broke
the surface. Sunlight blinded him. He kicked frantically, coughed, spluttered, caught a breath then
plunged to the bottom again.

What had they weighted him with? He had to get it
off, get it off. He could bend his arms at the elbow. He
groped with his fingers. Felt insulated wire wrapped securely around his chest. He pulled at it. Yanked, fought,
struggled. Shot to the surface again for another breath
of air.

On the bottom again. He realized the wire had loos-
ened. Had a knot slipped? Had he simply shifted position? He tugged at it and it moved an inch up his arms.
He ducked and twisted, lungs burning as he fought the
wire.

It snapped. The weight vanished. He rolled free in
the current. Which way was up? For a moment he
didn't know. Then he felt the bottom under his head.
He rolled over and pushed, bursting from the water in
a fountain of spray.

CHAPTER

9

Somewhere along the walk back to the warehouse, Phousita and Arif had come to an unspoken agreement. She should not return to the clan with him, at least not now. The children would be better off if they didn't see her in transition. Plague could be a horrible thing. Even if it turned out all right in the end, the hungers of transition could consume a personality. They'd all seen it: playmates eroding both in mind and body as the disease progressed. Phousita wouldn't subject them to that again.

So at the edge of the market district she'd said good-bye to Arif and set out on her own. Pedestrian traffic in the crowded streets moved slowly, held back by the fierce heat of the late morning sun as it steamed through the remnants of the rain clouds that had soaked the city earlier that morning.

Phousita moved at the leisurely pace of the crowd, and as she walked, she found herself examining the faces around her, looking for one with fair skin and blond hair who might be the angel. He seemed to be always in her thoughts. He was the only memory the evil sorcerer had brought to her. She didn't know if he was good or evil, or what his purpose might be, but she wanted to find out. The spirit inside her wanted to know. Twice she thought she saw him, and she hurried forward, only to draw up abruptly in disappointment as she realized her mistake.

Here in the marketplace only foot traffic could negotiate the narrow streets. People wandered from stall to stall, examining piles of merchandise, haggling, cursing, moving on. Vendors shouted the quality of their wares. Laborers groaned and coughed under the weight of goods to be transported on their backs. Phousita moved carefully through the maze, down the street of the jewelers, on to those selling cloth and spectacles, past the electronics alley and the tea shops. The commotion fascinated her. It seemed familiar and foreign all at once, as if she knew it well, but not in *this* life.

She looked in all the stalls. Stopped to finger the merchandise until the vendors cursed her and told her to move on. She was on sensual overload: the sights, sounds, smells—all gave pleasure to her. At a fruit stand she took out her last coin and purchased two bananas and a drink of river water.

She stood, slowly chewing, savoring the intense flavor of the fruit. Her eye delighted in its gross structure. Her tongue went further. With a sense she had never before possessed, she explored the essential structure of the fruit: the arrangement of its tissue, the careful order of its cells, the precise structure of its component molecules. As her vision shrank, her vocabulary vanished. She had no names for the treasures she discovered. No interest in their meaning or their use. She existed only to observe. And when she understood the most intimate details of the fruit's construction, she retreated until she stood once again amidst the jostling crowds.

Her chin lifted. She looked about, nostrils flaring as

she sorted the myriad scents born on the searing air. The Chinese doctor had opened his office. The crowd noises that had roared so ebulliently in her ears only moments before now seemed muted. Her gaze no longer wandered. She had a goal.

She glided easily through the throng, as if her sharp eyes could see, a moment before it happened, just where the crowd would part. She crossed the last street of stalls and entered a new section of the market. Here the buildings were planned, permanent structures, made of wood and preserved with a stabilizing resin. In the windows, brightly painted signs beckoned to the passers-by. Phousita could read none of them, but then, she didn't have to. She knew what each shop sold.

She came to Zeke Choy's shop. A line of customers already hung out the door. They were mostly women, mostly well dressed, with jewelry on their arms. Phousita took a place at the end of the line and stood cock-hipped, waiting patiently in the sun. The old woman stood at her side. Phousita started in surprise at her kindly face. Decades of sun had dried and bronzed the old woman's skin; her frail shoulders stooped with age. She wore her thin black hair in a tight bun held in place by tiny bone picks, and she'd carefully arranged her sarong to hide all sign of repair. She smiled at Phousita, revealing blackened gums sparsely occupied by teeth. Phousita clung to her skirts and sobbed. She was terrified. She was a waif, a freak, she had no right to be here with these finely dressed women. The old woman caressed her shoulder, mumbling unintelligible encouragement. In the pocket of her sarong she carried the money she'd saved over the past year from her business of selling charms and potions. Enough to buy the services of the Chinese doctor. Such a powerful man! Phousita quailed in fear. *I want to go home. I don't want to grow up. Please, Mother!* Though of course the old woman wasn't really her mother. But Phousita was eight years old in mind and body and could remember

no other parent. She'd been eight years old for thirteen
years, poisoned by her pimp because he didn't want her
charm spoiled by maturity. But today the Chinese doctor would command her body to grow. She looked up,
her vision blurred with tears. Who would she be tomorrow?

She reached for the old woman's hand, but there
was no one there. She spun around, searching. Behind
her stood a man with raw red sores on his face. Behind
him, a pretty woman cradling a tiny baby in her arms.
They waited in line, as she did. The old woman was a
ghost, dead now several years.

And Phousita had matured. She had the body of an
adult woman, though she'd never gained in height. A
toy woman. That's how she sold herself. The line crept
forward. Zeke Choy was a very busy man.

Late in the morning, Phousita grew suddenly restless. A realization had come upon her: the angel was
nearby. Somehow, she was aware of his presence. How
could that be? She hadn't scented him. She looked all
around, but he was nowhere to be seen. She chewed
her lip nervously, wondering how far away he might be.
How satisfying it would be to find him, to discover why
the evil sorcerer had given her this vision of his face.
Yet she couldn't search for him now. She must see the
Chinese doctor. That was urgent. She needed his advice, his knowledge. She craned her neck to gauge the
length of the line ahead of her. Ah, not so long now.
Only another two or three hours. Good. She would
search for the angel tonight.

At noon the shop closed. All the customers who'd
been waiting in the cool interior retreated to the streets,
forming a neat line beside those who continued to wait
outside. Last of all, the doctor came out. He seemed
very tired. People smiled at him and murmured *honored
sir*. He acknowledged them in a distant way as his gaze
swept down the line. He seemed ready to turn away,

hurry off to his lunch, but he hesitated. "Phousita?" he called softly. He stepped toward her.

She bowed her head deeply. *"Tuan."*

"You've changed. You look different. More . . . vigorous?" He seemed suddenly aware of the many people who listened. "Come," he said, crooking a finger. And she left her place in line to follow him down the street.

"Tuan," she said, hurrying after him. "I *have* changed. I think I'm becoming a witch. I see many things I never saw before. The old woman's spirit comes to visit me now. I think she's pleased."

Zeke snorted. "How many times do I have to tell you there are no such things as witches?"

Phousita nodded patiently. "Yes, *tuan.*" The doctor would always insist on that. "Still, I've come to ask your advice. Though there are no such things as witches, there are many here who practice the trade. And some of them are very rich and very fat. Since I've developed some talents, I, too, would like to practice the witch's trade. Though of course," she added hastily, "there are no such things as witches."

"Of course," he said dryly, leading her around the building and to the back entrance of his shop. He passed his hand across a white panel and the door popped open with a squeak. Using his foot, he nudged it open further and went inside. Phousita passed her own hand across the panel, but nothing happened. "Come in," Zeke called. "The door will close behind you."

Phousita had never been in the shop's back room before. She looked around curiously, but there was very little to see. Just the kit the doctor had brought to the warehouse, a small refrigerator, a telephone, a TV. On the TV, a picture of the shop's public area.

Zeke touched her arm. Startled, she turned. He had a rubber cord in his hand. "So you want to be a witch," he said. "Well, I don't know anything about witches, but I'm sure one of the charlatans in the market would be glad to find a talented apprentice." He took her hand. "Turn your arm like this." He tied the cord around her upper arm and picked up a syringe. "Make a fist. Good."

The needle slipped into a vein. She watched the dark red blood bubble into the syringe. "Witches practice deception, Phousita. They feed on hope and ignorance. Even the old woman, with her dried spiders and herbs, never cast a decent spell in her life." He withdrew the needle and turned to his diagnostic kit.

Phousita stared after him in utter confusion. "But a witch poisoned me when I was a child," she said. "Only you could break the spell. And a witch transformed Arif into a clown."

"No," he said, his back to her as he worked at the kit. "You were poisoned by a Maker, a tiny machine that tampered with your metabolism. Arif was poisoned by a different kind of Maker, one that wrote out a new genetic program for his face." He sighed and turned around. "Never mind how it works. Just believe that there's no magic involved. The witches in the marketplace don't know any more about magic than you do. They just know the black market address where a good chemist can be reached—

"Ah, I'm sorry. Of course you don't understand."

She bowed her head. "I'm stupid, *tuan*."

"No you're not, Phousita. You've just never had a chance to learn." The diagnostic kit chimed. He studied it, a frown on his face. "Have you had any more symptoms besides the hunger?"

"Yes, *tuan*," she insisted. "I see many things I never saw before. The old woman visits me now. I *know* things."

"You've been infected with a Maker," he said, as if he hadn't heard her answer. "It's very elusive. I haven't been able to determine its structure yet."

"I know what it is."

"Now, now. We don't *know* that it's plague."

"It's not plague, *tuan*. It's the spirit of an evil sorcerer."

He sighed. Putting down the diagnostic kit, he turned to her, his arms crossed over his chest. "We'll find a cure."

She shrugged. She didn't want a cure. "There are some things *you* don't understand, *tuan*, because you're not from the city. You're from the Commonwealth." Her lips parted in dismay as she realized, *"You used to be a cop!"*

Anger darkened Zeke's face like a cloud across the moon. Phousita felt the cold draft of his bitterness, his fury, his venerable sense of betrayal. She'd offended him! Horrified, she bowed her head, hunched her shoulders, threw her hands before her face to hide her shame. "Forgive me, *tuan*!" she sobbed. "Forgive me! I have a stupid mouth. I don't know what I say—"

A harsh buzzer interrupted her. She jumped, her heart pounding.

"Someone's tampering with the front door," the doctor growled. He turned to the TV.

Phousita followed his gaze and hissed. *"Police!"*

An officer wearing the black uniform of the Commonwealth Police pounded on the door with the flat of his hand. Two huge hunting dogs stood panting behind him. Phousita whimpered and began backing toward the door.

"Don't be afraid," the doctor said. "They won't hurt you."

"They *will*!" she squealed. Zeke Choy was a great man, but there really were things he didn't understand! Like the dogs. They were a sign of death; the old woman had said so. To see them twice in so short a time was a terrible omen.

"Phousita!"

She hid her face from his fury. "Forgive me, *tuan*. Forgive me. I will never disturb you a—"

He grabbed her arm in a gesture so shockingly rude

she almost cried out. "Is there something you're not telling me?" he hissed, leaning over her. "Have you been working for the Commonwealth?"

"No, no! Of course not, *tuan*."

"Who told you I was from the Commonwealth? Who told you I used to be a cop?"

"No one! I think—maybe you did?" She had only a vague notion of what the Commonwealth was: a magic place in an undefinable direction where food was so plentiful it could be fed to dogs and every child lived to grow up. "*Tuan*, you must have told me."

"No! I've never mentioned it to anyone." He stared at her, suspicion sharp in his eyes. "I won't go back with them. Tell them that. I resigned and I'm not going to change my mind." He pushed her away.

"Tell who, *tuan*?" she whispered, as she edged toward the door. Her hand touched it. It opened with a soft click. What could he be thinking? What work could she possibly do for the Commonwealth?

But he didn't answer. He was looking at the TV again. On its screen she saw the officer bending over to examine the front door. One of the dogs had disappeared. "I have to go," Zeke said. He started toward the front room.

"Don't go out there," Phousita cried. "They'll arrest you. Run away. Come with me. I can hide you."

"Nobody can hide from the dogs once they have your scent. If they're looking for you, Phousita, you might as well come with me."

She shook her head. Was he crazy? With one last backward glance she slipped out the door, into the street. Instantly, a hand clapped over her arm. She was yanked down behind some cardboard boxes stacked against the building. She started to scream but another hand fell like a clamp across her mouth. A voice hissed in her ear. *"Quiet, you stupid country girl!"*

Arif!

When she relaxed, he uncovered her mouth. "We've

been burned out," he growled. "The dogs came this morning and cleared out the warehouse before the 'Surgence torched it. It's all gone. There's nothing left but charcoal."

She sat for a moment, stunned. "The dogs were there? But they're here now." She twisted around to look at him. "Do they follow *you*?"

His lip twisted. "*Nothing* followed me. Maybe it's Zeke Choy they're after. Come on. Let's go."

Obediently, she rose to her feet and followed him as he ducked into the steady stream of foot traffic moving through the crowded alley. The sun stood high overhead. Its heat steamed in her lungs and burned into her muscles. She trailed Arif, darting through the crowd with practiced ease. A side street opened. Arif followed it. A few vendors had spread mats at the base of stucco buildings. The scent of charcoal filled the air, and the music of a gamelan. Behind them Phousita heard startled cries. She turned to look. "The dog's coming!" she cried. "Where can we hide?" She saw no shelter in this street, no open door.

"Stay close!" Arif ordered. He cut through the crowd with the grace of a practiced thief. She started to follow, but a fat merchant cut her off. They collided. He cursed and swung at her, striking her across the face with the back of his hand. She stumbled back, hunched over and tasting blood. When she looked up, Arif was gone. Behind her, a woman was screaming. Phousita hesitated in confusion. Then she caught Arif's scent, actually tasted it. It hung in the air, a thin, broken trail that blazed incandescent in her mind.

She plunged ahead, following it, picking it out of the thousand other scents of other people who'd passed through this street. At last the stucco buildings ended. A cross street ahead. She hurried past it, then stopped abruptly. The trail had disappeared. She backtracked. Swung her head. Caught the trace and cut right.

"Phousita!" He waited for her, crouching behind

the wheel of a dilapidated *becak* while the driver fidgeted nervously. "You see that?" Arif pointed down the street. A truck rumbled toward them, its sides marked with faded government insignia. The funeral truck. When the destitute died, its crew gathered up their bodies and hauled them off. Phousita did not know where. "Follow me!" Arif cried.

As the truck approached, he started cutting through traffic. The press of people parted slowly as it advanced. The truck driver sounded his horn at another *becak*, but the bum had waited too long to get out of the way. The truck's worn brakes engaged with a tremendous squeal. The two crewmen clinging to the back of the truck swung forward. One fell. The *becak* driver cursed and pedaled his rig to the side.

Arif picked that moment to jump. He landed on the tiny platform occupied by the remaining crewman. Finding a handhold, he crouched down and reached back for Phousita, ignoring the curses, threats, and blows rained down on him from the crewman. Phousita scrambled up beside him. He took her elbow and shoved her, sending her tumbling into the loading bin. Then he turned like a snake on his tormentor. He struck, catching the man's free hand in his. Phousita lay dazed in the bin, sickened by the stench. She stared up at him. He looked like a magic figure from a *wayang* vid. He moved his wrist and a purse appeared in his hand, the straps neatly cut. Phousita stared at it. Where had it come from? The crewman stared at it too, then turned a questioning eye to Arif. Arif nodded. "Let us ride to the river," he said. The man's hand closed over the purse. He nodded in turn. Arif dropped into the bin beside Phousita just as the truck lurched forward.

"The dog comes," Phousita moaned. "Smell it on the air?"

Arif scowled at her. But he peered over the edge of the bin to survey the street. A moment later he dropped back down, cursing. "It's at the crossroad."

"It's following *you*," Phousita accused. "Your scent's as bright as the sun! Anybody could pick it out. We have to change it."

"Huh. This stink should cover us."

She shook her head. "Not hide it. That won't work. We need to *change* it. I must change too." Her tongue darted out of her mouth, sampling his scent. His odor was a byproduct of the living processes of his body, the stamp of his metabolism. To change it much would destroy him. But the change needn't be extraordinary. A subtle adjustment would confuse the pursuing beast and give them time to escape. Her tongue darted out again, then she leaned forward, pressing her mouth against his wide clown's lips. He pulled away, startled. But the job was done. She lay back and closed her eyes.

Her body had a signature of its own, just as bright, just as unique as Arif's scent trail. She reached into her cells, into the metabolic pathways that nurtured them. She made adjustments. At her command tiny hands pulled at the molecules, making subtle changes. Then the hands turned to one another, adjusting their own structure too.

She opened her eyes. Arif was watching her with a suspicious scowl. "We must bathe in the river," she said. "When we have cleansed ourselves, the dogs will no longer know us."

Arif's scowl deepened. "Are you a witch, Phousita?"

She smiled. "Will we make it to the river?"

CHAPTER

10

The transmission time between Summer House and Earth averaged three minutes. Nikko stayed on the tether, clinging to a silvery tree branch with his long, prehensile toes, because the continuous tremor in his fingers had grown so bad he no longer trusted his hands to maintain a grip. He waited out the time that would have to pass before his ghost reached Sandor; before it could arrive on its emergency beacon and deliver its warning; before an acknowledgment could be composed and sent back to him.

He switched on his camera pack and directed the lens to focus on him as he tried to summarize what had happened. He sensed the scope of his documentary expanding as he spoke. "I learned today that I almost owned the Bohr Maker. Love and Nature! It hurts to watch a chance like this slip away. It'll never come again. Maybe that's why I tried so hard to salvage the situation. Tried *too* hard. The debts are still coming in. . . ."

Summer House moved through its long, slow spin.

The silver trees that sprouted on the outer walls of the tether turned their leaves to follow the light. The distant gold sparkle of the magnetic launch tube seemed to move in a swift arc overhead. Three minutes passed. Then four, then five. Nikko felt his heart begin to beat faster, harder, as the critical moment approached. He stumbled over his words. He couldn't seem to focus on a coherent thread of thought. His breathing quickened.

The count passed six minutes and his atrium's emergency signal resounded through his skull, again, for the second time in his life, the second time in an hour. Moments later a form coalesced into existence beside him. Tall, blue, manly figure; exaggerated fingers afflicted with a grotesque, insectile twitch; exaggerated toes curled securely over black branches; an emotionless face, like a mask. He gazed at himself.

For a moment neither himself nor his ghost spoke. Then Nikko felt the fiery heat of understanding grow with the relentlessness of ticking seconds, of passing time. If a destination address were unavailable, a ghost would automatically return to its origin.

So Sandor's atrium was unavailable.

Panic squeezed at his throat. He felt mildly nauseous and his heart rate seemed to instantly triple. Maybe Sandor was only crippled. Or maybe he was dead. "Go to Marevic," he croaked at the ghost.

Marevic Chun was his mentor. She was also the regional president of Summer House at Earth. She was a fossil—almost as ancient as Kirstin—a sly old dinosaur who'd fed off the entrails of police kills for a hundred years. Marevic would be able to find Sandor.

The ghost nodded agreement. It was himself. He didn't have to explain his intent. It downloaded without uttering a word.

Nikko's face had always been a lie, an emotionless mask. But now he wore it deliberately, hiding from even himself as he dropped back down through the forest to the nearest transit node and returned to his apartment. Fox came up the corridor from the other direction and met him at the door, his ruddy face creased with anger, his red hair wild. He followed Nikko silently through the door. When it closed, sealing them off from the corridor, Nikko turned. The camera lens floated on its tentacle, focused on Fox. "Something's happened to Sandor. The police may have him. I don't know."

Fox blanched. Into the shocked silence Nikko poured his explanation. He held nothing back, not even the theft of the Bohr Maker. There was no point now. Fox would still be here when Nikko was gone. Perhaps he could help Sandor. The camera recorded everything.

Nikko listened to himself speak as if he were a detached observer, a silent third person in the room. Now his voice wore the mask.

"Who was it?" Fox asked.

The question seemed to hang in the room, detached from all reference. Nikko cocked his head, then realized: Fox wanted to know who had attacked him. "I don't know. But he wasn't a cop."

That seemed to anger Fox further. "A civilian got past my defensive Makers? A civilian?"

Nikko almost laughed. Professional pride, even in a moment of crisis.

"I'll need tissue samples," Fox snapped. "Maybe I can identify the foreign Maker; get it out of your system." He stomped to the door. "I'll get my things. I'll be back." Tears glistened in his eyes. He hesitated at the door. Nikko braced himself for a gush of apologies; guilt-laden expressions of regret for his hubris in creating a son outside the human norm. But Fox was still working on his anger. "We think we can plan our lives," he muttered. "We think we can model reality. But chaos is an intrusive, inconsiderate bitch."

The door closed behind Fox.

Nikko stood frozen in place, at a loss for what to do next. His neck twitched a few times. The camera lens snaked around his shoulder, as the Dull Intelligence guiding it decided to record his deteriorating condition. He roared in rage, stripped the pack off his shoulders and hurled it into a corner of the room.

His blue hide began to itch intensely. That was the influence of the foreign Maker, he decided: a pollution in his body that his mind could not forget. He found himself acutely conscious of its presence, of the fact that he'd been colonized; controlled. It outraged him. He wanted to strike out at something, but the room offered no ready targets so he simply stood in place, while heat began building up inside him.

He felt feverish. He knew he had to calm himself, or take a sedative. He closed his eyes. Arms twitching at his sides, he ran through a breathing exercise, deep cleansing breaths.

Thoughts of Sandor licked at his conscience. He tried to turn away from them. He'd sent a ghost Earthside. There was nothing more he could do now.

Cleansing breath.

He could feel the heat pouring off his kisheer. He needed to take a sedative. He could die of overheating. That would be funny. Yes. But bad policy.

Cleansing breath.

He must confess to the police. Exonerate Sandor.

Cleansing breath.

Sandor was innocent.

He tried to coil his hands into fists, but his rebellious fingers would not close. His breath ran out in an angry hiss. Love and Nature, there had to be a way out of this mess!

He remembered what Fox had said about the biogenesis function. Could he really retreat into hidden code? But how was that different from dying?

The apartment door opened. He turned eagerly, expecting Fox. But it was Kirstin who stood in the doorway, dressed in police uniform, a hungry half-smile on her plain face. She looked heavier than she had on Castle, as if this incarnation were more strongly muscled.

At first Nikko was only amazed. Then he ran a check on his atrium, but no, she wasn't resident there as a ghost. "You've come," he whispered, his words afloat in a vapor of disbelief.

Hope surged through him. Had she reconsidered? Had she come to make amends? A warning voice seemed to whisper in the back of his mind: *This is Kirstin.*

His arms had been half lifted in tentative greeting. Now he let them fall back to his sides, where they danced and jerked like marionettes. He chuckled grimly. "Kirstin. What a pleasant surprise. Did you miss me so much? How touching."

Her smile faded. She stepped into the room. "Give me the Bohr Maker," she said. "I know you have it."

Nikko held himself very still. She must have found Van Ness. But if she'd found him, why hadn't she recovered the Maker? "You're wrong," he said cautiously. "I don't have it."

"Huh. You don't expect me to believe your little brother convinced Van Ness to run."

"Sandor?" Nikko stepped forward anxiously. "What about Sandor? What do you know about him?"

"He's dead. And if I have anything to say about it, he'll stay that way."

"No! You can't block his resurrection. He's innocent."

"So prove it. Give me the Maker."

"I don't have the Maker! If I had it, do you think I'd be standing here, wasting my time on a twisted old fuck like you?"

Her chin dipped. Her eyes glittered dangerously. "Give me the goddamn Maker, Nikko, or your brother is going to be thoroughly, utterly dead. The goddamn Maker and a full confession, you fucking whore. You fucking child murderer. How old was your brother?

Eighteen? You killed him. Good as sticking a knife in his throat. He's dead because of you. Have you fixed yourself up yet with Bohr's Maker? Are you happy to be alive?"

"I don't have it!" he screamed. "If I had it I wouldn't be shaking myself to pieces!" He turned away, his fingers clawing convulsively at the memory of the soft, vulnerable feel of her neck. The recollection intrigued him. He'd never really touched her before. But now, for the first time, she was real and he was real and Sandor would be better off in the hands of almost anyone but her.

But no. It would do no good. Kirstin was a creature of many incarnations. She'd just pop up again in another city, and swoop down on Sandor and Fox and Summer House like a harpy from hell.

He raised his hands in a gesture of surrender. But Kirstin must have misconstrued his intent. She hissed and darted toward him, a stun gun in her hand. He tried to dodge, but she was faster. Somehow she'd managed to time her move perfectly, despite the unfamiliar gravity. She tapped him in the back. A charge raced up his spine. His rib cage spasmed, driving the breath out of his lungs, and he sprawled hard on the floor, bruising his chin and chest.

In an instant she was on her knees beside him. "Confession time, Nikko. Where's the fucking Maker?"

"I don't have it," he growled again, forcing the words from his tingling throat. His arms and legs were quivering, out of control. The kisheer had shriveled into a painful knot. "Van Ness synthesized the bloody thing. He brought out a physical copy. I couldn't send that through the data Gates. So I don't have it. I never had it. Never!"

"And Sandor?"

He could feel the barbs of the stun against the back of his neck. If she fired it now, it could cripple his atrium. He sucked in breath after breath, feeling like a lobster, set to boil in its shell. "Van Ness knew me under Sandor's face, that's all. It was a convenience. Not everybody likes to fuck blue, you know. And besides, Van Ness liked boys."

She struck him across the back of the head with the stun gun's housing. "You dirty whore," she hissed.

He grunted at the blow. His teeth squeezed together, as if he could press out the pain. "Sandor's innocent," he croaked. "Didn't know anything. Didn't even know I was using his face."

"That could have been awkward for him," Kirstin said acidly, "if he'd chanced to meet one of your clients." Then, in a wheedling voice he'd come to despise, "Why should I believe you?"

Panic spread its wings in his belly. She had to accept his confession. "Why should I lie?"

Kirstin chuckled. "It does seem a bit out of character for you to play the hero. But technically, the possibility that you might be trying to save your brother's ass constitutes a mo—" She screamed.

The lights went out. Nikko felt a crushing weight fall across him, engulf him. He couldn't breathe. He couldn't see. He felt himself being lifted up; ferried away. Kirstin thrashed against him. They rolled together in a thick, liquid world as fiery *lancets* of pain began to pierce his body, a billion tiny knives carving his flesh into a billion tiny flakes, pieces of himself cut loose and abandoned, falling away into darkness. His structure was dissolving. Flesh was stripped away from bones. Bones eroded and disappeared. Thoughts shot round and round in his brain in terrified loops. He was being consumed alive by microscopic piranhas. Torn apart by a billion hungry sharks, one bite at a time. And he could do nothing to stop it.

CHAPTER

11

Kirstin sat in stony silence, staring at Nikko's corpse. It was sprawled in a dense patch of grasses on the edge of a meadow, the long blue limbs bent at awkward angles. His body had the slick, wet look of a newborn baby. But he was dead.

She huddled a few meters away, crouched against the warm surface of a rock that protruded from the brown meadow grass, the two-thirds G of Summer House pulling like an oppressive weight against her shoulders. Her skin and hair and clothes were still slick with the organic gel that filled the transit system of Summer House. The House was a fully organic habitat—an entity, some would say. And it had turned on Nikko. It had killed him.

She shivered despite the heat, remembering the sight of the apartment walls coming down around them, as if reality had suddenly melted, pouring in upon them like hot jelly. . . .

To escape the image, she forced herself to stand up, to pace the surface of the meadow. This incarnation was

heavier, bulkier than her primary on Castle, well muscled to withstand House gravity, but less graceful than
her accustomed form.

She flexed her arms and looked about. Except for
Nikko's corpse, she was quite alone. Birds sang in the
surrounding forest, undaunted by the oppressive heat.
A slight wind flowed in from a break in the broad-
leafed trees. With a shrug, she followed the breeze to
the edge of the meadow—also, she discovered, the
edge of a cliff.

Standing quietly a few steps back from the preci-
pice, she gazed at the wall of another cliff, some two
hundred meters away across a gulf of open air. It was
studded with windows, and it rose far higher than the
one on which she stood. Her gaze followed it up, until
she was forced to crane her neck, squinting against the
glare. Even then the summit eluded her behind a
slowly roiling bank of fog.

She looked down. The windowed cliff seemed to
descend at least a kilometer below her, rooted in darkness.

Kirstin grunted, impressed despite herself. So this
was the hollow interior of Summer House. She'd never
experienced it directly, though she'd studied it for
many decades.

The House was a mockery of Gaia. The "oceans"
were on the outside: walls composed of huge, discrete
cells of water that were maintained as a habitat for a
multitude of aquatic organisms while doubling as a
massive radiation shield. Inside this was the city proper,
a fairly conventional ring of apartments and parks,
shops and offices, and factories. The windowed cliff
that faced her across the gulf was the inner wall of the
city.

But it was the hollow interior cylinder that made
Summer House famous.

This massive space—over four kilometers high and
two across—housed a vertical forest hung on a sup-

porting structure of freely branching, curvilinear beams fifteen meters in diameter. This was the "heartwood," the bones of Summer House, a massive, treelike structure upon which all the rest of the House had been hung: the encapsulated oceans, the apartment complexes, the forest. The heartwood spanned the height of the forest, from bed to apex, and provided the rooting foundation for most of its trees. Its branches bridged the gap of open sky around the forest and fused with the surrounding walls. Inside the heartwood, a transit system piped nutrients, water, life-forms, heat, and light as Summer House actively maintained an equilibrium between its varied components. Myriad tiny, nonsentient brains regulated the system. Kirstin wondered if any one of them in particular had ordered Nikko's murder.

Her forced journey through the transit system had been blind, hot, and terrifying. There'd been no transit bubble to protect her from the heated fluids pumped through the circulatory system of this mindless behemoth. She and Nikko had been wrapped in a thin sac, like a chorionic membrane, two twins pressed together in the womb. His frantic struggles had bruised her. But his sudden stillness was worse. She'd panicked, certain that her turn was next. But no. The House had freed her, dumping her through a portal and into this meadow. Why?

A condor appeared in the gulf of open air, climbing up from below in a lazy spiral, its great wings hardly moving as it mounted higher and higher, rising on a convection current until it encountered a patch of sky: a horizontal platform the size of a small lake, mounted on a branch of heartwood. The sky emitted blue light from below, while supporting a treeless bog on its upper surface. Tendrils of fog appeared above the dense grasses, only to be whisked away by the wind.

The condor veered away from the obstruction, wheeling around the curve of the vertical canopy. The sight stirred memories in her, of times almost a hundred years past. She breathed in the scent of the forest, remembering the dangerous days with Leander, the Colombian rain forest, the guns that had flowed through her hands like water.

They'd fought for the Goddess then. And they'd won, in a way. The ravaged body of Mother Earth would need millennia to repair, but the Commonwealth tended what it could. Not out of devotion of course. But for purely economic reasons. Molecular prospectors were still extracting fortunes from the forest resource. Fox had been one of them. He'd made his fortune in Ecuador. Then, with exemplary human illogic, he'd abandoned the Mother to construct this rubber-doll mockery of the body of Gaia.

She spat contemptuously into the grass.

Summer House was not *real*. None of the life-forms here were natural. Every one of them had been genetically tailored to suit this artificial ecosystem. So the House could not even claim status as a museum. It was a fatuous experiment, and no more.

"Chief Adair!" The shout resounded across the meadow. She turned, to see three uniformed police officers emerge from the gray door of an arched portal set in a rough earthen bank—the same portal that had earlier spit forth herself and what was left of Nikko. "We got your distress call," the lead officer shouted. "But we had a bitch of a time finding you. The House didn't want to admit you were—

"My God," he said, as he almost stumbled over Nikko's body. "What happened to . . . ?" His question trailed off and he looked up guiltily. Kirstin knew he was weighing the possibility that his boss had performed an unwarranted execution.

She crossed the meadow. By the time she reached the huddled officers, the portal was active again. The silhouette of a human figure appeared in it. At first half-sized, it grew rapidly larger. A moment later a red-haired, florid-faced old man stumbled from the arch. She grinned as she recognized him: Fox Jiang-Tibayan.

She stepped aside, so that he might have a clear view of Nikko's corpse.

The sight seemed to transfix Fox. He uttered a little cry of anguish, then fell to his knees beside the body, his hands running in a practiced medical routine across Nikko's neck, head, and chest. Kirstin squatted across from him. "He's dead," she said, more to inflict another wound than to impart any information. "Your House killed him. Did you design it to behave that way?"

He spared her a solitary glance, then bowed his head against Nikko's motionless chest.

At the portal, yet another figure was emerging, and then another and another until there were six. All with the appearance of twenty-somethings, they huddled around Fox, talking in low whispers. Kirstin tossed back her gel-slicked hair and strode into their midst. They gave way before her, seeming almost as frightened of her as they were of Nikko's remains. She nudged at the still blue-china body with the toe of her shoe. "So who do I arrest for murder, Fox?" she asked. "You? Or the House? Who do I get to charge with the kidnapping and assault of a Commonwealth police officer?"

"It was an accident," Fox said, in a weak voice that was barely audible over the sound of the wind in the trees.

The twenty-somethings murmured angrily. "Leave him alone," one young man warned. "His son is dead."

Kirstin studied the body dubiously. Nikko certainly *seemed* dead. But in the modern world it was hard to be sure. She pinned the twenty-something with her gaze. "Why?" she asked. "Why is he dead?"

The young man seemed struck dumb. No matter. Fox answered for him. "He never had a mind for molecular detail. He would use my tools without understanding them. He would use them for things I had never intended." Fox finally looked up. His face was haggard. There were actual tears in his eyes. He looked every part the grieving father. But some inner sense told Kirstin she was watching a performance.

"Were you developing illegal tech, old man?"

"No!" He fired off the word like a bullet. "Your people watch me closely enough. You know that."

"Then what happened to him?"

"He was using tech illegally. He wanted to live. He wanted to escape from *you*. He expected to be arrested, you know. So he programmed the House to rescue him and record his pattern if it looked like his freedom was in danger. He thought he could hide his pattern in the House neural plexus."

Kirstin stiffened. She felt her lips pull back from her teeth. "Can he?"

Fox's eyes narrowed. His bitterness oozed through. "That would be illegal, now wouldn't it?"

"Can he, old man?" Kirstin pressed.

Fox's brief defiance faded. He seemed to sink in upon himself, and once again he was the weak, grieving, aged father. "The House was constructed under the guidance of the Commonwealth Committee on Technology. The plexus executes a search for unregistered programs every thirty seconds and evicts any that it finds."

"Nikko must have known that," she insisted.

Fox shrugged. "Nikko believed he could find a way around every rule—and generally, he could. But this time he didn't have a chance to work out the details."

"So it was Nikko who ordered the House to commit his own murder."

"He didn't want to be interrogated; he might have given himself away."

Kirstin stood cock-hipped, coolly evaluating the old man. She knew a piece of fiction when she heard it. Nikko wasn't dead. He was somewhere in the body of the House; he had to be. Because a devoted father like

Fox could always be counted on to shelter a wayward child.

Nikko's ghost stood hunched in anger in front of the desk of Marevic Chun, regional president of Summer House-at-Earth. "I almost had it, Marevic," he hissed. "Bohr's Maker. Here in my hand. But Van Ness let it slip away. And now Sandor's gone."

Marevic nodded grimly. She sat at her desk, a slightly built, dark-haired, fragile-faced woman who somehow looked her age, despite the youthful smoothness of her brown skin. Perhaps it was the eyes: cold and reptilian. Perhaps it was the antique bent of her mannerisms.

Or perhaps it was the coloring of his own prejudice. He loved Marevic Chun ... the same way a schoolboy might have loved his first-grade teacher—most respectfully. She'd taught him how to play tag with the police and she'd never been caught.

They shared a deeper affinity too, though neither admitted it aloud. When Fox had developed Nikko in his lab, he'd started with genetic material from himself and a female donor. Nikko had been eleven when he'd broken into that research file. He'd been inspired by Sandor's birth to see how much they had genetically in common. He recalled the pleasure and astonishment he'd felt at learning that Marevic figured in his parentage. Sandor had been conceived from different donor stock. Why? Nikko suspected that Fox had not been entirely happy with his first child, and that he'd seen no reason to repeat his original mistake.

Marevic had never shown the same prejudice. She'd always treated him in a straightforward way. "We received a distress packet from Sandor nearly half an hour ago," she told him. "He was in Sunda at the time. We haven't been able to trace him."

Nikko felt his mouth fall open. "So the police don't have him?" That was very bad. If Sandor were in the hands of the Commonwealth Police, it was reasonable to expect he would survive at least the few hours it would take to prepare a trial. But if he were simply missing. . . .

Marevic looked down at her desk, while her small fingers lightly stroked its marbled surface. "The municipal police may have him."

"Love and Nature."

If she replied to his oath, he missed it. He was already consulting the net, seeking out a mule to ride through the hell of urban Sunda. He would find Sandor. He had to find Sandor.

"Nikko!"

His gaze roved outward, briefly.

"Don't go," she said. "I want you to stay with me. It's only a matter of time before Kirstin runs over your trail. She'll have the Gate filters set for you. You have to take care. You could be the last surviving copy of yourself."

"Huh. If she's hunting copies of me, she's not going to overlook *your* head."

Anger flashed across Marevic's delicate face. "This is serious, Nikko. Big time."

He nodded. "Call me if you hear anything." Then he sent his ghost to Earth.

A few hours later, Kirstin's consciousness rejoined the body she'd left at Castle mausoleum. While she dressed, she checked in with Allende, voice only.

He told her: "The dogs followed the Maker's trail to a city herbalist. Zeke Choy, an ex-cop out of Haskin's."

Kirstin ran the name through her atrium notebook, but came up with nothing. "Never heard of him," she said, as she pulled on the black tunic of her police uniform.

"He was a draftee. Had a bad attitude; didn't last long."

She jumped into her shorts, then checked the drift

of her hair in the projection on the wall of the transition room. "He the Jiang-Tibayan contact?"

"No." Allende sounded puzzled. "He doesn't seem to have any connection with Summer House. But he has a patient—a young woman he calls Phousita—he believes she's been infected by an uncataloged Maker, but he hasn't been able to identify its structure. He seems very fond of her; very protective."

"You've picked her up?"

"Uh, no. We haven't been able to find her yet." After a heavy silence, Allende added reluctantly: "Actually, we haven't found a trace of the Maker since detaining Choy."

"Love and Nature," Kirstin hissed softly. "It's mutated." She studied her reflection in the mirror, remembering her days with Leander and how he'd used the Maker to change and change and change again, leading the police on a merry chase that only ended when she'd betrayed him.

What worked once could work again. "You say this Choy is fond of the girl?" she asked Allende. "Then ask him if he'll help us find her. Suggest to him that if he does not, we can't be responsible for her safety." She smiled at her image. Choy would understand the social structure of the Spill. And her ghost could ride an ex-cop as easily as it could ride any other dog.

CHAPTER

12

Phousita blinked as bright sunlight fell across her eyes. She sighed and stretched, watching sparkles of refracted light dance across her lashes. She'd gone to sleep in the shade, but the sun had moved across the sky until now her skin burned. Time to move.

Suddenly, a new scent came to her. She sat up abruptly, shoving her matted hair out of her eyes. It was the angel; somehow she knew it. He was drawing nearer.

She looked around cautiously, but saw no one. Where was Arif?

When they'd been running from the dog, she'd told him they must bathe in the river to erase every trace of their old scents. But *he'd* insisted they go for a swim. The river had been chugging between its concrete banks, swollen by rain in the distant mountains. She'd sobbed in terror as he'd dragged her into the muddy waters, fighting him with every step until she could no longer find the bottom. Then she had no choice but to cling to him as he rode the wild current nearly a mile downstream. The river echoed his raging mood. When he finally sought the bank, he carried her up the steep concrete slope, set her stumbling on her feet, then screamed at her for ten minutes, hitting her periodically with his cupped hand for emphasis. He screamed, but he said nothing. He was only venting his rage. The clan had lost everything, the children were scattered, dogs pursued them, and he'd sold himself for *her*. And for what? She'd be dead soon. Plague would take her. Despite his unfailing service in her behalf. Why, look what he'd endured for her today! And all because of *tuan*. (As if it were *her* fault.) Why did we plant *tuan*? he screamed. (He knew it was his fault.) What is happening to our lives?

She couldn't answer that. All she could do was calm him, concocting a spell in her tears that would enter his body and lull his mind toward sleep. She couldn't allow him to return to the clan now, not in this mood. He'd beat the children, hurt them senselessly, and maybe, *maybe*, the Knives would finally turn on him.

So she'd collapsed at his feet, sobbing apologies, declaring her unworthiness, begging forgiveness. He kicked her once and turned away. Then he seemed to reconsider, as she knew he would. He returned to her, crouched at her side, and slipped his arm around her shoulders. She looked up at him, raised her head to rest it against his shoulder. With her fingers she rubbed at her tears. Then she touched his lips, and moments later a veil seemed to fall across his anger. He sighed, and she could feel his tense body begin to relax. "I'm very tired," she said plaintively. "I can't go on, I need to rest. Please help me one more time."

He nodded. Together they explored the riverbank until they found shelter amongst the tumbled concrete blocks of a broken foundation. Arif picked out a patch of shade near the water. He dragged an old beggar out of it, then urged him away with a few hard kicks. Phousita watched him sorrowfully, but said nothing.

"Sit down, you stupid woman!" he barked. She obeyed and he settled next to her. They'd listened to the river flow as they gradually drifted into sleep.

But now the shade had gone, and so had Arif. Phousita stretched again, feeling renewed, refreshed. Not at all stiff from her nap on the unyielding concrete. So strange. Of course hunger had begun to gnaw once again at her belly. She tossed her head and her nostrils flared. She caught Arif's scent—very strong—and the scent of the angel, more nebulous. But he's coming, she realized with growing excitement. He'll be here soon.

She followed Arif's trail around a large block of concrete to the river's edge. He squatted in the sun, his feet in the water while his fingers strained the river for fluff. He'd already collected a fair pile of it on the concrete bank. Sudden fear set her heart pounding. "Arif!" she cried. "Get back! Get away from the water. You know the 'Surgence will shoot you. Arif!"

He looked at her calmly. "The Resurgence has done all they can do to us today. They're celebrating."

"They are not!" Burning the warehouse had been nothing to them. He knew that. He knew they'd be back. He'd chosen to disregard it. He'd been pushed beyond his limit, and he would hide no longer today, even if it meant his death.

"You're hungry again, aren't you?" Arif accused, turning around to gather up the pile of fluff he'd collected. "This is for you." He held it out to her.

She stared at it. Saliva started to flow in her mouth.

He laughed at her, then walked up the concrete bank and sat down, pulling her down beside him. "Eat," he commanded. "I won't have you running off again tonight."

She ate, staring at the water, too ashamed to look at Arif. As she finished the last of it, she suddenly realized the scent of the angel had grown much stronger. She stood, staring upstream, her nostrils testing the air. Arif watched her suspiciously. "He's coming," she said.

"Who?"

She shook her head. Arif cursed her. After a moment: "There. See?" She pointed up the river. But Arif was already on his feet, gazing at the spectacle approaching along the riverbank.

A raucous crowd of at least a hundred people waded through the edge of the racing water or negotiated the steep bank, whooping and yelling, stumbling into each other as they sought to keep up with an object being swept along by the current.

"It's him," Phousita said, her voice soft with amazement. "Look at his golden hair."

The angel clung—or he'd been trapped—in a tangle of deadwood. Only his head showed above the water. She couldn't tell if he was now alive. He'd been dead; she knew that. She could remember casting him in the river. There had been much fear and anger and a need to hide his body. *"The river."* Someone had said it. Afterward no one was quite sure who. *"The river will obliterate his corpse."*

She turned to Arif. "Look how they pursue him. They wait for him to wash up against the bank."

Arif's mouth turned in a wicked smile. "Sure. He must be rich. I'll take him myself!"

"Yes," she said, with a nod of satisfaction. "He is for us."

Arif leapt into the river. Phousita watched his hard body slice the water like a spear. He surfaced several meters away and struck off across the current. Smiling, she sat down to wait. The evil sorcerer had arranged everything so well.

The river seemed to be without end. Swollen by rain in the mountains, it raged through the city, sweeping up filth and debris that had accumulated on its banks, giving up nothing. Sandor couldn't escape it. He struggled to swim but he had no strength. The river rolled him over and over, filling his eyes and nose with grit, forcing silty water down his throat. He retched and sputtered, fighting to keep his head above the surface. Now and then he caught sight of the shore: dilapidated buildings leaning precariously over the water, fine estates, burned-out ruins, luxurious gardens, ramshackle structures whose function he couldn't guess. The river swept him past it all and he began to wonder if it would ultimately sweep him all the way to the sea. He imagined himself lost in the blue waters of the ocean, circling sharks below and gray seabirds overhead. The fierce light of the sun turning the waves to gold—

He cried out as something struck him in the head. He turned and lunged for the object, felt a solid something under his hands. He clung with primate tenacity to the broken stump of an uprooted tree. It felt like heaven to him, the perfect float. He kept his face out of the water for ten seconds, fifteen, twenty, breathing, pumping oxygen into his starving tissue. The shore began to look less distant. His shaking hands began to calm.

He pressed his head against a pillow of wood, wondering how long he'd be able to hold on to this precarious raft, how long before the river rolled it over. He found himself staring at his forearm, at a puncture wound where the local cops had ripped out his ID chip.

His eyes began to close. In his mind the roar of the river was transformed into the soft, pelting rush of rain falling in the vertical forests of Summer House. He clung to a tree branch to keep from falling in the easy gravity and napped while the monkeys foraged through the trees.

A hand clasped his arm and yanked him off his perch. He surged forward to keep from falling. Water closed over his head as his arm was twisted behind his back. Someone was holding him underwater! He writhed helplessly. Then suddenly he was jerked backward; an arm crossed his chest like a steel strap. Air washed into his lungs. *"Pay me,"* a gritty voice hissed in his ear. He could feel a rough hand searching his back, his buttocks, his abdomen. "Nothing?" his rescuer cried, a single word that exposed a mountain of frustration. "You have nothing! Why do they follow you on the bank if you've already been stripped?"

The arm that held him above the water was suddenly gone. He slipped beneath the surface. Water flooded his nose and eyes. He kicked hard and burst once again into sunlight. "Help me!" he screamed, his head swiveling wildly as he searched for the other. "I can *pay*. Don't leave me here."

Someone seized him by his hair. *"What can you pay?"*

"Money, goods, whatever you want." He reached back to grab his rescuer's wrist. He would not be left behind!

"I command many Knives. If you don't pay me, I will kill you."

"The House will pay. Take me out of the river. Need to call home. No rivers in Summer House. No fascists—" He choked on a mouthful of water. "Vertical forests . . . have you been there? I'm still there. Everything alive . . . but me. I live here now. Die here. . . ." He listened to his own babble, unable to stop it. Eventually, the roar of the river overwhelmed all other sound. Its voice poured through his ears and into his mind, dissolving his thoughts until they ran together in a pleasant, bubbling stream.

He lay on a hard surface that refused to conform to his body or yield in any way. The afternoon sun glared from a golden sky, blistering his bare skin, blinding him. He groaned and turned his head. A monster crouched at his side. A horrible yellow clown-monster with violet eyes, a hooked nose at least five inches long, and cheeks so round they looked as if they'd been stretched over billiard balls.

Dismissing the vision as a product of his injuries, he turned his head the other way. A pretty young woman smiled at him. She had lovely brown eyes and dark tangled hair tied loosely behind her neck. A worn blue breastcloth encircled a generous chest; a faded yellow sarong hid her legs. He suspected faulty judgment, for she seemed no larger than a child of seven or eight.

He smiled at her. Lifting a hand, he touched her flushed cheek just to be sure she was real.

But someone slapped his hand away. She pulled back, startled. Sandor turned his head. The monster still crouched on his other side. He swallowed hard, wondering if the rules that governed this fantasy allowed the monster to eat him.

The monster spoke: "Where's your money?" The same gritty voice that had pulled him from the river.

"Have to call home," Sandor croaked. His throat was swollen, his voice almost gone.

The pretty woman spoke to the beast. Her words ran like music, though Sandor couldn't understand them. The creature growled something in return. Strong hands grasped him under his arms, hauled him to his feet. With help he could stand. The pretty woman took his hand and smiled encouragement. With the assistance of her monster he began to walk. "My name is Sandor Jiang-Tibayan," he told her. "I belong to Summer House. Please, I must call home."

She looked distressed. Her gaze shifted to her pet.

"She doesn't understand English," the creature growled.

"What's her name?"

"Nothing, to you."

They climbed the bank and threaded their way through a village of crude shanties inhabited by dull-eyed, bony children. They reached a street. There were no vehicles, though foot traffic ran fairly heavy as shabbily dressed men and women pursued their business. "You have a phone, *tuan*?" Sandor asked.

The monster laughed. "*Tuan?* You are *tuan*, though the river almost had you. Call me Arif. I have no phone. I have no home. I have no money. But then, neither do you."

CHAPTER

13

Phousita strolled through a cloud forest, walking upright on the fifteen-meter-wide branch of a tree so tall it must span the distance from Earth to heaven. She looked up, and could see no top to the great tree. She looked down, and could see no ground, no roots, only more leaves and branches. Smaller trees (though still giants in her eyes) grew in the joints of the world tree. Ferns clung to their limbs, and the warm air was sweetly scented by a huge mass of brilliant red flowers borne by a trailing liana. The world tree also supported patches of sky: smooth puddles of light, each one as big as a neighborhood, aglow with a brilliant blue light like the sky over the Spill.

A monkey dashed past her, leaping off the branch-path, to land in the top of a banana tree. It reached down to a huge cluster of fruit, plump, and just turning yellow. *Good banana*, it signed, picking one. *Share with you?*

Phousita laughed. Sandor Jiang-Tibayan—for that was the angel's name—looked at her as if she were a police dog ready to crush his head. She sighed. "Forgive me. It's just that it's ..." *So absurd.* "So odd to think that a monkey could talk ... talk with its hands."

Sandor's eyes widened. He shrank further against the black, mildew-stained wall of the tiny room the Knives had rented in a row of tenements three-quarters of a mile from the river. Rats galloped through the rafters and a pool of rust-colored water collected in one corner of the dirt floor. Sandor sat on a low shelf, just large enough that two people could sleep under it and two could sleep on top. He was still naked. He'd turned sideways to her so that his legs would hide his genitals. The brilliant afternoon sunlight that filtered through the curtained rectangle of the door lent his skin a translucent, milky glow. His hair gleamed gold. His thoughts were clean and bright and delightful in her mind, and his scent tasted good to her. Sandor Jiang-Tibayan. Even his name pleased her tongue.

"What monkey are you talking about?" he asked, suspicion a gathering cloud in his blue eyes. "And when did you learn English?"

Phousita bowed her head. "The monkey you call Sax," she said softly. "I don't know when I learned English." She'd had need of the talent, and it had come. Another gift of the evil sorcerer. (*Why did he choose me? And what purpose did he have for this boy, Sandor?*) Fear fluttered in her chest. What was given could also be taken away. The evil sorcerer could abandon her at any moment. He could take Sandor away and leave her with nothing, once again. (*I will burn incense. I will pray to his spirit.*)

She devised a spell to calm the looming panic in her breast. Gently, she shooed away the tiny children who clustered at Sandor's side and knelt to examine his wounds. In the cloud forest the first monkey had been joined by another. They moved away from the banana tree to continue their meal on a fruit that looked like guava, though it grew on a vine. The inner vision and the outer vision: her mind observed both with equal clarity. Did a goddess see the world like this? Through many eyes at once?

Sandor winced as she touched the burns on his chest. She knew his fear: of her, of the rats, of the poverty that surrounded him . . . of what had happened to him in the police station. Softly, she said: "It's not your fault. Sometimes, it just happens. The cops hear a name, someone's arrested. It matters little to them if a crime has really occurred."

His face squeezed tight in remembered pain. Then his eyes opened and confusion filled his gaze. In his words she heard a desperate need to understand. "I didn't know what they wanted, or why they—" His gaze darted away, to fix on a wide-eyed toddler standing at Phousita's side.

"Perhaps they don't know the reason either." She pressed her fingertips firmly against the burns, and then against the shallow cut in his forearm. "I've touched you with a spell. These wounds will not sicken now."

"A what?"

"A spell." How could she explain to him the complexities of the invisible world that inhabited her fingertips? The tiny spirit-servants that could weave spells on command from infinitesimal grains of matter. She had no understanding of them herself, and possessed no words that might interpret them to others. For her, explanations weren't necessary. A new instinct had roused within her, and as she knew how to eat and drink, so she knew how to heal with a touch. She sighed. "You need food, but we don't have any now. If we can get more water, Sumiati will cook rice in the afternoon."

Sumiati had been a hero today. When the dog had attacked the warehouse, she'd grabbed the stove and the rice pot, while ordering the children to save the rice before they fled together into the street. The hammocks had been lost though, and most of the plastic jugs. Also the collapsible plastic crates and the tarp that had been their home before they found the warehouse.

"I need a telephone," Sandor said.

Phousita nodded. "Arif has gone to find one. But he has no money to pay the operator. He must find someone willing to provide the service on credit."

Where money was absent, sometimes skills could be bartered. The Knives had hired themselves out to pay the rent on this room. They'd earned their first night here by evicting the previous tenants: three men, all infected with a debilitating plague that gradually turned their skin into beautiful, inflexible golden shells like the skin of the Buddha that presided over the temple by the park. A statue cannot walk or work. The fat old matron who owned the line of tenements had related the unhappy fact that it had been a week since any of them had left the room, a week since the rent had been paid. The Knives carried the afflicted men nearly a mile to the Christian hospital, then left them at the end of a long line of sufferers.

Now Phousita's inner vision had shifted to a different forest, a different point of view. She crouched in the shadows, her whole body focused on the progress of a bright red, stilt-legged bug as it walked through a swath of sunlight that had fallen across her leaf. Instinct spurred her to action. She scuttled into the sunlight, snatched the bug in her jaws and bit hard. Horrible poisons flooded her body. Her mouth opened. She dropped the carcass and staggered back toward the illusory safety of her shady lair.

"Why do you live like this?" Sandor asked.

She looked at him in surprise. "What other way is there for us?"

Sandor's fists closed indignantly. "A thousand other ways! There are new ways being invented all the time. *It does not have to be like this.*" His hand swept the room in a contemptuous gesture. "There can be enough for everyone. It's just that your government has forbidden Makers. For religious reasons, I think."

Phousita shrugged. She didn't understand this. She wondered pensively if Sandor were completely sane. His memories were too wonderful. Who could live in a cloud forest with no canopy and no ground, where the monkeys talked like men? Who could have a brother who was not a man, but a blue china human spider? Her eyes flew open wide; her hand covered her mouth. The old woman had visited her this morning. The old woman had tried to warn her. She'd talked of such out-landish things so many times. . . . "Are you a god?" Phousita whispered.

Sandor closed his eyes, and for the first time since Arif had pulled him from the river, he seemed to relax. "Not me," he said easily. Then he opened one eye. "How about you?"

She ducked her head, her face flushing hot. Shame crowded her mind. Hadn't she just wondered if she'd been granted a goddess's vision? Stupid country girl! "I'm only a witch, *tuan*," she whispered.

He started to lean forward, then remembered his nudity and covered himself with his limbs as best he could. She sighed. Though she respected his modesty, she could do nothing to help him. The clan had no clothes to spare.

"How'd you know about Sax?" Sandor asked. "And don't just shrug, please. Who hired you? What do they want with me? What's going on?"

She turned away, startled at his accusation, so simi-lar to the harsh words of the Chinese doctor. "It's not like that, *tuan*." She couldn't imagine who would hire her, who would entrust her with the care of this stranger—so healthy, pure, beautiful—he must be the cherished servant of a great power. "I don't know any-thing. I'm just a witch."

"But that's something, Phousita. I've never met a witch before." He lifted his hand, wanting to touch her, though he didn't quite dare. What was the custom here? She seemed to be something of a shaman. Though she didn't demand respect, he wanted to offer it. He didn't know how. And the stifling heat in this shack had numbed his brain. Or was that a residual gift of the local police? He didn't know, couldn't think. He wanted to go outside, breathe clean air, eat. But he had no clothes and didn't want to offend anybody. Oh, Summer House, hurry before he ran the wrong code and somebody took mortal offense.

He looked up as the bright rectangle of the doorway darkened. Arif swept aside the thin cloth that served as a door and entered the foul little room. A boy with nut-brown skin and wispy blue hair followed him. Sandor forgot his vow of decorum when he saw what the boy carried in his right hand. He leapt to his feet, almost cracking his head on the rafters. "You got it!" he shouted, reaching for the precious telephone.

The boy snatched it out of his grasp with a vicious snarl. He jabbered angrily at Arif, then started to leave. But Arif barked a quick command, and two children blocked the door, a knife dancing silently between their hands, passed with the skill of practiced jugglers. The boy turned back to Arif, muttering something that sounded obscene. But he offered the telephone.

Arif took it. "Make your call," he growled, handing it to Sandor. "Make sure you get through. This boy's papa will use white skin in his brothel if he can't get paid any other way."

Sandor took the phone with shaking hands. He felt as if he'd slipped through the Looking Glass into a world that was an inverse of his own. Poverty, violence, exploitation: before today he'd never witnessed them. He hadn't really known they'd existed. Why? Why had the House kept him ignorant of this world?

He turned over the phone; stared at it a moment. "I, uh ... I don't know the number. The cops wiped that out when they—"

Arif said something to the boy. The kid sneered and rolled his eyes, but he took the phone back from Sandor and punched in a code. Arif listened to his explanation, then translated: "Information," he said. "The voice will help you. You do know who you want to talk to?"

"Sure." Regional headquarters. "Summer House-at-Earth," he told the computer, while keeping a wary eye on Arif. A moment later he was greeted by a pleasant, masculine voice.

"Summer House Incorporated: Achieving personal security through diverse and abundant life. You've reached our offices at Castle. How may we help you?"

"This is Corporate Member Sandor Jiang-Tibayan declaring a personal emergency. I have no ID. My codes are broken. I've sustained personal and system injury. Help me. I must speak to David Enberg, *now*."

"Please hold."

He closed his eyes, breathing slowly through the suspense. How would the computer answer? *Please don't tell me I'm dead*, he thought. *Just don't tell me I'm dead*.

David Enberg directed the regional security wing. *(Should I have asked for a subordinate?)* Maybe the computer would classify him as a crackpot. But he didn't know any of David's subordinates. Didn't know David, really. Had only met him for a few minutes nearly a month ago. Sandor came from Summer House, not Castle. First time Earth-side—

"Sandor?" a doubtful voice spoke from the telephone.

"David, it's me!" Sandor shouted. He paused long enough to nod triumphantly at Arif. "I was arrested! The municipal police. Oh, David, you don't know what it's like down here. They wiped out my atrium, and—and Nikko, too, I guess. Everything. Help me, David. Send somebody for me, please. Send money. They'll kill me if they don't get something."

"It'll be all right now, Sandor. Calm down. Calm

down. We got your distress packet. We know you had a
run-in with the municipal police."

"A run-in? David, they had me in their station." He
heard his voice going shrill; took a breath to calm himself. "Send somebody, David."

"Sandor?" A woman's voice this time. "This is
Marevic Chun."

His mouth opened in astonishment. Marevic Chun
was the regional *president* of Summer House-at-Earth;
she commanded all corporate operations Earth-side.
Why had she come on line for him?

"We're astounded to find you alive," she said. "Our
agents on the ground led us to believe the worst.
Where are you?"

"I don't know. In a slum somewhere. The cops
thought I was dead so they dumped me in a river. Arif
fished me out. You can trace this call, can't you,
Marevic? Send somebody for me?"

"Are you safe where you are?"

He frowned in confusion. Arif observed his change
of expression and stepped forward, his eyes hard. Turning away, Sandor hissed into the phone. "What's the
matter, Marevic? Why don't you just send someone?"

"We'd like to, Sandor. But things are a real mess up
here. Nikko had some trouble with the Commonwealth
Police, and unfortunately, your name got mixed into the
fray. If Kirstin Adair finds out you're alive, she'll have
you on trial in an hour. So stay put. Stay hidden. I need
time to sort through Nikko's notes and prepare your defense or the police will crucify you."

"But why? What did I do wrong?"

"Nothing, Sandor. You just got caught up in other
people's games."

"But you can't leave me here! You don't know what
they said they'd do to me!" Arif started to snatch the
phone. Sandor jerked it away from him. "Marevic, you
have to help me!"

Arif caught his wrist and yanked the phone out of

his hand. "You want this boy back, you will pay for him *now*," Arif growled into the receiver. He glared at Sandor while he listened to Marevic's reply. It seemed to go on so long. But finally, he nodded. "Sure, if that's what you want." He clicked the phone off and handed it back to the blue-haired boy, a wicked grin on his face. He uttered an ear-splitting whoop of triumph, then turned to Phousita, caught her up in his arms and kissed her. Incomprehensible words ran off his tongue, interspersed with laughs. Phousita appeared uncertain.

"You're going to stay with us!" Arif barked. Then he laughed at Sandor's look of dismay. "Marevic's paying us to take care of you. Hope you like it here in the Spill. She says it could be a couple of days before they can retrieve you."

The afternoon ground past with impossible slowness. Sandor's captors had left him alone in the shack. He could hear some of the children playing outside, but he didn't hear Phousita, and he didn't see her when he peered past the curtained doorway.

Where had she gone? Inexplicably, he found he missed her. He held his head in his hands. The heat and humidity were making him dizzy. Or maybe it was the lack of food. His belly growled. He wished he knew the local word for water. Yesterday, it would have been so easy to consult a library. Today . . .

He felt like a victim of tunnel vision. All he could see were the crumbling walls of this room. All he could hear was the brave laughter of the children out in the street and a blend of voices beyond them. These had become the boundaries of his perception.

What had Nikko done to get him into this mess?

He dozed.

Or at least that's how he accounted to himself for the time that ultimately passed.

He was roused by a shrill cry in the distance, a commanding ululation that rose suddenly over the slum's continuous low mutter of noise. The children outside quieted instantly. Sandor sat up. In their low whispers he heard Arif's name.

The whoop sounded again and this time the children answered with their own shrill cries. Sandor crouched in the shadows near the door and looked out.

Arif had come back. He'd brought Phousita with him. They each carried two distended plastic sacks. The children crowded and cavorted around them while Arif set the sacks on the ground. Sandor watched in fascination as he began producing treasures from the bags. Bananas—one for everybody—mangos, thin slices of meat on a stick, calorie bars, a bag of peanuts—

Sandor felt a wave of dizziness sweep across him. He pressed his forehead against the termite-eaten wood. Splinters jabbed at his hands. He tasted dirt in his mouth. Someone nudged at his shoulder. Pushed harder until he rolled over. He found himself lying on his back on the shack's dirt floor, looking up at Arif's laughing face a thousand kilometers above him. "Don't die on us, *tuan*. Marevic expects to have you back someday."

"Here, drink this," Phousita said. She knelt at his side, holding a plastic jug to his lips. "Forgive me, *tuan*. I should not have left you alone."

He drank. The warm water slid down his throat and the awful buzzing in his head began to recede. He pushed himself to a sitting position; held his pounding head in his hands. "We have food," Phousita said.

"I'm not hungry." He thought he might puke if he put anything in his mouth now.

Arif laughed at him. "Got one of those 'delicate' constitutions?" he asked. "Too bad. But we'll eat again tomorrow." He dropped a bundle at Sandor's feet. "Get yourself dressed. I'm tried of looking at your dick."

Arif had brought him a pair of khaki work pants, patched at the knees and butt and a little too small, but Sandor took them gratefully. He slipped them on, while a little girl stood in the door eating a banana and watching him.

Phousita brought him two bananas and a slice of meat on a stick. He took the food and ate ravenously, his nausea forgotten. Phousita watched him, a pleased smile on her face. He grinned at her, then drank more water. Outside, Arif produced another prize from his last bag. Some sort of confection, Sandor surmised, by the squeals of the children. Arif carefully divided the treat amongst the little ones, then squatted on the pavement, his clown face reflecting smug satisfaction as he watched them greedily devour his gift.

"Did you spend everything?" Sandor asked.

Arif scowled at him. "Stay out of sight," he warned. Then: "I spent only a tiny part of it." He patted the belt at his waist. "I've never held so much money before, not even that last night when I parted from my master. But it's nothing to Summer House, is it?"

A child pulled at the hem of Arif's shorts, interrupting him. The little girl who'd been watching Sandor dress. She rubbed her stomach and groaned, then sat down abruptly on the pavement. Arif's arm went around her shoulders as she began to jerk convulsively. She threw up on the ground, then stared in shock at what she'd done. A moment later she was sobbing hysterically against Arif's chest.

He stared past her, his absurd face stunned, helpless. The food had been too rich, Sandor realized. Her system wasn't used to it, couldn't handle it. Other children were already holding their middles, groaning in pain as their bellies cramped in protest at the unaccustomed feast. Arif had poisoned them with his gift.

"It's all right," Phousita said. Sandor's gaze followed her voice. She crouched beside a little boy who lay on the pavement, his knees pulled up to his chest, his face knotted in pain. She pressed her hand against his belly, and a few seconds later his face began to relax, his body began to straighten. Phousita left him to visit another child, then another. She touched each one of them, easing their pain with a soft stroke of her palm.

Sandor stared after her in amazement. Without thinking, he stepped outside the hut and approached her. She knelt beside the last child, the little girl who'd already lost her meal—the only meal she could expect that day. She said something to the girl, and the child smiled and nodded. Then Sandor was at her side. He caught up both her hands in his and turned them over. Tiny white glands glinted wetly in her palms just below the knuckles, along her fingers, and on her fingertips. Sandor touched them gingerly. He'd never seen a mutation like this one. She could heal with a touch. Somehow the glands must generate healing Makers that could cross the barrier of a patient's skin. But how did she program the Makers? How did she direct them to their tasks? (And how had she developed this remarkable talent amidst the degradation and ignorance of the Spill?)

She lifted her hands, staring at them as if she'd never seen them before. "I've changed them," she muttered.

He frowned. "You didn't know?"

She shook her head slowly, wonderingly. "There have been so many changes, so quickly, since . . ."

"Ah . . .": a soft sigh of disappointment. He'd imagined the healing touch to be a system of her own design. "You don't understand your abilities, do you?"

She bowed her head, her shoulders hunched as if in shame. "No, *tuan*. I've become a witch but I don't know what I can do, or why, or how, until the very moment something needs to be done. Even then, I do nothing but obey the spirit of the sorcerer that inhabits me."

Sandor nodded his understanding. He imagined that it could feel that way. "You command a very powerful Maker," he said. "How did you learn to do that?"

She gazed at him with a confused, disoriented face,

so that he knew immediately she didn't understand him. He bowed his head and sighed, his fingers rubbing at the stinging sweat that clouded his eyes. Her Maker had taught her to speak English; she knew every word he knew. Yet he sensed she did not *understand* the words. Raw knowledge without an adequate frame of reference.

"Leave her alone," Arif growled. He stood behind Sandor's shoulder. As Sandor started to turn, Arif placed his foot against Sandor's butt and shoved, toppling him to the pavement. Sandor scrambled quickly to his feet, anger rushing in discrete packets through his veins. "She's a sorceress and her powers are growing," Arif shouted at him. "*You* are the one who doesn't understand what's going on here." Arif stepped forward, closing the distance between himself and Sandor. "Look here. And here," he said, jabbing his steely fingers into Sandor's chest, forcing him to stumble back. "She touched you. Look what her magic has done."

Sandor looked. His chest was unblemished. His jaw dropped. Gingerly, he touched the site of the burns he'd received under interrogation, the laceration where they'd cut his ID chip out of his arm. . . .

All sign of the injuries had vanished.

Sandor's gaze jerked back to Phousita. "This is not magic," he hissed. "It's technology. A technology *banned* by the Commonwealth." The children crowded them anxiously. In their dark eyes Sandor read confusion, and fear. They couldn't understand his words, but like Arif they recognized his doubt. And they resented it. *Why do you question Phousita?* their earnest faces seemed to demand. For she must be as a goddess to them. A sweet savior ready to lift away some of the agony of their existence. And now he must condemn her.

He spoke softly, earnestly, knowing he had to convince her. "This talent that's taken you . . . it's not a blessing. This is not a way you can live. Phousita, you have to be careful. If the police discover what you can do, they'll extradite you. If they can't cleanse your body of the Maker, they'll terminate you. There's no mercy in this. The Commonwealth exists to stamp out the kind of talent you've become."

"Liar!" Arif shouted. "You want her for yourself."

"I'm not lying! I—" He broke off abruptly. What *was* he trying to do? He couldn't help her. He'd had some nebulous intention of offering her refuge at Summer House, but that was absurd. Even if she were willing to leave Arif and the children, she could never get through police Gates carrying an illegal Maker. "I just want you to live, Phousita. Get rid of the Maker now, if you can. All the money in the world won't stop the cops once they scent your trail."

Arif stepped forward, shaking his outrageous head. "Back inside," he growled. "You're the fugitive. Back inside before the police find *you*."

At nightfall the children started crowding into the shack, lying down upon the floor or under the shelf, giggling and whispering until Sumiati shushed them with a song.

Phousita came into the dark hut later, carrying a flashlight. Sandor watched her, his eyes half closed. She stepped carefully over the sleeping children; he didn't know how she found room to place her feet.

Suddenly, he realized she was coming to him. He stiffened, caught between anxiety and glee. What could she want of him? Where was Arif? In a panic, he closed his eyes and pretended to sleep. A moment later, he felt the touch of her hand against his shoulder as she lay down, squeezing in between him and a young boy of eight or nine. Where was Arif? He could feel her breath on his cheek. It was scented. It reminded him of the perfume of some exotic flower. Against his best intentions, he looked.

She'd slipped a brown cloth over the flashlight, so only a little light came through. It was enough to set her eyes aglow with an aura he'd seen only once, in an old Dutch painting. His heart raced. He tried to remember if Arif had come into the shack with the children. He didn't think so, but it was so hot. He couldn't be sure. What did she want from him?

Phousita frowned, a puzzled expression on her face. Then she touched a finger to his neck, and immediately, his body began to cool. Fear left him, tension began to bleed out of every pore, and the shack no longer seemed so oppressive. Her frown turned to a smile. "Arif won't be back for many hours," she whispered.

Sandor nodded, his mind toying with the possibilities inherent in that news. Her face was all that he could see in the world, and he wanted nothing more. "What did you do to me?" he whispered.

"A spell to soothe, that's all."

He smiled, delighted at her skill. "I want to touch you."

She seemed pleased. "Yes. Do."

With his fingertips he touched her cheek, her lips. Her skin was smooth and dry. "Who *are* you?"

The smile left her face. She looked away, and he was instantly sorry he'd asked. "No one."

"Phousita—" His hand was left hovering in midair.

"I'm only a servant of the sorcerer who rides me," she whispered. She looked at him again, took his hand and placed it once more against her cheek. He drew closer to her, until their foreheads touched. "He brought you here, you know," she said. "They were going to put you on the funeral truck, but he suggested they throw you in the river instead."

Sandor scowled, confused. "How—"

She showed him her palm again. "I have many tiny servants. They drift about the air like dust. They tell me of the world, and sometimes, they'll do things for me."

Sandor nodded his understanding. "They're like behavioral viruses, then."

"I don't know, *tuan*. I'm just glad that they—" Her gaze fell; she took his hand, pressed her lips against his palm. "I'm so glad you're still alive. I have never ... I—I. . . ." She closed her eyes and sighed. "I enjoy what I sense in you. It makes me happy." Her eyes popped open. "You're happy too? With me?"

He almost quailed before the earnestness of her gaze. He had never been happier, he wanted to tell her that, but it was too ridiculous to say. Proper words eluded him, until suddenly he realized he didn't need words. She smiled and nodded and they kissed. Her mouth was warm and inviting.

"Your face was in my dreams," she muttered. "I had to find you."

He kissed her cheeks and her neck. She was so tiny! He didn't want to go too far. There were children all around. His hand found a way inside her breastcloth though, and he stroked her nipples, while her tongue performed delightful acts on his ear.

"Come back to Summer House with me," he begged.

She drew back, her eyes aglow with pleasure. "I will dream of that."

"No! I'll make it real." His own determination frightened him. He didn't understand how his feelings for her could be so strong, so soon.

Sensing his hesitation, she pulled away. "I still don't know who *you* are," she said. "Why are you important to the sorcerer? When he first came to me, the only thing he could remember of all the world was your face. Why?"

Sandor shook his head. "I don't know. It doesn't matter. Come to Summer House with me." He started to kiss her again, but she turned her face away.

"*Don't,*" she said, a cold chill of fear in her voice. "I was wrong. Arif is coming *now*. He despises you. Please go to sleep."

Sandor bristled. "I'm not afraid of Arif."

She touched her fingers to his lips. "Then *be* afraid, for me." She flicked the flashlight off, then wriggled over so that her back was to him.

"*Phousita!*" he hissed. He touched her shoulder. "*Phousita!*" But she refused to answer. By her breathing, she seemed to be already asleep.

Sandor sighed and lay back against the wooden shelf. He didn't find the transition to sleep so easy. He stared into the dark, listening to the sounds of the sleeping children, wondering what magic it would take to get Phousita out of the Spill. After a while, the cloth that served as a door rustled, and Arif came in. His face glowed an eerie yellow in the dark. He crouched by the door, staring into the hut as if he were trying to find someone. Sandor watched him until fatigue finally closed his eyes.

He awoke at dawn, Phousita still beside him. He stood slowly, cautiously, unsteady on his feet, then picked his way carefully to the door through a tangle of sleeping bodies. He must relieve himself in the street. His hand touched the soft, splintered wood of the door frame. He lifted the cloth door aside—and swayed in shock!

A mass of humanity filled the street. Intent. All eyes on him. Except for a meter-wide demicircle around the door that they'd left respectfully void, he couldn't see how another individual could squeeze into the alley. He shivered in the eerie silence and ducked back inside the hut.

Arif stood at his shoulder. "They've come," he said quietly, as if he'd expected this.

"Why are they here?" Sandor whispered.

Arif stepped past him, to peer around the edge of the cloth. "To see the messiah. The fools. But I'll make her their queen."

CHAPTER

14.

Kirstin's ghost stood with Zeke Choy on the edge of a preternaturally silent crowd that packed a narrow alley deep in the Spill. She and Choy were both far taller than most of the people jammed into the alley, so she could see easily over their heads. Far down the crooked little street the morning sun blazed against the face of a long, dilapidated shed. Doorways opened into the narrow building at intervals of three or four meters, each of them—save one—crowded with spectators. It was the one curtained doorway upon which the crowd focused its attention.

"This is very bad," Choy muttered. "Very bad."

Kirstin had to agree. People were jammed in so tight, there was no way her officers could force a passage through the mob. If Phousita really was in that curtained hovel, as the rumors on the street claimed, they'd have to walk on the shoulders of her fans to get to her.

And what then? It wasn't hard to imagine how the

crowd would react if the Commonwealth Police tried to arrest their newest messiah.

Choy turned to look at her. Deprived of his visual input, the shifting crowd froze in Kirstin's sight. She scowled at him in annoyance. But he took no notice. "Call your people off," he said. "You can't get to her now. You're going to have to wait for a better time."

"What's on the other side of the shack?" Kirstin asked.

Allende, who was listening from his post on Castle, answered: "A narrow alley; about two meters wide. But it's jammed too."

"Bring up the dogs," Kirstin told him. "We can't do anything until these streets are cleared."

"No!" Choy cried in outrage. He grabbed her wrist. She was a ghost, but she existed within *his* atrium. She was real to him. "Bring in the dogs and you'll start a panic. Anything could happen. People will die."

"I don't think you understand how serious this contamination could be," she told him calmly. "If we don't contain it quickly, we'll have to consider radical measures, even thermal sterilization. A lot more people will die then."

Choy's mouth dropped open. He gazed at her in open horror.

"Look at the crowd," she told him. "I need your eyes to see what's happening."

Sandor crouched by the curtained door, squinting against the glare of the morning sun as he gazed out past the cloth at the crowd. The sight terrified him. He'd never seen such a gathering before—so many people, silent, intent. Slum-dwellers. Each one of them painfully clean and neat despite worn and faded clothing. Somehow they'd heard of Phousita, and overnight this little shack had become the focus of their desperate lives, a place to find salvation.

Could they believe that?

He knew they could. He could see it in their stance, in their determined eyes. And he felt tiny before them. He knew he could easily be trampled here. He turned to Arif, but the other had moved away. Sandor had no desire to be left at the door alone. He turned to follow.

The sun had found its way into the torrid little hut. In its light, Sandor could see Phousita sleeping peacefully on the wooden shelf, a slight smile on her face, while a little boy cuddled against her belly.

"Get up, country girl," Arif growled, laying a heavy hand on her shoulder. "The day is here, and you have a thousand clients waiting to buy your talents."

Her eyes opened blearily. She looked at Arif, a tiny scowl of confusion on her face. Then her gaze shifted to Sandor, her wide dark eyes aglow with concern. "Are you all right, *tuan?*"

"Sure," Sandor said. He tried to smile, but instead he glanced nervously toward the door. "There's a problem, though. Things have gotten out of hand, and—"

Arif turned and cuffed him. His head snapped back as a hot wave of pain sent colors dancing in his eyes. He stumbled half a step. Little hands pressed desperately against his thighs to prevent his falling.

"Don't let this boy scare you," Arif said to Phousita. "There are some people here to see you, that's all."

She scrambled to sit up, fear bright in her eyes. Sandor hated to see it there. He wanted to help her, hold her. Hide her perhaps? If only they could both vanish like ghosts. Reappear together on the other side of the sun, in some cultivated city where no one ever went hungry. Why were they stuck in this hellhole?

"Is it the police?" Phousita whispered.

Arif laughed at her: contemptuous, mocking laughter. *Stupid, stupid, stupid,* he seemed to say, while she hung her head in shame. And Sandor wanted to kill him. For the first time in his life, he felt hate strong enough to ignite the desire to kill. His hands flexed, fingers curved like claws. A growl rolled up from deep in his throat. He laid a rough hand on Arif's shoulder; yanked him around.

Suddenly Sandor found himself without breath, on the ground, on his back. He could feel children wriggling desperately to get out from under him. His sternum was ablaze with pain. Arif had hit him. In retrospect he saw it: one sharp blow to the chest, no more effort than it took to shoo a fly and he'd gone down. How could the man move so fast?

And now? Already Arif had returned his attention to Phousita. Sandor knelt, racked with shame and self-derision while Arif took Phousita's hand.

"The police wouldn't dare touch you now, my magic princess." Arif pulled her to her feet. "Come have a look. See how your reputation has spread."

Sandor watched, befuddled, uncertain, wanting to interfere yet hesitating while Phousita found a path between the children. She tentatively lifted aside the entrance cloth. Immediately she drew back, uttering a tiny cry of alarm. "What have you done?" she whispered to Arif.

Arif flashed an ugly leer of triumph. "All I had to do was talk about you in the right places. You and your healing powers. A hundred other people did the same—everyone who saw what you did last night—it's in the nature of people to talk. By tonight there'll be no one in the Spill who hasn't heard of you. You are a goddess."

He reached out and ripped the cloth from the door frame. Morning fell across him like a benediction, yellow clown aglow in yellow light. Brave and absurd lord of nothing, wanting everything. He reached a hand toward Phousita.

A low murmur ran through the street, rapidly rising in volume. People surged forward. Hundreds of hands stretched toward her. The crowd was an entity, demanding her presence. Sandor could feel its need, its desperation like a brittle wavelength shuddering through his mind.

Phousita seemed stunned. But she took Arif's hand.

The children were all awake now, jabbering like small birds in the dawn. They pressed around her, staring out the door, and suddenly Sandor couldn't see her anymore. She'd disappeared amongst the kids and once again he realized how truly tiny she was. He scrambled after her, trampling toes and earning curses until he was at her shoulder. He swept up her free hand in his. "Phousita?"

She turned to him, her eyes glittering with excitement. "Come," she said. "You and Arif must shelter me."

He swallowed against the pressure of fear in his throat. He didn't want to go into the crowd. But he would not tell her no.

He pressed Phousita's arm under his and together the three of them stepped forward.

Immediately the crowd flowed around them, cutting them off from the shack. Bodies pressed against him. Intent, frightened faces jostling on all sides. The air was thick with a stench of sweat and perfume and incense. Someone shoved him. He stumbled against Phousita, struggling to keep his feet. His heart was racing, aquiver with a contagious panic that seemed to be sweeping through the mob. And he could see no way out of this. No way at all.

Then suddenly everything changed. The morning light seemed less stark. The faces that whirled around him began to soften. The press of the crowd eased, and smiles flashed from face to face. Sandor felt his own heartbeat slow. He drew a deep breath, eager to pull in more of the magic that Phousita had loosed upon the air.

He could see the wave of her influence traveling outward in a demicircle through the street, a spirit of peace, sweeping through the mob. People relaxed.

They no longer shoved against each other. They stood quietly, eyes bright with expectation, all anxiety gone.

Those nearest still reached for her. Countless fingers stroked her face and hair, the folds of her sarong, the dark skin of her arms, the soft curve of her hands. Fingers like the close press of vegetation, touching and sweeping past, giving way as she slowly moved through the crowd.

As she passed, joy blossomed on face after face. Sandor could feel his own mouth turned in a giddy grin. He didn't know what Phousita was doing, if she really was casting healing spells or only charming this audience. He didn't care. This moment seemed to outweigh his whole life. He was beyond questioning; beyond fear. He could have continued in this state forever.

Kirstin's ghost hovered on the edge of the crowd, watching as Phousita emerged from the shack, escorted on one side by the clown-faced goon she'd seen the day before, and on the other by a tall blond youth.

Sandor Jiang-Tibayan! Kirstin realized with a start.

But he was supposed to be dead, the victim of an overzealous municipal police officer. And besides, Nikko had sworn Sandor was not involved.

Yet here he was.

She felt the rush of a strong emotion, something fierce, between fury and delight. Nikko had lied to her again. He'd lied to protect his brother. But to no purpose. Because here was Sandor Jiang-Tibayan, exposed in guilt that would follow him all the way back to Summer House.

Allende called. "The dogs are coming in on a truck. Twenty of them. They should be in the vicinity within three minutes."

Kirstin beckoned to Zeke Choy. He stood transfixed by the sight of Phousita. "Look how she controls the crowd," he said in awe. "How can she do that? How?"

"Come," Kirstin said. "The dogs will be here soon. We need to get out of the street."

"No."

She glared at him, annoyed. Then she shrugged. What did she need with Choy now? She shunted her electronic pattern into one of the approaching dogs . . .

. . . and trotted beside the animal as it left the truck and entered the streets. Its great head swung from side to side, scanning its surroundings. The few people still in sight fled at its approach.

It passed an intersection. Kirstin caught a strong whiff of gunpowder. The dog stopped. It lifted its head, its nostrils delicately combing the air.

A truck approached from the cross street. Olive-drab, and painted with the raptor insignia of the local government. The dog stood in the vehicle's path. The truck roared toward the animal. At first, Kirstin thought it would refuse to stop. But at the last second, the driver slammed on the brakes. It squealed to a halt just a meter from the beast.

Municipal police officers dressed in light green combat fatigues began to pile out of the back. Each one of them carried an automatic rifle.

Outraged, Kirstin opened a line to Allende. "What are the local cops doing here?" she shouted. "Don't they know we have an operation going on? Call them off!"

The municipal cops gave the dog a wide berth as they moved down the street. Still, many of them gestured menacingly at it with their rifles, muttering ugly words. One spoke in English. "This is *our* city," he warned. "*We* will maintain order here."

Sandor noticed a sudden change in Phousita. Her chin lifted. Her body stiffened. She turned to look over her shoulder, eyes wide with fear.

He followed her gaze to the low roof of the long shack. Three police dogs trotted along the canted surface, tongues lolling. Their eyes seemed to be fixed on him.

A little cry of fear escaped Phousita's throat. Sandor felt it as a physical sensation, the same way he'd felt her joy. So did the crowd around them. A ripple of terror ran out from their locus, rapidly growing more strident. It swept through the crowd like flash fire.

Arif tried to shout instructions, but his voice was lost in a sudden cacophony of panic. People screamed and started running, stumbling. Cries of agony rang out as some fell, and were trampled beneath panicked feet. A dam might have broken at one end of the alley, so rapidly did the mob drain away.

Sandor felt himself running too. Phousita's arm was still tucked under his. Arif's clown face bobbed on her other side. "No!" she screamed at them, fighting their forward progress. "We have to go back. The kids—"

Bodies flowed past them, pummeling them. Uniforms began to appear amidst the ragged dress of the street people. Sandor recognized the insignia of the municipal police. Guns went off, almost on top of them. A whiff of smoke ran in the air, and suddenly a deep-voiced *whump* followed by a low roar.

Phousita screamed in agony. She doubled over and fell to her knees. Sandor thought she'd been hit by gunfire. But she was on her feet again a moment later. *"The kids! The kids! They're still in the shack,"* she screamed.

She leapt away, running back up the street, against the flow of the crowd.

Sandor gazed past her in horror. The shack was an inferno. He thought he could hear shrill screams from inside it. He bounded after Phousita.

She raced toward the door of their tenement. But it was curtained with a sheet of flame! Child-sized, fiery figures seemed to move within the incandescent light. "Phousita!" Sandor screamed, when he realized she wasn't slowing down. She was going through the door, inferno or no.

He dove for her ankles, tackling her. He brought her down in the filthy street, the searing flames only meters away. She clawed at the ground to get away from him, struggling toward the fire. "The kids," she sobbed. "The kids are still inside."

He fought to hold on to her. His nails clawed into her legs. His hair began to smolder, the fire was so near. "Phousita," he pleaded. "Phousita, please."

She hit him with a spell. It was only a behavioral virus. He knew that. But it struck him like a bullet. He felt her despair explode inside him. It seemed to rupture his nervous system. He cried out, and fell to the side. For a moment, his heart stopped beating. The fire seemed to arch over him. He gazed up at it in wonder, welcoming its searing truth.

Then the spell broke. A municipal cop was standing over him, leering. The bastard kicked him in the ribs. He heard bones crack. He screamed and curled in on himself. The next kick landed in his back. He braced himself as best he could, but the third kick never came. Then Arif was there, yanking him to his feet and pitching him into the street, away from the fire.

He didn't remember hitting the ground. He opened his eyes, to find himself lying in the muddy street, staring into the still, bloodied face of the municipal cop, the green combat fatigue and brass badge marbled with red. Phousita's soothing hands were stroking his face, her voice a sweet burr in his ear as she muttered, "*I am sorry, I am sorry, I am sorry,*" over and over again in a soft, hysterical chant.

He turned his head to look at her. He could hear bones scraping in his rib cage. But he could feel no pain.

He gasped when he saw her face. It was burned red, her cheeks and forehead covered with blisters. He started to sit up, and she helped him. Then Arif appeared and urged him to his feet. He stood with their help. His lungs were gurgling as he breathed, but he felt no pain.

Except for the bodies the street was empty. Mixed in with the trampled human corpses, Sandor counted the bodies of at least fifteen police dogs. Some of them were twitching and snuffling, the way dogs do sometimes when they dream.

At Arif's urging, he moved forward one step. Then another. His legs wobbled under him. His lungs felt peculiarly full and heavy. Suddenly, he coughed hard. Blood filled his mouth and he spat it out on the street. But he felt no pain.

He laughed, suddenly giddy. Then he was on his knees. Phousita and Arif were arguing over him. "You have to leave him!" Arif was saying. "He's dying."

"But I can heal him!"

"There's no time, stupid country girl!" Arif's voice was high and frantic. "Your tricks frightened the cops away, but they'll be back. They'll come armored next time. You have to run from them. You have to hide." His voice cracked. He was screaming through tears now, begging. "Don't let the cops take you, Phousita, please. You're all that's left. You're all that's left."

"But I can heal him. I can, I can."

Sandor blinked, and found that his cheek was resting in the mud of the street. He was staring at the burning shack. The roof had collapsed. The fire had spread to the buildings beyond.

Then Phousita bent down beside him. Her lips met his, there on a pillow of mud. Her tongue darted into his mouth. A moment later, the joy of her benediction exploded once more across his brain. "You will come back to me," she swore. "You will come back."

Then she was gone. And still, he felt no pain.

CHAPTER

15

A snaking line of fire ran through the city. The black smoke that rolled off it was choking, toxic. Helicopters buzzed the air, dousing flames where they could. Below the aerial assault, Nikko's ghost fled with his mule to the broken concrete bank of the river. They clambered past shattered foundations and sprouting banyan trees to a sheltered spot by the water, where they huddled, hemmed in by thousands of stunned residents of the Spill.

Nikko shuddered against an assault of foul odors: the stench of smoke, the urinal stink of overcrowded humans, the sickening smell of burned hair and flesh. He hunched his shoulders against the olfactory assault, against the nerve-grating cries of human misery that mobbed the air, while his rage grew helplessly greater.

He hated this place! Love and Nature, how he hated it. And as he crouched beside the river, invisible to everyone except the corpulent, balding, unwashed scoundrel he'd hired for a mule, he began to consider for the first time that he might not be able to escape the Spill. Kirstin must have already set the Gate filters against him; he wouldn't be able to upload to Castle. He'd have to hire a mule with an unregistered atrium to carry him up the Highway. But how would he pay for it? If he accessed his accounts now, Kirstin would know it. She'd trace the transaction back to the source.

He slapped the ground in frustration. And he hadn't found a trace of Sandor! He'd been here hours, chasing rumors, each one more absurd than the next. Yes, a thousand people had seen Sandor. No, no one knew where he was now. They spoke of a witch. It was said she'd cared for Sandor after he'd escaped the local police. Perhaps she'd lifted him to Heaven.

Perhaps she had, Nikko thought. And where was Heaven?

A call came in for him. It was a recorded voice message from Marevic—meaning she didn't want two-way communication. Very bad. The pressure was on.

Nikko, Sandor was picked up in the Spill nearly two hours ago by the Commonwealth Police. He's being transported to Castle for trial. I'll defend him myself; with your testimony, he should be all right.

I'm more worried about you. A substantial bounty's been put on your ghosts, and the Gates have been set to filter your pattern. You can't get out of Sunda unless we smuggle you out.

But there is some good news. Our security team may have located the Bohr Maker. According to police files, it's infected a young witch named Phousita. The police have been trotting in circles to come up with her, but so far she's evaded them.

It might be easier to find the man she runs with. He's called Arif. He was once a slave, and he still carries an illegal atrium. A slave atrium, Nikko. You could inhabit it. You could control him through it, and you could control her through him.

I bought the address of Arif's atrium from the estate of his former master. I'm giving it to you.

•   •   •

Phousita huddled with Arif in a metal culvert that ran under a street on the northern side of the city. A garish green stream trickled across the bottom of the culvert. The fumes that rose off the water were dizzying, so that even the neighborhood beggars refused to shelter here.

She crouched on the slick, curved floor, trying to keep her feet from sliding into the water. She felt like a tree that had been stripped of its leaves by typhoon winds, uprooted, tossed into the air, now falling, falling, falling past the edge of the world. Fire danced before her eyes. The voices of the children wailed to her from the afterworld. Sumiati with her unborn baby, Sri and Maman and Pieter and all the rest of them.

And Sandor. She'd abandoned Sandor to the police.

She could have saved him. She could have saved all of them. Her spells had subdued the police dogs, sending the beasts into a harmless deep sleep. Her spells could have similarly calmed the municipal cop who'd started the fire, if only she'd been alert enough to notice him sooner, if only she hadn't lost herself in the celebration of healing, if only she weren't so slow and stupid and unworthy of the evil sorcerer's powers.

Arif sat across from her, on the other side of the vile green stream. He hugged his knees against his chest, his head bowed, his shoulders trembling with quiet sobs.

Arif hated her. She could feel the searing heat of his emotion; another blazing fire.

She wanted to comfort him, but he'd warned her not to touch him with her spells and she didn't dare disobey him. Now he wouldn't talk to her at all.

And she was so hungry. She leaned back against the curved wall of the culvert, struggling to keep from sliding into the green stream. Hunger was making her faint. It angered her that she could think about food *now*. But the spirit of the sorcerer was beginning to command her as it had that first night when she'd run away with Arif. How much longer before she must run away again?

Arif stirred. She eyed him warily as he rose to his feet. The culvert was low; he couldn't stand up straight. So he bent over the stream and stared at her with his violet eyes, as if he'd never seen her before.

Her heart began to beat in deep, powerful strokes. She drew her feet up, watching him closely, ready to run.

"You—are—Phousita?" he said stiffly, in English. His voice sounded forced, as if he were saying the words against his will. "You—are—Phousita?"

She moaned and began to slide away toward the mouth of the culvert.

"No, wait! Don't—run." He sat back down, his body unnaturally stiff. "See, I don't want to hurt you. I want to help you. I want to see you to a safe place."

"Who are you?" she squeaked. For it was obvious to her that a ghost had possessed Arif just as it had on that night long ago when she'd first met him. Arif was terrified of ghosts. His master had used ghosts to control him.

"I'm sorry to come to you like this. I'm sorry to frighten your friend. But there was no other way." Arif's mouth shaped the words, but it wasn't Arif talking. "You are Phousita?" it asked again.

She nodded slowly. She could sense nothing of the substance of this ghost. But its words were polite. Nothing like the ghost Arif's master had employed.

"My name's Nikko."

Phousita felt her heart trip. "Nikko?" In Sandor's memories she'd met a brother-spirit of that name. "Do you belong to Sandor?" she asked. "Did he send you here?"

Arif's body leaned forward, to glare at her. "You were the one with him, then. He's been arrested. But he'll be all right."

"They've taken him away."

"They've taken him to Castle." The ghost's speech flowed more easily now. "But he hasn't really broken any laws. He'll be all right. The police won't go so easy on you, though. You have to get out of Sunda."

Leave the city? Sandor had suggested the same thing, but even yesterday she'd known it was only a dream. Her place was here. The spirit of the old woman had visited her to remind her of that. In life, the old woman had cared for her, asking nothing in return. Phousita could give of herself in the same way. She knew she could. Why else had she been given such a great gift? But after today—

The brother Nikko must know she was unworthy of the sorcerer's gift. "But I can hide from the cops now," Phousita said. "I'm a slow learner, but the evil sorcerer is very powerful. He's taught me better how to hide, and how to soften the hearts of the cops. I will do better. I promise. What happened today will never happen again. I will make up for it. I will give everything I have to those who need me—"

But the brother Nikko was shaking his bulbous yellow head. "You don't understand. The police *will* find you. And when they do they'll be ready for you. They won't be subdued by your talents again."

He crept closer to her; held her with his violet eyes. "I've heard people talk about you, Phousita. They say you're a healer, and that you've been blessed with extraordinary powers. But the power that possesses you is not a blessing. It's a curse. It will bring the Commonwealth Police down on you, and everyone around you unless you run away. What happened today could happen again. Don't let any more people die because of you, Phousita. Trust me. Put yourself in my hands and let me hide you. There's no other way."

She felt stunned. The words of the brother Nikko so closely echoed what Sandor had told her. Sandor had warned her that the police would come. But she hadn't heeded him, and now the children were dead. It was her fault. She'd been too proud to listen.

Now she bowed her head in acquiescence. "Where will you take me?" she asked softly.

"To Summer House."

Her head came up. Her heart beat faster. "I've been there in visions," she whispered. "I've seen it through Sandor's eyes. It is Heaven . . . isn't it?"

Nikko didn't answer for a moment. Then he nodded thoughtfully. "It could be," he said.

A few minutes later a car stopped on the street above the culvert. Nikko led her out of her hiding hole. They got into the car. It was driven by a dark-haired young woman. She stared for a moment at Arif's grotesque face, then she turned her attention to the road. Some twenty minutes later the car drove down a ramp into a dimly lit garage. Another woman met them. She handed Nikko an Arabic woman's veil and gown and helped him put them on. Then they all got out of the car. Phousita felt wobbly on her feet; desperately hungry now. She followed Nikko onto an elevator. It rose up a few floors, and then its doors opened on a palatial suite. She was offered a bath; fine clothes; rich food.

Nikko commanded a thing that looked like a rearing cobra with a glassy face. He said it was a camera. He asked her many questions as the camera looked on.

She told him about the evil sorcerer, and about Sandor, and about how she'd learned to disguise herself and Arif from the dogs. This last seemed to amuse him. He asked her if she would change both of them again. So she did. After that there was another bath, and more food.

As her strength returned, her senses seemed to awaken. She became aware of Arif once again. He was an imprisoned consciousness, a slave inside his own body: terrified; furious; helpless. She saw herself through his eyes. Felt his raging sense of betrayal. "You must let him go!" she told Nikko.

"No. I need him. His atrium's unregistered. The cops may overlook it."

"But—"

"No. I won't hurt him. But I have to do this."

She pretended to sleep. But while her eyes were closed, she used her talents to investigate Nikko. She could still sense nothing of him, but after a while she located the evil filamentous growth in Arif's head where the ghost kept itself. She left some of her tiny servants there to watch and learn.

Nikko didn't seem to notice. He got a needle from one of the two women. "If you're going to pass as a Commonwealth citizen," he told her, "you'll need an ID chip." He injected something under the skin of her forearm, and pleaded with her to let it alone and not change it.

Later, they both dressed in the robes and headgear of women of strict Islamic faith. Arif's bulbous face disappeared behind the veils; only his violet eyes were visible. "If anybody asks," Nikko said. "I'm going up the Highway for treatment."

They took the elevator to the roof. Night had fallen. They boarded a waiting helicopter. As the craft rose into the air, Phousita caught sight of the city lights. She gazed in unabashed wonder at the towers of brilliant gold, the incandescent white rivers that swept around their bases. A sense of displacement swept across her. Was this the same city she'd known all her life? But how could it be? When night had always seemed so dark in the Spill.

Hours later she stood at another window, her gaze fixed on another view. She felt herself trembling, caught by an emotion somewhere between fear and marvel as she looked out on *the world*.

So the brother Nikko had named it. *The world*.

Palms and forehead pressed against the cold glass of
the window-wall, she saw the world as a jet would see
it, a cloud, a goddess, a satellite. The huge foreign city
they'd left only an hour before had vanished to nothing
in the immensity of this vision. The land that had
seemed so vast when the helicopter had flown across it
now seemed small enough to cradle in her arms. The
clouds were tiny scraps of white silk unraveling in the
wind. She grew somber as she considered the ocean.
Alone on the world, the ocean remained immense.

"*It's so beautiful,*" she whispered. She glanced shyly
at Nikko. The ghost had said very little since they'd
started this journey on the Imperial Highway.

She'd heard of the Highway all her life, never understanding it. The Imperial Highway: a legend, a story,
so she'd thought, like the tales the old woman had spun
to keep her from crying on dark, hungry nights long,
long ago. Yet here she was, a passenger in a building
that rose higher and higher, climbing a magical thread
stretched taut between the sky and the world.

She and Nikko were safely ensconced in a private
room with two huge beds, a kitchen, and a TV. To
Phousita it seemed both grand and alien. But it was
only one room among a hundred, on an elevator car the
size of a multistoried building.

Nikko sat cross-legged on the carpet, gazing out
the window-wall. He'd taken off his woman's clothes.
He was shirtless, dressed in close-fitting pants, the camera pack strapped around his shoulders . . . Arif's shoulders. Its glass eye gazed at her.

The ghost had been afraid when they'd passed
through the police Gate in the port city. The terminal
had been very crowded. The Gate had scanned their
new ID chips and surveyed them for illegal substances.
Nikko said that sometimes the police took days to an-
alyze the scans. They wouldn't know for sure if they'd
made it through until they'd passed the second Gate at
the top of the Highway. But for now they could relax.

Phousita walked over to one of the beds and sat down on it tentatively. It was plush and so comfortable, but the associations it stirred in her mind were not pleasant. A sense of entrapment closed around her. She left the bed and returned to the window, stretching out on the carpet beside Nikko. His violet eyes shifted to gaze at her. Arif's mind-numbing fear pulsed in her consciousness.

She was beginning to understand the slave atrium. In her mind, she was comparing it to the atrium of Zeke Choy. She'd found that she could recall the structure of Zeke's atrium in detail, though the last time she'd been with him in his shop, she hadn't been aware of its existence. One of her spirit servants must have learned the device and brought its secrets to her.

Nikko seemed unaware of her efforts.

Her gaze roved out across the world again. "In the Spill they say that if you lead a good and generous life, when you die your soul will ride the Highway up to Heaven."

Nikko was silent for a moment. Then: "I think *I've* died. Marevic won't tell me of course, but I think it's really happened."

It was two and a half days later when they finally approached Castle. *Up* and *down* had reversed during the journey, and the car had actually turned over to compensate for this, so that they seemed to be descending rather than rising, sliding down toward a mountainous temple of white stone, its slopes studded with intricate towers divided by winding parks that made Phousita think of green, flowing rivers of vegetation. A transparent bubble enclosed the city. The elevator car slipped into it. The window clouded white. Seconds later they were on the other side, dropping down amidst the city towers toward a terminus at the center of a huge, circular plaza roofed with the woven branches of living trees. She could see people beneath the pleached canopy.

The elevator settled imperceptibly to rest. Phousita jiggled experimentally. Through the journey she'd felt increasingly light upon her feet, at one time even drifting off the floor. She still felt as if her arms and legs were winged by invisible fairies that tried to carry her into the ceiling with every step; as if her material substance had declined, and she had become more spirit than mass, a being caught partway on the journey between Earth and Heaven.

The room's voice warned that they had one half hour to exit the elevator car before it was shifted onto an Earth-bound track where it would receive passengers for the return journey.

Curtly, Nikko told Phousita to put on her Islamic garb. He did the same. Then he stowed the camera pack in a small suitcase, and they left the room.

The hallway was narrow, and crowded with other passengers eager to disembark. They held on to handrails and moved in single file. At the end of the hall, a door opened directly onto an arrival corridor in the multilevel terminal. They found themselves in a passage slightly wider than the hall on the elevator car. A friendly female voice spoke from overhead, offering advice on the best way to move in the near-weightless conditions.

"That's the Castle Gate," Nikko said, his voice low as he nodded toward a black arch at the corridor's end. He took her hand and held it in a painfully tight grip. She could scent the fear on him. It was his fear, not Arif's. He commanded the body more every hour. It was becoming his body. Arif was beginning to fade.

She mouthed a silent prayer for Arif to hold on. Even now her tiny servants were at work on his atrium, changing it to more closely resemble the atrium Zeke Choy had kept. In time, Arif would be able to force Nikko out. She'd take the ghost into her own head then. By then, her own atrium would be ready.

She looked straight ahead at the Gate. It was a

black-walled tunnel about five feet long, narrow, but
well lit. Stewards at the entrance instructed people to
pass through it one at a time. Phousita listened to the
other passengers laugh as they moved through the
Gate, joking about being picked up by the cops. Then
it was their turn. Nikko was first. His hand squeezed
hers even tighter, slick with sweat. Then he let go, and
stepped through. She followed him, and a moment later
they were on the other side, swiftly descending on a
moving ramp into the open-air plaza that she'd seen
from the elevator window only a few minutes before.
The plaza was lightly shaded by its lacy canopy of
woven tree branches. And there were no cops in sight,
no cops at all.

Phousita laughed in joyous relief. She tried to hug
Nikko, but he would have none of it. "It's not time to
celebrate," he growled at her.

She smiled at him in turn, understanding his fear,
but not sharing it. Fear seemed a superfluous emotion.
What was there to fear? She'd already died, there in the
Spill, when the children had burned and her world had
come apart. Now she was a spirit halfway to Heaven,
enjoying the light, fine air of this city.

An empty bench moved up to them from an under-
ground tunnel. It floated a finger's width above the
plaza tiles, as if buoyed on a cushion of air. It seemed
to offer itself to them. Phousita stared at it, her eyes
wide. Nikko took her elbow in a firm grip. "Sit down."

She obeyed him.

"Destination?" the bench asked.

"Gold Wing terminus," Nikko said.

They sat shoulder to shoulder, while the bench ferried them across the plaza. Phousita grasped the edge
of the bench, twisting in her seat as she sought to see
everything at once: the people, colorfully dressed, traveling swiftly on benches and chairs to disappear down
dark tunnel mouths set in the plaza's white floor, or into
bright open-air alleys roofed in twining branches. The

birds, as colorful as the people, flitting through the branches, filling the air with raucous songs. The tresses of flowers: purple, white, yellow; exuding pockets of scent into the air. And overhead: she craned her neck, peering beyond the network of branches and flowers to the city's tall, sculpted white buildings with their hanging gardens; and beyond that, to the black thread of the elevator cable. The sky was a deep, dark blue, its periphery studded with a few dull stars, while directly overhead there loomed a dark circle, illuminated on one side by a wide blue crescent aswirl with white. That was the world, she realized. And by the stars she knew that night had fallen. Yet it seemed to be daytime here in the heart of the city.

The bench suddenly slid downward. She gasped, as the light dimmed. They sped through a tunnel. A few minutes later the bench emerged on the edge of a small lobby, brown carpet on the floor, three rows of padded chairs, a window on the far side of the room that looked out on a gray metal wall only a few meters away. "That's our ship, Phousita," Nikko said, nodding toward the window. The room was empty. The bench ferried them across the carpet to a metal door. Nikko urged her to stand.

On the wall beside the door was an alphanumeric pad. Nikko punched a code into it. The door hissed and then swung open in slow majesty, a shield of steel as wide as Phousita's forearm. Beyond it, a short hallway edged with handrails led to an opulently furnished living room. "Home sweet home," Nikko said. He started to lead her across the threshold, but she pulled up in sudden alarm.

One of her tiny servants had come home to her. From where? Back in the Spill, Nikko had commanded her not to release any to the open air until they were far beyond the reach of the police. And she'd obeyed him. Yet the servants were here, drifting like dust upon the air.

"Come on," Nikko growled. "The ship's ready. We need to go."

"But Sandor is here."

"Of course he's here. I told you the cops were bringing him up to Castle." He tugged at her wrist.

Phousita fought his demanding hands. "No! I have to find him. I swore to him I would."

"Leave him alone! He's safer without you."

"He's not!" She shook her head, trying to make sense of the news her tiny servants carried. "That's not what I feel. He's afraid. He believes he's to die very soon. The trial—it went badly."

Nikko froze. He dropped her hand and edged away. Then he turned, grabbed a handrail, and launched himself into the ship.

She followed him into the living room. They were alone. There would be no one else aboard the ship. Computers would guide it.

Nikko leaned over a console set into a wooden desk on one side of the living room. He barked orders at it as she came up behind him. She touched her small hand against his back and felt him flinch. "You're right," he told her in a hollow voice. "The court found Sandor guilty of conspiracy. A party to the theft of the Bohr Maker." He turned to look at her, violet eyes searching, as if she kept the answer that eluded him. "But Sandor's *not* guilty. The cops have to know that."

"Maybe they want to draw you out," Phousita said.

He nodded slowly. "That's it. That must be it."

"Don't go to them." She put a gentle hand on his arm to stay him. "Let's wait here a few minutes. Things may change."

CHAPTER

16

Sandor sat huddled in the corner of a bunk in a windowless cell on Castle. He stared at the walls. They were a plush, soft gray, very businesslike. He pulled his knees closer to his chest, breathing shallowly. It hurt to move. It hurt to breathe. The medic who'd been in earlier said his ribs had been broken. The shattered bone ends had punctured both his lungs. He'd been more or less dead, there in the Spill.

He shifted, trying to find a more endurable position, but only managed to shove himself away from the wall in the almost nonexistent gravity. His last memories before waking here were of a painless state of grace, lying in the mud at Phousita's feet. He had no idea how much time had passed between now and then.

The cell door slipped open. Two police dogs entered the little chamber, shuffling forward, their feet never breaking contact with the floor, so that Sandor knew they'd been dealing with the micro-G all their lives. One took up a post by the door. The other glided to him as if it were the family pet, shoving its hideous head into his face, its nostrils whuffing hot air. He started to twist away, then winced in pain.

Behind the dogs came a uniformed cop. She paused at the door, studying him with eyes the color of honey in a pot. Her hair was long, full, kinked and coppery; she kept it off her face with a black sash across her forehead—a style that seemed vaguely African. He recognized her, of course. Most citizens of the Commonwealth would. She was the Chief of Police, Kirstin Adair.

She approached him, then knelt at the side of the bed, her gaze still fixed on his face, studying him as if he were some mindless exhibit she'd come to view, and not a self-aware being at all. He felt his heart hammer in his chest. His lungs burned.

She said: "I knew your brother Nikko. We were very close, you know."

Sandor's voice cracked. "The medic told me he was dead."

She nodded. "He is. Even his ghosts are gone."

Sandor thought about the copy of Nikko's ghost that had accompanied him on the flight to Sunda, wiped out by the kem-wand of the municipal police. That had been his fault. If he'd followed Nikko's advice, if he'd stayed in the terminal, maybe things would have been all right. Maybe the local cops would have left him alone and—

"Why did you let Nikko get you involved in this mess?"

He blinked and looked up at Kirstin, suddenly aware that his attention had wandered. "What mess?" he asked. "Why am I under arrest? I didn't do anything. I was assaulted by the municipal police in Sunda. Why aren't you following up on that? Why am I here?"

Kirstin's heavy lips turned in a slight, hungry smile that belied her kindly voice and made him shiver. "You're involved in a very serious crime, Sandor. You're presently in possession of an illegal Maker that is functioning as a beacon inside your body, continuously shedding information packets that advertise your position. We've identified it as a derivative of an antique Maker whose pattern was stolen from police files." Her eyebrows rose in question. "Are you expecting a rescue?"

"No!" Sandor blurted out. He gazed at her in stunned disbelief. "I don't know anything about a stolen Maker. I've never accessed police files. I don't—"

His protest broke off in mid-sentence. Once again he was seeing the odd little glands on Phousita's hands. He felt a cold sweat break out across his face. "She was poisoned," he whispered. "She didn't know what she had."

"You mean Phousita, don't you?"

He stared at Kirstin, dread flowing like cold water through his veins. "Did you arrest her too?"

Kirstin's expression stiffened into a macabre facsimile of a smile. "You're in very serious trouble," she told him. "The research scientist who committed the theft named you as a willful accomplice."

"No! That's a lie. I don't even know—"

She interrupted him, her voice gentle, sympathetic, insistent. "You resisted arrest by the Sunda police."

"No. They never gave me a chance to—"

"You refused to cooperate with their lawful interrogation. You escaped from their custody by employing an illegal physiological modification. Immediately following your escape, you joined your accomplice, this *Phousita*. How long have you known her?"

"She wasn't my accomplice. I didn't know her at all, until then. The municipal police assaulted me! She helped me survive."

"Helped you? By turning over to you an illegal Maker. How much did you pay her for that?"

"I didn't pay her anything. I'm not part of anything. Neither is she."

"You deny it?"

"Of course I deny it."

"Yet you carry an illegal Maker. How do you explain that?"

"Have you ever been down there? It's a sewer of illegal Makers. Why don't your officers do anything about *that*?"

"Why were *you* named as an accomplice?"

"How should I know? I don't even know the person who was supposed to have—"

"Enough!" Kirstin said. She rose to her feet, her eyes flashing. "I was hoping you'd give me some reason to stay your execution. After all, you're only a child."

Sandor felt his heart trip. "*Execution . . . ?*" he whispered.

"The judiciary has already ruled against you. Your original body at the mausoleum on Summer House has already been destroyed."

"You can't—"

"We have to, Sandor. The laws of the Commonwealth were not made lightly. And it is the duty of the police to enforce them with an absolute hand."

Kirstin felt a trifle dejected as she left Sandor's cell, the two police dogs at her heels. She'd had Sandor interrogated before he'd been returned to full awareness, but he'd revealed no more under the unconscious influence of drugs than he had under the conscious influence of fear. Whatever he might have known must have been lost when the municipal police destroyed his atrium. She liked her cases to close neatly. A confession would have quieted the protests from Summer House. And a confession might have led to bigger game in the corporate hierarchy.

A motion sensor followed her progress down the corridor, past other, unoccupied cells. After assessing her identity, it opened a second locked door, and let her through. A handler waited on the other side. He leashed the dogs and led them away, leaving her alone in the narrow passages of the detention facility. The musky scent of the animals clung to the air. For a moment, Kirstin wondered if Sandor might really be innocent of conspiracy. Not that it mattered.

Molecular law was not a system of justice, it was a system of enforcement. Personal innocence could not be a mitigating factor. The judiciary could only be concerned with personal *involvement*. If an individual carried an illegal Maker, that individual must suffer the consequences, or the use of illegal Makers would spread beyond the ability of the police to control them. In this way, molecular law was analagous to natural law: shove someone over a tall cliff, and that individual, though personally innocent, would still die. There was no mercy in the application of the law of gravity. There could be no mercy in the application of Commonwealth law.

Sandor Jiang-Tibayan was in possession of an illegal Maker derived from the Bohr Maker. The seriousness of this association alone had persuaded the magistrate to consider this as a potential capital case. When police attempts to eradicate the derivitive Maker failed, the verdict of execution was assured. But at that point the case might have been considered only second-degree terminal: Sandor's original physical copy at Summer House as well as his ghosts might have been spared if they could be shown to be free of a similar violation.

Enter the factor of willfulness: Sandor had been named by Van Ness as an accomplice. He'd escaped from the custody of the Sunda municipal police, thus avoiding arrest by the Commonwealth Police. And upon his escape he'd immediately appeared in the company of Phousita, the mule Van Ness had used to carry the Maker.

Sandor's protestations of innocence didn't count for much against the roster of his actions. Besides, memories could be edited. Even if he couldn't recall participating in a conspiracy, he obviously had. Willfulness elevated the case to a first-degree capital offense, in which all physical and electronic manifestations were forfeit.

Kirstin might have introduced some doubt by reporting Nikko's confession at Summer House. But why confuse the issue? At that point, Nikko had known himself to be a condemned man, and he'd had nothing to lose by lying about his brother's involvement. She'd thought it best to omit his testimony from her report.

With no legally acceptable proof of Sandor's innocence, the verdict was unavoidable: execution in entirety, with sterilization of all remains.

Alone in the corridor, Kirstin's thoughts turned to Fox, and she smiled. Thirty-one years ago he'd mocked the law, using bribery and coercion to win the research permit that allowed Nikko's existence. Kirstin had been making him pay for that victory ever since. This was one more installment on the debt. But not the last. Oh no. The score wasn't even yet.

The termination chamber was another cozy gray room, equipped with soft white furnishings. Six chairs had been arranged in an arc for the audience. Three of them were already occupied by uniformed police officers, chatting idly as Sandor was led into the room. Kirstin Adair was one of them. She glanced at him, then leaned over to whisper with the other two officers.

The guard who escorted Sandor nudged his elbow, indicating that he should sit in a seventh chair, one that faced the others. He obeyed numbly, pulling himself down into the chair. The pain in his ribs was excruciating. He watched as his arms and legs were strapped into place. Then the medic came and inserted an IV into his forearm.

He closed his eyes, telling himself that this was only a dream. It could not be real. Very soon now he would wake up. But the fiery pain around his lungs belied that. Why hadn't the medic given him something for the pain? Love and Nature. Love and Nature. They'd give him something soon enough.

He tried to slow his ragged breathing, knowing he'd feel better if he could manage it. But he was too scared to concentrate. His heart fluttered unevenly. He felt nauseous. *Wake up!* he commanded himself. *Wake up!*

He heard the chamber door slide open. He looked up, to see Marevic Chun dart into the room. Immediately, his hopes fixed on her. Lovely, fragile Marevic Chun. The president of Summer House at Earth. She knew the cops. She knew the system. She could get him out of this. She had to!

She glided straight to Kirstin; touched the arm of Kirstin's chair to stop her forward motion. "Chief Adair, you must delay this barbarous execution! Stop it at once, or I warn you, you'll endanger your position. I have a magistrate considering this case. I've offered you copious notes derived from Nikko's own files that *prove* Sandor had no involvement in this case. You must reconsider."

Kirstin looked around irritably. "Marevic. Have you found a copy of Nikko's ghost?"

Marevic froze. Her dark eyes became obsidian.

Kirstin said: "A magistrate has already ruled that the notes which you claim belong to Nikko cannot be admitted as evidence. They are as likely to be forgeries as anything else. It's too easy to blame a dead man. Unless you can produce a ghost to testify to the validity of your evidence, it can't be considered."

"But a court *is* considering it. And you have a moral duty to delay this execution so long as that court is still perusing the issue."

The Chief of Police gazed up, her expression annoyed. "The only issue in this case," she said, "is whether or not the Board of Directors of Summer House—yourself included—had prior knowledge of this crime."

Marevic's lips met in a thin, hard line. "We had no

involvement." She sat down in one of the empty seats. Her angry gaze fixed on Sandor. "I'm sorry," she said in a calm, cold voice. "I've done everything I could."

It took a moment before he realized she was addressing him. When he did, his whole body began to shake. Marevic was giving up! She was giving up. His breath surged in and out of his lungs. He felt himself straining against the straps. "You can't say that!" he screamed at her. "I didn't commit any crime."

"It's all right," Phousita said.

His head snapped up as if it had been yanked in a noose. His wild gaze searched the room, but she was nowhere to be seen.

"It's all right," she said again. "I know how to carry you now."

He had no functioning atrium. *She* had no atrium. She could not be with him.

Phousita? he thought.

She didn't respond. He tipped his head back and studied the ceiling. Odd, silent tears slipped out of his eyes. He thought of his walk through the airport terminal in Sunda, of the little girl with the begging bowl and of how much his life had changed. It seemed like magic.

Phousita believed in magic. Where was she now?

A wave of dizziness swept across him and he sagged back against the chair. *"It's all right,"* Phousita whispered again. He smiled. He didn't believe her, but it was good to hear her voice.

Someone tugged lightly on the IV line. His eyes fluttered open. He half expected to see Phousita. He blinked hard, struggling to focus his sight. But it was only the medic, adjusting the flow rate on the IV. "The pain is gone," he told the medic. His words were slurred. She looked at him fearfully and backed away. He stared after her. Something *was* wrong with him, he realized. The dizziness was getting worse. It filled his ears with a roar and a rush. . . .

His head snapped up. He was awake again, alert. His gaze swept across the gallery. Kirstin was staring at him, a dark, suspicious frown on her face, as if he'd suddenly become something dangerous. Marevic looked scared, her small frame pressed into the seat as if she could hide herself there.

One of the uniformed officers sitting with Kirstin cleared his throat impatiently. Kirstin glanced at him, then nodded. "Proceed," she said.

Sandor looked around. The medic had left the room. A stranger in surgical scrubs stood in her place. At Kirstin's word, he plucked a syringe from a waiting tray. Calmly, methodically, he injected the contents into the tube feeding into Sandor's arm.

Sandor's eyes widened. He stiffened reflexively as the poison rushed down the tube. His thoughts fled home. "I'm sorry, Fox," he whispered.

He tried to keep awake, tried to count. One, two, three, four, f—

Phousita stood swaying, just inside the lock of the little ship. Nikko stood behind her, hardly breathing, his anxiety a drug exuded into the air to keep her alert.

Phousita felt herself looking down upon towers, upon gardens. Her vision was as wide as the city. Somewhere, not far, her tiny servants steamed off Sandor like vapors off a volcanic vent. They returned to her in gusts:

She saw him walking a narrow corridor, his hands shackled to his sides, police dogs at his heels. Every breath made fierce by pain.

She saw him seated, bound, terrified.

Knew his hope; his despair.

Then she was inside him.

She became an insect, no larger than a grain of dust. On her back, like a minute pearl nestled between her wings, she carried an empty world. She set the world down and began to pray, and soon a snake wound down to her from out of the firmament, a thread of story, twisted, knotted, turning back upon itself, mile after mile of it coiling down toward her. She scuttled aside and watched the head of the snake fall into the basket of her world. The threadlike body followed, settling in neat coils. She guided it with her insect feet and watched her world fill with days, with years. More. With life. Down, down, down the thread of the snake came, until she began to fear it would be too much, more than she could carry. Then the last link of the snake collapsed into her globe and it was full. She looked up anxiously, but the sky overhead was empty. So she rubbed her papery wings together and swallowed the world. Then she rose into the sky and flew home.

Phousita turned to Nikko. She felt as numb and cold and sterile as the air that nurtured this city. Whoever had started the rumor that Heaven could be found at the end of the Highway had been a fool. She looked into Arif's fearful eyes, still waiting for a sense of joy, a feeling of triumph to envelop her. It didn't come. Perhaps she was too tired to feel anything.

"Sandor's with me now," she said to the ghost that parasitized Arif. "We can go."

CHAPTER

17

As Chief of Police it was Kirstin's prerogative to fill all the executive positions on her staff, save one—the Director of Internal Security. Allende was a Congressional appointee; his loyalty was given to the Committee on Molecular Law and Police Matters, and not to the force itself. So it came as no surprise to Kirstin when the Congressional dog finally howled to his masters. Indeed, she'd anticipated it. The time was right to bring the matter of the Bohr Maker to the attention of a wider audience.

So she took her place willingly at the witness table in the Congressional hearing room, her expression attentively polite as the obscure senator chairing the investigation finally came round to his point.

"Chief Adair, this committee has been charged with investigating the report of a serious breach in police security. We've asked you to attend today to confirm or deny whether such an incident has taken place."

Kirstin nodded slowly, still absorbing an abstract of the senator's biography from her atrium. Congressional representatives could serve only a single, one-year term in the Commonwealth offices on Castle. They were as ephemeral as celebrities, and Kirstin rarely came to know them as individuals. According to his bio, this one was a conservative corporate member out of Julevy-On, a professed staunch supporter of molecular law enforcement who'd voted to her direction three of the last four times she'd bothered to make her opinion known in the capitol rooms. She anticipated an easy afternoon.

"Yes, Senator," she said. "An incident has occurred."

He nodded, as if to congratulate himself for having gone straight to the source by summoning her here. "Would you please explain the exact nature of the incident?"

"Yes, sir." She'd be happy to do that. The raw facts would be enough to frighten these senators and buy her a free hand in the investigation. "You may be familiar with a device popularly known as the Bohr Maker. It's an enhancing Maker that was retrieved from the body of the convicted criminal, Leander Bohr. It's an adaptive artificial intelligence, imbued with Bohr's talents in molecular design. It will modify the body of its host, allowing that individual to become a literal molecular factory, capable of producing Makers for nearly any function, including camouflage, espionage, and assault. Although it's an antique, the police have never been able to devise a Maker of similar talents, because to do so would require the revocation of current statutes limiting the independence of artificial intelligences."

The committee chair frowned, his expression one of open concern. "So in effect you're saying the Bohr Maker is an illegal artificial intelligence."

"That's right. Its capacity for independent action exceeds statute limits."

"So it's smarter than police Makers."

"Intelligence is a thorny issue, Senator, intelligent behavior being so dependent on natural instinct, which this Maker lacks. Let us say instead that it would be more *adaptive* than police Makers."

"And better armed."

"It's possible," she admitted, with deliberate reluctance. She didn't want the populace to think she lacked confidence. They would be voting for her again in a year.

"Could you explain that answer?" the senator asked.

"Of course. The Bohr Maker has no core personality and therefore it has no inherent ambitions or instincts. Its developmental direction is determined entirely by the personality of its host. If it attaches itself to a warrior, it will develop a warlike demeanor."

"And has that happened, Chief Adair?"

"Our best evidence indicates not. On the contrary, the Maker seems to have taken up residence in the mind of an illiterate prostitute."

There was a titter from the gallery—a small corporeal audience, mostly students come to observe government in action. Of course the electronic audience would be immensely larger.

Kirstin waited for the sounds of amusement to subside before she continued. "The lifestyle of this prostitute has led her to instinctively hide from the police. She's used the Maker's talents to aid her in this process, making her apprehension difficult."

"Isn't it true that your one attempt to arrest her resulted in disaster?"

Kirstin smiled indulgently. "Police operations are always unpredictable, sir. Our investigation led us to the location of the suspect. Because it was in a territory outside the Commonwealth, it was legally necessary for us to inform the local government of our activities ahead of time. Unfortunately, a sense of nationalism afflicted the local police force. They resented our intrusion, and sought to settle the problem themselves, in their own way. Their interference prevented us from making the arrest."

"But isn't it true that this 'illiterate prostitute' incapacitated over twenty police dogs?"

There was a gasp from the gallery, and for the first time Kirstin felt a flash of annoyance. That bastard Allende hadn't left anything out when he'd squealed to his Senate masters.

"Isn't this true?" the Senator pressed.

"Yes, sir. It is true. The dogs were drugged into a temporary state of somnolence."

"They were made to sleep?" Again, a titter from the audience.

"Yes."

"And where is this illiterate prostitute now?"

"We don't know, Senator. She could be anywhere."

In hindsight, the flaw in the arrest procedure was obvious. They'd pushed Phousita too hard. They'd forced her to strike back. Like a game of coevolution, when predator shapes prey and prey shapes predator, they'd forced her to adopt an aggressive defense. And now that she'd become acquainted with her capacities, would she maintain her newly acquired aggressive nature? Or would she revert to her inoffensive former self?

To answer that question, Kirstin had detained Zeke Choy once again, questioning him extensively on the subject of Phousita's personality. His final comment still haunted her: *"I can tell you what she was like. But that isn't going to mean much anymore. Because when I knew her she wasn't a messianic healer. When I knew her, she hadn't yet seen her family burned alive. When I knew her, she feared police dogs. I don't know her now."*

Phousita had literally disappeared. The dogs could recover no trace of her. The Gates reported no sign of her. Even the rumor mills in the Spill were helpless, running on false, frantic tales that failed to explain the fate of their vanished sorceress.

The trail was worse than cold. It was nonexistent.

Kirstin thought of her days with Leander Bohr. Leander had always used the Maker righteously, in the service of the Goddess. He'd never used it to violate the body of the Mother, or sought to change her natural order. There'd been no harm in him. But how many people could she say that about?

She'd dreamed of Nikko this morning. In the dream she'd entered his apartment at Summer House. Not alone this time, but with a contingent of officers as backup. They'd all worn isolation suits. They'd bombed the room with assault Makers, the best in the police arsenal, programmed to destroy any Makers not bearing the latest police identity code. Nikko had been hanging by his long blue toes upside down in a tree. He'd laughed at her. Then he'd waved his hand in the air. A moment and her isolation suit began to dissolve. He waved his hand again. She felt her body changing. When she raised her fist against him in a gesture of defiance, she was aghast to find it armored in enameled blue.

She did not believe Nikko was dead. Somehow, somewhere, his consciousness must still exist.

Somehow, somewhere, he must be pursuing Phousita just as she was.

She no longer believed Phousita was still in the Spill. Messiahs were notoriously difficult creatures to hide, yet Phousita could not be tracked even through rumors.

So Phousita had left the Spill, and that meant she could be anywhere, in contact with anyone.

Fear was an emotion Kirstin had not experienced in many years. It caught her by surprise when it came. When she realized what this pounding heart, this fluttering gut meant, she reacted in irritation. She was too old for fear! If she couldn't find Phousita directly, then she'd have to do it in a roundabout way—by finding Nikko first, whatever was left of him.

To Summer House, then.

She prepared her ghost, and departed.

• • •

Over three minutes elapsed in objective time, but to her it seemed only a moment before she arrived in the atrium of the police captain on Summer House—an undistinguished administrator who had command of a handful of on-site officers. She continued to consult his biography. The captain had been born in the EC sixty-seven years ago and so he had no natal corporate affiliation. He'd been assigned to Summer House for the past year, and was presently due to move on.

"Have you enjoyed your stay here at Summer House?" she asked him.

He seemed taken aback by the question. Several seconds passed before he came up with an answer. "It's been a nice assignment," he managed at last.

"Corporate membership in Summer House is notoriously difficult for outsiders to obtain," she said. "Yet many of our officers who've served here have been offered that privilege at the end of their tour of duty." She let him think about that, while she watched the anxiety grow in his eyes. "Such a situation naturally leads us to wonder what favors our officers might be doing for the Board of Directors here, to earn the privilege of corporate membership."

His cheeks seemed to go hollow. "The ranks of the Commonwealth Police are full of many fine individuals. Just because the House recognizes that, it doesn't imply a crime."

"Have you been offered a corporate membership?"

Sweat actually appeared on his brow. "I have been," he said stiffly. "I haven't decided whether to accept it."

Hadn't decided? Right. It amazed her that such a transparent man had risen so far in the ranks of the police. But if his loyalties had already been taken over by the House, she would need to find another mule for her investigation.

"There are some things I'd like to look into here,"

she told him. "But I know you're much too busy to assist me. I'll summon one of your officers instead."

"Yes, ma'am." He seemed more nervous than ever.

She turned her attention away from him, to scan the personnel roster, checking the political backgrounds of the on-site officers. She moved from one entry to the next in growing dismay. *Every one of them* harbored radical sympathies! Apparently the House had been exerting considerable influence over posting procedures.

She made no effort to hide her anger from the police captain. But apparently he didn't trust his comrades in her presence, because he stepped forward with a political solution.

"Might I suggest instead ... well, it sounds like an insult, but you could access the House plexus in complete privacy if you rode one of the animals." Kirstin must have looked puzzled, because the captain immediately added an explanation. "Monkeys and birds and such," he said. "The House has doctored a few of 'em with slave atriums. You can ride inside their heads and send 'em where you want to go. And of course you'll have full access to the plexus."

"I'm familiar with slave atriums," Kirstin said. "They've been used by corporate pirates for decades in the rape of Mother Earth."

"Yes, ma'am."

"But I suppose the House uses them only for research."

"We're far from the Mother here, ma'am."

Kirstin raised an annoyed eyebrow. Yet the proposal intrigued her; it would allow her to examine the House plexus without interference. And despite the captain's fears, she had no interest just now in investigating the disloyalties of her forces on Summer House.

"We've all kinds of animals," the police captain said, sensing her interest. "But the baboons are best. Big and smart. Let me roll a catalog for you."

Data fed into Kirstin's mind. It felt as if she were

remembering in a linear way the highlights of a long list of animal hosts. "What's that?" she asked suddenly, and the roll paused. "Back search for Jiang-Tibayan," she said, and found herself considering a baboon by the name of Sax.

"Oh," the officer said, as if Kirstin had committed a social blunder. "Some of the monkeys are, well . . . kind of like pets, I guess. See, it says in the listing, that one belongs to Sandor Jiang-Tibayan."

"Not anymore," she pointed out coldly. "I'll have that one."

"Ma'am—"

She didn't stay to hear the captain's objections. The routine was easy enough to adopt. She issued a code for the monkey's address, and downloaded.

Sax woke up with a start. He'd been sleeping with his head on a female's rump, but when Kirstin entered his atrium, he stood up abruptly, stretching like a dog and sniffing expectantly at the forest air. Awaiting an old master? Kirstin wondered.

The baboon pair was at rest on what might have been a horizontal section of heartwood, part of the supporting "bones" of Summer House. The humus-covered surface was heavily forested and oppressively hot under a shimmering blue swath of artificial sky that hung not a hundred meters overhead. Sax sat back down on his haunches and started grooming the female.

Kirstin took a few minutes to accustom herself to her new sensory environment. She enjoyed sight of a human quality while scenting with a baboon's skill—a fascinating change. The captivating odor of the female mixed with intoxicating vapors from overripe fruit, and a heavy, pervasive sweetness so intense that it must be issuing from some tree in full flower. Other scents she couldn't even guess at, because though the baboon's perceptions belonged to her, its knowledge did not.

Not yet. She sought an atrium notebook, wondering if it might house a dictionary that she could subsume.

The atrium notebook.

Sandor's atrium notebook. The boy had been guileless by all reports, yet devoted to Nikko. What personal information had he seen fit to record?

She summoned the index and began to look through the listings. She found the dictionary. And a file on the behavior of the baboons (they were an artificial descendant of an African species of forest baboon). There was an extensive collection of private material: reminiscences, poems, descriptive writings on the forest, half-formed ideas for research, molecular histories, a calendar. And several short files with peculiar names: *Bird Park, Rat Heaven, Budding Bears, Eve's Wall.* . . . And then: *Nikko's Score.*

Kirstin opened this last file. It was another list of similar nonsense: *Lizard Fruit, Bat Berries, Fish Stones.* . . . Each entry was accompanied by a brief description, as *Solar Flies: observed hatch out from grapelike fruit cluster on seed tree in outer forest, prox. 400m S. tether center-point, 60m W. Silver wings unfurl like butterfly, but crawl, don't fly. Designer: C. Furui. Background check fails! Christy never got approval on solar flies! No genesis. Nikko, you liar.*

But the other entries had apparently been corroborated. Animals sprouting from plants, or hatching from rocks, or emerging from heartwood. Biogenesis of adult organisms.

Nikko and Sandor seemed to have enjoyed a running competition to see who could locate the most sites of active genesis. Why not simply consult corporate records? Kirstin wondered. She queried Summer House. But no matter how she phrased her question, the House denied her any information on biogenesis. *Corporate privilege,* she was told. The House was not at all impressed by her status as an investigating police officer. *All queries into this subject must first be authorized by corporate officials, or information will be denied.*

Corporate privilege. Limit the available information, and locating sites of biogenesis became a kind of Easter egg hunt. She reviewed the list again. *Eve's Wall* sounded provocative: *Evita Rodrigues doubled herself here! Sax scented her the day before she emerged. This has to be worth two points. More, if you're a cop.* But an entry under a later date dampened Kirstin's interest: *Board of Directors furious; site dormant.*

Amongst the other entries, *Bird Park* was closest. *Chandelier tree, protected from predation. Adults of various avian species observed emerging from genesis pods. Nearly inaccessible; birds safe from predators while plumage dries. Designer: P. Cartmin.*

Kirstin decided to have a look at it. She was wondering how to steer Sax in the proper direction when the animal stood up again and started walking slowly down the branch.

Kirstin had never utilized a slave atrium before. Never had she encountered such an intimate form of transportation. She experienced the play of the baboon's strong, lean muscles as it walked on all fours down the forest highway. The soft, cool feel of the humus under powerful hands. The rough, gnarly texture of bark against furred skin as Sax clambered over a tree root. The grunt of the female as she finally got up and began to follow. Fascinating.

Sax jumped suddenly, taking Kirstin by surprise. He leapt off the heartwood and caught a large branch heavy with fruit. The branch grew from a tree rooted in a meadow some fifty feet below. Sax plucked one of the fruits and took a bite out of it while the branch bobbed and swayed under his weight. Kirstin recognized the taste and texture of mango.

She felt herself being drawn in by the charm of this place. Forcefully, she reminded herself that this forest was not the Mother. It was an artificial construct, full of artificial life, designed by Fox Jiang-Tibayan who thought he could improve upon the Goddess.

She slipped into command mode and tried to forcefully guide the monkey's limbs toward Bird Park. The method worked for about three seconds. She got Sax to drop the mango seed. He looked up, and reached out with a monkey paw for an overhead branch. But she overestimated his reach and the poor animal's hand closed on nothing. Sax fell forward, tumbling out of the tree. Kirstin fled command mode, returning control of the body to the monkey. Sax recovered instantly, catching a lower branch in his paws, then clambering back up to the female who was screeching at him from the heartwood.

Kirstin sighed internally. Obviously, the monkey should guide itself. But how to get around? She examined the system. Between passive observer and active command modes there lay an intermediate level of communication with the monkey. This would allow all specific movements to come under the baboon's control, but the rider could influence the monkey to move in a desired direction, or even to proceed to a preprogrammed destination. How thoroughly had Sandor trained this monkey?

Bird Park, Kirstin urged experimentally. And to her surprise, Sax began to move. *Bird Park*, she thought again, more passionately this time, and Sax began to scamper along the heartwood with the happy abandon of a child at play. *Bird Park!* The female pursued, slapping at his rump whenever he allowed her to catch up.

Along the heartwood they ran, for nearly a quarter mile before it finally branched. Sax took the smaller fork, followed it for only a few hundred yards until they'd cleared the patch of sky just overhead, then he started to climb. Once Kirstin ordered him to stop, so she could gaze at the glowing blue oval, one of hundreds of little bits of sky that brought light to all levels of the vertical forest. This close, Kirstin could see the faint shapes of aquatic creatures moving inside the light. Curious, she consulted the House. Yes, the skies were also aquatic habitats, populated with organisms adapted to the bright, warm waters of tropical seas. Artificial constructions in an artificial world.

Bird Park! she commanded Sax, and the monkey sprang upward.

They climbed beyond the sky. A meadow grew on its upper surface, cut through by a tiny stream that fell in a misty spray of water to a clear pool hollowed out of a branch of heartwood. There was no visible outlet from the pool, so Kirstin surmised that the water drained into the heartwood's transit system.

They went on.

The forest changed gradually as they climbed, becoming wetter until Sax began to slip on the mosses that clothed the branches of the trees. A breeze started to blow, and tendrils of mist floated past. The breeze freshened, setting the branches swaying slowly up and down.

What happened when a tree fell? Kirstin wondered. She'd seen the trunks of small trees that had fallen, clothed in moss and fungi and epiphytic plants, wedged against the roots or branches of other trees. But what happened when a forest giant, rooted in the heartwood, toppled? Or was the House too young to have ever experienced that particular disaster?

The girth of the branches Sax chose to climb had thinned. They'd gone up as high as they could on a tree whose canopy blazed in orange flowers. Sax looked down. Kirstin saw a thin weave of branches below him, and then a route of heartwood, at least three hundred feet below. She quailed. Sax leapt.

Kirstin wanted to close her eyes and scream, but of course neither response was possible. The monkey remained undisturbed. It caught a flexible green branch no thicker than Kirstin's finger, and hung on to it, bobbing up and down like a child at the end of a bell rope.

His presence startled a flock of large fruit bats that had been roosting on the pendulous branches. They flapped away with cumbersome strokes, disappearing briefly behind a thin veil of leaves before they emerged into the open air, wheeling in great circles as if they couldn't decide where to go. Beyond them Kirstin could see the window-perforated wall of the apartment complex.

Sax climbed the pendulous branch. It was part of a tree that grew upside down, hanging like an elegant chandelier on a trunk barbed with thorns and glinting with a moist gel. The trunk was suspended from heartwood; it looked to be at least two hundred meters long. The branches were all pendulous, whip-thin green cords like the one Sax climbed. They were sparsely leafed but heavily in fruit with green, gourdlike pods that ranged from the size of a fist to the size of a coconut. A few of the pods had turned red. Sax climbed until he drew even with a large green pod. Then he leapt through space once again, grabbed a branch, and sat down upon the pod like a child seated on a swing. He didn't seem inclined to journey further.

Bird Park? Kirstin wondered, but of course Sax didn't respond.

If this was Bird Park, it certainly didn't deserve its name. There were almost no birds around. Just a pair of little finches in dull green plumage squabbling over a perch on a tiny red pod. Kirstin watched them, and after a moment she noticed that the red pod had a crack in it. Another pod, farther down on the same branch, had already split open, its shell peeling back like the petals of a flower. A bird hung inside it. A little green bird. It was suspended by its feet, twitching occasionally, its wings making frantic flapping motions every few seconds. Its plumage looked unkempt, somewhat wet and sticky. At first Kirstin thought it had been trapped by the flower/pod, which must be of a carnivorous nature, and if she sat here the whole slow afternoon, she would see the petals close over the sorry victim. But no. As she watched, the bird's movements became more vigorous. Soon it was swaying back and forth as if it hung from a trapeze, and finally it dropped free, flapped its wings, and shot into the forest, the other small birds in noisy pursuit.

So this was a biogenesis tree. Kirstin watched the red pod with the crack in it for over an hour. When the flower finally opened, it revealed a tiny brown hummingbird. The creature revved its wings for a few minutes, then flew off into the forest.

She watched it go, her mind troubled by the implications. Automated biogenesis. An artificial world that could bring forth its own life, almost instantly, apparently without immediate supervision. Dangerous. But not illegal, so long as the biological machinery wasn't developing the design. That would be a violation of Commonwealth covenants. Nonhuman intelligences could not be self-aware or act without strict direction. This was probably just a manufacturing process, under strict control. And yet, and yet . . .

She finally pinpointed the source of her growing alarm. This talent had no purpose. Not here on Summer House anyway, where the forest community was reportedly self-sustaining or so the line of propaganda went. Then where?

The answer came to her immediately: anywhere; everywhere.

If the corporation wanted to duplicate the House, what would be the best way to go about it? Follow the same process of trial and error, setback and failure that had led to the original? Or create a program employing all that had been learned in the design of Summer House? Could all of that be coiled into one package? An egg that could hatch a world? Delivered by automated machinery.

Another thought swiftly followed; an even darker thought. In all that great, winding, cross-referenced

chain of data, might the pattern and persona of one
Nikko Jiang-Tibayan be hidden?

The possibility left her oddly calm. She could feel
the hand of the Mother guiding her. *Caution*, the Goddess seemed to whisper. *Move slowly*. Indeed. She must
not alert Fox to her suspicions. He must have no
chance to erase evidence before she could investigate.
But how to conduct an investigation? The staff on Summer House could not be trusted. No, a new staff *must*
be brought in.

She would route a police ship to Summer House,
one with a proven commander. It might be several
weeks before the new staff could reach the city, but the
evidence would wait. Given the political climate, Fox
couldn't be thinking of recovering Nikko for tens, possibly hundreds of years. She would have more than
enough time to trap Fox in his own schemes.

CHAPTER

18

Nikko awoke with a start. How could he have been sleeping? It wasn't possible. Even when Arif's body subsided toward sleep, his own consciousness would continue. He was an electronic program, a ghost. He was not Arif. And yet he'd been sleeping.

He sat up. He found himself on a plush pallet, on the floor of one of the ship's two cabins. The walls were tuned to a mock-up of the forested interior of Summer House in simulated moonlight; soft insect sounds rolled out of the air. The bedding was crumpled, and it stank, as if he'd inhabited it for days.

Phousita stood in the door, watching him. She was dressed in new clothes: a gold breastcloth, and a white sarong stitched with flowers of red and gold. Her hair hung down her back in a long, black cascade. Nikko felt his fist clench. "What did you do to me?" he growled.

"I'm sorry," she said. "But I had to. You're killing Arif. Can't you feel what you're doing to him? You're violating him. He can't stand it. He can't."

"So you made him sleep? You made me sleep too? How'd you do that?"

"I wove a dream for you, and fed it to the atrium."

"You synthesized the sensory input? For how long? How long, Phousita? I don't even remember leaving Castle!"

"Three days," she said. "We're far from Castle now. We're safe. You have to let Arif go."

His bladder felt ready to burst. He staggered to the head and relieved himself. Arif's body still seemed awkward to him: too short, too tightly muscled. But very strong. Strong enough to put his fist through the wall. He resisted the impulse. Instead, he pulled on a pair of shorts, then dug the camera pack out of his briefcase and strapped it on.

As an historian, he was very conscious of the political shock waves the theft of the Bohr Maker might generate. At minimum, the historical record he was compiling would demonstrate to every citizen what a gauzy thing police "security" must always be. Beyond that, anything was possible. In a world where police Makers were no longer supreme, what law could be enforced? He could envision the Commonwealth crumbling around him, an outmoded fortress to be ripped apart molecule by molecule, opening the way to a new and unpredictable torrent of social change.

He touched the small control pad on his chest strap. The camera lens reared up on its tentacle, then the Dull Intelligence guided it around to focus on his face. He gazed at the glassy eye, then began to dictate.

"Phousita tells me I've been asleep for three days. If that's so, then I've commanded Arif's body six days." He hesitated at that statistic. For six days he'd kept the slave atrium in command mode. Without respite. Never letting Arif assert his own will. Actually denying him existence.

Six days.

"Love and Nature," he whispered. "I would never have done that to the animals on Summer House."

The camera stared blankly. His gaze cut away. He glanced at the cabin door, then wandered out to the living room in search of Phousita.

She emerged from the kitchen, carrying a tray that held a huge, steaming platter. A sweet, spicy odor filled the room. Nikko suddenly realized this body was very hungry. But Phousita had already known that. He felt a sudden flash of anger at the way she'd anticipated him.

She set the platter on a low table. "The ship's kitchen has made food for you. Come eat. You must care for Arif's body."

"I had no choice, you know," he told her defiantly. "It was the only way I could get you out of the Spill."

She glanced at him, her gaze softly chiding. Even Phousita knew that it was possible to ride an animal without being in command mode; that it was possible to occupy an atrium only as an observer. "Please eat."

He glared at her, stubborn as a child, refusing what he really wanted. "What happened to Sandor?" he demanded.

"He's with me." She knelt beside the table, across from the platter of food. Her hands lay palm up in her lap, one nested in the other. The tiny glands shone like drops of water.

"What do you mean he's with you? Did they execute him?"

"Yes. But I contain him, like a seed."

"His pattern?"

She nodded. "There is a way to reduce the information of a man into a long, knotted string."

"Condensed data. Can you really do that?" *Could one tiny cell contain all the information necessary to construct a human being?* That was the myth he lived by. He swallowed hard. "Can you restore him?"

"I don't know yet." Her gaze shifted minutely, as if

he'd touched a sore point. "Come eat. You must care
for Arif's body."

Arif's body. She wouldn't let him forget it.

He sat down on the carpet. She'd brought him
diced white meat laden with oils and spices, served in
a papaya shell, with fruits all around. He picked up the
chopsticks and began eating.

The flavor seemed to explode in his mouth: lus-
cious fats; protein-laden meat. As he ate he watched
Phousita. She sat beside him, her eyes demurely downcast. But she would glance at him occasionally from
under her long lashes, with an inquiring look, as if to
ask *Was the food good? Was everything all right?*

He'd come to know her on the long ride up the elevator. She was a precious thing. So sweet. So pretty.
Yet she made him nervous. He was afraid of her.

Not because she held the talents of Bohr's Maker in
her hands—though he might have to reevaluate his attitude there. She'd just shown him she could be a tyrant like any other individual, sending him into sleep
for three days to teach him what it was like to be *controlled*.

Or had she only sought relief for Arif? The solace of
sleep. Kindness glistened like water in her hands.

Yet he feared her. Because despite her pliable, inoffensive nature, she still held him to account for what he
was doing to Arif.

He took another bite of chicken, but it didn't taste
so good anymore.

The situation couldn't be helped, he told himself. It
was him or Arif. He had nowhere else to go. If he tried
to move through the net, Kirstin's filters would trap
him.

But Phousita was there with him, her sympathetic
gaze grazing him like a soft ray of solar radiation, which
felt warm and good in the moment, but would inevitably develop into a burn.

He laid the chopsticks down on the table. His belly felt mildly nauseous.

"*Tuan?*" Phousita asked in concern.

He stared at his hands. *Arif's* hands. To be helpless was a horrible fate.

"Too much of my life I've used people," he told her. "It's an old habit. I excused myself on the grounds that I was a dying man. I had to do what was necessary to survive, you see?"

She only gazed at him. She didn't even nod. But he knew she understood. She understood everything. She told him: "I'm making a home for you, *tuan.* Here in my head. You'll be able to be yourself there."

He nodded. She'd told him this before. She'd started a Commonwealth atrium growing in her head. He would inhabit it, and he would feel real. But he would not *be* real. He was dead. "How long until it's ready?"

Her gaze slid away guiltily. "Several more days, I think."

"Arif won't be able to survive me that long, will he?"

"He will, Ghost-Nikko. If you let him go."

Arif was being slowly crushed out of existence by Nikko's dominating presence. Even if he survived, he would not be sane after such a long time as a prisoner in his own body.

Nikko let a shaky breath slide out of his lungs. *Arif's* lungs. "All right," he said. "I'll let him go."

He instructed the atrium to disengage command mode. Control slid away from him. It was a peculiar sensation. He'd half expected to feel divorced from his body, but no. Its physical presence continued unchanged. He felt everything as he had before. The input remained just the same. But he could no longer output his own will to the apparatus of this body. It no longer reflected his emotions. He could not speak or blink or scratch. It was a terrifying sensation.

He almost seized command mode back again. But he refrained. Arif had felt this way for days. *For days.* Love and Nature.

Disorder seemed to sweep across him as he thought about it. So many days. How could he have done this to any man?

The body began to stir. Its heart began to race. All the muscles seemed to tense at once and then Arif screamed: a long, long roar of agony. Love and Nature.

Abruptly, he lunged at Phousita. He grabbed her by the hair, struck her viciously across the face, berating her savagely in a language Nikko did not understand.

Nikko plunged back into command mode. The body froze, its lungs heaving in exertion. "Listen to me!" Nikko bellowed, knowing that Arif would hear and understand him. "I am still here. I have not gone away.

"I am haunting you.

"Move against Phousita like that and I will enslave you again. And I will never let you go. Never."

Phousita stared up at him from the floor, wide-eyed, a bruise darkening her cheek. "Please let him go, Ghost-Nikko."

"I won't let him hurt you."

She nodded. "Just please let him go."

Despair was difficult to avoid. Nikko felt himself caught in a nebulous existence. He had no way to interact with the world. He was chained to Arif, yes. The slave atrium forced him to experience every move Arif made, every breath, every itch, every time he took a shit. Everything. Unremittingly.

But he couldn't manifest as a fully realized ghost—the stunted slave atrium didn't allow for that.

He couldn't divorce himself from Arif's senses—the atrium wouldn't permit that either.

He could not sleep—not even when Arif slept. Those were the worst times. He could see nothing then. Behind Arif's closed eyes the world was endlessly dark. All he could do was listen to Arif breathe, until the slow, drawing, hesitating grumble of air in and out of lungs he could not command threatened to drive him from the atrium.

But he couldn't leave the atrium. There was no place to go but into the net, and that would be deadly. All the data Gates would be set to filter his pattern. Kirstin would pluck him out of the lightspeed transfer of data and erase him. Or worse, hold him in a prisoner plexus, jacketed by a program that would not let him write his own destination.

So he was trapped in a hyperconscious hell.

Arif was alone in the living room. Phousita had gone into the bathroom to shower. They'd been in the ship two weeks. Arif was much calmer now, calculating. He lounged on the carpet, his gaze locked on the smooth ceiling. Nikko experienced with him the sensations of his body. It was changing. Phousita must have touched him, because the livid yellow glow of his clown face had faded. His cheeks weren't so prominent. His huge, hooked nose had begun to recede. Nikko was aware of all this. But he had no access to Arif's thoughts.

"Can you hear me?" Arif said, in a gruff, unforgiving voice.

Phousita was out of the room.

"Can you hear me, Ghost-Nikko? When my first master sent ghosts to enslave me, they would talk to me sometimes. Can you?"

Nikko thought about it. After ceding control of this body he'd felt helpless. But the slave atrium must have functioned, at least in part, as a voyeur's habitat. It would make sense to have equipped it with at least this level of communication. He explored the system, and shortly, found a voice link.

Like this? he asked.

"That's right," Arif said. "I can hear you." He chuckled darkly. "Do you like this body?"

Nikko felt repulsed by the question. *Not much*, he growled.

"No? My master's clients paid a lot to experience this body. But then, they were always fascinated with freaks."

You're beginning to heal, Nikko pointed out, in an effort to be friendly.

Arif overlooked it. "You being a freak yourself," he said, "maybe it's not so interesting to you."

Nikko's patience was never more than a veneer. *What do you want, Arif?*

"You owe me. I got you out of the Spill."

Ha. I got you out.

"Then *you* are my new master."

The accusation stung with truth. Nikko denied it anyway. *No!*

"I am not your slave?"

Of course not. He found the direction of this conversation excruciating. He didn't want to think about where he was or what he had done to Arif. What he was still doing. Love and Nature. To be haunted by an unwanted ghost, to have your every action, your every move surveilled by someone you *loathed*. It was intolerable.

Arif chuckled. "You need me to survive, don't you, Ghost-Nikko?"

Grudgingly, he admitted it. *Yes.*

"Then you owe me."

In the equation of their relationship, Nikko knew he did owe something. *What do you want from me?*

"Teach me about your world. I want to know everything you know."

Nikko reacted with open surprise. *Do you?*

"Of course, Ghost-Nikko. Even with such a fine master as you, I don't enjoy being a slave."

• • •

They started with the ship's systems. Nikko withheld the command codes that would permit a change to be entered into the ship's navigation system. But he taught Arif how to use the console to access the Commonwealth net. *If you had a legal atrium, you wouldn't need the console*, Nikko told him.

"Then I could throw you out, couldn't I?"

I'll go as soon as Phousita's ready to take me.

"Think of another plan, Ghost-man," Arif warned. "She's not for you. I won't have you fuckin' her in dreamland."

Anger was a difficult emotion to maintain without the physical expression of a body. But Nikko managed it anyway. *You're the slave, Arif. Not me. I'll leave you whenever I please.*

"Not for Phousita. You won't be curling up inside of her while I'm alive."

Think you can stop it? You're not her master.

"You say that? You don't know her at all."

It went on like that a lot. They were two rats gnawing at each other in an empty cage. It was horrible.

But it was better than the helpless isolation he might have had. And by teaching Arif, he bought himself access to the data net.

After the Congressional hearing, news of the Bohr Maker's escape had gone public. It had become a favorite subject of talk shows. People claimed they were frightened, but most grinned when they said it, as if they were caught up in the giddy hysteria of an interactive horror flick and not dealing with reality at all. Maybe life in the Commonwealth was too secure.

Phousita sat with Arif, watching the shows in her quiet, patient way. She seemed tired most of the time. She didn't say much, and she wouldn't let Arif move on her in a sexual way—much to Nikko's relief.

Days passed, and they drew nearer to Summer House. Arif began to look like a real man. As the goon's mask faded, his true face emerged: a smooth, powerful

visage, bisected by the harsh ridge of his nose, shad-
owed by heavy brows. A sparse black beard sprouted on
his chin. Nikko convinced him to record the slow transition on the camera pack.

Phousita was changing too. Day by day she grew
taller. Already her head reached Arif's chest. Kirstin,
Nikko thought, would be pleased at this surfeit of nor-
malcy.

They were four days out of Summer House when
Phousita made her announcement. She and Arif had
just finished dinner. Now they were lounging on the
soft carpets, watching an Asian medieval drama that
was playing on the net. Arif had his head pillowed in
her lap. She looked down at him, and spoke suddenly,
without preamble. "My atrium is ready. I can take
Ghost-Nikko from you now."

Arif looked up at her. Nikko could feel the sudden
tension in his body. "No."

One word. Phousita's lips started to tremble.

Arif raised his head. His hard fingers pressed against
her throat. "If you say the address, I'll tear your tongue
out," he warned her. "Nikko is not going to have you."

"But it's best, Arif. It's torture for him to be with
you. He has no body. But he'll be able to feel real if
he's with me." She moved her hands toward his face.
The glands on her hands glistened in the low light.

Arif sprang away from her with feral speed. "Don't
touch me with your spells," he warned.

Her hands closed into fists. She crouched in front of
him, a spark of anger in her eyes. Nikko watched it all,
debating with himself. He wanted to slip into command
mode; to scream at Phousita, demand that she tell him
the address so he could come to her now. But that
would enrage Arif.

Arif glared down at Phousita. "Stupid country girl.
You think you don't want me anymore. You'd rather be
fucking Nikko. Or that dead boy I found for you in the

river. New gods and heroes for your bed. Queen of witches. You'll have to kill me first."

Her anger burned like a black fire in her eyes. "Like I killed our children?"

He sprang into the air. His leg shot out. The ball of his foot struck her cheek a terrible blow. Her head snapped back and she crumpled to the carpet. "Queen of witches!" he screamed at her. "You killed all of us with your spells!"

Nikko tried to slip into command mode. Tried again, but he couldn't find the proper path.

It was gone.

Arif seemed suddenly aware of his efforts. His body went still, his head cocked as if listening. "Ghost-Nikko?" he asked in a soft, dangerous voice. "Aren't you going to stop me from beating her?"

Phousita lay motionless on the floor. Nikko tried again for command, but the mode no longer existed. Arif's atrium had changed. Phousita had given him his freedom.

Arif seemed to realize this in the same moment as Nikko. His cheeks stretched as a grin spread across his face. "Ghost-Nikko, the Queen of witches has given me a rich man's atrium. Now I'm free—to throw you out. Go now. Or I will erase you."

You bastard. You can't go on treating her like this—

"Get out of my head!" Arif roared. "Get out now! Right now! Or I'll wipe you out of existence."

There was no sanctuary in the net. Kirstin would be waiting for him there. *You goon-faced bastard!*

"Go!"

He had no choice. He addressed himself to Fox, at Summer House—though he had no expectation of actually arriving there.

He downloaded.

CHAPTER

19

"Get up, Phousita! Get up!" Arif screamed. His voice seemed to come to her from the other side of distant mountains, muted thunder rolling in from over the horizon to fill the air above this forested valley with a gloom so thick it threatened to bow the treetops.

Phousita huddled between the knees of a monstrous tree, its surface roots enclosing her like walls. She was naked, soaked and shaking. Her own disembodied voice wailed far above her head, haunting the rain-soaked canopy. The treetops tossed in storm winds.

Too much! She'd tried to do too much. There were limits to everything, even the power of the evil sorcerer.

"Get up!" Arif's distant, monstrous voice continued to demand. "Come back to me. Please. I need you."

She'd tried to divide her attention between too many tasks. She'd set herself to healing Arif's atrium and face. She'd set her own body back on its natural course of growth, enhancing it with an atrium of her own design that went far beyond the pattern laid down by the Commonwealth. She'd filled up the atrium with this forest world synthesized from her borrowed memories of Summer House—and then she'd set herself to reconstructing a ghost of Sandor from the knotted string of data that pretended to describe him.

It had been too much.

Sometimes in the Spill there would be only a handful of rice for the evening meal. Phousita would divide it. Everybody got a taste; nobody got enough to matter.

Someone touched her cheek. She flinched. Sandor crouched beside her, the whites of his eyes reflecting his natural horror. He'd tried to warn her she was going too far. A Commonwealth atrium could support one ghost in good detail, or two, if resolution and verisimilitude were sacrificed. Phousita had set herself to constructing an atrium that could contain three: herself, Sandor, and Nikko. Her mind had been fixed on the effort of construction for so long, so intently, that she'd essentially forgotten Arif. She'd wanted to forget him. She'd been so tired of his anger, his latent violence.

Sandor brushed his rain-chilled lips against her forehead. "I'm sorry, Phousita. I should have let you go. I'm sorry. It was my fault."

"*No.*"

His hand slipped between her legs. His fingers swiped at the threads of sticky semen he'd left there, as if he could remove that evidence of himself, recover it, change what had happened. But to change the past was beyond anyone's power.

"I didn't want to leave you!" she cried. "I didn't want to leave you."

Shattered. Shattered. She'd given all but a veneer of her attention to Sandor, his body and hers, illusory ghosts tangled in mock-reality. He'd wanted it so much. Just once more, he'd begged her. Just once more, before Nikko comes, while we're still alone.

But something had told her to be afraid. She'd held

Sandor tighter, but she'd let a wisp of herself go, a breath of mist drifting up out of the forest in search of her other self—

—where she sat cross-legged on the carpet of the living room, her hands tenderly stroking Arif's hair as he lay with his head pillowed in her lap, watching a medieval Asian drama. She didn't want to be here. His presence cut her like an accusation, a reminder of the children she'd lost for him. She didn't want to spend any time at all with him. So she spoke quickly, without thought, wanting only to return to Sandor and screw, screw, screw, forever seeking the orgasmic ecstacy that enclosed her like a swaddling cloth, insulating her from the bitter, bitter world. "My atrium is ready," she said without preamble. "I can take Ghost-Nikko from you now."

"Phousita!" Sandor said. His hands on her shoulders, his fingers pressing painfully into her flesh. She gazed up into his deep blue eyes, wanting to wrap herself in their color, so clean, like a twilight sky at the end of a rainy day when all the pollutants had been washed out of the air.

Her hand knotted into a fist. She pounded her thigh in impotent anger. "How can you come to me?" she cried. "How can you bear to look at me? I killed your brother. I was too slow. Too stupid. I killed him."

She wrenched away from him. But he tackled her before she'd gone a step, rolling her down into the humus, her back pressed against the spongy, rotting layers of decay, the feet of a hundred wriggling insects tramping across her skin. Rain fell in her eyes. "But I love you," he said.

It was too much. She dissolved in his arms, rising up out of the forest in a drifting pillar of mist.

Her eyes were closed, but she could feel the gravity of Arif beside her. He raised her up, cradling her in his sinewy arms, rocking her like a baby, sobbing over her.

Her head throbbed where he'd kicked her. She sent tiny servants to ease the pain and a moment later her eyes fluttered, focused.

"Phousita," he sighed. His relief stung. She couldn't meet his eyes, so she looked away.

Queen of witches.

"I'm sorry," he whispered. "I'm sorry." Maybe he really was. "You're all I have left." Again, that sense of latent accusation. Curtains of fire seemed to blaze across the field of her vision. "We don't need Nikko," he said.

She flinched.

He held her tighter. "Forgive me," he begged. "I'd be lost without you. Don't leave me. Don't ever leave me alone."

She felt smothered by his touch; his need. It felt mechanical, impersonal. He wore her like clothing; a utilitarian garb to keep the sun from burning his skin. He didn't need *her;* only her talents, the thin comfort she could offer him. "What am I to you?" she demanded.

He didn't hesitate. "You belong to me. You are mine."

The despised object of his desire. A talisman he'd held close on dark nights in the Spill when she'd been able to offer him the faith he lacked. "You don't want me," she told him. "You want what I have. And that's all right. I'm happy to give it to you. I can do that now."

He drew back, the handsome lines of his renewed face reflecting a sudden wariness. She noticed that his eyes were a little violet still. She told him: "Sandor warned me that the spirit of the evil sorcerer was dangerous. Nikko said the same thing. But we're far beyond the reach of the cops now."

They were in a tiny room on a tiny vessel that sped at unimaginable speeds across a great abyss of utter emptiness hostile to all natural life. Beyond the walls of this ship there was *nothing* for miles so numerous they could be comprehended only in dreams.

"If you want to take the spirit of the sorcerer into your own body, I can give it to you. You can heal yourself, Arif. You won't need to keep me anymore."

"It's not like that," he objected, his voice pained.

But she was tired, irritable, insistent. "Do you want it?"

His arms shook as he held her, but he nodded.

So she began to weave a spell between her hands that would pass the seed of the sorcerer to Arif.

"But it's not that easy. It can't be."

She sat up, startled by the sudden presence of a stranger. He crouched on the carpet, not an arm's reach away, a small, lean man, with a breathtakingly precipitous forehead and astonishingly fair skin. His fashion was European, his white-blond hair arranged neatly about his shoulders.

"What is it?" Arif hissed.

"A ghost," Phousita whispered. Then louder: "You are a ghost?"

"Yes, it's true. I'm a ghost," the gentleman acknowledged. His lips twisted in an uncertain little smile that was quickly washed away by a sigh. "I've had a world of trouble getting in touch with you. I almost gave it up as hopeless, if you want to know the truth. Then I remembered Zeke Choy. It would be natural for you to try to copy his atrium, I thought. Even duplicate it down to the address. And so you did ... duplicate the address, that is. But you've designed your own atrium, haven't you? An awfully complex one. Two levels of synthetic reality. Very impressive."

"Who are you?" Phousita asked. Her hands still prepared the spell for Arif. The task divided her attention.

"Ah, forgive me." A red blush crept across the stranger's cheeks. "I'm Leander Bohr. I guess I'm responsible for your troubles in a rather roundabout way. I designed the Maker, you see. Though I hadn't intended it for general use."

"You're the evil sorcerer?" she asked, incredulous.

"Is that what they're calling me now?" He laughed nervously. "Seriously. Don't give away the Maker. Not until we've had a chance to talk. I thought you might come visit me. Soonest, you understand? I wouldn't want to give away your position to the police, but if I have to, I will. This is my address. Do come, please. Good-bye." He vanished as abruptly as he had appeared.

Fear set in as soon as the sorcerer was gone. Phousita stared at the soft, blank face of the carpet. Her hands began to shake, and she dropped the spell she'd been trying to weave. It dissolved into harmless traces. Numbly, she communed with her atrium, instructing it to withdraw her soul from her body in the way Sandor had explained.

Arif plucked at her arm. "What is it?" he hissed. "What have you seen?"

She turned to look at him, her eyes wide with dread. "The evil sorcerer has summoned me."

Arif swallowed hard. "You aren't going to him, are you? You can't go. You know he only wants to steal his spirit back. Then he'll destroy you."

Phousita feared this. She didn't want to lose her soul. And yet Sandor had carefully explained that the spirit now forming in her atrium wasn't really her soul at all, but only an image of herself, something akin to the image she might see in a mirror. Perhaps. Yet she knew from the old woman's teachings that the soul wandered free of the body in dreams. . . .

She shook her head. She knew so very little. With all that she'd learned, with all that had been revealed to her, she still knew almost nothing. Worse, what she knew was in pieces, and she didn't understand how to fit them together. "I have to go," she insisted. "The sorcerer has summoned me."

In the old woman's stories the world had always been strictly divided between gods and human beings. The one to command and challenge and torment. The other to struggle, to obey. Phousita was a minor woman, at best. The evil sorcerer though: she suspected he might dwell on the other side of the divide. How could she not obey him?

"He said he would tell the police where we are, if I didn't go to him."

"Can the police still reach us?"

"I don't know."

Arif looked away. "Be careful," he said. "Don't let him—"

"Oh, you came. Oh good. I didn't want to scare you."

It was the sorcerer who spoke. Phousita blinked at him in confusion. Just a moment ago— But no. Though it seemed as if no time had passed, somehow she knew that many hours had gone by since her spirit had left Arif. How did she know that? She couldn't say. Some new sense. A tiny servant . . .

The sorcerer stood before her, clasping and unclasping his hands, his bright blue eyes seeming anxious as if he wanted her to speak.

They were in a courtyard. There were walls of white limestone on three sides nearly obscured by a lush garden. The air was heavy with the scent of flowers. Dark wooden doors led through one of the walls, presumably into a building. A fountain bubbled merrily under a large frangipani tree. The courtyard was U-shaped. It opened onto a view of a barren, jumbled slope of cold black lava that fell away at a steep angle until far below the slope vanished abruptly as if cut off by a knife. And where there should have been something beyond that—a valley or mountain, an ocean or a desert plain—to meet the jagged, lifeless slope, there was only a sea of stars. And overhead a great round moon loomed, like a huge sea as blue as the sorcerer's eyes. Phousita gasped in fear, expecting it to pour down upon them at any moment. But for now, it held.

Shivering, she looked once again at the sorcerer.

"This is my home," he said softly. (Almost shyly, she realized with a start.) "It's not real, of course. But then you must have guessed that. No atmosphere on a rock like this, is there? Shouldn't be, anyway. But since my home is a fiction, I can furnish it with fictional elements. Everything you see is a ghost, including me."

Phousita calmly rearranged the folds of her sarong as she weighed the implications of this confession. She understood the structure of this place. It was very similar to her own inner world. Too simple for a god. Could that mean the sorcerer was only human? Drawing a deep breath, she decided to find out. "*Tuan*, you have summoned me, and I have come. But could you please tell me, so that I might offer you the proper respect, are you a god? And is this the spirit world?"

The evil sorcerer laughed, but only for a second. Then he seemed to grow thoughtful. "I'm not a god, no," he said. "I'm just the ghost of a man called Leander Bohr. He died quite a long time ago, you see, and I'm all that's left of him. But is this the spirit world? I never thought of it that way before, but I like that idea, I do. Certainly the physical basis of this existence is very small. And there's always room for a new mythology, isn't there? The spirit world. Yes, I like that very much."

Phousita frowned at this answer. Did he toy with her? It was too much to think that one as learned as this sorcerer might be ignorant of the structure of the world and his station in it. The spirit world, the world of people: they were two parts of a whole, a fundamental that ran through every tale the old woman had ever spun. She studied this Leander Bohr thoughtfully. Had some god stripped him of this most essential knowledge? Oddly, she began to feel a bit sorry for him.

"*Tuan*," she asked, when the silence had grown long and she sensed he waited for her to speak. "Are you that which inhabits me?"

He shook his head. "No. That's a thing I made. You've kept it to yourself, haven't you?"

"Yes, *tuan*."

"Good. Good." He smiled: shy and charming.

She wasn't lulled by his expression. She knew she'd trespassed on his interest. He *must* want the spirit back. Why else would he have summoned her?

His smile faded. He seemed confused; concerned. "You mustn't give it away to anyone else, you know. It would be very dangerous. You wouldn't want to be responsible for that."

His warning seemed to conjure bright waves of fire: a sea of flame that rolled in and surrounded her, licked her legs, kissed her skirt. She squeezed her eyes shut, fighting the vision.

"The Maker's brought you nothing but terrible pain," Leander said, his voice gentle, persuasive. "I know you'd never wish that on another."

She stiffened. Anger edged her thoughts as she began to see beyond his words. Yes, she'd trespassed on his interests. But the spirit was hers now! It had come to her. It was a gift, not a curse, and she would share it out as she liked.

She met his gaze. "I won't give it back to you. My people need this thing."

That startled him. "Your people?"

His doubt seemed to fuel the flames. They leapt again on the edge of her vision. But her anger quickly chased them back. *Did he believe she had no people left?*

"My people!" she shouted in open defiance. Her finger thumped hard against her breast. "The people of the Spill. I will share what I have with every one of them."

His eyes widened in sudden panic. "You can't mean that!" he squeaked. "You can't meant to release the Maker on Earth."

"But why not?" Her frustration twisted like a wire through her voice. "With this spirit, every person would be able to heal his own life. If that could happen, then naturally the world would be well too."

He shook his head, his gaze reflecting deep fear. "Other people aren't like you, Phousita. They don't want to be healed. They want to be more than human. They want to remake the world. They will murder the spirit of our Mother. You must destroy the Maker. I have to ask you to destroy it."

Her lips pressed together in a bitter line. "I cannot do that, *tuan.*"

She would not betray Arif and Sandor, her vanished children, everyone she'd ever known who might benefit from this thing, even the memory of the old woman, just to satisfy this man. Just because he didn't want to share his talents? He said he wasn't a god . . . yet he acted like one. She told him so: "I've heard that gods are stingy with their gifts, that they enjoy the suffering of the people . . . it makes their own lives more sweet."

"Ah." He turned half away, to stare dejectedly at a fruit tree laden with huge, colorful bats. "Well, at least now you know my wishes. Perhaps you can be persuaded, I don't know."

"Will you torture me?" Phousita asked.

"Oh. I never—I—" His moon-white skin blushed a shy pink and he spoke as if his tongue had suddenly grown thick and clumsy. "Yes. Yes, it may come to that. You can't leave until I let you go, and you can't erase yourself, you know. I've edited your persona that way. Bit of a fascist, I guess. So sorry."

Oddly, Phousita wasn't afraid anymore. How could she be? Of this man who seemed like a shy and demure little boy and not a great sorcerer at all. Perhaps this was only a guise he wore to put her off her guard. That would be a familiar ruse; the old woman had told her countless tales in which demons masqueraded as friends. So she held on to her suspicions, even while she tried to approach him. "You don't seem evil," she said.

His gaze shifted nervously, never meeting hers. "Don't be too confident of that. I'm a coward myself, but I can command Makers to do the dirty work."

"Why do you want to destroy this spirit you've made?"

"Because if it becomes naturalized, it will destroy our past." He immediately suppressed her first objection. "Oh, not our memory of the past," he snapped. "Of course the Maker remembers everything. That's one of its functions. But it will destroy our *connection* with the past. The biological continuum. The billions of years of change, the billions of deaths of human and nonhuman entities, the constant, unconscious improvisation of a trillion genetic lines. The body of our Mother will be laid to waste. After the Maker there will be no place left for chance and no history."

Phousita turned away in disgust. This man made no sense. He had to be a man. No god could be so foolish.

"You see the Maker as a savior," he said, speaking from behind her. "And I commend you for that. I don't condemn you at all. You've seen horrible sufferings, I know, and it's a credit to you that you want to end them. But the Maker's a destroyer, not a savior. It will preserve the individual, but not the continuum of life."

The continuum. What was that but pain passed from one generation to the next? She turned on him suddenly, anger flaring sharply from her tongue. "No one suffers in the Commonwealth—"

"Fah! The Commonwealth is not important. *You* are important. You are real. The Spill is important. And so is every other place that refuses the insured existence of the Commonwealth. Life needs risk. It needs uncertainty. Or it becomes passive; vulnerable."

Phousita forced her hands to her side. Her gaze wandered out across the starry sea while she drew three calming breaths. Somewhere, a frog began to softly call. "You live alone, don't you?" Phousita asked at last.

The sorcerer backed off a step; cleared his throat as if she'd brought up something unpleasant. "Well, I, uh, yes, I do."

Phousita scowled her contempt. "Forgive me, *tuan*, for my stupid question. You have already told me you are a ghost. And ghosts don't live at all. Do they?"

His fingers began to tremble against his thigh. "Not in the way you mean, of course—"

"Of course. I didn't mean to distress you. I am a stupid woman."

"Stop it, please."

"Yes, of course, *tuan*. But tell me something first, if you can. After you've tortured me, and persuaded me to exorcise the sorcerer's evil spirit— Oh, oh, pardon me for my clumsy tongue. After you've rid me of the *Maker*— (How foolish of me to think of it as your spirit!) What will you do? Will you remain in this empty world, and not-live in your nonlife and not love and not be horrified at death? *Tuan*, who are you to command the world?"

At first he offered no answer. He stood before her, eyes downcast, his toe tracing circles upon the ground. Then a parrot squawked in the tree overhead. He looked up at it and waved his hand. It fell silent as he met her gaze. "I made this thing, Phousita. It's my responsibility, my *fault*. I should have destroyed it long ago, but I couldn't get to it. So I thought it was safe. Then that damned Nikko Jiang-Tibayan turned it loose."

Her heart seemed to stop cold in her chest. She didn't want to ask him, she didn't want to be beholden to him, but she had to know. "Nikko? Do you know of him?"

He looked at her in surprise and sudden suspicion. "Do you?"

"He's dead," she said.

"Yes."

From his face, she knew it didn't matter to him. She stomped her foot in anger. What acquaintance did this man have with death that he could think it led to anything better than despair?

He seemed to hear her thoughts. He stepped closer to her, though he had enough respect not to touch her. "I'm not evil, Phousita. I'm not cruel and I am not heartless. I've been hungry too. I had three sisters. Plague took them all within a month of birth. My mother abandoned me when a trick offered her a ride over the border. I lived with my best friend until his mother discovered I had a little talent with molecular design and then *she* sold me to a clan of criminals. *I know how horrible the world can be.*"

"Then why won't you change it?" she pleaded.

"The world is changing itself. I know the agony. I feel it every day. But every parent knows a child must be allowed to suffer."

"So much that the child never grows up?"

"The world will go on, one way or another."

Her head jerked up. "Oh yes! The Commonwealth will see to that! We still have things they want."

"So long as they leave your natural cities alone."

"You *are* heartless."

He nodded reluctant agreement. "I suppose you're right. You put an honest name on everything. That's refreshing, and I won't insult you by pretending to less. I must torture you now."

Her heart thundered, but she didn't let it show. She wondered if he knew anyway. Did he spy on her mind? "What will you do?" she asked.

"I will rewrite your ghost and infect you with part of myself. My beliefs and my convictions will become yours. It's the same result I've tried to achieve today through persuasion, though obviously I've failed miserably at that. You will carry these convictions home to your original and you'll act on them in the best manner you can."

"You will possess me."

"Yes."

"You *are* evil."

"I never thought so before, but now, well . . . you may be right."

CHAPTER

20

K irstin started her investigation anew after the
news of the Bohr Maker's escape became public.
There had been some calls for her resignation
after the Congressional hearing, but the complainants
were quickly hushed. Her reputation for ruthless per-
sistence still made her the favorite candidate to find the
Maker.

Allende knew that, and kept his distance. But he
still dogged the investigation. As Director of Internal
Security, it was his job to investigate cops. His role in
the case had begun with the defection of Jensen Van
Ness and should have ended there. But he'd hung on,
investigating the cops who investigated the case, developing a report that would ostensibly explain why the
Maker was still missing. He watched Kirstin. He reported to Congress that the Chief of Police had mishan-
dled the case. He sought to wound her. But she had the
agility to turn his assaults to her own advantage.

Allende had engineered her appearance in Congress. But Kirstin had benefited from the publicity. No

longer did she need to conduct a subtle investigation. After the hearings, she commenced a series of massive data searches, inspecting every form of surveillance recorded since the original theft.

So much information was transcribed in the Commonwealth that a known fact could disappear as easily into the sea of data as an unrecorded fact could vanish into the past. Nevertheless, Kirstin commenced her investigation. Never before had such a thorough survey of records been contemplated. As the weeks passed and the monumental procedure ground on, the news feeds began to mock it as "the slow eye of God."

Kirstin continued to pursue her quarry.

DI's were instructed to review all visual records collected at the Gates, searching for:

(1) an optical identification of Phousita and Arif

(2) an optical identification of all individuals approximately the body sizes of Phousita and Arif.

The first target achieved zero results. The second achieved three hundred thousand in the first week, each requiring a secondary evaluation.

A human investigator was assigned the task of developing a projection of what Arif would look like if his face were healed. Another human investigator was given the objective of developing a psychological profile of Phousita that would predict how she might change her physical appearance. Kirstin regarded this assignment as the ultimate soft science. Little more than witchcraft, really. She had no faith in it. It produced no usable results.

Another DI checked scents recorded at the Gates and on the Highway. Another investigator developed a projection of the possible evolutionary scenarios of Phousita's and Arif's changing scent profiles. The DI was instructed to search for those, as well. Again, no results.

Another DI was given the task of performing background checks on all identity chips recorded at the

Highway Gates, to ensure that each one led back to a
real person with a verifiable history. No anomalous results.

Another DI was set the task of combing through all
the surveillance data recorded on Castle: every bit of
information pulled in by the filters, cameras, and micro-
phones set to watch over the city at the end of the elevator. Every public area and many private ones were
covered by the surveillance net and the quantity of data
collected was immense. The time needed to sort
through it was measured in days. But in the end the effort paid off, with the discovery of a single word uttered
within range of a microphone at the Castle docks:
"Phousita."

Though Nikko had written Summer House as his destination when he fled Arif's atrium, he had no expectation of actually arriving there. He knew the cops would
pick him up in transit. In all likelihood, Kirstin would
greet him herself.

So it came as no surprise when he found himself
seated across a desk from a uniformed cop, in an environment so close to weightless that he had to be on
Castle. He did feel a mild jolt when he realized the cop
was not Kirstin.

The officer scrutinized him with small, dark eyes—a
stout man with heavy hands that rested tensely against
the desk. By his uniform, a high-ranking cop, a section
commander. With a legal atrium.

For the first time in weeks, Nikko found himself
physically manifest. The sheer joy of experiencing his
own existence almost overwhelmed his rational mind.
He hardly noticed the annoying twitch in his hands.
Then his gaze met that of the hard-eyed cop and he
knew he must seek a measure of the situation. "I know
you," he said bluntly.

It was half true. He'd seen this man before. He

searched his memory for a name to match against the
face.

"It's Allende," the cop said. "I've been waiting a
long time for you to show." He looked up and down
Nikko's long blue body with an expression that wa-
vered between admiration and disgust.

"And Kirstin?" Nikko asked.

Allende smiled coldly. "You don't want to see her,
do you?"

"No."

"She's been hunting hard for you—but under a false
pattern. You see, I revised your file. Now I'm the only
one who has your true pattern." He grinned. "We can
deal with each other, I think. You have the Bohr
Maker?"

Nikko studied him, feeling his way into the situation. Was Allende looking to cross the cops? "The Bohr
Maker," Nikko said. "You want to deal for it?"

"You have it, don't you?"

Nikko leaned back in his chair and drew a careful
breath. He took a second to explore the atrium that
held him. He discovered the prisoner's jacket Allende
had written around his electronic pattern. He was
trapped here—unless Allende freed him.

"What are you prepared to offer?" Nikko asked.

"I'll open the Gates for you. You can go where you
like."

"Why?"

"Kirstin wants to destroy the Maker."

Nikko nodded, understanding. "And you don't."

"Give up our finest weapon?" Allende asked. "It's
absurd."

"I do have it," Nikko said, cherishing his blank,
blue, expressionless face—it could never betray him.
"But not with me."

"I traced your path," Allende said. "I know you
originated on a ship in the void."

"The Maker is there," Nikko agreed.

Allende's lips pulled back in a hungry expression. "Then it got past two Gates and all the filters on Castle! Incredible!"

"It is the Bohr Maker," Nikko reminded him. He leaned forward. "I can give you the ship's command codes. But the rest will be up to you."

"Then do it."

Nikko shook his head. "I want to get through the Gates first. When I'm on Summer House, I'll give you the codes."

Allende's eyes narrowed. "But Jiang-Tibayan, I don't trust you either."

Nikko nodded. He'd dealt with similar situations before. "Then I'll leave the codes here," he offered. "But electronically sealed. Jacket me with a rebound signal. When I reach the House, the signal will bounce back and release the codes."

Allende nodded slowly. "That'll do," he said. "That'll do."

Kirstin had encountered hundreds of false leads during the weeks-long data search. She no longer had the capacity to get excited when an investigator brought her the latest, not even when it was the clearly recorded name of the primary suspect: "Phousita."

But her interest grew as further investigation revealed that the name had been spoken in a concourse lobby serving (at the time) a ship belonging (through a complex trail of subsidiary corporations) to Summer House. After that it was a brief operation to call up the identities of the two passengers as recorded from their implanted chips. Not surprisingly, their documented names were meaningless; their life histories generic. But when their route was backtracked, it led to the Free Trade Zone.

A few minutes later it was discovered that Marevic Chun had issued the ship's guidance program.

Kirstin decided to visit Marevic Chun in person.

She assembled a cadre of uniformed officers to accompany her. At the last minute, Allende showed up and included himself in the party.

Marevic's home territory was high up in the Castle tower that belonged to Summer House. She rarely emerged from her suite of offices there. Naturally, by the time Kirstin had led her officers past the maze of security devices and secretaries set up to impede the progress of any outsider through the corporate grounds, Marevic had ample warning of their impending arrival. She greeted Kirstin coldly, but without surprise, from her seat behind a large wooden desk. "Chief Adair. I'd thought your investigators were through examining our corporate records."

Kirstin grinned. "No, Marevic. In fact, I've just obtained a warrant to open your personal files. You are under arrest."

Marevic's delicate face didn't change expression. "On what charge?"

"Forging identity chips."

She blinked at that. "Do you have evidence?"

"I have two individuals entirely unknown to anyone in their professed hometown."

"And what connection do they have to me?"

"You wrote their travel orders."

Nikko had half expected Allende to betray him to Kirstin. But apparently the Director of Internal Security really did have his own agenda, because when Nikko manifested again, he found himself in Fox's apartment at Summer House.

A holographic simulation of a vertical cross section of Summer House filled the center of the room. Fox stood beside it, regarding Nikko with a comical expression of mingled suspicion and astonishment.

Nikko whooped in joy, slapping his projected blue palms against the ceiling. "I made it, Dad!" His amazement at his own good fortune bubbled over in a hearty laugh. "I actually made it home!"

The past weeks had not treated Fox well. He looked considerably older. Gray streaks ran through his thinning red hair, his shoulders were stooped, and deep lines of worry tracked across his face.

"Hey Dad," Nikko said. "Things aren't as bad as you think."

Fox took one step forward. His hand came up. "Where did you come from?" he asked, in a hoarse voice that was barely more than a whisper. "When did you originate? How did you get through the Gates?"

Nikko glanced away, uneasy at the distress he saw in Fox, uncertain how to respond to it. His gaze fell on the holographic display, and lingered there, drawn in by the exquisite detail. He could make out birds flitting through the canopy of the forest, and people walking in the corridors. He glanced at Fox again. Fox wasn't paying any attention to the simulation, yet the atrium followed the changing display with no loss of resolution. How many times had Fox watched this simulation run?

He shook off the thought. He had more pressing business. "I need your help, Dad."

But his gaze was drawn back to the simulation. Something had gone wrong with it. He watched as the House deteriorated: its inner features dissolved; the forest rotted away; people disappeared. The scene unsettled Nikko. It was like looking at a time-compressed video of natural decay, except that the decaying body was that of Summer House.

Within seconds, a dark lattice appeared as corridors expanded vertically. A few seconds more, and the House had been divided into cells of varying sizes, from a few tens to hundreds of meters per side. The cells clustered into groups, separated by narrow, black-walled channels. There was a moment's pause. Then the cells split apart and spun off into the void.

"Love and Nature!" Nikko exclaimed, shaken by the destruction. "Fox, what is that?"

Fox glanced over his shoulder. His eyes opened wide in a startled expression. "Display off!" he barked. He looked back at Nikko, his brow furrowed with anger. "It's nothing," he snapped. "Just a project one of my students submitted."

Nikko didn't believe him. "It's more than that. Have you found something wrong with the House? Is it unstable?"

"No, no. The House is fine. What you saw was a survival strategy." He chewed his lip nervously. "Look, Nikko. You're a fugitive. The less you know, the better."

But Nikko's guesses were already leaping ahead. "A survival strategy? Does it have to do with the biogenesis function, then?"

Fox didn't answer, but his expression gave him away.

"It does," Nikko said. "But why destroy the House? A survival strategy?" His kisheer pulled in close around his neck. "Those were reproductive cells, weren't they?" He shook his head, incredulous. "A survival strategy, in case of disaster. That's what you're working on." He laughed in disbelief. "Do you really think the House can be *seeded*?"

Fox shrugged. He looked unhappy.

"Listen," Nikko said. "I really do need your help. There's a ship just a few days out of Summer House. Aboard, in the possession of one of the two passengers, is a physical and psychological record of Sandor. But the ship's not going to stop here. It'll pass the House and return to Castle. I have to get the passengers off before that happens. You'll help me, Dad? Won't you?"

Marevic's defensive Makers were very, very good. Also unregistered and therefore illegal. It took the police research division several hours to define their structure and develop an assault Maker that could overcome them. But after that it was easy to introduce a psychoactive drug to her system. Minutes later, she reached a state in which she could not resist answering any question put to her. She sat on a couch in an isolation chamber at police headquarters, her lawyer at her side. Her tiny mouth was turned in a foreboding frown. She wasn't at all tipsy. Merely irresistibly talkative.

Kirstin stood in the center of the room, studying her, weighing the possibility that research had missed something. Could Marevic be faking her cooperative state?

Research insisted they really had her. And they were Kirstin's people. She had to trust them.

She glanced at Allende. He stood in one corner of the room, ostensibly observing. But his gaze was fixed on the floor, while a worried frown played across his face. Kirstin's brows rose in sudden suspicion. Was he afraid Marevic might reveal something about him? She determined to study the record of this session and gauge his reactions. But for now, she sat down with her team on a couch across from Marevic.

The interrogator took that as a cue to begin. He leaned forward, his gaze fixed on Chun's face. "Marevic Chun. You're aware of the case against you. Tell us the real identities of the recipients of the false ID chips."

Marevic shuddered, and shifted in her seat. "They're nonentities within the Commonwealth," she growled. "They have no identities."

"Tell us the *names* of the recipients of the false ID chips," the interrogator said in precise, measured words.

Marevic's breathing suddenly became deep and husky as she fought to resist the biochemical urge to speak. "Phousita," she grunted. "No known last name. Arif. No known last name."

Kirstin grinned, while her officers muttered in quiet triumph.

"Phousita and Arif," the interrogator said, the only one in the room who hadn't changed expression. "Are these two presently aboard a vessel bound for Summer House?"

Marevic's hands had been lying still in her lap. Now they suddenly grasped each other, the fingers working madly. "They're bound for Gold Wing," she said, between clenched teeth.

"And is Gold Wing an on-site subsidiary of Summer House?"

Her face was turning red; her expression was furious. "Yes."

"Is Phousita or Arif presently in possession of the artifact popularly known as Bohr's Maker?"

"I don't know."

The interrogator didn't stumble. "Do you *believe* that they are presently in possession of the artifact popularly known as Bohr's Maker?"

"Yes!" The word emerged like a small explosion.

Kirstin leaned forward. "Are you aware of the location of any ghost of Nikko Jiang-Tibayan?"

"That question does not pertain to this investigation!" the lawyer protested.

But Marevic answered it anyway. "Yes."

"Admission of a felony," Kirstin said. "We're broadening the investigation."

"Not without a warrant." The lawyer rose to his feet. He stood in front of Marevic, as if he could protect her.

From his corner, Allende spoke in a deep, angry voice. "This forced interrogation is for the sole purpose of investigating Marevic Chun's involvement with the forged identify chips. If you venture beyond that specific without a warrant, Chief Adair, I will have you removed from the police force."

Kirstin felt a chill run up her spine. Allende was hiding something. She was certain of it. "Request a warrant," she instructed one of her officers.

There was silence in the room for several minutes. Then the warrant arrived simultaneously in the atriums of everyone present. The lawyer sat down again beside his client. The interrogator repeated Kirstin's question. "Marevic Chun, are you aware of the location of any ghost of Nikko Jiang-Tibayan?"

"Yes," she said again.

"What is that location?"

"An atrium."

"*Whose* atrium?"

"Arif."

"This ghost is aboard the ship that—"

Marevic's chin came up. Her eyes squeezed shut as if she'd been lanced with sudden pain.

Kirstin rose to her feet, sensing disaster. "The control codes!" she shouted. "What are the ship's control codes?"

The alphanumeric sequence emerged from Marevic's throat in forced, guttural, monosyllabic bursts. After twelve digits she collapsed against the back of the couch. Her head lolled on the cushions. Kirstin stood over her, fists clenched as she resisted an urge to slap her awake.

One of the medics skidded to her side. The lawyer tried to shove him away, but Kirstin signaled to her uniforms, and they hauled the lawyer out of the way. "Tell us what's wrong with you, Marevic," Kirstin commanded.

"I don't remember."

"Tell us your name," the medic said in a gentler voice, as he pressed a series of dermal patches against her neck.

"Marevic Chun."

"What are the ship's control codes?" Kirstin growled.

"What ship?" Her eyes were open now, fluttering.

The interrogator tapped Kirstin on the shoulder, inviting her to step back so that he could resume his job.

She cast him a scathing glance. But this was his specialty. She stepped aside.

Ignoring the lawyer's protests, the interrogator crouched in front of Marevic. "The ship we've been discussing," he said gently. "You remember it, don't you?"

Marevic slouched in her seat, a confused frown on her face. "No, I don't remember."

"How can she lie?" Kirstin demanded.

"She's poisoned herself," the medic said. He examined one of the dermal patches on her neck. "There are indications of brain tissue destruction."

"Where do you live, Marevic?" the interrogator asked.

"Ecuador."

Kirstin's teeth came together in a hard line. Marevic and Fox had lived together in Ecuador almost eighty years ago. "How old are you, Marevic?" she asked, in a voice cold with fury.

"Thirty-four."

The interrogator settled back on his heels. He looked up at Kirstin. "We can keep trying if you like, but it's fairly obvious she's induced extensive—and probably permanent—amnesia."

Kirstin's hands clenched behind her back. "Issue a warrant for her ghosts." Not that she expected to find any. Not at this late hour. But she had twelve digits of the ship's control codes. It should be possible to work out the remainder through trial and error. And once they had control of the ship, it would be a small task to program a missile to destroy it.

She glanced again at Allende. He was glaring at Marevic, his yellow teeth bared.

Fox wanted to say no. Nikko could see it in his posture. He paced back and forth across the wheat-colored carpet, shoulders bowed, hands clasped behind his back, his red hair bouncing up and down around his ears. He did not want to cross the police. But he wanted Sandor. Fox was a devoted father.

He stopped abruptly in the middle of the room and straightened his shoulders. Sweat shone on his wrinkled forehead. His eyetooth bit down so hard on the inside of his lip that Nikko was sure it must have drawn blood. "I can't act autonomously," he announced. "I'll have to get the approval of the Board of Directors."

Nikko felt the first flush of triumph. "You can sway them."

"The rescue should be as secretive as possible."

"Sure."

"I've got a scheme in mind, but it requires *you* to go out after them, in a small ship, without life support."

"Really?" Nikko found the notion both appealing and frightening. He'd never been away from Summer House. Not physically anyway. Then he remembered: "What can I do on my own? I'm a ghost."

"We can address that. I recorded your pattern, you know." His brow wrinkled uncertainly. "No. You don't know. This ghost originated before that event. . . ." He started pacing again. The sweat on his brow began to bead on the crests of thoughtful furrows.

"You're saying you can resurrect me, then?" Nikko pressed.

Fox looked put out. "The biogenesis function," he said. "Remember?"

"You preserved my code. But it'll take months to develop a physical clone."

"No. It'll only take a day and a half."

"You said a day and a half."

Fox frowned. "Maybe not that long," he admitted. "Maybe thirty hours."

"But that's impossible. It takes half a year to grow a clone in the mausoleum tanks."

"The biogenesis function involves a modular growth system. We've tested it on various animals. The assembly takes place in segments, under low temperatures.

The available work surfaces are enormous and of course the nutritional matrix is kept fully supplied." He stopped pacing again to look at Nikko. "But I'm allowing myself to be overconfident. I won't mislead you. We've never done it quite this way before. You see, after Summer House mapped your cell structure, the data was scattered in packets throughout the biogenesis function to make it harder to detect. The linking codes were highly redundant of course, and reassembling your physical structure shouldn't be a problem. Still, reality remains the only good check of a virgin system."

"Thanks for the shot of confidence, Fox. Are you going to be able to correct the nervous disorder?" He held up his trembling hands.

Fox stared at them resentfully. "You'll be exactly the same as you were when you went in. I won't introduce any modifications until you're whole again. After that . . ." He shrugged. "No point in holding back now, is there?"

"I *never* saw any point to it." He wondered for a moment if Fox would have bothered to go after the fugitive ship if Sandor had made it back to Summer House, and Nikko had been the one stranded on the robotic vessel. But that wasn't fair. Fox had preserved his pattern in defiance of the law—although at very little risk to himself. Nikko's fingers tapped against his thigh. "So tell me, Dad. If this ghost hadn't made it back here, how long would you have kept me dormant?"

Fox shrugged. "Until you were safe."

Nikko didn't like the vague feeling that answer gave him. He visualized himself, tucked away and forgotten. "And how long did you think that would be?" he pressed. "A year? Fifty years? A few hundred?"

A guarded expression slipped across Fox's face. "I hadn't worked up a projection."

"No, of course not. The cops might have been looking over your shoulder. They might have caught on. Right, Fox?"

"There's no point in snapping at me, Nikko. I'm on your side."

But Nikko hadn't had physiological responses in so long—even simulated ones—that he felt overwhelmed by them now. Bitter. Angry. Almost out of control. He could feel himself sliding into a reflexive verbal assault. "You're on my side so long as it's safe for you and the House. *That*'s how it's always been with you."

Fox gazed at him, his expression oddly calm. "I know you think I'm a coward. But you don't have children. You don't know what it's like to really be afraid."

"Right. Well you didn't fight too hard to keep me around. And now that Sandor's gone, you don't have any children at all, do you, Fox? Not anymore." The words emerged out of anger. But once spoken, they were impossible to recall.

Fox went very still. His chin came up. "It's true I could have done more for you, Nikko. I guess I probably should have. But revolutions have a way of consuming their originators. I was afraid for myself. I was afraid for the House."

"The House: that's your first child, isn't it?"

Fox didn't deny it. Instead he returned to the business at hand, as if he could eliminate the hurt by pretending it didn't exist. "I want you to download into your physical construction as soon as the brain tissue is adequate to support you. If the police suspect your ghost exists, my atrium is the first place they'll look."

CHAPTER

21

Ghosts could claim no freedom. While Summer House developed his physical clone, Nikko could do little except tag along with Fox. It was an awkward situation. They'd never been able to put up with each other's company for long. But they both tried hard to ignore the history between them while Fox went about designing the craft that would rendezvous with Phousita's ship. Nikko looked over his shoulder, and offered suggestions when he could. His ghost still imitated the tremors that had afflicted his now-vanished body, reminding him of why he'd gone after the Bohr Maker in the first place.

Shortly before the scheduled departure they took the elevator up through the core of the tether to the central docking ring. The local police captain was there. But he worked for Fox now, assigned to clear the area of any police Makers.

With Fox, Nikko examined the little ship. It was a jury-rigged vessel, composed of three coffins from the mausoleum, set end to end and attached to a fusion motor that Nikko would control through his atrium. Smart glue knit the molecular structures of each piece to the next. The craft would be secured with a temporary bond to the side of a robotic cargo vessel that had been held back in port for a day. It would remain coupled to the cargo ship for the taxi out to the magnetic launch tube and the subsequent burst of acceleration. After that, the bonding agent would wither, and Nikko would be on his own.

It was a dizzying sensation to see his inert body being loaded into the lead coffin. He watched as a pink-tinged, semitransparent acceleration gel was hosed in on all sides. A quick system check followed, confirming that all was well. Then the lid was closed and sealed.

Fox said: "I'm still working on the Maker that was used to sabotage your atrium."

Nikko had almost forgotten about that; it seemed so long ago. "You haven't cracked it?"

"It was elusive. Very sophisticated. Self-protective. The original sample is long gone, of course. I'm trying to deduce its structure from environmental clues."

One of the workers approached Fox. "We're done here. Time for Nikko to download—if he still wants to go." Only a handful of Fox's assistants were aware of Nikko's return. They seemed ambivalent about the situation—exhibiting an underlying resentment because they'd compromised themselves with the police, but at the same time enjoying their act of defiance. That was Summer House: strong on revolutionary talk, uneasy with action.

"Tell him I won't be backing out," Nikko said. "Tell him, if he's getting nervous, he can always reformat his memories and forget I ever happened."

Fox smiled uncomfortably. "Take care, Nikko."

"Sure, Dad."

Was that all they could find to say? The tension between them weighed in multiple G's, but it was too late to change that now. Nikko wrote himself to his home address.

There was a moment of blankness, and then a growing, vague awareness of the cramped feel of his body, the slow breath in and out of his lungs, the claustrophobic press of the acceleration gel that stole any possible movement from his limbs.

He remembered his last living moments on Summer House, when Kirstin had come to visit him. He remembered his weeks with Phousita. So the ghost had already assimilated. He must have been unconscious for a while. But peering out the transparent cover of the coffin, he could still see the lights of the loading bay.

His heart began to beat faster. He'd never ventured beyond the outer walls of Summer House. He knew absolutely nothing about boarding a reluctant ship.

Fox rapped on the transparent lid. *Okay?* his silent lips asked. Nikko nodded. From this point on there would be no radio communication.

As if to enforce his isolation, his kisheer responded to the declining level of O_2 in the coffin by sliding past the restrictive gel to fuse with the papillae of his mouth, nose, and ears. No more atmosphere for him. He would breathe through the kisheer until he reached the target ship, or until he died.

Fox withdrew. The coffin shook as a tractor engaged. A pump hummed, then gradually faded into silence. A gentle nudge of acceleration from the tractor sent the ship drifting out of the bay. After a few minutes it engaged with a clang to the robotic cargo vessel that would carry it piggyback through the launch.

It took nearly two hours to taxi out to the magnetic launch tube. That was a long time to be awake, and unmoving. A long time to think about what he was doing.

The acceleration came without warning. Nikko wasn't even aware the two ships had entered the launch tube when suddenly his brain slammed against his skull. A huge weight crushed his heart. His lungs were a joke. He blacked out.

When he came to, the coffin lid was fogged. The acceleration gel had been absorbed by the coffin's maintenance system and he was free to move in the cramped space. He raised his arm and wiped at the transparent lid. He saw stars beyond. In the coffin it was very dark. He checked his atrium clock. Four hours had passed since he'd left Summer House. He had a headache.

He ordered the coffin to open. It depressurized, then the lid popped free. He felt cold for a moment, then the feeling was gone. He climbed carefully out.

His hands were already shaking badly under the influence of his advancing palsy. Fox had given him a Maker to correct the disability, but it hadn't done a thing yet. He found it a challenge to grip the handholds.

Fortunately, he'd been fitted with a shoulder harness and tether before leaving Summer House. It kept him secured to the little vessel as he clambered back to the next coffin. He opened the lid, then pulled out the camera pack he'd ordered stashed there. He slipped it on, then drifted out on the tether's slack. The camera hovered on its tentacle, recording an image of the little vessel.

While on Summer House, Fox had helped him recover the data from the camera pack he'd used before his "death." When he combined that with the data stored in the camera pack aboard Phousita's vessel, he'd have a continuous history of events surrounding the Bohr Maker's liberation.

"That's my ship," he said, continuing his documentary. He subvocalized the words. The atrium translated them and sent them on to the camera. "Absurd-looking, isn't it? But functional, I hope."

He went on to describe how it had been designed and assembled. Eventually, the radiation from the sun began to upset his thermoregulatory system, so he pulled himself in on the rope and sought refuge in the shade of the lead coffin, as far from the engine as he could get. He was concerned about radiation. Fox had insisted it was safe enough, and he had Makers to repair any damage. Still, he didn't like being close to the engine.

He was hungry. He popped the lid off the coffin and withdrew a long tube. He wrapped his toes around a handy grip, then struggled with his palsy until finally he was able to stick the end of the tube into a socket Fox had fixed in his forearm. Nutrients began to flow directly into his bloodstream. His mood improved briefly, though he was hungrier than ever when he removed the tube. His belly did not appreciate being cut out of the feeding cycle.

He began to record:

"The emptiness and silence of the void are beginning to weigh on me. I feel utterly alone, with Summer House unimaginably far behind."

His words opened a cavern of emotion. Suddenly, he felt every kilometer of separation like a minute in time, hard and real, but impossible to cross again once he'd gone by.

But gradually his perspective changed. "As the hours pass I find myself growing used to the isolation. It begins to seem less threatening, more beneficent. I understand now why Fox insisted this ship be as small as possible. Because I am tiny, I'm almost invisible in the vast empty reaches that surround me. I'm so far from anywhere that it's unlikely anyone will notice me, even when the fusion engines finally fire on schedule. Some astronomical instrument may record my presence. But will any human eye ever review that record?"

He checked the time. Not long now.

He was just about to return to the coffin and prepare for the next leg of acceleration when a ghost came to him.

"You again!" Nikko hissed, as he recognized the odd little gentleman who'd sabotaged his atrium so many weeks ago.

His visitor sat cross-legged on nothing, his lithe figure floating in vacuum about a meter off Nikko's right shoulder. His blond hair waved as if he were underwater; he wore no vacuum suit. "Success," he said. "My assault Makers were replicated along with your body. I guess Fox didn't notice that."

"What do you want from me?" Nikko demanded.

The man's lower lip swelled in an angry pout. "I wanted you to stay away from the Maker!" he said. "I warned you weeks ago, but you wouldn't listen. Oh, you're good. But now you've forced me to move against you. I'm sorry for what I have to do to you. Slave atriums repulse me. But *you* should understand their occasional necessity, better than most. I can't change the course of this silly ship you're on. But I *can* control you. I can prevent you from taking on any passengers."

Nikko stared at the little gentleman, feeling brutally, utterly terrified. The kisheer reflected his emotion. It swelled up in his throat until he thought he would choke. "Slave atrium? But you can't—"

"I'm sorry. I really am. But you've left me no choice. My assault Makers are modifying your atrium now."

"But you don't understand what's going on!" Nikko protested, the atrium working an interesting croak of panic into his voice.

"Oh I'm sorry. But you're wrong. I do understand. Phousita's aboard that ship, and she has my Maker."

"Your Maker?" Nikko blinked in astonishment. Was this little man really . . . ?

"Phousita has to stay aboard that ship! So the police can recover her. Kirstin's finally figured out how you got the Maker out of Castle, you know. Marevic gave her the ship's control code, or most of it, anyway—"

"Kirstin?" Nikko echoed dumbly. "Marevic?"

"Your scheme's falling apart," Bohr said. "It was a valiant effort, though."

So Marevic had been arrested. She was probably dead by now. And Kirstin . . .

"Kirstin will have Phousita executed," Nikko said, wondering what it would take to elicit sympathy from this ghost. "Do you know Phousita? Have you met her? There's no harm in her. She doesn't deserve to die."

The ghost looked suddenly uncomfortable. "Nature can be so unkind," he admitted. "But it has to happen. She's told me she will share the Maker with anyone who wants it. I can't let that happen."

"Why not?"

Bohr seemed to curl into himself like a spider that had been knocked from its web. "Look at yourself," he mumbled, his eyes averted as if he were embarrassed to speak of these things. "I don't have anything against you personally, understand. But you're not a child of the Goddess. You don't belong to the Earth. You're not a part of the continuity of life that is unique to our Mother. What's to stop the development of more like you if my Maker is widespread? The lineage of the Goddess will be broken. The natural continuum shattered."

"That's crazy!" Nikko hissed. "Nature is blind and deaf and dumb, a reactive machine, no more. It doesn't matter if we change it! It's a good thing. Look at Summer House. The technology that made Summer House can fill the void with life. That can't be bad."

Bohr's chin came up in a little boy's stubborn gesture. "What's crazy," he said, "is our presumption that *we* have the vision to be the guiding hands of evolution."

"But—"

"I'm sorry," the ghost interrupted.

"But my brother's pattern is on that ship. If the police recover it—"

"I'm sorry," the ghost repeated. He seemed truly apologetic. "This whole affair has become so ugly."

Nikko's kisheer fluttered across his face. He struggled to calm it. "But Phousita will die if—"

"Phousita made her choice— What's this? What's this? Oh, damnation! Your dad's got a new Maker in you. It's attacking the atrium. Smart move. That'll get rid of me, won't it? More effective than attacking me direct."

The ghost was gone.

What for the love of Nature?

Nikko stiffened. He'd meant to speak the words. But they were a thought, no more. His voice was gone. He ordered a check on his atrium, but his command went unacknowledged. He tried to access his atrium notebook. He tried to get a reading on the time. The atrium didn't respond. He felt suddenly dizzy. Pain flared through his skull. What had Fox done to him? He pressed his head against the deep cold of the coffin, trying to hold on to consciousness.

Fox had destroyed his atrium.

Fox had saved him from slavery.

Fox had stranded him in the void, because without a functioning atrium, he had no way to signal this absurd little ship to begin the voyage home.

He blacked out. When he came to, he found himself in the coffin. He didn't remember climbing in. But the engine had kicked on, so it was good that he'd managed it. He tested the atrium. No result. He drew nutrients from the coffin and mulled his problems and grew hungrier, until he could think of little else but his hunger. If the atrium were working, he could suppress that physiological reaction. . . .

The atrium was gone.

He didn't climb out of the coffin again. He felt weak, and vaguely dizzy. The shaking in his hands was beginning to be replicated in his toes. There was noth-

ing he could do about it. There was nothing he could
do about anything. He couldn't even dictate to the
camera.

His was a miserable existence. Yet it could have
been worse. Fox had looked to his bodily functions. He
didn't have to defecate because he had no food in his
intestinal tract. He didn't have to urinate, because his
genital organ recycled his urine, while the excess fluids
and toxic excretions were sweated off in a thin film of
ice.

After a day the engine slowed. The steering mech-
anism turned the vessel about. Deceleration. Nikko was
a piece of baggage, badly packed. Another day passed.
The engine cut off for the last time, and Nikko blacked
out, a victim of exhaustion.

He woke up only when his little vessel banged
against the target ship. The hull of the coffin immediately fused with the hull of Phousita's ship. The glue
would hold until he sprayed the bond with a little can
of propellent stashed in the middle coffin.

Clumsily, he reached up to his chest panel to acti-
vate the camera. The gesture sent waves of cramps
through his hands. His numb fingers were yanked into
sudden, excruciating circles. Slowly, he exercised them,
opening and closing his hands. At first his long fingers
tangled with each other, but after ten or twelve repeti-
tions, they began to remember what they were for.
With the camera on, he opened the coffin lid, then
climbed out, craning his neck to get a look at the ship
that had carried his ghost out of Castle.

It was a squat, ugly cylinder, just large enough to
contain three decks. The engines were working to
produce a comfortable deceleration. Recessed sensory
equipment studded the hull, but there were no windows. Nikko pulled out some slack on his tether and
clambered around the hull, using handy grips installed
for the benefit of maintenance personnel. He found the
air lock. The outer door was closed. Access was con-

trolled by a numerical keypad affixed to the hull, minimum security for a vessel that would dock in crowded
inner cities. He'd recorded the access code in his
atrium notebook—but of course the notebook had been
destroyed along with his atrium.

He punched experimentally at the keypad, but it
rejected his attempts. He wondered if there was a door-
bell. In the end, he decided to knock.

Phousita sat huddled in the living room of the little
ship. A soap opera was playing, but the volume was
turned down. Arif was asleep on the floor. She watched
him, his handsome face so calm in sleep. What to do?
What to do?

She still waited for her ghost to return from the evil
sorcerer. It had been almost three days now. She'd begun to wonder if it had been lost. Perhaps it would
never return.

What to do?

She'd thought it wise—for the time being, until she
knew more—to obey the evil sorcerer. So she'd reneged
on her offer to share the Maker's talents with Arif. He'd
flown into a rage. He'd hit her again. But that was the
last time. She made a spell that would send him to
sleep any time he moved against her—an absurd solution that did nothing to heal the deep wounds inside
him. The Maker could do that. She wanted to share it
with him. But she was afraid of the evil sorcerer and so
she waited for the return of her ghost.

A dull, distant banging intruded upon her consciousness. Her chin lifted as she listened to a barely
audible pounding that seemed to roll up from the deck.
She tested the air, but sensed no change aboard the
ship. Arif stirred restlessly in his sleep. The pounding
continued in a slowly varying rhythm. It seemed to
come from the lock, from the door. She swallowed hard
as an unreasonable fear gripped her. There was *nothing*

on the other side of the door. There would be nothing, until the ship docked at Summer House.

The pounding went on.

She got slowly to her feet and walked to the lock. The door itself was only a colored outline. Its material had bonded with the inner hull of the ship. Using the terms of address Nikko had taught her, she asked it politely if it would open. The outline faded away. A thin crack appeared in the gray surface. Several seconds passed as the crack deepened, then the door slid aside, out of sight.

When Phousita had boarded the ship at Castle, there had been a short passage between double doors. Now the passage was filled with a curious, semitransparent wall. She reached out to touch it. It was cool to her hand but not cold, and it yielded to her touch, like soft flesh. She could see the hazy points of stars through its mass. So the outer door must be open too. She pushed harder and her hand sank into it. It was very broad, more than the length of her arm, but if she leaned forward, perhaps she could reach all the way outside. . . .

A bitterly cold hand grasped her arm from outside and shoved her back into the ship. She screamed in surprise and stumbled backward. A moment later she saw Nikko pulling himself through the membranous wall on a succession of handgrips. Despite all the weeks she'd spent with his ghost, she'd never actually seen him herself. But she recognized him from Sandor's memories. He slipped out of the gel, the familiar eye-tentacle of a camera pack hovering over his shoulder.

His own eyes were occluded behind dark lenses. But the lenses cleared rapidly and in a few seconds she could see the blue of his true eyes. He towered over her, his tall blue body like a china sculpture. Beads of water condensed on him from out of the air. The living kerchief that covered his mouth, nose, and ears shivered, then unfurled until it lay like a mantle across his shoulders. The alien profile of his scent set her trembling.

He looked past her.

She followed his gaze, to see Arif crouched on the floor. Quickly she turned back to Nikko and laid a hand on his arm. His smooth skin was icy cold. She could feel the muscles quivering under her palm. His fingers were in constant, erratic motion. "Please don't kill him, Brother Nikko," she whispered.

"I don't need you to defend me!" Arif shouted. He rose to his feet, his body flexed, ready. She sensed then that he would not be unhappy to die.

Nikko's contempt was a bitter perfume on the air. But he showed no interest in fighting. He shrugged, and a wave of shimmering blue ran from his shoulders to his knees. "The police have taken control of this ship," he said. "It's not going to Summer House anymore. It'll probably be brought back to Castle. If you want to dodge the cops, you'll have to come with me."

Phousita frowned at the gel membrane. She could sense no duplicity from Nikko. Still . . . "How can we leave?" she asked. "Outside there's nothing. It's death." She looked at him in surprise. "You have a ship?"

"You could call it that. It'll get us back to Summer House, anyway. You still have Sandor?"

She looked down in sudden shame. She hadn't been back to visit Sandor since Nikko had gone. She'd been too mortified to face him. But Nikko wasn't gone. He was here. Alive and whole.

"Phousita?" His voice was worried now, riven with a hint of anger. "You still have Sandor's pattern, don't you?"

"Of course," she whispered.

"And you'll come with me?"

She gazed up at him again. She could feel tears standing in her eyes. Her chest was filled with a great sadness. "I want to go home, Brother Nikko. Can you help me go home?"

The taste of his regret flooded her senses. "I don't know if you can ever go home again," he said. "It depends on you, and how well you can hide from the cops."

She nodded her understanding. "The cops haven't called on me yet. But I have had another visitor. The evil sorcerer sent a ghost to me." She felt his alarm, and nodded again. "He gave me his address, Brother Nikko, and he told me to visit him. I sent a spirit there, but it hasn't come back."

The chill in Nikko's voice made her shiver. "Did he give you his name, Phousita?"

"He said it was Leander Bohr."

Nikko hissed his anger. "And do you still have his address?"

"Yes, Brother Nikko." She shared that with him, while the camera looked on.

Then abruptly the scent of Nikko's mood seemed to change: anger leavened with something like shame. He turned to Arif. "I need your help," he said.

Arif stiffened. His face went hard, locked down in a stubborn expression that Phousita knew too well.

Nikko seemed to sense it too. His kisheer went still across his shoulders. His reluctance clouded the air. "My atrium's been destroyed," he said. "I have no way to initiate the autopilot aboard my ship. But you can do it."

"You need to get inside my atrium again?" Arif growled.

"No. I need you to command my ship."

Arif was silent for a moment. And then a grin slowly spread across his face.

Nikko retrieved two pressure suits from a locker in one of the bedrooms. He shook them out, revealing two long white coveralls, much too big for either Phousita or Arif. "You'll have to remove your clothes before you put this on," he said.

Phousita nodded and began to strip. After a brief hesitation, Arif followed her example and soon they were dressed in the baggy garments. Phousita looked down at herself.

The suit covered her body from toes to neck. Even her hands were hidden inside baggy gloves at the ends of long sleeves. She found the sense of enclosure deeply disturbing. Her senses seemed to shrivel beneath the dense cloth. Then Nikko touched a panel on the breast of the suit, and it began to shrink. She gasped a little. "Don't worry," Nikko said. The suit pulled tight. Within seconds, it had achieved a snug fit.

Phousita held herself stiffly, repulsed by the garment. She felt violated, as if she'd taken on someone else's skin. Her heart fluttered in her chest. She sent servants to investigate this disturbing cloth, but they quickly returned to her, unable to penetrate it without damaging it. Arif watched the process warily, then repeated the gesture with his own suit.

"This is your helmet," Nikko said. He handed a globe to her. It was solid white plastic on one side; the other side was transparent plastic. "Goes over your head."

Her heart thudded in dull fear. The helmet would complete her enclosure, and cut her off from the world. She watched Arif place his own helmet over his head. Nikko locked it down and turned to her. She swallowed her fear. She could not go back and she could not stay here. A path had been laid out for her, and she must follow it. She slipped the helmet over her head. Nikko locked it with his clumsy, trembling hand. A hiss of air, a sudden change in pressure. Then silence.

She drew a deep breath to calm herself. The air tasted slightly different from that of the ship. She thought of all the tiny servants that still roved the room. She couldn't recover them now. Nikko beckoned with a long, curling finger.

"Let's go." Arif's voice growled in her ears, both

ears at once, as if he stood on two sides of her, his lips but a breath away.

He took her arm and steered her toward the gel membrane, eager to be off. Nikko had taught him to speak to the new ship with his atrium. He would command it. He seemed to have drawn new life from that simple role.

Nikko spent a few seconds fussing over his old camera pack, then he shrugged his kisheer up over his face, and backed into the membrane. It closed around him as he slipped outside. Arif went next. Phousita watched him closely, then she reached into the membrane, caught a handgrip, and pulled herself through. Outside, the suit seemed to stiffen slightly. It squeezed her body ever so gently.

Nikko had waited for her. He showed her how to climb using the handgrips. He hovered close beside her as they clambered across the hull to his tiny ship. He helped her lie down in the coffin. Then he closed the lid.

CHAPTER

22

K irstin headed home after Marevic's execution, bone-tired but aglow with a sense of triumph. The Bohr Maker was hers again—not in hand yet, but under her control. Her staff had extrapolated the ship's control codes from Marevic's aborted testimony. They'd communicated briefly with the ship, obtaining video and auditory images that confirmed the identity of the two passengers as Phousita and Arif.

And she'd ensured the ship would never come back to Castle. Already the police ship *Galapagos*, routed toward Summer House, was moving into position to launch a missile at the outlaw vessel. Nikko's desperate caper was nearly at an end.

For a moment a darker mood eclipsed her triumph. Nikko's ghost was aboard that ship too. She had no direct proof, but every instinct told her it must be. She would have liked to visit him; let him know that he was not so clever after all; that in the end his treachery had failed.

But the ship's communications systems had been

shut down to prevent any ghosts from escaping, and she wouldn't compromise that.

She smiled as she reached the welcoming door of her apartment. She would not let Nikko steal her pleasure. No, the only real disappointment in the case was that Marevic's testimony had offered no links to Fox.

The majordomo program greeted her as she stepped inside, informing her that she had two hundred ninety-seven calls or ghosts waiting, one hundred thirty-four of them coded urgent priority. She returned the greeting with a few choice epitaphs.

After a bath and dinner, she replayed an atrium record of one of Nikko's visits, then slept contentedly. So another full day passed before she finally turned her attention to the backlog of calls and waiting ghosts. Even then, she failed to notice his presence until she'd worked through nearly half the urgent list. The majordomo program had taken no special notice of the waiting ghost's identity. But the tag caught *her* eye, and brought her up sharp.

Leander Bohr.

She blinked in shock that quickly turned to anger, then to cynical amusement.

It was a hoax, of course.

Still, it had got her attention. She called up the ghost, curious to see what cocky bastard would dare use Leander's name.

The ghost appeared for her.

"You!" she hissed.

He shrugged deferentially. The white-blond hair, the cool blue eyes, the milky skin . . . just the same as she remembered. Just the same.

But it was impossible. He'd died so long ago. He could not have hidden from her all this time.

Fury set in. He'd played her for a fool! But no longer. Now she knew he was extant, she would find him. But she kept these thoughts hidden.

"Leander," she said coolly. "Or a damn good imitation."

He seemed confused, but that was always his way. "Kirstin. You look imposing. More grand than I remember. Oh, but you've kept me in the tank so long. Have they made it to Summer House? Are you watching closely?"

She shivered at this haunting from the past. But it *had* to be Leander. The mannerisms were perfect.

"It's a bit of a surprise to see me, isn't it?" he went on, when she failed to answer. "Sorry. I hadn't intended to stick my nose into your business, but the truth is, I'm beginning to doubt you. You let them take the Maker."

"What do you know about it?"

"I've talked with Phousita."

"You—"

"I've talked with Nikko."

She went very still. "The ghost, you mean. Marevic admitted that."

"No, the man. You're not aware of him? That's bad. He'll have taken the Maker from you by now, then. I tried to stop him, but Fox had booby-trapped his atrium."

"You idiot! Try to make some sense."

He smiled as if she were an embarrassing child. "Nikko will have taken the Maker from you by now. That's all. Can't you stop him?"

The ghost was transistory. It answered her questions about Nikko and about the little craft Nikko had been piloting toward an interception with Phousita. Then it dissolved itself, leaving no trail, no hint of where it had come from, not even a pattern that she could feed to the Gates.

The experience left her shaken. She no longer felt sure of the extent of her powers. Leander had duped her all these years. Now Nikko thought he could fool her too? Her doubt turned to hot anger. She checked the time. The police cruiser had fired its missiles several hours before. They were scheduled to strike the ship in approximately twenty-three minutes. She ordered communications with the ship reestablished. She had to confirm Leander's warning.

A machine can't duplicate human senses. This was neither a philosophical statement nor a scientific opinion, but a law within the Commonwealth, and Kirstin experienced its severity when her ghost arrived aboard the police ship. She "heard" through the ship's audio pickups, "saw" through its video eyes, "smelled" through its molecular filters, and felt nothing. She had no body and no fixed position, either mental or physical. She saw the whole ship at once, heard it, smelled it. At once she knew that it was empty.

She wanted to breathe.

Instead, she reviewed the ship's memory, scrolling rapidly through the days since launch until the moment the visitor was first detected. Now she perused the records more slowly. She watched as the strange craft approached and locked to the hull of the police ship; she saw a familiar figure emerge from it. She listened to conversations aboard the ship.

She wanted to breathe.

Nikko Jiang-Tibayan mocked her. A dead man, now heartily alive. Like Leander, he'd played her for a fool.

She must breathe.

She went home.

Immediately, she convened a closed-door meeting with select members of the Congressional Committee that oversaw police activities. "It's the biogenesis function," she told them. "I filed a report on its potential weeks ago; now my worst fears have been confirmed. Fox has stored illegal code in the function and used it to recreate a proscribed life-form."

"You don't know that for sure," one of the politicians objected.

Kirstin glared at him. "That's why I'm here seeking a warrant," she growled. "So I can conduct an investigation. I want a warrant that will allow me to review every line of code in the function. I want another warrant that will allow me to arrest Fox on unspecified charges. I don't have any proof of his involvement at this point, but if I postpone the arrest, he's going to disappear. We're not talking about an ordinary citizen here. We're talking about Fox Jiang-Tibayan. And he may have already armed himself with the Bohr Maker. We simply can't afford to wait."

The Congressional people looked worried. Good. Get them scared enough, and they'd let her do anything.

"All right," the ranking representative said. "You can have your warrants. But you will take no punitive action without our approval."

Kirstin gave him a look of open contempt. "I appreciate your delicate moral sensibilities," she said. "But the situation is critical. We will do what is necessary."

"Within the bounds of the law!"

"We'll try."

CHAPTER

23

Nikko's condition steadily worsened as the craft neared Summer House. He couldn't fool himself anymore. The medical Maker Fox had devised to correct his degenerating nervous system simply wasn't working, and he could guess why. The journey through the void had been arduous. His metabolic rate had climbed steadily in a furious effort to keep him warm, to power chemical exchanges in the kisheer, to maintain even a lethargic level of motor activity. He was left in a state of perpetual exhaustion. There simply wasn't enough metabolic fuel available in his body to satisfy the threshold energy requirements of the medical Maker, and so it remained dormant.

His consciousness blurred, so that it didn't seem so long before he could pick out the winking blue star that would resolve into the rotating body of Summer House. He left his coffin and pulled himself along the tether. The muscles in his hands felt weak. He could hardly close his trembling fingers around the line. He moved slowly, carefully, concentrating on every gesture until he reached the control panel on Arif's coffin. He battled with his fingers to enter the short sequence that would initiate Arif's awakening. Guided by its Dull Intelligence, the camera hovered at his shoulder, recording it all.

He went on to Phousita's coffin and did the same. By the time he managed it, the blue star of the House had resolved into the distinct shapes of the mother asteroid and the blue teardrop of the enclosed ocean, rolling down upon him in a threatening circular motion, like rotating hammers fixed to a nearly invisible spoke.

The sight mesmerized him. He shook his head, striving to focus his concentration. Barely visible beyond the House was the gold metallic glint of the magnetic launch tube. And something else. A gray point. A ship, he realized. Moving out of the shadow of the launch tube. A new arrival. Robotic merchant ships visited the city every couple of weeks, sometimes more often.

Slowly, carefully, he made his way back to Arif's coffin. He could sense movement in there, so he popped the lid. Lights fixed on the coffin rim illuminated Arif's features beneath the clear faceplate of his helmet. He studied Nikko calmly. His gaze narrowed as he watched Nikko reach for the umbilicals and miss, reach for the umbilicals and miss again. Nikko cursed himself. His kisheer went taut against his face in a reflection of shame. He closed his rebellious hand into a tangled fist and slammed it against the coffin hull ... as if pain might force his muscles to obey him.

But he hardly felt the blow, and that scared him more. He tried again anyway, summoning all his will and this time his fingers closed in a clumsy grip around the bundled umbilical cords. Arif's gloved hand covered his and together they disconnected the suit from the coffin.

Nikko pulled back, his body quivering in exhaustion. Arif climbed out. He stretched stiffly, while checking his harness to see that it was secure. He looked pointedly at Phousita's coffin. Nikko nodded. He flexed his hands a few times, then began to make the laborious three-meter journey.

Phousita awoke with a terrible awareness of age, her own age. She'd grown so very old. Lifetimes of experience weighed upon her, pressed upon her. She knew more about the human condition than anyone had ever known before her. She'd lived the lives of men, the lives of women, she'd known poverty and wealth, joy and suffering, she'd been frivolous, melancholy, devoted, treacherous, loving, despairing, curious, petulant ... everything that a person could ever be. She'd distilled all this experience until she'd become the paradigm of humanity, the spokesman of a world, the one best suited to judge what path they all should take.

Except that it was not *her* experience ... this was her second thought. No, these lifetimes belonged to another, to Leander Bohr. He'd laid the weight of them upon her, transforming her into a lesser copy of himself. This was how he'd tortured her.

She cried out in anguish. She pounded her gloved fist against the transparent plastic shield that kept the void out of her coffin and screamed. Her tampered soul had come home sometime in her sleep, had slipped quietly in through her atrium. She hadn't even been aware of it as it dissolved itself into her mind. She'd slept on, while the memories it carried became hopelessly entangled with her native mind, until the two could never be separate again. Leander Bohr had colonized her, and she screamed at the agony of his life.

She hit the plastic shield. It bubbled under her fist. She hit it again. The bubble deepened. Again. It broke. A pinhole. Air screamed through the tiny opening. Her ears popped, and then the suit pressurized. She hit the shield again.

Dimly, she was aware of movement eclipsing the

stars. Nikko's passionless face stared at her through the glass. His camera hovered above his head like an intelligent snake. She cringed at the sight of him. His presence repulsed her. *This creature isn't natural*, she thought. He wasn't made of Mother Earth.

An irrational fury began to build in her as she looked at him. Hissing air became the voice of her anger. She yanked the umbilicals free, then struck at the plastic shield again just as Nikko popped the lid on the coffin. She exploded out of her prison.

Nikko recoiled instinctively as Phousita dove at him. But he wasn't fast enough. Her helmet struck him in the chest, knocking him off the coffin. She clung to him. They shot out together the length of his tether, then snapped back. They hit the seam between two coffins with a thud. He caught an unsteady grip with his toes, arresting their motion. Then he glimpsed Phousita's face. Her features were twisted in an expression of unreasoning fury. Her gloved fingers found his kisheer. She tore it, as if she were trying to rip it off his neck. A muffled howl of fury reverberated in his throat. Blinded by pain, he tried to slap at her, to thrust her away. But she clung like a burr. Her strength amazed him. A wispy cloud of minute red ice crystals drifted past her face. He felt the bite of intense cold in his kisheer, and he knew he'd taken damage. He thrust at her with both hands.

She was gone. He threw himself in the opposite direction, scrabbling along the hull until he reached the lead coffin. A searing pain pulsed through his kisheer. His heart hammered in a war-beat and he could hardly breathe. He pressed his face against the hull of the coffin and tried to stifle a scream that threatened to rise from the growing nausea in his belly.

When he finally lifted his head, the coffin's hull was coated in a rime of red ice.

He looked down the length of the jury-rigged craft.

Some five meters away, two space-suited figures huddled at the end of a tether.

"What's wrong with me? What's wrong with me?" Phousita sobbed. Her voice rang shrill inside the artificial confines of the helmet. Arif held her in a strong, steady grip while they drifted at the end of the tether. "I hate him. I want to kill him. He's not natural. He must die. Help me, help me, Arif. These are not my thoughts. I don't want to feel this way. I hate him. Let me go. Let me go."

Her ranting was insufferable in her own ears, yet she couldn't stop. Tides of hate pumped through her blood. Bohr had poisoned her; polluted her. She was not herself. Her thoughts were not her thoughts. Her feelings were alien. She leaned back against Arif and moaned in heartfelt agony.

"It's all right," he kept whispering, his voice a warm buzz in her ears. "You'll make it all right. It was a nightmare, that's all. Calm down. It'll be all right."

"It won't," she cried. "It won't. Not until he's dead."

Some part of Nikko whispered that he'd misread Phousita's attack. It had been an accident, a nightmare carried into wakefulness, nothing more, and that he should go back and check on her, see that she was uninjured. But a more basic instinct kept him frozen in place. The hate on her face had been focused on him, and him alone.

Motion drew his gaze around. He looked, to see that the rotating hammers of Summer House had drawn appallingly near. They rose overhead and plunged downward like some hellish machine bent on crushing the tiny craft on its slow approach: fist of rock, fist of ocean, in a slow booming rhythm that drew ever nearer, more menacing.

The merchant ship had drawn much closer too. He

could make out its shape now: cylinders bundled in a diamond pattern. It was no robotic vessel, he realized. This craft was manned. And too, it was no merchant ship. He stared at the formal Chinese characters on its side that identified it: this was the *Galapagos*, a ship of the Commonwealth Police.

He wanted to believe its presence was a coincidence, but that was too much to ask.

A sense of helpless fury rolled over him. He'd come so close to bringing the Bohr Maker home. So close. But the cops had caught on. *How?* Suddenly he knew. Bohr's ghost had turned him in. That sniveling, limp-spined bastard.

The fist of rock came hammering down, occulting his view of the police ship. The rock swept past, less than a kilometer away now. He could see the clawlike pattern of the ceramic pipes that drained the asteroid's artificial frosting of cometary ice. It plunged away. The police ship had turned its prow to face him. A white light bloomed against its belly.

Nikko jerked in shock. The fucking cops were shooting at them! He scrabbled at his harness, his tangled fingers resisting. But terror had steadied them somewhat. The clasp snapped open. He dove aft. Phousita and Arif were still drifting on the end of the tether. They hadn't seen what was coming. Probably wouldn't understand, even if they had seen.

Holding on with his toes, Nikko perched on the rim of the middle coffin and worked at the anchor that held Arif's tether. Got it loose. Turned his attention to Phousita's and freed that one as well.

Phousita felt a jerk against her harness. She twisted in Arif's arms. Nikko had the end of the tether in his hands. Over his head, the huge fist of a blue ocean was plunging down faster than a falling star. "Arif!" she screamed, in a violent combination of rage and terror.

Nikko heaved on the tether. He was holding on by

his toes. She felt the harness jerk, knocking the breath
out of her lungs, then she and Arif were shooting helplessly toward Nikko. He let go of the tether and
ducked. Her arms flailed as she tried to reach him. Arif
was screaming manic threats. They shot past Nikko,
past the little spacecraft. Their tethers trailed after
them like broken strings from a kite as they swept
under the path of the plunging blue fist. She screamed
in utter terror, knowing that the hand of God had
reached out to crush her from existence.

But the hand swept past. She blinked in amazement. Her perspective seemed to shift. The silvery
scars on the receding wall of encapsulated water became distant trees, the airless forest of Sandor's memories.

Still clinging to Arif, she twisted around to look
back.

Nikko had jumped. He dove after them like a blue
arrow in the void.

It was a suicide leap. Nikko knew it, but he took it anyway. What choice did he have? The police ship had
fired its missile. A sudden wave of light and heat
washed over him, and he knew the missile had found
its target. He curled his body into a ball as chunks of
debris swept past. Smaller bits of shrapnel peppered his
back and shoulders, igniting fires of bitter cold. Something struck him hard in the shoulder, sending him into
a violent spin. He almost blacked out from the bruising
pain.

He caught a glimpse of the distant, entangled figures of Phousita and Arif. A halo of frozen vapors surrounded them. So one of them, at least, had taken
damage. But the suits would self-seal.

The fist of rock swept down on them. It looked like
a falling world. Nikko had never seen the House from
this perspective. It horrified him: this merciless image

of stone-cold power. He fully expected to be swept up, crushed, like an insect beneath a rock.

But the rock swept past. It hurtled beneath him. Or he tumbled past it. At jet speeds he spun over the plain of ice and rock and back into open space, wobbling in a mad, helpless rotation. He caught a glimpse of Phousita and Arif. They were far beyond him now, at least half a klick, small white entangled figures. A shadow swept over them. They disappeared. Then reappeared moments later, black silhouettes against a blue ocean. They were going to hit the surface. He knew it. They were going to hit. He spun away.

He felt the presence of the House at his back like a thousand gravities. When he completed his rotation he was facing a wall of blue. He could see the spongy surface texture of the lower House. It couldn't be more than twenty meters away. It seemed to fill the Universe. He'd seldom come exploring here. There were no trees. Nothing to hold on to. Just a curving plain of blue that seemed to fill the Universe. Home. Only fifteen meters away. Then ten. Then unbelievably, five. He stretched his body out, reaching for it, knowing the impact would kill him and not caring, wanting only to go home.

His long fingers brushed the surface, meeting no more resistance than he might have met from atmosphere. He cartwheeled into an insubstantial blue sea. Blue light blazed on every side. Then suddenly, darkness. The sea rapidly thickened. His spin slowed, then ceased altogether as the gelatinous matrix enfolded him with all the protective warmth of a mother's womb.

CHAPTER

24.

Kirstin's ghost arrived in the atrium of the commander of the *Galapagos*. Beryl was a hard-line cop with a buzz cut and a system-wide reputation for molecular intolerance. She and Kirstin went back a long way, and they welcomed each other with a hearty hug. When the clinch eased, the commander leaned back and treated Kirstin to a wide grin. "Fried his glass ass," she announced.

"Nikko Jiang-Tibayan?" Kirstin asked eagerly. "You got him?"

Beryl nodded. "It was close. He was only a few klicks off the station when we got a video ID. We had to fire a sweetie right through the arc of rotation. Real cute. Nailed him in his nuclear ass."

Kirstin felt a thrill of triumph. Nikko had almost sneaked past her again, but not quite. "Nature. I wish I could have seen it happen. Bet the BOD's screaming about the rads, though."

The commander frowned. "You'd think so, wouldn't you? But except for a little grousing from traffic control,

Summer House hasn't said a word. You'd think we were exterminators they'd hired to do a job."

Kirstin felt a brush of concern then. It wasn't like the board of directors to lose an opportunity to file a complaint against the police. "You sure you hit them?"

"Sure. They're dust."

She kissed the commander on the cheek. "Dock the ship, then. I've got a corpse warming up and a warrant to arrest Fox. I'll meet you in the city."

As soon as Kirstin emerged from the mausoleum, she summoned the contingent of officers stationed at the House. The *Galapagos* was still in the process of docking, but she could begin her investigation with the staff on hand.

"The first thing we do is find Fox," she told the reluctant police captain, the same man she'd visited weeks ago on her first inspection of the House. His tour of duty was nearly over now. He'd already submitted his resignation and accepted full House citizenship. Obviously, he didn't like the situation one bit.

"They're hiding him," the captain said. "The House won't say where he is."

Kirstin's eyes narrowed in irritation. "We have a warrant," she informed him. The data Gates had already been instructed to filter his ghost.

The police captain nodded nervously. "That's fine. We'll need to take it to the corporate offices and get someone to open the House security system to us."

Her frown deepened. "We've got Hunter Makers. We can find him on our own."

The police captain averted his gaze. "Could be," he said. "But the hunt will be easier if we go through channels."

She glared at him in open indignation. "You're saying our Hunter Makers won't work here?"

He glanced at her, then quickly looked away. "No,

no, I'm not saying that at all. If that were the case, I would have reported it, wouldn't I?"

"Damn right." If he hadn't reported it, she'd have *him* up on charges.

"It's the organic nature of Summer House," he explained. "We can't just flush our Hunters through the air system. There's a lot of undifferentiated tissue to inspect. It could take hours."

She was not convinced. But for the moment, she agreed to go along. "All right," she said. "To the corporate offices, then."

The corridors seemed oddly empty. When they did encounter people, it was mostly children, playing tag and hide-and-seek and other games. The few adults they saw were openly hostile, scowling at the contingent of police officers.

They found the corporate offices nearly deserted. A few kids were playing in the outer rooms. They scattered when the cops showed up. The desk consoles had all been shut down and wouldn't reactivate when Kirstin punched in an experimental command. She glared questioningly at the local police captain, but he only shrugged, his face creasing in worry. "I've never seen it like this before," he said. "They're usually fully staffed here, round the clock."

He led them on. The doors to the various offices stood open, but one after another, they found each room empty, the consoles unresponsive. Finally, they came to the president's office: Fox's old haunt. This door was closed, but it slid aside at the request of the police captain.

A red-haired figure sat behind the desk, idly swiveling from side to side in the office chair. For a moment Kirstin thought she'd found Fox. Her eyes widened. She started forward. Then the chair's occupant looked up.

He was a teenage kid. His gaze met hers. Amusement glittered in his eyes. His face was a study in insolent self-assurance, as if he'd discovered the big bad wolf had rotten teeth. When she saw that expression, she felt a sharp pang of worry.

"We're looking for Fox," the police captain said.

The kid's gaze remained fixed on Kirstin. "Fox is gone." He had the effrontery to actually grin.

Kirstin carefully pulled a wrap over her outrage. "Gone where?" she asked between gritted teeth.

"Well, nobody knows. He's just gone. All his personal files, too, if you want to know." The kid leaned back in his chair; kicked his feet up on the desk. "Sound like a suicide to you?"

Kirstin glared for a long, cold moment. "Where's the corporate staff?" she asked. "Who is acting president?"

"Well, the staff stepped out for a few minutes, you see. But I'm still here. I'm the new president." He laughed again, then popped a stick of gum into his mouth.

Two hours of searching turned up no sign of Fox, or any other member of the corporation's Board of Directors. Sometime during that interval, the police captain also disappeared. After Kirstin discovered his absence, she ordered the rest of the local officers aboard the *Galapagos*, which had finally completed docking procedures at the central tether. House personnel had not assisted in the process. The staff was ostensibly on holiday and officially the dock was closed, while all corporate citizens observed a day of grieving over the supposed suicide of Fox, their corporate father. There didn't seem to be any formal ceremonies.

The police manhunt continued. When a few members of Fox's staff turned up, Kirstin summoned them to the *Galapagos* for questioning. But nobody would admit to knowing where the missing corporate members had gone, or who had overseen Nikko's resurrection.

They gave her no useful information at all, and when she threatened them, they showed no fear.

So she released the Hunter Makers into the city—three waves of them over a ninety-minute period. Six hours later none of them had obeyed their programmed limit and returned, leaving her with the inescapable conclusion that something out there was eating them. It seemed impossible. She should have had the best arsenal in existence. Yet her finest molecular devices failed to return.

The hunt took on a critical feel. Summer House was not like other cities. She couldn't just run the dogs through the corridors. The corridors represented only a small part of the body of Summer House. Manufacturing facilities and secure labs were set away from the inhabited levels and could only be accessed through the transit system. The multitudinous levels of the forest had to be accessed on foot. But what concerned her most was the uninhabited and unimproved zone between the outer oceans and the inner city. The area consisted of little more than mass: an undifferentiated gelatinous medium through which the lanes of the transit system passed. Fox could hide a world in that vast, interstitial space. But without the Hunter Makers, she had no way to inspect it.

Her frustration grew with the passing hours. Instinct told her a whirl of activity was proceeding just beyond her perceptions, yet she couldn't access it. The situation was slipping out of her control.

CHAPTER

25

Phousita felt herself cradled in a warm, thick darkness. She was alone. Arif had been torn from her arms when she'd died. She *must* have died. And been reborn, or at least conceived in the womb of a new mother. Her memories trailed after her, a continuous stream linking her to a life now past. She surveyed that fact with wonder. The darkness shifted around her. A voice spoke in her mind. No. It was no voice. It was the memory of a voice, someone questioning her: who are you? A voice as warm and reassuring as the darkness.

"Phousita," she whispered. But she couldn't speak. Her own voice went out through her atrium. In that moment, when she spoke her name, she understood that she had not been reborn. She was still the same unworthy creature she'd always been. "But where am I?" The words were a subvocalized whisper, but the darkness understood.

She'd entered the body of Summer House: the knowledge came to her not as a voice, but as a memory, newly retrieved.

Summer House.

She must learn more. She began to compose a spell of tiny servants to explore this place, then stopped. She still wore the suit, the helmet, the blinding gloves. "May I remove these garments?" she asked.

It would be safe. The House would evacuate a transit bubble around her.

The gentle pressure of the darkness seemed to recede. She could feel soft walls forming under her hands, like smooth, boneless flesh. She felt herself sink until her booted feet touched a curved floor. Then a thin blue phosphorescence developed around her, gradually brightening, illuminating the interior of a spherical chamber barely large enough to hold her.

She worked at the clasp of her helmet until it snapped open, then she lifted the burdensome thing from her head. A puff of warm, moist air greeted her. She breathed it in deeply. Ah, so much better than the nasty cold stuff in the suit.

She punched experimentally at the control panel of her suit until the garment finally released its form-fitting grip. It sagged into a thin, oversized unit. She peeled it off and stepped out, leaving it in a heap on the floor. Her hands glinted in shiny, moist patches. She clapped them gently together, and her eager servants leapt away in a minute cloud of mist. From the House she sensed a sudden disquiet, but she chose to ignore it. "Where is Arif?" she asked.

Arif: the House had established communication with him. He'd entered the House with suit damage and was being transported to the infirmary for treatment of his injuries. The House expected a full recovery.

Phousita swallowed hard against a sudden knot of tension. "And where is—" It took a discernible effort even to say the hated name. "Where is *Nikko?*"

She'd glimpsed him just before the ocean swallowed her up. His trajectory had changed. He'd been hit by a piece of debris that sent him careening in a wild spin over the edge of the world.

The House needed clarification. Did Phousita refer to the corporate citizen Nikko Jiang-Tibayan?

"Yes." An unsettling mixture of delight and dread ran through her veins as she anticipated the House response.

The House was unaware of the present location of Nikko Jiang-Tibayan.

She sagged down against the floor of the transit bubble, her naked body pressed against the discarded suit. So Nikko had never returned to the House. He'd plunged past the edge of the world. He'd missed this sanctuary and fallen into the void.

She felt a pious joy, a righteous triumph at that terrible accident. But why? How could she despise him so?

Abruptly, she sensed an approaching presence. She sat up, as the illumination began to fade from a tall section of the sphere. The curved wall seemed to thin, then it drew apart like contracting flesh, revealing the interior of another blue-lit sphere and an old man with wild, gray-streaked hair that took the color of old blood in the cold light.

"Fox," she whispered.

He looked at her askance, perhaps embarrassed by her nudity. The lines in his face were deeper than she remembered. . . . No. These were Sandor's memories. He seemed gaunt, his shoulders bowed. He reeked of grief.

"You made it," he said, as if he could hardly believe it himself. "We were watching for you. We saw it all. We tried to warn you, but Nikko wouldn't answer."

"His atrium was dead," Phousita said.

Fox stared at her, aghast. Fox had engineered the destruction of Nikko's atrium. Phousita wanted to say something to comfort him, but an alien sense of contempt held her back. Leander Bohr did not like Fox any more than he liked Nikko.

Fox swallowed hard. He seemed to gather himself.

"I don't suppose . . . in all the chaos . . . you managed to—" His lips trembled. His forehead shone with sweat. "Sandor?" he croaked.

Phousita turned half away from him, repulsed at the thought of giving Sandor to this man. Until she realized he'd asked for Sandor, not the Maker. He was the first person she'd encountered who hadn't shown an active interest in that talent. She blinked, and quickly looked back at him. "Can you make him live again?"

"If the code is good, maybe. Maybe. But time's growing short. The biogenesis function's been initiated. We have to bring Sandor back now, before it's too late."

Phousita nodded slowly, uncertain of his intent.

"It's a dangerous time," Fox explained softly. "The cops have guessed Nikko came out of the biogenesis function. They've got a warrant to inspect the code, and of course to interrogate me—though I'm not going to be around to talk to them. We have to keep them doubting long enough to make good our escape."

"Your escape?" Phousita asked. She had thought Summer House might be a kind of sanctuary.

Fox nodded shakily. "We've taken a vote on it," he said. "And we won't give up what we've gained. The biogenesis function is our only insurance, and we aren't going to let the cops take that away from us. Here. Here's the electronic address for Sandor's code."

She recorded the address in her atrium. There was an awkward silence. "You'll send it soon?" he asked.

She nodded.

He seemed ready to go, but he hesitated. "Your friend Arif was injured by shrapnel," he offered. "He's in the infirmary. He'll be all right. The cops won't recognize him. It's best, though, if you stay here. The cops think you're dead. They didn't see you jump ship. They won't be looking for you, so you'll be all right, too, if you stay out of sight."

Again, he seemed ready to go. But again, something held him back. "We can't find Nikko," he said.

She felt herself stiffen. "I know."

"I can bring him back, of course. His code's still in the biogenesis function. But it won't be the same. His memories will be antique. He'd changed a lot, you know. He'd learned a lot from you."

She shuddered. Nikko had tried to murder her. That's what she'd believed when he'd flung her and Arif from the ship. But moments later the ship had exploded. So really, he'd saved her life. And he was Sandor's brother. She loved him too. She knew it. She didn't hate him. The contempt was Leander's, not hers. She bowed her head, as a storm of conflicting emotions welled up inside her.

She could not go on like this.

She hadn't visited the valley since the terrible storm. When she finally returned, she was surprised to see how much the forest had recovered from the assault of winds. The trees were sending out new leaves of soft green and dull gold. The air was still. And the sun, where it filtered through the canopy, nourished with its heat.

She coalesced out of mist, to stand on a smooth spill of rock just outside the mouth of a small cave. She was nude. The sunlight touched her brown skin with tender hands. Her hair hung loose and long, brushing the small of her back. She felt strong, but dirty too.

Sandor seemed to sense that. He'd been sitting just inside the mouth of the cave, cross-legged, his skin a little darker than she remembered. He jumped to his feet when he saw her. "Phousita!" He started to reach for her, but stopped, put off perhaps, by the expression in her eyes. "You've been hurt," he said. "You've been changed." He backed off a step. His voice shook. "What's been done to you?"

Her chin dropped slightly. She was caught off balance. She'd expected anger from him. Didn't she deserve it? She'd abandoned him for days. But there was no anger in his eyes, only horror, as he seemed to look past her face and into her soul, to recognize the evil sorcerer: the true spirit of Leander Bohr now. Not simply his servant anymore, but *himself*.

His hesitation hurt her more than his anger ever could.

"I'm possessed," she whispered. "The evil sorcerer lives inside me. I'm not myself anymore." She raised her hand tentatively. "Do you remember me? Do you remember who I was?"

He reached for her then, and enfolded her in his arms. His scent swept around her in an intoxicating cloud. She wanted to make love. She wanted to feel the false promises that came with orgasm, the lying certainty that everything would be all right, all right. But she knew that nothing would ever be all right so long as the spirit of Leander commanded her.

She clung to Sandor. She pulled him against her with all her strength, as if by sheer physical pressure she could force him to become part of her, so that his soul might dilute the influence of Bohr. "Help me, Sandor, please. Bring me back. Bring me back to what I was. You knew me best. You can do that."

He shook his head slightly. His lips brushed her cheek. His breath washed against her skin, warm and full of life. More life than most living men could command. He was only a ghost. She could taste his regret, like a bitter tea. "I don't know what's happened to you," he whispered. "But I do know there's no going back. I've learned that at least. You taught me. You've pulled me past all the horrors, Phousita. God, you have to pull us past this too."

"But I can't," she moaned. "I can't get rid of him." Leander couldn't be exorcised. He was too thoroughly entangled in her memories. She could never remove him.

"It's true," Sandor said. "You can't get rid of anything. It all stays with you, becomes part of you. I remember—" But he caught himself. He wouldn't speak of it. Still, she knew. She'd lived his memories

too. "You can get past it," he insisted. "Set yourself
apart from your memories. Make yourself new. It's the
only way to move on."

Make yourself new? She clung to him, savoring this
idea.

Could it be possible to simply—

—leave Leander behind?

But if she did that, wouldn't she risk losing other
things along the way? Sandor's arm tightened around
her. She could smell his fear. He sensed the danger too.

She pressed her head against his chest. "I have to
send you away," she whispered. "We've come to Summer House. They're waiting for you. They want to
make you real again."

He sucked in a harsh breath. His grip tightened further. "Come with me."

"I'll follow. I promise."

He didn't believe her. "Phousita!" he pleaded, his
doubt palpable. "You come and go, and go and go. I
can't hold on to you."

"No," she agreed. "It's useless to try."

They were insubstantial ghosts, ever-changing vapors adrift in time, impossible to hold on to anything
with the damnably infirm grip of a human hand. "But
I will follow," she swore. "I will." She kissed him
deeply, then let him fade away.

She left the rock shelf to stroll among the trees. The
humus felt coarse beneath her feet, warm, and full of
living things. She knelt down, and scooped a handful of
it, breathed upon it to blow some of the finer particles
away, then watched the tiny, crawling beings that inhabited it as they went about their instinctive business.
She must go beyond instinct, beyond any pattern set
down in her cells. She must write her own future. Was
it possible?

She gazed at the tiny crawly things, with their many
legs, their simple lives, and tentatively, she began to

weave her spell. The effort was spontaneous, not intel-
lectual. She worked with a visceral sense, feeling, never
planning. How could she plan? She'd descended into
the handful of humus and become a worm, blind and
dumb and living in darkness, chewing through the humus of the forest floor, eating experience, her own, and
that of others. Digesting memories. She spun the silk of
her spell, wove it around herself, wrapped herself up in
it until she could no longer move. She became a pupa,
outwardly quiescent, sheltered in darkness. Changing.
From the pupa hatched a small brown moth. It crawled
up through the humus to the surface of the forest floor
and stretched its wings. Suddenly, she shuddered. Everything was so much brighter here, more intense. She
caught the fading scent of Sandor's love upon the air.
She drew it into her mind, and as she held it there it
seemed to swell and grow, filling her until she thought
she would burst; a terrible, sublime ache that spilled
across the plain of her experience like cold moonlight,
touching everything she knew.

And then it was gone. Her eyes flew open; she
gasped for breath. Her soul was a small brown moth, and
everything was brighter, more intense. And she realized: *it
must be so*. If she would fly above the plain of her experience, then every sensation must fall across her with the
intensity of a first encounter. But like rain on the scales
of a moth's wing, the experience would flow away, a flash
flood of emotion awash on the plain below.

Far above the flat Earth, her wings dried rapidly in
the sun. She grew lighter, flew higher. She had no master. Certainly not Leander, though he was part of her.
And not Arif, or the old woman, or the pimp who'd
owned her long ago. Or even Sandor. They were all
there below her. She could see them, taste the scents
they'd given to her life, but they couldn't hold her. She
was a small brown moth fluttering so far above their
heads they couldn't see her. She was free.

CHAPTER

26

The biogenesis function was an awesome assemblage of information. As Kirstin watched the investigative staff aboard *Galapagos* wade through its complexities, she began to feel as if they were attempting to decode the entire history of life on Earth. Hours passed. No one was allowed to go off duty. Sleep suppressants were passed around. Meals were served on the bridge. The work continued.

Odd reports began to come in from the scattered officers sent to patrol the House. Most of the animal life had disappeared from the rain forest. The trees were beginning to wither, and the light to fade. Most of the adult human population had also vanished, leaving the children to run about the corridors of the House, unattended. And the kids wouldn't come near the cops, wouldn't talk to them. They were like wild animals, loose in a deteriorating habitat, refusing the help of human hands. A few officers had tried to catch some of the errant children. But the kids had slipped out of sight and disappeared. Just disappeared. Not knowing where they went—that was hard on the officers. They could rationalize it; intellectually convince themselves that nothing bad had happened to the little ones. But there were always nagging doubts. And after a while, the cops left the kids alone. No one wanted to be responsible for the loss of a child.

The House itself continued to cooperate with the police except when their inquiries trespassed on "secure information avenues." But those roads seemed to become more and more common as time wore on.

Kirstin could not foresee a neat end to the situation.

She watched the newsfeed out of Castle. Like most major corporations, Summer House operated its own public information channel. The kids had taken that over too, suspending the usual programming, and replacing it with roving footage gathered from around the eerily empty House. There was no narrative. Just endless pictures of the silent kids, the fading city, leaving the viewer to doubt and wonder and doubt. Always, the invisible conductor behind this orchestrated decline seemed to play on doubt.

The general newsfeeds loved it. They picked up the vids for system-wide audiences, and added narratives of their own—shameless speculation about the role of the police in initiating "The Incident."

The Incident: that was what the debacle at Summer House was being called, a vague term for a vague event that no one outside the House could really explain.

And the system-wide audience grew steadily larger. Billions hung on every lurid speculation, and increasingly, convoluted logic worked up the police as the culprits, the instigators, the party responsible for this slowly unfolding disaster. Kirstin watched the programming and felt her coin shrink. She knew that even on Castle, the very heart of the Commonwealth, the mood was turning against the police. People feared the police reaction more than the odd events on Summer House. Even Congress had publicly called for a cautious response, as if the party to be mistrusted was the police and not the deviant House. It was a masterful feat of propaganda, engineered by an invisible hand. And it worried Kirstin. If the time came, would she be allowed to carry out her duty to safeguard the Commonwealth?

Thirty hours into the investigation, with these and other thoughts on her mind, she was on the bridge of the *Galapagos*, huddled in a strategy session with that ship's commander. A staff of twenty investigators surrounded them, all working on a three-tiered horseshoe ring of consoles facing the command podium. Above the general speculative mutter of the investigators, one voice suddenly rose in masculine triumph: "We found your nemesis, Chief!"

Silence immediately enveloped the room. Kirstin looked up. Her gaze fixed on the speaker. "Which nemesis?" she growled.

"Nikko Jiang-Tibayan," he announced. "The one who instigated this whole affair."

Nikko? Kirstin straightened, hardly daring to breathe as she approached the console. "You found him?" She glanced at the display, but all she saw was a screen full of genetic code.

"Yep, that's him," the officer said. "That's the DNA sequence coding for the enamel in his carapace—or at least a major segment of the gene. As soon as I decode the end markers, we'll be able to tease out the sequence defining his entire composition. We've got him."

She turned away, a cold feeling in her chest. She didn't bother to point out to the officer that Nikko was already dead, that he'd been killed a day ago by the *Galapagos*'s missiles, that the genetic description just found was that of a deceased being, and that what she really wanted was the *author* of that description. She didn't bother. Congress had convened its daily session less than an hour ago, and if this fool couldn't deliver her Fox, she could at least use his fool's gold to blind the eyes of Congress. "I want a Congressional report ready in five minutes," she said. "Forward it to my mule on Castle."

As she returned to the command podium, she felt the gaze of the *Galapagos*'s commander. "What are you up to, Kirstin?"

"We've just proved Summer House has used the biogenesis function to disguise illegal data. I'm going to petition Congress for permission to destroy the function. That'll either force the Board of Directors out of hiding or inspire them to move against us."

Either way, it would bring the issue to a head.

The Congressional response came twenty minutes later in the form of an order to proceed. Kirstin read through it grimly, then opened a line to the acting president of Summer House. The gum-chewing kid appeared on her console. His desk had already received a copy of the order. "We're coming," Kirstin told him.

Judging from the cold glare on his face, he was finally taking the police presence seriously. He cracked his gum, his gaze reflecting the considerable passion an adolescent could muster. "You can't touch us," he said.

Kirstin bit down hard on her retort, reminding herself that this kid was not Summer House. He was just a dumb terminal plunked down in front of a camera to frustrate her. Arguing with him would be the equivalent of arguing with a piece of furniture. "We're coming," she told him again, fulfilling her legal duty to notify.

He only shrugged. "Come ahead. We won't stop you. 'Cause you can't touch us. You can't touch the biogenesis function. It'll be a real laugh, watching you try."

The gum popped and cracked. He glared a lost-rebel glare. And then he cut the connection.

A sudden commotion broke out on the bridge. Kirstin whirled around, to see several of the investigators on their feet. Others were hammering at their consoles. "We've lost it!" one of them shouted. His voice rose above the general cacophony.

"Silence!" Kirstin barked. The black-uniformed mob froze obediently, but fury showed in the eyes of more than one. She pointed a finger at the senior officer. "Report."

"We've lost the biogenesis function," he said. "It's disappeared from the House plexus. Disappeared, just like everything else in this house of horrors."

"Love and Nature," Kirstin swore softly. "Why are they going this far? Don't they believe we'll respond?"

The officer grunted his disdain. "What do they need to worry about?" he asked curtly. "They've eaten every one of our assault Makers like so much caviar. They've got the molecular arsenal to beat."

She stared past him, gathering her thoughts. The situation was out of control, and her options were narrowing.

CHAPTER

27

Sandor approached consciousness gradually, first aware of himself, then more slowly, his surroundings. He found his gaze fixed on the curved wall of a transit bubble only a few centimeters away. He stared at it in confusion. How had he come to be in a transit bubble?

Lifting his head, he looked around. It was a large transit bubble, at least eight feet long. He lay on the floor. Fox sat cross-legged beside him. Tears stood in the old man's eyes.

Sandor stared at him a moment. He couldn't say he was surprised to see Fox. Not intellectually, anyway. Phousita had told him they wanted him back. Still, he felt viscerally astounded. Emotionally confused. Not well grounded in reality anymore, he suspected.

"Fox!" he blurted out, sitting up. "I never thought I'd—" But words failed him, so he simply spread his arms and they embraced. "I don't know what's real anymore, Fox. I'm so glad to be home."

He felt the old man stiffen a little. But then Fox

tenderly stroked his head. That's when Sandor noticed
they'd forgotten the hair. His pate was as barren as the
moon. The rest of his body, too, was smooth and hairless. His finger and toe nails were stumps. "They'll
grow out in time," Fox assured him. "See?" He rubbed
Sandor's head again. "I can feel a hint of stubble already."

"Where's Phousita?"

Fox's momentary good humor vanished. "She's
nearby."

"Is she all right?"

Fox's arms dropped from around Sandor. He backed
off a little. "Not really. She's withdrawn. She's—" He
frowned unhappily. "Truth is, she's comatose. She's
been that way since she delivered your code. I don't
know why."

"I do. Where is she, Dad?"

"Nearby."

"You said that. What's going on? Why are we in a
transit bubble?"

Fox sighed. "Well, the police are here, and we're in
hiding. Actually, the House is in revolt."

"What?"

"Yes. Well, the cops guessed Nikko's code was hidden in the biogenesis function. They've found it at last.
Of course we knew they would, if they really started
looking."

"Have they erased him?"

"They want to erase the whole project."

"Oh."

"We won't allow it, of course."

"No?"

"The decision's been made. The people seem to
agree."

"I don't understand, Fox."

Fox glanced away for a moment. He seemed mildly
troubled, mildly pleased, like a father at the start of his
wife's labor. "We knew it had to happen sooner or later.

This is a bit sooner than expected, but we're ready just the same.

"The House is coming apart, Sandor. This is what the biogenesis function is all about. The House is already in the process of absorbing all interior structures. When that's done, it'll divide into a thousand propagules, little vehicles of life, each one capable of regenerating a new House once it latches onto an appropriate substrate."

Sandor blinked, astounded. Fox had never talked about this vision before. "And the people?" he asked, too stunned to disbelieve anything Fox said.

Fox smiled and nodded. "It didn't sit well with a lot of the citizens to be reduced to code. You've been through that. Guess it's a helpless feeling."

Sandor shrugged. He hadn't done so well when he was corporeal either.

"Well, that's the general feeling anyway. So most of us will continue to exist in the tissue of the largest propagules." He grinned. "Like legendary homunculi embedded in the ovaries of a fecund mother." Sandor stared at him blankly. "Well," he said with a shrug, "you were never much for biology. But the point is, there'll be too many of us to police. That's the beauty of it. The status quo will have to change." Fox's eyes shone as he spoke of it. But he sobered quickly. "The cops are hot on us, though. If that Kirstin Adair suspects what we're doing, she could finish us with one missile."

"I've met her," Sandor said. They were silent a moment. Finally, he thought to ask: "Did you get the Bohr Maker from Phousita?"

Fox shrugged. "We don't need it. The House can do more than Bohr ever did. Much more."

Sandor looked at his father with a measure of suspicion. The cops had pursued Bohr's Maker so relentlessly that he'd been forced to assume it was of stellar importance. How could Fox dismiss it so easily?

"Oh, I don't dismiss it," Fox explained when pressed. "The Bohr Maker, from what I've heard, is an amazing adaptation. But you see, the House represents a completely different solution to a similar problem: how to harness the powers of molecular technology. The House is an external solution. It can be used by great numbers of individuals as an external creative and computative organ, and because of its vast size, its complexity, and the sheer volume of resources it can command at a mature stage, it will always represent a superior solution to an internally contained modification such as the Bohr Maker. The limits imposed by the minute volume of a human body will always dictate a lower limit on creative and computational abilities."

"With the trade-off being individual freedom," Sandor said.

"Yes. That's right. I'm a conservative old man. I don't mind limits, so long as I impose them on myself. And I'm pretty typical of the population here."

"Phousita wants to go back to Earth."

"Does she?" Fox seemed mildly surprised. But then, he'd never been able to understand why anyone would want to go there.

"She'd be taking the Bohr Maker with her."

"Yes. I suppose she would."

Sandor could almost feel the heat rising off Fox's head as his fine brain mulled this bit of information. "You don't object, do you?" Sandor pressed. "You're not on the cops' side in this?"

Fox looked startled. "No. Of course not. She can do what she likes with it. It's her business. In fact, it could benefit—" He caught himself. His cheeks reddened.

"What, Dad?"

"Sometimes I think I've run too many equations in my life," he said. "Everything that enters my mind seems to emerge in terms of costs and benefits. I don't intend it that way. It just happens. But I'll say it outright. If Phousita takes Bohr's Maker back to Earth, that'll be one more distraction to pull the cops off our tails. And if she manages to keep her freedom and her life, then the status quo will have to change. Every new House that grows from the propagules will look hopelessly conservative next to the society she could create."

"Will you help her, then?"

"I'll take it up with the Board," Fox said.

Sandor frowned at him. That was a Fox stock response.

"Well, it shouldn't be a problem convincing them," Fox said defensively. "Assuming, of course, that any of us live."

They were silent for a while. Then Sandor asked tentatively, "Dad? Nikko didn't know any more about this than I did, right?"

Fox stared at his hands for several seconds. "Secrecy was so important," he muttered. "Until a few days ago, only a handful of us knew."

"Nikko never would have gone after Bohr's Maker if you'd let him in on your plans. But you didn't trust him, did you?"

"Nikko had his own agenda. I—" His voice broke off. He bowed his head into a framework of fingers made clawlike by tension. "It wouldn't have made any difference," he muttered. "Nikko would have gone after the Bohr Maker anyway. He wanted to live. He didn't want to be reduced to code. He went after the Bohr Maker—and he forced us to act."

Sandor found it hard to be angry. He'd paid in plenty for Nikko's adventurism. But he'd found Phousita too. "Where is she?" he asked Fox.

The old man nodded, his mood dark and heavy, as if he sensed he would soon lose his son again. "I'll take you to her."

She was stretched out on the floor of a transit bubble, in the comatose state Fox had described. Sandor kissed her and called her name until she smiled. A moment later her eyelids fluttered open.

• • •

Phousita stretched and looked around, to find herself in an expanded transit bubble, one that was tall enough to stand in, long enough to walk five or six paces. Sandor gazed at her questioningly. She turned her hands palm up and shrugged. "You were right," she said. "I have learned to move on." The glands on her palms glistened in the cold blue light. She reached out to touch Sandor's face, relishing the sense of his reality. Not everything had been left behind.

He pressed her palm against his cheek. "I heard you were under a long time. I'm so glad you came back."

"It was hard. Sandor? I want to go home."

"I know. I told Fox. The House will help you." He kissed her hand. "I'm going with you."

She smiled. She already knew that, but it was good to hear. "I've been exploring the House."

"Then you know it's coming apart. I can't believe it. Fox never even hinted that anything like this was possible. I knew the biogenesis function was a way to replicate the House, but I never thought— Well, it's my home. It's been my home. And it's about to tear itself apart. That's staggering. It's like I'm a ghost inside a dream world. Sometimes I wonder if any of this is real."

She closed her eyes and sighed. She could taste reality in every molecule that crossed the thresholds of her body. Sometimes, it was all too real.

"The funny thing is," Sandor went on, "I'm not afraid. We can't stop what's happening. We just have to ride with it. I just wish Nikko was here."

CHAPTER

28

"**S**omething big is happening in there."

Kirstin stood on the bridge of the *Galapagos*, studying the young officer who'd made this statement. He'd just returned from the city—or what was left of it—and fear showed in his eyes. "The House is dissolving. The forest is dying. Things are just . . . *vanishing*, being sucked up by the walls." His eyes were wide with horror. "Even the people. We encountered a group of children. We tried to get them to come with us, but they ran away. I know we should have let them go, but—*everything's falling apart in there*! So we pursued. They couldn't outrun us. So they just stepped into a wall and disappeared."

He shook his head in grim disbelief. "They never came out again. The wall hardened behind them. Then the passage started to close. The walls pressed in on us from both sides. So we fled. We ran. And the corridor sealed behind us.

"Everything was changing. Connecting passages that had existed only a few minutes before were gone.

We didn't know where we were, or where we were going. But it was obvious that we were being driven, with no option to turn, or go back, until finally we entered a huge cavern. Half a klick high but no more than a hundred meters wide. We met some other patrols there. Their experiences were the same as ours.

"Together we moved through the hallway. Tremors shook the floor every few minutes. A few civilians began to show up, looking dazed and scared. None of them were corporate citizens. They were all here on visas. We escorted them. Not that we could have offered them any protection against the sheer power of this place. It could have closed in at any time and crushed us so easily. But it let us go. I'm convinced of that. We were being forced out.

"The hallway eventually brought us to the elevator. It was the first recognizable feature we'd seen in hours. And it was working, praise the Holy Mother. We came up the tether without further incident."

His breathing was harsh and labored, and he paused in an obvious effort to gather his composure. When he spoke again, his gaze fixed on Kirstin. "I don't know if we can go back. This place doesn't want us. It's like a monster, out of control."

Kirstin retired for an hour to a small cabin aboard the *Galapagos*. She turned the lights down low and sat in darkness for several minutes, considering her career. It would be over if she could not somehow retrieve Summer House from the brink. She shuddered to think of the political consequences if she were forced to use the nuclear missiles carried in the armory of *Galapagos*. But use them she would, if it came to that.

Ongoing footage of the debacle on Summer House was still being transmitted to the newsfeeds, though the pictures seemed to be coming from robotic cameras now. She watched them for a while, trying to understand what was happening. Why had the House reacted so powerfully when wrongdoing had to be limited to only a few, albeit powerful, corporate citizens? Summer House was a graduated democracy. It made no sense.

Unless . . . could one of her assumptions be wrong?

Her heart began to beat in powerful strokes. She'd come here in pursuit of the Bohr Maker. It had eluded her for months. But in the end it had been destroyed by the *Galapagos*'s missiles, in a firestorm worse than the one that had consumed Leander . . . or at least that's what she'd been told. She'd hadn't checked the records herself. Maybe it was time she did.

She called up the video record of the missile strike on a wall display, then frowned at the lousy image. The police cruiser had been standing off nearly a hundred kilometers when it fired at the absurd little vessel. The magnification resulted in a slightly blurred image. And the passengers were in shadow. Still, she could make out two tiny figures floating at the end of a tether. And there was no mistaking Nikko's spidery frame.

The *Galapagos* fired its missile. It was moving almost too fast to follow. But obviously Nikko knew it was coming. Kirstin watched him bound to the prow of the ship, detach the tether that held his two human companions, and fling them toward the station's arc. She watched him jump.

Seconds later, the missile reached its target and the little ship evaporated in a fireball. But the passengers were already far away. The video didn't follow them as they fell toward the station.

Kirstin couldn't be certain they'd made contact. But a chill ran through her just the same. In a sudden gestalt vision she imagined the Maker taking up residence in the organic neural network that controlled the House. If the Maker could transform a pathetic prostitute like Phousita into a witch capable of eluding the best efforts of the police to capture her, what could it do in the vastly larger and more complex neural system that regulated the physiology of Summer House? What better explanation for the sudden, disastrous demise of a thriving corporate entity?

But had it really happened?

She might never know. Every effort by her staff to penetrate the shield of defensive Makers that guarded the hidden portions of the House had failed. She could make no detailed assessment of the situation. But the mere possibility that the Maker had colonized the neural structure of the House was enough to ignite in her an instinctive terror.

Her thoughts turned to the remaining missiles in the *Galapagos*'s armory. *Nobody* would be able to tell truth from rumor if the House were to vanish in a fireball of its own.

Sterilization was a word the police rarely used. It didn't sit well with the civilian population. But they understood its necessity.

Kirstin viewed the video once again, watching Nikko with a sense of grudging admiration as he deliberately dove into the abyss. Who else but Nikko would arrange for ten thousand innocent lives to share his funeral pyre?

But Kirstin was moving ahead of the game. It was not too late. She might still be able to convince some corporate citizens to abandon their lost cause before the police strike. She could at least try. Such a show of magnanimity under extreme circumstances would be good for her image. The Congressional inquiry that would inevitably follow this affair would be blunted if she could show she'd taken every possible step to save lives, if she could show that in the end the citizens of Summer House had decided their own fate.

She summoned the commander of the *Galapagos* to her quarters. Beryl arrived, looking tired, worried, and older than a Commonwealth citizen should. Kirstin had felt that way only a few minutes ago. Now that she understood the situation, though, her vitality had returned. She looked forward to the next few hours.

"Recall any of our people who are still in the city," she instructed. "The *Galapagos* will disengage from the docks within half an hour. You will take the ship at least a hundred klicks off the city and you will wait there, with your remaining complement of missiles poised to fire."

"What have you found?" Beryl asked, her expression carefully neutral. But Kirstin could almost scent her sudden fear.

"I have evidence that the House neural systems have been colonized by Bohr's Maker."

In reality the "evidence" was no more than speculation, but she needed to be sure of Beryl's unhesitating cooperation. It was not every day a police commander was asked to destroy an entire city.

Her old friend was quick to point this out. "If you're considering sterilization, we're required to seek Congressional approval."

"I've already applied informally, and the response was favorable. But you know how slow the committee works. We might not be able to wait for an official sanction. There may be no time."

Nobody knew the committee better than Kirstin. The Congressional representatives would never have the spine to order the necessary job done. After the fact, though—that was different. When the deed was complete and there was nothing left to fear, the committee would cooperate. It would be in their interests to shore up the good name of the Commonwealth Police.

Still, the commander hesitated.

So Kirstin leaned. "Even if the formal approval fails to come through, we are first sworn to protect the Commonwealth, and only secondly, to uphold the letter of the law. If you believe as I do, you won't hesitate to risk a reprimand in the interest of the state." For a moment she thought she'd been too heavy-handed. But no. The circumstance called for extreme professions of faith.

"All right," Beryl said slowly. "You'll be with me anyway. You can give the final order."

Kirstin charmed her with a slight, indulgent smile. "I'll give the final order," she agreed. "But I won't be with you. I'm going down into the city to see if I can persuade any of the inhabitants to come out. We'll hold off as long as we can. There are thousands of human lives at stake, after all."

Beryl's brow furrowed with doubt. "But we've tried persuasion. No one's responded. You could be trapped in the House."

Kirstin shrugged. "This corpse is disposable. I'll stay until we're forced to launch the missiles. Then I'll upload a ghost."

Her old friend nodded slowly. "As you say then, Kirstin. But damn, this is a bad end."

CHAPTER

29

Nikko had been taken in by dreamtime for a long, uncertain era. The House nourished him, and he began to heal, at least partially. He sensed Phousita's presence in the darkness, a fleeting awareness, no more, nothing he could pin down. He dreamed of Sandor. Strength seemed to be returning to his fingers, his hands, his arms. Or maybe that was just part of the dream.

Then change set upon him. He felt the darkness grip him with a determined tide. He began to see occasional lights: nebulous blurs of electric blue that flowed past him, always too far away to touch.

Then ahead, the darkness finally began to ease. Blackness became a dark gray that rapidly lightened to blazing white. Firm ground congealed under his feet. The tide pulled away from him. His kisheer shivered and peeled away from his face. He felt the light touch of air against his skin. He breathed it in: it was supercold and terribly thin. Immediately, he knew that something was wrong.

He tried to look. The light wounded his dark-adjusted eyes. He squinted against it, to see where he'd emerged.

Astonishment took him. He gazed at a vast, utterly empty hall. The nearest walls stood at least fifty meters apart. They rose in parallel, like the faces of a deep chasm, until far overhead they finally curved together to form a rounded ceiling. Even in the easy gravity of Summer House, he didn't think he could throw a ball far enough to touch that roof.

The hallway was long too. He couldn't see either end. It curved away at an impressive distance on both sides.

The walls were smooth, a fleshy brown surface marbled with black. Light came from oblong, glowing panels set high overhead. His eyes were adjusting now, and he realized the brightness he perceived was only an artifact of his night-adjusted vision. The empty hallway was dimly lit. And even as he watched, the level of light seemed to slowly fade.

His camera snaked over his shoulder, dutifully recording the scene. Nikko's gaze fixed on it while his heart boomed in deep, frightened beats. There was something familiar about this hallway.

Then he remembered. It was only a few days ago. He'd seen a holographic simulation running in Fox's apartment. The House had consumed all its inner structures while dividing itself into hundreds of discrete cells designed to part along the open channels that separated them.

He felt as if he'd been transported into that simulation. This hall was a channel between groups of cells. When the process reached its conclusion, this great chasm would peel open to the void.

He spun around and threw himself at the wall from which he'd just emerged. No longer was it soft and pliant. The camera reared back, recording his hands as they scrabbled in panic at the rapidly hardening surface. He pounded his fists against the wall, leaving small indentations. "Take me back!" he screamed. "Take me back."

His voiced echoed through the cavern, startling him. "Fox!" he cried. "Hear me."

But how could Fox hear him? Nikko had no atrium. His voice could not get beyond these walls.

He stood, shoulders heaving. He'd become an invisible man. Without the atrium, Summer House could not recognize him. And if Summer House didn't know him, then Fox wouldn't even be aware that he was here. . . .

A sense of estrangement washed over him. He felt as if the pleniverse had cast him out, locked him somewhere outside itself in dreadful isolation.

The camera slowly drifted across his field of view. He glanced up at it. The lens was focused on him. The Dull Intelligence must have tired of the view of the darkening hall. He stared at it, an icy fury running through his veins. His hands twitched, blue fingers knocking against his thigh as he fought an irrational urge to tear the tentacle out of the camera body!

Suddenly, his hands went still.

The camera. The camera could send transmissions into the House plexus . . . if the plexus still existed . . . could he communicate with Fox?

He reached for the chest panel. He couldn't remember Fox's address. That had been lost along with the atrium. It didn't matter. He coded the transmission emergency priority, continuous feed. The camera hovered in front of his face, sending his image out in real time to whoever chose to receive it. "Fox," he said. "It's Nikko."

A tremor shook the great hall. The floor buckled under his feet, tossing him to his hands and knees. The walls groaned. The ground subsided. Or perhaps the ceiling rose, he couldn't be sure, but the lofty space seemed to grow even taller.

The walls were changing too. The black marbling

seemed to be expanding. He touched a vein of it on the wall behind him. It was smooth and very, very hard.

In the simulation it had taken only a few seconds before the House was ready to divide. In reality he should have more time. But how much? Surely when the wall became all black, fission would not be far behind.

Startled, Phousita opened her eyes. "Nikko?" she whispered. Sandor gazed at her, his eyes wide. He'd picked up the transmission too.

"It's got to be a fake!" he hissed. His gaze was focused inward, to the image of Nikko. "Some trick of the cops to lure us out."

But Phousita wasn't sure. As she studied the image of Nikko in her own atrium, she felt touched by a sense of déjà vu, as if on some level she'd already *known* of Nikko's presence in the House. She reexamined her memories, and discovered a packet of data that had come to her sometime during her sleep. It described Nikko. There was no doubt. He'd been adrift in the basal tissue of Summer House while his injuries and debilities gradually healed. She looked at Sandor's anxious face. "The House doesn't recognize him."

"Summer House!" Sandor commanded, sending his words out through his atrium. "Locate corporate citizen Nikko Jiang-Tibayan."

The response arrived in both their atriums simultaneously. Nikko Jiang-Tibayan was not resident at the House.

"Then who is the being who shares his pattern?" Phousita asked softly.

The House couldn't answer.

"He has no atrium," Phousita said. "The House doesn't know him."

"Then he's been here all the time? We have to get to him!"

Phousita shook her head. "It's too late," she realized. "The walls have gone up."

• • •

Nikko spoke to the camera for several minutes, hoping for some kind of response, some kind of acknowledgment. Hoping that the walls would dissolve and take him in again. It didn't happen. After a while he waved the camera lens away and turned his mind to his predicament.

Perhaps there was something about this section of the chasmal hall that prevented him from contacting the plexus. He should move down the corridor. Sooner or later he had to come in range of someone's atrium. There had to be people still awake, still aware. The whole city could not have gone dormant yet.

The moment the thought formed, he sprang away, loping down the hall, not in a panicked sprint, but rather, at a fast, determined pace, his gaze scanning the walls for any discontinuities as he moved around the hall's slow curve. He continued to transmit, muttering a monologue, still composing his documentary:

"The dim illumination is fading. The light tubes are dissolving, being taken in by the obsidian walls. If you can hear this transmission, please alert Fox. This is Nikko Jiang-Tibayan. I'm alive, and trapped in a hall. Love and Nature! The light's gone!" He stumbled, then caught himself. Picking up his pace again, he bounded forward in the dark.

"I can't see a thing. It's pitch-black in here. The only sound is the rhythm of my footfalls, the harsh wash of my breath. The air seems to be thinning rapidly. Is that good? It means the walls here are still active. Can anyone hear me? Find me, please. This is Nikko Jiang-Tibayan."

His throat burned as the fiercely cold air dragged in and out of his lungs. His kisheer began to lap up around his cheeks. The low O_2 had confused its sensory system, so that it hovered uncertainly, ready to engage.

"I'm running blind. Doesn't this corridor have an end? Doesn't anybody hear me? Am I alone?" He stumbled, shaken by the possibility. Suddenly, he felt like the last man on the last day of the Universe. "Where have you all gone?" he shouted into the darkness. "Why have you forgotten me? This is Nikko Jiang-Tibayan. Respond if you can."

Sandor called Fox. Fox assembled a quorum of corporate officers. Everybody's atrium was tuned to Nikko's ongoing broadcast as they huddled together in a cramped transit bubble and debated what to do.

"It's got to be a trick of the cops," insisted Caroline Bukey, the corporate vice president in charge of security. Her choleric temper was reflected in the grim set of her face. "We have no corroboration that this transmission is actually originating with Nikko."

"You're not listening!" Sandor snapped. "Phousita has already provided independent corroboration."

Bukey turned a skeptical gaze on Phousita. "After the fact," she said. "And I'd like to point out that she's not a corporate member. We don't know what her motives are."

"Nikko is alive," Sandor said, barely reigning in his temper. "Phousita wouldn't lie."

"But it seems impossible," Fox said. "If Nikko had survived, the House would have reported it."

"The House can't recognize him without his atrium, Dad! And his atrium was annihilated. He didn't have an ID chip because he never traveled. *He has no identity,* so the House evicted him along with every other noncitizen. We can't even talk to him."

"He's in one of the interstitial halls," Phousita said.

Fox shuddered in open horror. "Those halls are the seams along which the House will fission."

"We have to retrieve him, Dad. You know it's him. Just listen to his monologue. It's pure Nikko. The cops couldn't fake that."

Fox looked doubtful; scared. "Where exactly is he?"

"Moving parallel to cells 412 to 433, Dad."

Fox blanched. "Love and Nature," he whispered. "There are nearly three hundred walls between this cell and Nikko. It'd take hours to get through them."

"And we have only twenty-three minutes," Bukey said.

"We don't have to go through them," Sandor insisted. "All we have to do is open one of the walls and let him through."

But Fox was shaking his head. "It's not that simple. Those cells are all tiny, uninhabited units. There's nobody there! Their interior mass has been reduced to undifferentiated matrix, and there isn't enough of it to support a corporeal person anyway. Even their industrial Makers are dormant."

Sandor frowned. His head moved slowly back and forth as he sought a solution. "But all noncitizens were evacuated in the vicinity of the primary elevator column, right? Can Nikko access the elevator? Is it still operational? Could it take him to a habitable cell?"

Caroline Bukey held up a hand for quiet. Her habitually grim expression had deepened to a forbidding solemnity. "The House plexus reports that *Galapagos* has begun to disengage from the station," she announced. A stir went through the small assembly. "Time is critical. Do any of you doubt what the ultimate solution will be?"

"You want to abandon Nikko, don't you?" Sandor demanded.

Bukey looked at him as if he were a petulant child. "We don't even know if it *is* Nikko."

"I believe it is," Fox said. He caught Bukey's eye. An inaudible exchange seemed to pass between them. "Clear?" Fox asked tentatively.

Bukey scowled and nodded. "Command priority one," she said aloud, though her unfocused gaze made it clear she was speaking through her atrium. "Modify fission procedure: delay disassembly of prime elevator column until further notice. Restore any sections which

may have already been disrupted." Her cold gaze fixed
on Sandor. "There's a cluster of large cells near the bottom of the elevator column. They're not inhabited, but
we will modify the programming of their industrial
Makers to develop a life-sustaining habitat—if we can
get him down to that level."

Kirstin had half expected the elevator to be inoperable.
But it was still functioning when she disembarked from
Galapagos. She took two police dogs with her, each one
inhabited by the ghost of a police officer. Their artificial eyes would record everything that happened below.
Since the House plexus would no longer relay police
communications, she strung a land line along her route,
an ultra thin cable that would carry her transmissions
past the radio-opaque walls of the House. The line was
wired to one of the dogs. If communications failed, *Galapagos* was under orders to fire without hesitation.

Kirstin entered an elevator car and descended the
tether, letting the land line unreel with fiery speed
through the shaft. She emerged from the elevator near
what had once been the corporate offices, only to find
herself in total darkness. Switching on the headlamp of
her environment suit, she keyed its broad beam up to
a brilliant maximum.

The light ran out in a semicircle around her, illuminating what appeared to be an immense hallway. The
nearest walls were perhaps a hundred meters apart.
Like the floor, they appeared to be smooth, hard, and
dark as obsidian.

She tilted her head back and the beam swept overhead. The light rays grew diffuse with distance. She
couldn't make out any ceiling. Slight tremors testified
to the hallway's unstable situation.

The dogs whined nervously. "God, it looks like the
end of the world in here," one of the ghosts said
through Kirstin's atrium. One dog snuffled at scents
wafting from the hallway beyond the reach of the light.

The other appeared to listen. Kirstin couldn't hear anything beyond her own ragged breathing. Her lungs felt touched with fire. The air must be very thin. Certainly, it was supercold.

"Can you pick up anything?" she asked the ghosts.

"Nah," the same voice said. "It's a blank out there. Sensorially empty. Spookiest thing I've ever sensed, like every molecule more complex than carbon dioxide has been sucked right out."

The second cop made no comment.

"I'm going to try making contact," Kirstin announced. *But with whom?* Was there really anybody left alive? She adjusted her atrium, then sent a call through to the House. "This is Chief of Police Kirstin Adair, requesting communications with the corporate offices of Summer House." She received no answer. Similar hails on different bands brought no more success.

They set off down the hall, but there was nothing to be seen besides the radio-opaque black walls. Several minutes later they reached the hall's end: a vertical obsidian wall that confounded her search for a door, a passage. "Those poor, dumb bastards," the same ghost muttered. "They've really done themselves in this time."

They jogged back to the elevator, reeling in the land line as they went.

Kirstin explored another level, another hallway as vast and empty as the first. Her attempts at communication, both with the House and its inhabitants (did they still own a corporeal existence?) continued to produce no results.

As she stepped onto the brightly lit elevator car once again, the dogs at her heels, she began to regret the ploy of magnanimity that had brought her here. She was achieving nothing. And the prospect of facing her own death no longer seemed quite so easy, now that the time was drawing near. It was true that her ghost would escape, her persona would survive the nuclear

immolation she planned. But another copy of her consciousness would be trapped here, forced to face the
blast.

For a moment she considered recalling the *Galapagos*. But that would be the equivalent of backing down.
Bad PR for sure, and after the city blew, she was going
to need all the public support she could muster to keep
her job. So she'd just have to stick it out.

But there was no reason to explore every empty
hallway. Beryl was reporting that the blue oceans that
had once sheltered Summer House from cosmic radiation had blackened, congealing into the same dark material that walled the interior of the House. It was an
eerie, unsettling end to a great city. What was under
construction here she couldn't guess, but she sensed
the transformation was nearing completion. She would
have to act soon, if she wanted to be sure of annihilat-
ing this dangerous little world, so frighteningly out of
control.

But she had her own role to finish first, that of the
magnanimous police chief, striving through the last moment to rescue the doomed citizens of Summer House.

She scratched one of the dogs behind its ear. "Let's
go to the lowest level," she said. If the situation there
echoed what she'd already seen, there would be no
point in further delay. She would order Beryl to carry
out the strike.

They'd just stepped aboard the car when the same
ghost spoke up again. "I'm picking up some untranslat-
able radio activity."

Kirstin scowled. She didn't really want to find anybody. She didn't want a reason to hold off on the strike.
"Someone trying to contact us?" she asked, suspicion in
her voice.

"Probably not," the ghost admitted. "Just a leak
from the plexus, maybe."

The land line glistened like a spider's thread where
it hung down from the elevator shaft, an unblinking

witness to the play of events. Kirstin knew her role in the drama. "Let's go lower," she said, in a deliberate effort to please her invisible audience. "If we change position, we may get a better signal."

Fox, Sandor, Phousita, and even Caroline Bukey listened in silence to Nikko's ongoing transmission. Fox and Sandor were grinning. Phousita felt her own heart lighten despite Nikko's apocalyptic mood. Nikko was jogging toward the elevator! He was going to find his own way out. In a few minutes he would step aboard the car and be whisked away to safety.

Suddenly, Phousita stiffened. Like the others, she was continuously monitoring House progress reports. One had caught her attention.

"Did you hear that?" she whispered to Sandor. "There are police dogs in the city."

Sandor smiled absently. "That's good," he said. "If the cops are still trying to root us out, then they'll hold off their assault a bit longer."

But Phousita shivered. In the Spill, police dogs had always been a harbinger of death. She remembered terrible fire; lost children. "It's a bad sign," she whispered.

Sandor didn't seem to hear her. She raised her hands and gazed at the sparkling glands there. She'd learned the dogs' pattern on that horrible day. She'd sent them into sleep there on the edge of the conflagration. Almost instinctively, she began weaving the spell again.

Then she hesitated. How could the tiny servants pass through nearly three hundred impenetrable walls?

Nikko's breath was whistling in and out of his lungs now, raking his throat with painfully cold fingers. It was getting harder to speak. But up ahead: his gaze fixed on something.

"What's . . . that?" he gasped. "A tiny green light . . . in the darkness."

His eyes had played tricks on him before, reacting

antagonistically to sensory deprivation by filling the dark with false colors. But this light did not diffuse or float away. It held steady, a small green point that gradually resolved into a numbered column. He approached it with a sense of wonder and laid his fingers upon it, forgetting, for the moment, to speak. He could feel a vibration in the wall surrounding the panel. The elevator shaft! he realized. And it was working.

The camera peered over his shoulder, reminding him of its presence. "You see this, Fox?" he shouted. "I'm on the twenty-first level. By the elevator shaft. Come get me, Fox. Send somebody for me."

In the descending elevator car, Kirstin caught Nikko's transmission, static free. She slapped the stop button and chuckled incredulously. "Nikko?" she asked aloud, studying the dim picture that came in over her atrium.

"That transmission originated only a few hundred meters away," the ghost cop announced.

"Sure," Kirstin said. "On the twenty-first level." She punched the revised destination into the panel and the car began to ascend.

"The cop!" Phousita cried. "The cop is tracking Nikko. Look! Look at the House reports. She's gone to meet him."

Her frantic gaze swept round the small group in the transit bubble. Fox looked stunned. Sandor confused. Caroline Bukey had turned a ghastly pale color.

"Nikko knows enough to recognize the biogenesis function, doesn't he?" Bukey asked.

"He won't give us away," Fox said.

"Maybe this is good," Bukey muttered. "He can engage the cops' attention while the House completes fission."

"You can't sacrifice him," Sandor said. "You can't."

CHAPTER

30

Nikko was blinded by the light that spilled from the elevator car. He ducked his head and backed off a step, as his eyes fought a painful struggle to adjust. When he looked up, Kirstin stood bathed in the white glare like some foul goddess emerging from the netherworld.

"You!" he growled.

She studied him warily, a half-smile on her face. "Who were you expecting, Nikko? Were you expecting Fox?"

Nikko's worldview seemed to undergo a sudden convulsion. The chasmal hall had left him in a state of psychic isolation. Now Kirstin was here, intruding on his fantasy of apocalypse. In an instant the outside world became hard reality once again. If Kirsten were here, then the *Galapagos* with its nuclear missiles could not be far off. Real apocalypse faced the House if those missiles were fired.

The camera hovered beside his face, studying Kirstin with its unblinking eye. Nikko noticed the glistening thread of the land line then, as it hung down in front of the open elevator door. So Kirstin had a link to the outside world. She could command the *Galapagos* to fire . . .

Or to hold its fire?

His ragged breathing was not entirely from exertion or the declining levels of oxygen. He wanted to get past Kirstin, past the dogs, onto the elevator and lose himself in the depths of the House. But with visceral certainty he knew it was too late. He could not leave Kirstin now, not when she held a voice trigger on a nuclear missile aimed at the heart of the House.

The only thing left for him to do was buy time for the process of fission to reach its own conclusion. It wouldn't be long now.

He drew in a deep breath, and with a mental effort steadied his kisheer. "So you received my transmissions," he said, his voice only slightly hoarse.

Her hands twitched in a slight gesture. The dogs responded by moving out on either side of him. "What's going on here, Nikko?" she asked, in a voice held carefully neutral for the cameras. "What's become of the corporate citizens? Are they dead?"

"No, they're alive. You have to help them." He surprised himself with his own words. They emerged instinctively. But a moment's thought convinced him he'd stumbled on the right strategy. If he could plant doubt in her mind, she'd have to hold off on the nukes. The land line would carry a record of this transmission to the *Galapagos*. It would be part of the public record. She could not destroy Summer House while there was still a chance the city could be saved. . . .

"Where are they? And why don't they respond?"

"It's a long story." He raised his hands, intending to unbuckle the camera pack. But the dogs mistrusted his intentions, and growled a warning. He froze. "I want to take off the pack," he said. "I want to give you what I know."

She scowled at him in dark suspicion. "You say the residents of Summer House are alive?"

"Yes. Though they're probably all in cold sleep by now."

"Why?"

"It's an emergency response," he said. "I don't know what initiated it, but when the perceived threat is past, the House will regenerate. That's the biogenesis function. You've heard of it, haven't you?"

She skewered him with her cool gaze. "Could the House be reacting to the presence of Bohr's Maker?"

Nikko held himself very still. So she knew Phousita had lived. "It's possible," he lied. "It's possible the House is defending itself against the depredations of Bohr's Maker. Yes, that could be it. If the Maker threatened to contaminate the House neural system, that could stimulate an emergency response."

She looked openly doubtful. But what could she do? He'd just implied the House might save itself. As Chief of Police she was morally obliged to investigate that possibility.

Quickly, he reached for the fastenings on his pack and started loosening them again, despite the dogs' growls of warning. "Listen, Kirstin. I know there's no way I'm getting out of here alive. But still, maybe we can bargain." He shrugged the pack off one shoulder. The dogs tensed. One stepped forward.

He ignored them, and held the pack out to her. "I have information in here that you'll want. For your future security, you'll need to know how I escaped with Bohr's Maker. And I, being an historian . . . I want everything on the record. Everything. Down to the address of Leander Bohr."

Her eyes widened just a little, and he knew that he had her. She asked softly: "What do you know about Bohr's ghost?"

"I know the bastard ratted on me. He warned you about me, didn't he? That's why you're here."

Desire burned in her eyes. But he saw doubt there too. "How could you have Leander's address?"

Nikko chuckled. "Even the best of us make mistakes. He gave his address to Phousita, and she gave it to me." He hefted the camera pack. "Disconnect the land line, Kirstin. Plug it into my camera pack. The data can be transferred in only a few minutes, and you'll have Leander for your very own." His kisheer rippled as he passed the camera pack to her hand. It hurt to give it up. The pack contained the entire history of the Bohr Maker's liberation. But more than dry fact, the records he'd accumulated were solid proof that the Commonwealth could be successfully undermined. He held in his hand the soul of a revolution . . . and he was about to trade it for a few minutes' time.

Would a few minutes be enough?

"We have to attack them," Sandor said.

"No!" Bukey held up her hand. "No assault Makers. That cop is Kirstin Adair, Chief of Police. If she senses she's being attacked, she'll order the *Galapagos* to fire its missiles immediately."

"We strike fast and hard!" Sandor said. "Never give her a chance to—"

"The *Galapagos* is monitoring her every move via that land line," Bukey interrupted. "If the commander senses anything amiss, you can bet she's under orders to fire."

Phousita closed her eyes. Nikko's camera pack continued to transmit as he removed it and handed it to the cop. She watched him speak: *The data can be transferred in only a few minutes. . . .*

"Why is he helping her?" Sandor asked, a high note of confusion in his voice.

"He hates Bohr," Fox said. "He wants revenge."

Phousita shook her head. "It's more than that. He's trying to . . ." She groped for the right word as her eyes blinked open. "To blind the cop? No. He's trying to blind the *Galapagos*."

"Love and Nature," Fox said. "That's it. If he can get her to unplug the land line, he'll have a few minutes to—"

"To do what?" Bukey demanded. "To get past two police dogs and a rabid cop, using only his bare hands? Even Nikko knows better than to try that. He's buying us time, that's all."

"Can't we help him?" Phousita asked. She held up her glistening hands. "I have a spell that will mesmerize the cop and the dogs. But I can't get it there."

Fox's eyes went wide. "Yes you can!" he shouted. "The code can be routed to the industrial Makers poised on the elevator shaft. Transmit it to one of the supervisory Makers there. I'll authorize. The molecular equipment can synthesize as well as disassemble. Here's the address. Quick. Time's running out. Do it now!"

Nikko could almost taste Kirstin's suspicion, like a sour aerosol contaminating the thinning air. Still, she accepted the camera pack. The palms of her hands were slick with sweat. She wanted the data it contained. No doubt about that. But there was only one way to get the data out. She looked at the dog carrying the land line. "I'm going to do it," she said. She was not speaking to Nikko. "I'll be out of touch for a few minutes, but just sit tight. I've got protection. It'll be all right."

Nikko watched as she keyed a release and popped the line out of the dog's pack. She found the proper site on the camera pack, plugged in the line, punched in a command on the pack's control panel, then sat back on her heels, a cold smile on her face. The camera lens hovered on its tentacle like an uncertain cobra, watching her.

She opened her mouth as if to say something, but then she stopped. A glassy look came over her face. At the same time, one of the dogs sagged heavily to the floor. The other one followed a moment later. They lay together, their eyes closed while they panted, huge wet tongues leaving shiny streamers of saliva on the floor.

Nikko gazed at them, astonished, while cold fear washed through his belly. Was this the moment of final disassembly, then? Would everything not a registered part of Summer House be taken apart?

His chin jerked up as if he'd been slapped. A sudden urge overcame him, an almost irresistible desire to step aboard the elevator. His body flinched as he struggled against the suspect impulse. He glanced at the elevator, then at Kirstin. She was staring at the floor, her mouth open, her eyes unfocused.

His breathing grew ragged as he fought the urge to flee. His kisheer was shivering. What was going on?

Then he knew. He'd been hit with a behavioral virus. What else could explain the sudden, demanding intensity of his desire?

But who had tailored the virus to his system? Who had released it? Surely not Kirstin. She still stared at the floor, as motionless as the two dogs.

His body shook. Back in the Spill, Phousita had found a way around the dogs' defensive Makers. She'd proved then she could overcome the best defensive Makers the police had.

"Kirstin," Nikko whispered.

She didn't respond.

He drew a shuddering breath. *Phousita*.

So the young witch had cast a spell to mesmerize the Chief of Police.

He started for the elevator doors, then hesitated. Turning back, he bent down and grabbed the camera pack by its strap. Then he remembered the land line. If he disconnected it, *Galapagos* might fire. He studied the spool strapped to the dog's back, then tugged experimentally at the line. It came smoothly off the inside of the spool. He suppressed a grim chuckle and picked

up the pack. Then he stepped into the elevator while
the land line fed out behind him.

He glanced up. The other end of the line came
down into the elevator through an access panel in the
ceiling. It was as thin as the secondary strands of a spider's web. Thin enough to feed cleanly through the elevator doors even when they closed.

"Take me down," Nikko said. "Lowest—"

Another quake shuddered through the decaying
body of the city. Nikko grabbed at the handrails to
keep from falling. With the doors still open, the elevator suddenly dropped nearly a meter. A knee-high wave
ran through the floor of the corridor, bending it like water and knocking Kirstin onto her side. He saw her
body stiffen with the sudden return of awareness. The
dogs sprang to their feet. Kirstin rolled onto her belly,
her head swiveling as she took in the situation. She had
it in a glance. "*No!*" she roared, and scrambled for the
elevator car, diving forward as the doors began to close.

Nikko jumped to block her. If the doors touched
her they would open again! The dogs would get
through.

They met at the doorway. It was too late to shove
her back. So he grabbed her instead, one hand in her
hair, the other on her collar, and hauled her through just
as the doors whispered shut behind her feet. A great
weight thudded against the door's exterior, and then
the car began to drop.

Kirstin scrambled to the camera pack. She flipped it
over, reaching for the switch that would free the land
line.

Nikko fell against her. His long-fingered hand
closed around her wrist. "I'm real this time," he
growled in her ear. He caught her other hand. His fingers were tremendously strong.

"It's too late!" Kirstin screamed at him. "The transmission's done. When I don't pick up, *Galapagos* will
fire."

"How romantic," Nikko said. "You'll get to die in my arms."

The elevator's smooth descent faltered. It seemed to hang suspended in zero gravity for a moment, then it plummeted. The walls rattled. Nikko felt himself bouncing crazily around, Kirstin under him, then on top of him. Then the car was still.

Nikko let Kirsten go. He leapt to his feet. He could still feel the pseudogravity of the House spin holding him to the floor. But how long could it last? He felt as if the walls around him were holding their collective breath, waiting.

Kirstin stared up at him from the floor. "It's all over, Nikko darling," she growled—and yanked the land line out of the pack.

The elevator doors creaked open a few centimeters, then stopped. Nikko bounded to the gap, thrust his long fingers in and pulled. The doors grudgingly gave way. He wedged his shoulder in. A wall blocked the opening. Kirstin saw it and laughed. "Too late," she said, her voice soft and menacing. "You're going to die."

"Not before you," Nikko whispered. He could feel the wall's soft, yielding texture against his shoulder—a welcoming touch that told him Fox had heard him, and prepared the way. His foot shot out. He grabbed the strap of his camera pack with his long, prehensile toes, yanked it to him, then shoved it against the wall. It sank into the dark, gel-like substance, until only the lens protruded. The Dull Intelligence focused on Kirstin as she started to her feet. "Summer House has won," Nikko told her. "The Commonwealth is dead."

The camera recorded the twisted look of horror that bloomed on her face as Nikko thrust himself into the wall. He felt the wall grasp him. His kisheer rolled up over his shoulders as the gel wrapped around him like a woman's smooth muscles, and pulled him in.

•   •   •

Kirstin still felt sluggish from the assault Maker that had hit her on the twenty-first level. It had spoiled her reaction time, so that she hesitated a second before diving after Nikko. Too late! The wall had already hardened. She rammed it with her shoulder, roared at the pain of the impact, and skidded to the floor, her fists pounding helplessly against her thighs.

Why hadn't Beryl fired? What was she waiting for? *Clearance,* Kirstin thought, as her lips twisted in rage. Beryl didn't have the guts to authorize the destruction of Summer House on her own.

A tremendous quake shook the elevator car once again. Kirstin clutched futilely at the smooth floor, while the quake bounced her like a marble in a box. Then suddenly, she could hear Beryl's voice screaming in her head: "KIRSTIN! What's happening in there?"

Beryl might have said more, but Kirstin couldn't hear her. Her auditory nerve had been overwhelmed by a deafening, drawn-out screech that howled from the walls around her, followed by a sudden, harsh clap. She felt her eardrums burst. Something seemed to suck the air out of her lungs. She clawed at the floor. But suddenly it wasn't there anymore. She could see stars. She could feel a tremendous, crushing cold, pain flaring in every nerve of her body. With her last thought, she ordered her ghost to flee—

—manifesting on the bridge of the *Galapagos*, where she fell to her knees, screaming. Her hands slapped frantically at the blood she knew must be bubbling from her ears. She couldn't stop screaming. Then Beryl was there. Her hands closed over Kirstin's wrists. "Come out of it!" she shouted. "You're a ghost. You're not hurt. Come out of it, Kirstin. I need an order. I need clearance to fire."

Kirstin threw her head back. She breathed deeply, striving for composure. Her teeth were pressed together in a death-head's grimace.

With an effort she fixed her gaze on the display screen, and gasped.

The inhabited portion of the House had come apart like a child's three-dimensional puzzle. She could see flashes of sunlight between the separating pieces. Hundreds of pieces. Then suddenly, the tether snapped, and the puzzle exploded apart, the individual pieces careening off into the void. Each piece as dark as the void, disappearing almost instantly. "FIRE!" Kirstin howled. "Fire, fire, fire. NOW!"

Two missiles darted out across the screen almost faster than the eye could follow. One second ticked past, and then another. The missiles found targets simultaneously and exploded, bathing the ship in hard radiation. The staff murmured in deep concern.

"What did we hit?" Beryl asked.

"Two small fragments," one of her officers replied, his voice laden with disgust. "At a rough estimate, I'd say there's over nine hundred left."

Epilogue

(1)

News Release/Congressional Office of Public Information:
A Congressional investigation has concluded that
the destruction of Summer House was caused by a
runaway molecular event. While details will probably remain
forever unknown, investigators now believe that a program
designed to record and store biogenic information was deliberately released into the House plexus without adequate testing. It malfunctioned, converting all living physiological tissue
to electronic code. Only those foreign residents not listed on the
corporate roster were spared. Eventually, the organic body of
the House itself was attacked, a process that ultimately led to
catastrophic collapse.

Numerous fragments of the House have been surveyed.
None have shown any indication of further biogenic function.
Investigators believe that exposure to vacuum denatured the
aggressive Makers.

Rumors of survivors have proven unfounded.

No survivors. That was the official police response. And
it was true, in a way. Because after a few days even the

most stubborn inhabitants of the dispersing cells had to admit that given the limited resources and energy of their arks, there was no possibility of long-term survival in physiological form. Gradually, they transformed themselves into a vast haunting of electronic ghosts, each cell plotting its future in quiet isolation.

Except Nikko. He was alone and he had no atrium so the electronic world was closed to him. But being alone, he caused no great drain on the cell's resources.

Time passed: abstract minutes to abstract hours to abstract days. He spent a lot of that time asleep. There wasn't much else to do. He talked to the camera, and watched the pictures play back on the little monitor and meditated to stave off depression and wondered every waking minute: *What's going on?*

Until after three weeks his incessant query finally brought a response. Knowledge flooded into him as his newly developed atrium established a communications link with the Dull Intelligence that supervised the cell. He discovered a ghost of Fox waiting for him in the cell plexus, and immediately, he issued an invitation.

"Dad."

Fox smiled at him. He looked strained, but happier than the last time Nikko had seen him. "It's all on the table now," he said.

Nikko nodded. The cops were still out there. But for how much longer? "We'll rebuild the House, won't we?"

Fox's eyes seemed to shine. "Of course. At least those who stay." He shrugged. "Some have chosen to move beyond the solar system. The solar sails are already being spun."

Fox seemed so proud when he said this. Nikko felt a stab of loneliness, more intense than he had ever known. "You, Fox?"

"No." Fox shook his head. "Not yet anyway. I want to try it here one more time." He smiled shyly. "There's an Apollo asteroid that some of us have an eye on. We've nudged a few of the cells onto intercept courses. It's slow going. Not much propellant available. It'll be a few years before any of us make contact. But the more time that goes by, the better. The Bohr Maker's out there. It'll be changing things." His gaze cut away. "We, uh, took the liberty of instructing this cell to rendezvous at the asteroid too." He looked up quickly, concern in his eyes. "You're free to change that, of course. If you want to leave the system, or, or . . . anything. You're free, Nikko."

Free. He mouthed the word like soft candy. The research permit was void. His days were not numbered. He still faced a death sentence in the Commonwealth, but at least now they'd have to catch him first!

Free.

Suddenly a world of potential seemed to expand around him, almost at the speed of light. His kisheer shivered against his neck, and for the first time in years he found that reaction inadequate. He wished that he could smile. Instead, he shook his head. "Don't change a thing, Fox."

He turned to the watching camera lens, wanting to put an end on his documentary, eager to do that now that he knew this one would not be his last. Now that he knew he could start another.

He took a deep breath, and his kisheer spread smoothly out across his shoulders. "This is Summer House Corporate Citizen Nikko Jiang-Tibayan," he said, "back on line."

(2)

Phousita awoke in darkness interrupted by a thin, vertical wire of muted sunlight. She was upright, cradled and supported by a smooth, solid cocoon precisely fitted to her body. She wriggled her shoulders a little. The wire of light seemed to widen. She tasted the air and discovered the heady scents of jungle and natural decay. She called to Sandor over her atrium, once, then again. On the second try he responded, his voice groggy. "Wha—? 'Sita, y'all right?"

"All right," she reassured him. The strip of sunlight was definitely getting wider. She could get her fingers through the crack now. From far away came the chortling of an unknown bird. Quickly she concocted spells and blew them through the crack (now wide enough to admit her arm) hoping she might learn something of the bird's nature.

As the gap widened, she forced her shoulder through, then her head. After that the rest of her body slipped out easily, like a baby spilling from a birth canal.

At the touch of sunlight against her face, she burst out laughing. Then she turned to hug the tree that had produced her, this great and ancient machine. For perhaps two hundred years it had given birth only to seeds of itself. Then a tiny meteorite had come to ground here, after evading the watchful eyes of the police. Inside the meteorite, biogenic Makers had carried her quiescent pattern.

The Makers had changed the tree's biological programming, causing it to produce a new body for her in only three years from the energy collected in its living solar panels. In admiration she turned her eyes upward to gaze into its canopy, then stepped back, aghast. Sunlight burned against her face.

The tree's canopy had withered. It was a skeleton, worn out, exhausted by the effort of her creation. She was its last fruit. All around her, seedlings of the rain forest sprouted in the sudden glut of light.

Somber now, Phousita called to Sandor once again, and after a few hours of wandering about the forest preserve, they found each other. He'd engineered a dark brown complexion for this latest incarnation. Protection from the sun, he told her. His hair was still blond, his eyes blue. They kissed and made love and Phousita was glad she'd designed herself to be of moderate height.

"We'll go down to the village tonight," she said, as twilight fell across the forest. She'd scented the settlement earlier that day. It was over a ridge and down a long slope, very near to the edge of the forest preserve. At the boundary they'd have to pass through a cloud of toxic Makers maintained by the Commonwealth to protect the preserve from humans and human machines. But they were up to it.

"We'll force no one," Sandor said.

"Of course."

They arrived at the village just after midnight, when the moon was full. Dogs ran out and barked at them. Phousita calmed them with a touch. Worried faces peered out past the torn straw mats that served as doors in the moldy plastic shacks. Sandor beckoned to them. He used no spells, but nevertheless they came. Women and children and men, speaking in a dialect Phousita had never heard before. She gave them her thoughts and they listened. She offered them her sight, and ultimately, they accepted. Their poverty made them brave.

ABOUT THE AUTHOR

LINDA NAGATA's short fiction has appeared in *The Magazine of Fantasy & Science Fiction* and *Analog*. She lives on Maui, Hawaii, where she shares with her husband the joys and challenges of raising two active children. THE BOHR MAKER is her first novel. A second novel, TECH-HEAVEN, is scheduled for publication by Bantam Spectra in December 1995.

If you enjoyed Linda Nagata's *The Bohr Maker*, stay tuned for an exciting preview of her next novel, *Tech-Heaven*—a tale of a world poised on the brink of awesome changes, where the potent powers of nano-technology are only beginning to be exploited. . . .

**Coming in December 1995 to
a bookstore near you**

L.A. FLOW—News & Information

Flash Call Line Anonymous Message—Recorded 3:17 A.M.

"Here's one for you. You know Senator Ilene Carson, that East Coast hotshot on the National Health Care Committee? You know—'Cost-Cutter Carson'? Her baby brother, Tom Kishida, died tonight. His wife's about to have him cryonically preserved here in L.A.—frozen in liquid nitrogen . . . like a cure for death will ever be found. You might want to ask the good senator how that kind of 'health care' treatment fits into her budget. A hundred fifty thousand dollars just to put a dead man on ice . . ."

DEAD MAN ON ICE

Corvette. Beemer. Porsche. Jaguar. Lamborghini. Lexus. Z-car. The names rolled together in a potent chant as Katie Kishida counted the company on the freeway. Even at four A.M., I-5 was busy. A lot of fine cars out in the night. And why not? Traffic flowed at four A.M. It was a great time to drive.

"I do it sometimes," Harlow said.

His voice touched Katie like a searing light in the darkness. She flinched; she hadn't even realized she'd spoken out loud. Must be tired. She touched her forehead, as if she could feel brain burn. Funny, she didn't feel tired.

Her gaze shifted to her brother-in-law. She could see his face . . . just barely. Lit from below by the dash lights that he'd turned way down. He looked so much like Tom.

"Sometimes I get up in the wee hours," Harlow went on. "And drive for a hundred miles or more . . . in any direction. It doesn't matter where I go, 'cause I just turn around and come right back. It's the driving. Gives you a chance to lose yourself for a while. Zen meditation."

"I'm not tired," Katie said.

"It'll hit," Harlow promised.

"Look at the cars." Thousands of cars. So much power. White lights coming, red lights going, lanes of life flowing forward, back. A landscape utterly transformed from its primeval design. Nothing here as nature intended. Nothing at all. No. This great freeway was a human thought, rolled out smooth and laid across the countryside, the uppermost sedimentary deposit of time. So much power. Nature didn't have a chance.

She chuckled in grim satisfaction. Nature had designed Tom's body so that it couldn't heal the injuries he'd suffered. Nature had decreed that her husband should die. So Nature was the enemy now.

"Katie, you all right?"

She stared past the flow of traffic to the lights of the ambulance almost a hundred yards ahead. "Did you know that every day the average American consumes two hundred and fifty thousand calories in food and fuels used to produce that food? That's equal to one hundred and eighty quarts of Häagen-Dazs ice cream a day." A mirthless chuckle rolled past her lips. "Now that's power."

"Do you still see the ambulance?" Harlow asked, an edge to his voice.

Katie nodded. "Three ahead," she said, as a motorcycle passed them on the right. Thoughts slid round and round inside her head, as if caught on the rim of a whirlpool eager to pull her consciousness under. One hundred and eighty quarts of Häagen-Dazs ice cream. The freeway seemed fantastical, alien. Threads of thought flowing between the ocean and the mountains. California's cogitation. Nature remade.

I love you, Tom. You belong to me.

A light snapped on overhead. She leaned against a lamppost, chomping on a smelly cigar, the cold weight of a readied gun heavy in her pocket: a Hollywood-issue New Jersey hood, doing bad Jimmy Cagney. *You want to take him, God? I won't let you take him.*

Tomorrow she would consume two hundred quarts of Häagen-Dazs ice cream, and the day after that two hundred and fifty. And her power would grow. The spectacular thought that had made this freeway would be nothing but an infant's first analysis of the difference between *smooth* and *rough,* compared to the thoughts that *would* be, when the thinker learned to command the disposition of individual molecules.

Nature didn't stand a chance.

She grinned like a death's-head, her empty hands closing on a dream. Nanotechnology. An ugly, ungainly word. But the dream spun bright in the long night on the freeway. Nanotechnology: the promise that one day thinking machines could be built on the scale of bacteria. Acting machines. Working on command to reshape the world. To raise the dead. To rewrite the limits of life. To make the universe her playground. A child-safe playground. And she and Tom utterly safe there. "They're heading for the off-ramp," she said.

"I see them."

Dawn began to pale the light show. Bright signs advertising motels and all-night convenience stores faded. Headlights winked out. Traffic thickened at once on all sides as commuters left early to beat the rush. Harlow slowed, squinting worriedly as the ambulance made a left turn one block ahead. "It's all right," Katie said. "I know the way."

She guided Harlow the last few blocks, instructing him to pull into a crowded parking lot in front of a squat, gray building almost unnoticeable in its basic ugliness. "Forward Futures," Katie said with a grin.

"So I see," Harlow responded, nodding at the sign done in letters drawn to look as if they'd been swept by the jet stream.

The building was three stories high, basic cinder block, remarkable only for its scarcity of windows. There were offices on the second floor. A few lights showed through the windows there. Otherwise the building might have been the proverbial black box, smooth-walled, contents unknown. "The ambulance will pull up to a bay in the back," Katie said. She could feel Harlow's measuring gaze, and smiled to herself. He didn't feel the power yet. Not yet. But he would.

"You sure you're up for this, Katie? How about getting some sleep first?"

"I'm not tired." She opened the door and stepped out, stretching, breathing the sour Los Angeles air. She wasn't tired at all; she was feeling downright giddy. She slammed the car door with an eager *crack!* "We made it, Harlow!" She stomped the ground for emphasis, then turned to him with a grin. "So many things could have gone wrong! Tom could have died at the crash site, and then some coroner might have wanted to autopsy him. He could have died at the hospital hours before Gregory could get there. He could have had massive damage to his brain. He could have had impaired circulation. Someone in the family could have made a stink about this whole thing.

"But none of that happened! Ha! I won this round, Harlow. *I won.* And I'm going to fight fate every step of the way to get my Tom back."

Harlow carefully locked the car. "How do we get inside?"

As if in answer, keys rattled in the glass door fronting the building. Katie looked up as a young woman pushed the door open from the inside; she beckoned to them. Katie didn't hesitate. She started up the steps, hearing Harlow follow close behind. "Hi. My name's Maryann," the young woman said as they approached. "I'm so sorry to hear about the accident." Maryann had wide sympathetic eyes, short blond hair, and a bold nose and wore no makeup at all.

Katie swept past her. "Have they unloaded him yet?"

"They're just starting. But he's received all his transport medications, and his temperature's already down to twenty-two degrees C."

"Is that good?"

"Yes. The sooner we can get his temperature down, the less ischemic damage he'll suffer."

"Ischemia . . . lack of blood flow?"

"Yes." She locked the door behind them. "Most of the staff is here, and we've already prepared the perfusate. Your husband is relatively young and has experienced general good health, so we're hoping surgery and perfusion will proceed easily."

Maryann led them through a lobby equipped with three obvious security cameras, past the entrance of a small auditorium, to a heavy steel door. Again the keys. She unlocked the door and let them through. Harlow was beginning to look nervous. "Tight security," he muttered.

"A lot of people object to what we do here," Maryann responded, tension in her voice. "We have a responsibility to protect our patients." She looked over at Katie. "Gregory said you wanted to observe the surgery and perfusion. You realize it'll take several hours to complete."

"I want to see it," Katie said. Because to see it was to be part of it. To know that everything that could be done for Tom *was* being done.

"And I'm sticking with Katie," Harlow added, almost belligerently.

Maryann had them change into surgical scrubs, then she led them to a surgical unit. "He's in here," she said, indicating a table, only half-visible past the medical team surrounding it. Katie craned her neck to see. The HLR had been removed. The body was packed in ice and draped in surgical cloth. It might have been anyone under there.

She recognized Gregory behind one of the surgical masks. He eyed her doubtfully. "You doing all right?" he asked.

"Fine." She moved closer. Uneasy. Determined not to get in the way.

"We're going to perform surgery on the femoral artery to connect a heart-lung bypass," Gregory said. "We'll use a perfusion pump to remove his blood and replace it with a perfusate that'll better support his tissues and inhibit edema. The fluids will circulate through a cooling bath, and that'll keep his body temperature dropping. We want to get him down to a few degrees above freezing, and then we'll introduce the cryoprotectants."

His tone was optimistic. But Tom's injuries slowed the process. There were mutters of concern over the next forty minutes, but the staff worked efficiently; the team did its job. Katie started to get wobbly on her feet and Harlow found her a chair. Finally, Tom's body temperature reached five degrees C. A stainless steel hand drill was used to open a small burr hole in Tom's skull. Katie came over to watch. She felt uneasy about it, like she was trespassing, illicitly viewing a part of Tom that should never have been exposed to her vision, that never would have been exposed if somehow she'd managed to protect him.

Guilt, she thought, was not a logical emotion.

Gregory showed her the brain. It looked white and shiny. The blood in the cerebral vessels had been completely replaced with the clear perfusate. "Looks good," the chief surgeon said with an air of satisfaction. "Let's prep him for the heart-lung machine."

Tom's chest was exposed, and the surgeon cut a line down its center, slicing through the breastbone, and finally, carefully exposing the heart. Tubes were placed in the aorta and the heart, and then connected to a larger, more complex heart-lung machine than the one that had been used in the hospital. And once again Tom's circulation was restarted. Now cryoprotectants were gradually added to the perfusate solution, mostly glycerol and mannitol, to minimize ice formation and reduce freezing damage. It was a long process. The concentration of cryoprotectants could not be allowed to rise too quickly, or osmotic pressures across the cell membranes would further damage the body's tissue.

Four hours passed. Harlow had finally gone home, promising to be back before the end of the day. Katie found herself sitting in the building's lunchroom, across the table from Gregory, an untouched sandwich on a plate in front of her. "Eat," he said.

She picked up the sandwich and took a small bite. It seemed tasteless. She drank some skim milk. The morning's euphoria had faded, but she still felt a strong undercurrent of happiness. "It's going well, isn't it?" she asked.

"Quite well," he agreed.

They returned to surgery just as the cryoprotectant perfusion was judged adequate. Katie stood aside, watching, while Tom was taken off the heart-lung machine. The surgeon closed the incision in his chest. Then, using the burr hole in Tom's skull, the surgeon placed a temperature probe on the surface of Tom's brain. He closed that incision. Another temperature probe was place in Tom's throat, and a third in his rectum.

Then the ice packs and protective wrappings were removed. For the first time since the hospital, Katie could see Tom's face. It had a yellowish cast beneath his tan, and its texture seemed stiff, almost waxy. Like an artificial copy, she thought. Exact detail, but unquestionably inanimate. She felt something give way inside her, like a strut snapping beneath her emotional architecture.

Tom was gone.

Then two large plastic bags were wrestled over his body, eclipsing her view. She stared at a white wall until her breathing had steadied and her composure had self-repaired.

Finally, Tom was submerged in a tank of silicone oil. Wire leads from the temperature probes in his body were connected to a computer. "The Silcool bath is at minus ten degrees C," Gregory explained. "We'll be adding dry ice to it over the next day and a half to slowly bring Tom's temperature down. After that he'll be transferred to liquid nitrogen storage."

"I want to see that too," Katie said.

For the first time since she'd met him, Gregory really smiled. "Somehow I expected that. But right now you must be about ready to collapse on your feet."

"Really, I'm not. I'm so glad I came here . . . but I should be going home. The girls will need me. I've already stayed away too long."

"Let's go out and get something to eat first," Gregory said. "You haven't had anything all day. Unless you get something in your system, you're going to get the shakes when this adrenaline high wears off. After we eat, I'll drive you back."

"Oh, no," Katie said, shaking her head. "I'm not riding with you. You haven't had any more sleep than I have."

"I've had catnaps," he said defensively.

"I'll take the shuttle."

"Well, at least let me take you to dinner."

Katie was surprised to see that it was already dark outside. She sat in the passenger seat of Gregory's old Toyota as they drove about six blocks to a vegan restaurant situated on one end of a convenience mall. He was wearing his Mars pin again.

The restaurant was dimly lit. Indian music played softly in the background. The dining area was about half full, mostly with a yuppie clientele. Katie stopped at the pay phone to call Harlow. His wife answered. She said Harlow was still alseep, but that he was determined to drive Katie home as soon as she was ready. Katie gave her the address of the restaurant, then called home. She talked to her mother and then each of the girls. "I'll be home in a few hours," she promised. "Wait up for me." They said they would.

She found Gregory in a booth at the back of the restaurant. He'd already ordered for both of them. She sat down across the table from him, and suddenly felt as if she might never move again. Gregory quickly shoved a basket of crackers toward her, and she ravenously devoured four packs. The waitress brought a glass of milk, and she drank half.

"This does not feel real," she said after a minute.

"Be thankful for that," Gregory said.

She shook her head, confused at her own dispassion. "I can't accept that he's gone."

"He's not gone. He's just away for a while."

"A long while."

"Maybe." He picked up his fork aimlessly, set it down again. "When were you born?"

She gave him a scowl of mock suspicion. "Why?"

"You're still young. But I'd be willing to bet that when you were born your parents didn't own a color TV, nuclear war was expected at any minute, no human had ever been in space, any pregnant, unmarried teenager was shunned, computers were made with vacuum tubes and occupied whole rooms and couldn't perform the calculations my twenty-dollar pocket calculator can do today, the thought of blacks in elected office was laughable, commercial jet travel was just beginning—"

"All right, all right. So I'm an antique."

He grinned. "The point is, you're not. You're only in your thirties, and yet the world has undergone immense technological and social changes in your lifetime. And the rate of change is accelerating. Thirty years—"

"Thirty-four."

"If we can hold this world together that long, who knows where we'll be?"

"Mars?" she teased.

He frowned disapprovingly, as if she'd made a sacrilegious joke. "Yes," he said quietly. "That's exactly what I mean. We could be on Mars. You. Me. Tom. With bodies that won't easily succumb to injuries. With bodies that we can control precisely, and shape to suit our needs.

"Thirty years. Maybe fifty. Maybe more. But it will happen. You need to keep a perspective on time, all the immensity of time that's available to us."

"If cryonics works."

He shook his head. "No. If *nanotechnology* works. And why shouldn't it? Our bodies are already maintained by molecular machines, naturally occurring.

When we've developed artificial analogs, we'll have won."

"What are you going to do on Mars?"

He looked startled, as if she'd caught him at play in a children's romance. Then he leaned across the table. This was not a fantasy, not to him. "I want to see Mars transformed into a real world. Add an atmosphere. Find water. Design life-forms, plant a forest. Make it live."

"Paradise found."

"Paradise *made*. The human need for creative action satisfied."

"And to go where no one's gone before. How long do you plan on living?"

"As Gregory Hunt?" he shrugged. "I doubt I'll last more than a thousand years before my growth and change make that identity meaningless. But something new will come of me. Evolution in the individual, rather than the species. A thread of life stretching, changing through the eons. Different at every point from what has gone before, yet all the points connected through time. In time anything can happen. And it will all have started right here—" He rapped the table.

"In southern California. Yes." She smiled gently. "You dream fine dreams, Gregory Hunt. I need a dose of your confidence. I do."

They talked more—about cryonics, about Mars, about Tom and what he'd meant to Katie. The food came, and Katie found that her appetite had been restored in full. They were finishing a last course of herbal tea when Harlow arrived. He came hulking up out of the restaurant's dim aisles like a stiff-legged bear. She stood up to greet him. He hugged her and kissed her on the cheek, then shook hands with Gregory. "Ready?"

"Yes." She reached out a hand to Gregory as he stood up. "I'll call you tomorrow." Then she hugged him. "Thanks for everything."

Out on the street, the traffic seemed uncommonly noisy; the air smelled foul. A panhandler accosted Harlow. Harlow told the old derelict to shove off. "Gregory wants to live forever," Katie said.

Harlow raised an eyebrow. "A bit ambitious."

Katie tried to imagine the old panhandler endowed with immortal life, with the kind of control over nature that Gregory envisioned. She frowned, speculating, then suddenly turned back. "Hey! Old man!"

"Katie! What are you—" Harlow started after her, but she ignored him.

"Hey, old man." She positioned herself squarely in front of the man and waited until she was sure his gaze had focused on her. His eyes were blue, bleary and red-rimmed, almost hidden under his sagging eyelids. He had a good growth of salt-and-pepper beard, a ragged ski cap, and the usual odd assortment of cast-off clothes. He smelled of tobacco, body odor, and alcohol and his face was inflamed from scratching. It suddenly occurred to her that he probably wasn't much older than Tom. "Can you spare a quarter, fifty cents?" he asked. He nudged a guitar case with his foot. "I usually sing for a living, but I've only got five strings. This is a six-string guitar."

"What would you do if you could live forever?" Katie asked.

The man stepped back suspiciously. "You from the devil?"

"I'm not offering. I'm asking. Ten dollars for an answer. What would you do if you could live forever in good health?" She dug around in her purse and pulled out a bill while the old man hemmed and hawed. "Answer?" she wheedled, holding it out for him to see.

"I'd fuck women like you." He snatched at the bill, but Katie quickly yanked it back. Her eyes narrowed.

"Okay. You just spent a hundred years fucking women like me. Now what?"

"Hey!" he whined. "I answered your question."

"It was a boring answer. What would you do next?"

He took another step back. "I . . . I'd like to have a sailboat," he stammered. "I lived one year in Tahiti, back in sixty-nine. No one believes me, but it's true. I'd . . . like to go back there."

"And do what?"

He shrugged, the set of his body telegraphing a growing resentment. "Just live. That's all. What's it your fucking business anyway?"

Katie nodded. She gave him the money.

Harlow waited a few feet away. He shook his head at her. "I don't know you, Katie," he said.

She craned her neck to look at the stars overhead. There wern't very many visible through the city's glow. "You're interested in astronomy, aren't you, Harlow? Where's Mars?"

He sighed. "You know, I think it's below the horizon right now."

"Oh." The disclosure carried more weight than it should have. She looked down at the sidewalk, scuffed her feet. Took a first tentative glance at the void in her heart that she'd studiously ignored over the past day.

She shuddered. "I don't think I want to live without him," she whispered.

Harlow quickly put his arm around her. "Come on. You're tired. The car's right over here."

But it was too late. She'd already started crying and she didn't think she'd ever stop.

BANTAM SPECTRA

CELEBRATES ITS TENTH ANNIVERSARY IN 1995!

With more Hugo and Nebula Award winners
than any other science fiction and fantasy publisher

With more classic and cutting- edge fiction
coming every month

Bantam Spectra is proud to be the leading publisher
in fantasy and science fiction.

KEVIN ANDERSON • ISAAC ASIMOV • IAIN M. BANKS • GREGORY BENFORD
• BEN BOVA • RAY BRADBURY • MARION ZIMMER BRADLEY • DAVID BRIN
• ARTHUR C. CLARKE • THOMAS DEHAVEN • STEPHEN R. DONALDSON •
RAYMOND FEIST • JOHN FORD • MAGGIE FUREY • DAVID GERROLD •
WILLIAM GIBSON • STEPHAN GRUNDY • ELIZABETH HAND • HARRY HAR-
RISON • ROBIN HOBB • JAMES HOGAN • KATHARINE KERR • GENTRY LEE •
URSULA K. LE GUIN • VONDA N. MCINTYRE • LISA MASON • ANNE MC-
CAFFREY • IAN MCDONALD • DENNIS MCKIERNAN • WALTER M. MILLER,
JR. • DAN MORAN • LINDA NAGATA • KIM STANLEY ROBINSON • ROBERT
SILVERBERG • DAN SIMMONS • MICHAEL STACKPOLE • NEAL STEPHENSON
• SHERI S. TEPPER • PAULA VOLSKY • MARGARET WEIS AND TRACY HICK-
MAN • ELISABETH VONARBURG • ANGUS WELLS • CONNIE WILLIS • DAVE
WOLVERTON • TIMOTHY ZAHN • ROGER ZELAZNY AND ROBERT SHECKLEY

AA 1 3/95

Bantam Spectra publishes more Hugo and Nebula Award-winning novels than any other science fiction and fantasy imprint. Celebrate the Tenth Anniversary of Spectra—read them all!

HUGO WINNERS

A CANTICLE FOR LEIBOWITZ, Walter M. Miller, Jr.	_____27381-7 $5.99/$6.99
THE GODS THEMSELVES, Isaac Asimov	_____28810-5 $5.99/$6.99
RENDEZVOUS WITH RAMA, Arthur C. Clarke	_____28789-3 $5.99/$6.99
DREAMSNAKE, Vonda N. McIntyre	_____29659-0 $5.99/$7.50
THE FOUNTAINS OF PARADISE, Arthur C. Clarke	_____28819-9 $5.99/$6.99
FOUNDATION'S EDGE, Isaac Asimov	_____29338-9 $5.99/$6.99
STARTIDE RISING, David Brin	_____27418-X $5.99/$6.99
THE UPLIFT WAR, David Brin	_____27971-8 $5.99/$6.99
HYPERION, Dan Simmons	_____28368-5 $5.99/$6.99
DOOMSDAY BOOK, Connie Willis	_____56273-8 $5.99/$6.99
GREEN MARS, Kim Stanley Robinson	_____37335-8 $12.95/$16.95

NEBULA WINNERS

THE GODS THEMSELVES, Isaac Asimov	_____28810-5 $5.99/$6.99
RENDEZVOUS WITH RAMA, Arthur C. Clarke	_____28789-3 $5.99/$6.99
DREAMSNAKE, Vonda N. McIntyre	_____29659-0 $5.99/$7.50
THE FOUNTAINS OF PARADISE, Arthur C. Clarke	_____28819-9 $5.99/$6.99
TIMESCAPE, Gregory Benford	_____27709-0 $5.99/$6.99
STARTIDE RISING, David Brin	_____27418-X $5.99/$6.99
TEHANU, Ursula K. Le Guin	_____28873-3 $5.50/$6.99
DOOMSDAY BOOK, Connie Willis	_____56273-8 $5.99/$6.99
RED MARS, Kim Stanley Robinson	_____56073-5 $5.99/$7.50

Ask for these books at your local bookstore or use this page to order.

Please send me the books I have checked above. I am enclosing $_____ (add $2.50 to cover postage and handling). Send check or money order, no cash or C.O.D.'s, please.

Name _____

Address _____

City/State/Zip _____

Send order to: Bantam Books, Dept. AA 2, 2451 S. Wolf Rd., Des Plaines, IL 60018
Allow four to six weeks for delivery.
Prices and availability subject to change without notice.   AA 2 2/95

Also from BANTAM SPECTRA